RUNNING
FIX

RUNNING FIX

M
Gib

TONY GIBBS

RANDOM HOUSE
NEW YORK

Library of Congress Cataloging-in-Publication Data
Gibbs, Tony.
Running fix / Tony Gibbs.
p.   cm.
ISBN 0-394-57580-6
I. Title.
PS3557.I155R86   1990
813'54.20—dc20   89-29115

Manufactured in the United States of America

2 4 6 8 9 7 5 3

First Edition

For the family:
Elaine, Eric, Bill, Michelle, and Jessica

RUNNING
FIX

The yacht heeled at a gust from the west, and Sarah's hand shot instinctively to the grabrail above the chart table. She was still feeling terrible, but a small, pleasurable twinge of pride momentarily eased the ache in her head. Two months before, a lurch like that would have sent her flailing helplessly across *Sea Horse*'s cabin. Now, thanks to Roger, she could call herself a sailor. Reminded of him, she glanced across the darkened cabin to his bunk. Its canvas lee cloth was raised, laced to the grabrail in the cabin overhead, and all she could see of him were bony bare feet sticking out beyond the rough fabric at one end, and a tangle of damp brown hair at the other. Over the last six months, he had become the center of her universe; she loved him utterly.

Her nose was streaming and her eyes blurred, but it was the headache that was hardest to bear. Never mind. Roger had promised her an answer for that problem. In a few hours they'd both be back in the groove. She had stopped wondering how he would arrange it. His assurance was enough.

A few hours. The thought brought her back to what she had sat down to do. Over the chart table in front of her, the glowing green face of the loran projected two sets of numbers; meaningless, six-digit numbers she was supposed to be watching. 41179.7 the upper panel read; 13982.4 responded the one below. Together, they translated to *not yet, but soon*. She turned on the VHF-FM transmitter, checked its display, as Roger had instructed her, to make certain it was set on Channel 16. Up on deck, a spatter of spray rattled against the mainsail: a good, brisk breeze. Sarah leaned away from the table and glanced up the companionway. Against the rectangle of starry sky, the helmsman's head was an oval silhouette. The glow of the binnacle light bathed the underside of his jaw in red. A narrow jaw—it went with his narrow face and close-set eyes: André. Sarah had disliked him from the moment she'd met him.

On the windward seat, sheltering against the after end of the deckhouse, was what looked like a pile of wet, dirty clothes, until it stirred and emitted a giggle: Dawnstar Perigee, deckhand and nominal cook. How on earth, even in Southern California, could someone get a name like that? Another giggle. Sarah had already learned that it was a completely meaningless sound, like saying "uh" at the beginning of every sentence. Just the same, when she thought about listening to that giggle all the way back to New York—six hundred and seventy-odd miles—her head ached even harder. André and his flower-child sweetie were a seedy pair, typical pierhead-jump crew, but Sarah had had no choice, what with Roger too sick to stand, and the self-steering system broken, and sailing day irrevocably upon them.

On the loran screen, both numbers changed together, catching Sarah's eye. 41180.0 the top one read. And under it, 13990.0. She picked up the microphone and cleared her throat nervously. "Bermuda Harbour Radio, Bermuda Harbour Radio, Bermuda Harbour Radio," she said, speaking a little louder than felt natural and enunciating carefully. "This is the American yacht *Sea Horse, Sea Horse, Sea Horse.* Over."

Silence. Had she got it right? She wiped her dripping nose with the sleeve of her sweatshirt. Her stomach began to knot itself ever more tightly. Roger had told her over and over how important this message was. Something must be wrong. She was halfway to her feet, already turning toward his bunk, when the voice, faintly Cockney and seemingly right beside her, came back, speaking fast: "*Sea Horse,* Bermuda Harbour. Switch sixty-eight."

It was exactly what Roger had told her to expect, but it took her several moments to respond. Then she reached for the radio's tuning knob and turned it until 68 glowed in the little display. The radio operator was there ahead of her: "*Sea Horse?* Bermuda Harbour."

The next was what had to be done exactly right. Pushing down the throbbing pain right behind her eyes, Sarah spoke slowly and loudly. "Bermuda Harbour Radio, this is the American yacht *Sea Horse*, off Kitchen Shoal, outward bound for New York."

The voice was friendly enough but not impressed. It probably heard this speech a thousand times in a year. "Roger, *Sea Horse*. How many in your crew, please?"

"Four people."

"And do you carry an emergency position-indicating radio?"

"In the life raft. Yes, we do."

"Roger, *Sea Horse*. Please confirm that your anticipated next port will be New York City. And when do you expect to arrive?"

"July fourth, and New York is correct."

"Thank you, *Sea Horse*. We hope you've enjoyed Bermuda, and that you'll have a good voyage."

"Thank you, Bermuda," she said. "Good-bye." She reached for the on-off switch, just as another yacht came on the air, also clearing out of Bermuda, also bound for the States. There would be at least a dozen tonight, Roger had told her, most of them heading back to New England after the Bermuda Race. She got carefully to her feet and stepped across the cabin. In the dim light from the companionway, Roger looked a million years old, all pouched eyes and tangled, matted hair. She bent to kiss his gleaming-wet forehead. "We're all set," she said.

"You're sure we're on course? Did you check?"

Why can't you trust me? she wanted to ask, but she knew what had skewed his mood. He read her expression and managed a death's-head smile. "Well done," he whispered. "Just check the course, love."

"I will." She climbed two steps up the companionway ladder until her head and shoulders were framed by the hatchway. Compared to the warm, damp, sour-smelling cabin, the air on deck was clean and cool, with an occasional touch of spray borne on the strengthening wind. *Sea Horse's* wake was a double line of phosphorescence stretching out astern, pointing back toward Bermuda. Most of the islands' lights had already sunk below the horizon, and only a scattering of aero beacons still flicked across the sky behind them. As Sarah watched, the lighthouse on St. David's Head glowed white, subsided. Despite the boat's heel, André stood easily behind the wheel, leaning against the mizzenmast, with his weight on one outstretched leg. "You're steering three-ten, right?" she said to him.

"*Entendu*," he replied, glancing down quickly at the compass card. "You allow a lot for the Stream," he added after a moment. "Three-twenty would be better."

"I'm not the navigator," she snapped, liking him even less than when she'd hired him two days before. "Roger is. You can talk to him about the course. In the morning."

André smiled, sharp-looking teeth tinted pink by the binnacle light. "One hopes the skipper will be able to talk in the morning. When we sailed, he looked to be at death's door." Dawnstar giggled.

Sarah could think of no effective answer. But she knew she ought to rest. She would be on watch, probably alone, in less than two hours. Her bunk, whose foot formed the seat for the chart table, was on the leeward side, so at least she was spared the need for rigging and then climbing over the lee cloth. She stretched out on the cushions, propping herself against the row of lockers that formed the berth's outboard side. There was, she knew, no chance she could sleep.

André's panic-stricken yell half woke her, but it was the shuddering crash, right next to her head, that spilled her from the bunk and sent her clawing up the companionway ladder. On deck, the sails were luffing wildly, thundering in the stiff breeze. Another boat was alongside them, a sloop about their own size, with no sail up and no running lights. The other boat's side was lined with rubber fenders, and they squealed like injured animals as she butted at *Sea Horse's* side, forcing her up into the wind. The moonlight silhouetted one figure in the cockpit; a second, crouched on the side deck, was suddenly lit up by the green glow from *Sea Horse's* starboard running light. Sarah watched, stunned, as the second figure leveled a gleaming pistol at André.

"Up forwards!" he yelled, his hoarse voice pitched to cut through the noise. "Drop the sails, fucker!" Letting the wheel spin free, André cast off the mizzen halyard, then scrambled forward to the mainmast. The main and jib came down with a run, the mainsail cascading over Sarah's head. She fought her way free of the heavy, hard, slippery fabric. Now she could see that the person at the other boat's helm was a frowzy-looking young woman with a hard, flattened face. André, watched by the man with the gun, was lashing the two boats together—bow and stern, and two springlines set up hard with the sheet winches. The sea was lumpy, and the boats ground and scraped together.

The man with the gun turned to the woman at his helm and rapped out a command; it sounded like Spanish, but there was so much noise Sarah couldn't be sure. The other boat's engine slowed, and the two yachts swung slowly into the wind, pitching badly. "Wha'd you mean, four people? Where's Roger?" the man with the gun demanded, as he vaulted over the two sets of lifelines to board *Sea Horse.* "Who the fuck are you?"

André's lips were drawn back over his teeth in a tight smile. Sarah realized, with a thrill of fear, that he was terrified. "Crew," he said. "In Bermuda." He pointed to his feet. "Her, too. Sarah hired us."

The man with the gun shook his head angrily. "Fucked up. I knew he do it." He waved the gun at Dawnstar. "Get up, you." She got cautiously to her feet. Her eyes were wide with fright, but a giggle escaped her nevertheless. "Jesus," the man said. "A goddamn halfwit." His eyes lit on Sarah. "How about you? You halfwit, too? Where's Roger, anyway?"

"Down below," Sarah said, hearing her voice tremble. "He's sick."

"Sick?" The man with the gun let out a harsh, barking laugh. "I know that kind of sick. I can fix that."

Dawnstar giggled. The man with the gun regarded her thoughtfully. "Well, we don't need *you* no more," he said, and shot her. The bullet took her between the breasts, hurled her backward in a spray of blood. As her shoulders slammed into the boom, she doubled over and vanished down the companionway.

"Hole in one," the man with the gun said, smiling. André put his hands out in front of him, like a man trying to fend off a closing door. He was making a wordless, whimpering noise; it ended in a gurgle as the bullet hit him squarely in the throat. A look of surprise widened his narrow eyes, and he began to collapse slowly forward, blood spurting from between his fingers as he clutched at his neck. The gunman reached out and gave him a slight push, toppling him to one side, then out of sight down the hatch.

Sarah stood frozen beside the companionway. The shots had made so little noise over the din of waves and engine and the boats grinding together. The man with the gun smiled at her, his teeth bright in the moonlight. Somehow it broke the spell that held her. "Roger!" she screamed, diving down the companionway. "Roger, help me!"

"Oh, shit," said the man with the gun, and he followed her slowly down the ladder.

BARR:
FRIDAY NIGHT,
EAST NORWALK,
CONNECTICUT

When the vibrating silence in *Glory's* main cabin finally became more than Jeremy Barr could stand, he slipped quietly up the companionway into the cockpit. Though it was a warm night for early June, the air had enough chill in it to keep his calloused hands cupped around his glowing cigarette as he sat with his back against the coaming and listened to the gentle creak of the yachts straining against their docklines, and the slap-slapping of wavelets against the pier. Forward, the skylight over *Glory's* low deckhouse was open slightly, but no sound emerged. Fifteen years as a professional sailor had, he thought, immunized him to moods, whims, and tics in fellow crewmembers, but the heavy-breathing tension between Gillian Verdean, *Glory's* owner, and Patrick O'Mara, the mate, had abraded his nerves to a point where he almost wished himself ashore.

It had come to a head in Antigua, two weeks earlier, the night after *Glory's* last charter party of the winter season had left for home. A three-day bout of cleaning and refitting lay before them, and then the voyage back to New England: ten days on the open ocean, free at last from the daily need to find a sheltered anchorage well before the cocktail hour, and from paying guests demanding to know when there would be more hot water in *Glory's* shower or why there was no single-malt scotch in *Glory's* bar.

Still, the winter behind them had been a financial success, and Gillian deserved most of the credit. Her meticulous planning supplied the unobtrusive (invisible, as far as the customers were concerned) logistics that a good charter yacht had to have. She could also resolve personality clashes with the brisk cheerfulness of a first-class nanny—albeit a nanny whose boyish figure made her look like somebody's nice teenage daughter, and not the tough and accomplished young woman who could climb to the masthead, dive for a snagged anchor, or face down a bribe-hungry customs agent.

To Gillian's attributes the mate added some of his own—a carefully rationed sensuality for the female charterers, most of whom went kittenish in the presence of a blond, square-jawed Adonis with just enough rough edges to be interesting; a sympathetically respectful ear for their husbands, bitterly accustomed to being scorned by their own sons; and a talent for impromptu entertainment, from tarot card readings laced with double entendres to salacious sea chanties accompanied on the yacht's guitar.

But of all Patrick's social skills, the one Barr found most impressive was his ability to conceal from the world at large his passion for Gillian. Even Barr, who shared *Glory*'s tiny, triangular fo'c'sle with the mate, had been unaware of his state for several months—would have been oblivious still, if he hadn't overheard a cattily perceptive remark from one female charterer to another. At first Barr put it down to envy, but as the season went on he slowly began to accept the clues the woman had spotted—Patrick's tendency to stare fixedly at Gillian when he thought she wasn't looking, to invent errands that would put or keep him near her, to take needless physical chances in her presence. Gillian herself seemed not to notice, immersed as she was in learning the details of the charter business, and particularly its special West Indian convolutions. As she gradually mastered the tricks of her new trade, however, she began to develop a perceptible skittishness at Patrick's approach, though Barr was still unsure if she was aware of the mate's feelings.

To Barr, whose social graces were distinguished by their total absence and whose definition of gourmet provisioning was canned roast beef hash, fell the job of moving *Glory* from one enchanted isle to another. The navigational demands were next to nonexistent, the level of seamanship childish; most of the time he felt like window dressing, necessary only because of Patrick's lack of sailing experience and Gillian's sex: though she was an able, competent sailor, the charterers still seemed to feel more secure with a male skipper, even one who was monosyllabic to the point of rudeness.

The night the last charterers had gone ashore, though, Barr had found himself in a rare, tearaway mood. Partly end-of-term exhilaration, of course, but what really galvanized him was the prospect of the sixteen-hundred-mile blue-water passage back to Connecticut, even though its purity would be compromised by Gillian's insistence on a stopover at Bermuda. (Not that Barr objected to Bermuda— just, in principle, to stopovers.) He had been cold sober, or very nearly, for three and a half months; he would be sober again once *Glory* was at sea. That night, he was going to get plastered.

He hadn't bargained on Gillian's determination to corner him. Though he'd known for some time that she had a crush on him (funny, old-fashioned word, but it seemed right in this case) he'd managed so far to keep her from bringing it into the open. The whole situation embarrassed him, this stubborn infatuation of a worldly young woman for a misanthropic seafarer ten years older. When Barr looked in the mirror the poker face that stared back was all planes and sharp angles, burnt to the color and texture of a Top-Sider; his oddly light blue eyes were hedged with two decades' worth of squint wrinkles, his straight hair bleached to straw by the same West Indian sun that had rendered off every ounce of surplus flesh, so the sinews and muscles of his short, wiry frame stood out like rope just beneath the skin.

He had decided that what attracted Gillian—as it always did— was a skill she herself didn't yet possess. Typically, she'd hurled herself into learning the nuances of seamanship, as she had hurled herself into the business of chartering; it was no use telling her that only time and experience would give her a feel for the helm or the mood of the sea itself. Having absorbed what could be learned and finding herself still not Barr's equal, she'd convinced herself that he was some kind of nautical magician, and that she was in love with him.

To Barr such feelings were just misguided hero worship; he was doing only what came naturally to him, while Gillian's own determination to master everything she met seemed to him far more admirable, even when her stubbornness nearly drove him crazy. Still, he trusted her, respected her, had come to like her. That was as far as he could go, but he found himself unable to tell her why. She had discovered—it was no secret in the islands—that Barr's wife was dead, flayed to ribbons two years before by the coral knives of Anegada's Horse Shoe Reef, in the wreck of Barr's own charter yacht. Gillian probably also knew (it was the sort of thing she would ferret out) that Barr had been off watch, asleep, at the time of the accident, and it was his wife's inattention that impaled the boat squarely on the reef.

Gillian could not know, and Barr would have died before telling her, that his own sixth sense had brought him up on deck half a minute before the crash, and he'd been frozen by the sight of three naked bodies, a tangle of heaving flesh, in the corner of the cockpit. In that moment, most of his emotional fuses had certainly blown. On the reef two hours later, painfully injured himself, he had stumbled across her torn and bloodless corpse awash in a tide pool and felt . . . nothing. In the months that followed, scar tissue slowly formed, inside and out, until he was able to face all the ways he had been a fool—believing she loved him (or anyone), convincing himself that marriage would steady her, ignoring the manifold evidence she never tried to hide.

After a year or so, he became aware that feelings were beginning to return, but he took pains to bury them under the shyness he had been born with. It was far safer—and not, he discovered, that difficult—to regard himself and the world with a carefully detached amusement. And if you were looking for laughs, he sometimes reminded himself, the pattern of affections in *Glory*'s crew provided plenty. Barr wondered if their triangle was common gossip yet in the charter fleet. If it hadn't been earlier, that last night in Antigua had probably made the three of them into a public anecdote.

The evening had begun ungluing itself, as Barr vaguely recalled, in a rum shop outside the charter base at English Harbour. It was a rickety shanty, open on three sides to the cool trade winds; under the rusty iron roof the customers could huddle on warped benches around bare tables or dance, on a splintery floor, to a pickup country-and-western trio that provided a merciful change from the pervasive steel-band bar music of the islands. The place was jammed with white faces, mostly skippers and crews noisily unwinding from

charter parties just ended, and Barr found himself nodding to sailors he had encountered in waters as far away as Nova Scotia or
Bermuda.

Patrick, predictably, had gravitated to the band's enclosure, and
quickly possessed himself of someone's acoustic guitar. In just one
season he'd become known through the fleet as a first-class amateur
picker who knew all the words to everything, and the customers
loved him. Even the owner of the guitar looked reasonably happy.

Barr had settled at an isolated table, his back to the only wall,
where he could survey the crowd while he loosened up enough to
deal with company. Gillian immediately dropped onto the bench
facing him, and clearly had no intention of moving. They were
drinking rum swizzles, matching glass for glass in lieu of conversation. Gillian had a hard head for a woman, but she was soon well
back in Barr's wake. On the bandstand, Patrick was accompanying
himself to "Going Down That Wrong Road Again," pulling the
audience into the choruses. Gillian at last broke the silence between
them. "You're glad the season's over, aren't you?" she said, slurring
only a little.

"I'm glad the charterers are gone," Barr replied.

"So'm I." She seemed to be weighing him, her dark eyes alight.
Her face was triangular, like a cat's, with slightly angled cheekbones
and a neat chin. She had cut her chestnut hair short, as a concession
to the limited fresh water in *Glory*'s tanks and the even more limited
supply of hairdressers ashore. Brushed smoothly back along the sides,
it suited her eager spirit in some way Barr had tried and failed to
define. Now, as she waited for him to say something, it occurred to
him that she looked like a streetwise elf. "So'm I," she repeated, when
he said nothing. "You know why?"

"Not really," he said dismissively, realizing as he spoke that she
wouldn't be warned off, that she'd nerved herself up for confron-
tation. Across the dance floor, a large, familiar-looking blonde had
raised her glass to Barr in salute. After a moment's fuzzed recollection
he placed her, a delivery skipper named Joliet Cain, universally
known as Captain Jolly. She would do for a lightning rod. He
beckoned her over.

"Because I've wanted to talk . . ." Gillian stopped as she followed
his gesture. "Oh, *no*, Barr. Not her. Not Jolly the boat cow."

"Jolly's an old friend of mine," he said, not trying to keep the annoyance out of his voice.

"Jolly's an old friend of anything in pants," Gillian snapped. "Who else would shack up with Herman the Hun?"

She had a point: Jolly's most recent lover was a captain whose arrogance was so monumental even other Germans couldn't stand him. The one before had been a mechanic who was said to bathe only (and rarely) in the Marvel Mystery Oil he used to lubricate carburetors. But Jolly's appetites were her own business, and Barr found himself bristling. "She's all right," he said. "We've sailed together."

It was, he knew, a cheap way of putting Jolly off limits for comment: In the mythology of the sailing world a shared ocean passage was supposed to forge some kind of sacrosanct relationship, like blood brotherhood. Barr had made far too many voyages not to know better, and Gillian, in a cooler moment, might well have seen through his trick. As it was, she only shifted her ground: "I just never thought she was your type, that's all."

"My type?" He could feel his temper beginning to slip, and he forced a smile. "What's my type? I'd like to know."

"So would I." She colored, as if her words had taken her by surprise. "But really," she continued doggedly, "I don't get it. Jolly makes a lot of noise, and you don't like noisy people. She's always part of a crowd, and you hate crowds. Not to mention she's about fifteen pounds overweight. So what's the attraction?"

"Hi, guys. You're not having a fight, are you?" Jolly had come up soundlessly behind Gillian and now straddled the bench beside her. She leaned across the table to peck Barr's cheek, giving him the full impact of her awesome decolletage, barely contained in a scarlet tank top. She was an inch taller than he, and her broad face was boldly handsome. But too much tropical sun was having its usual effect on light skin, and next to Gillian she looked ravaged.

"Hello, Jolly." Gillian's chin was up, a dangerous sign. "Join us, won't you?"

"Just one quick question," said Jolly, answering her tone rather than her words. She turned to Barr: "You going to have any spare time this summer, Jeremy? I've signed up three deliveries from the

Virgins to the States, via Bermuda. Ex-bareboats from the belly-up fleet—you know what that means."

He certainly did. Undercanvased tubs for the most part, with performance sacrificed to fancy accommodation; after five years' brutally hard charter service they would now be going back to the optimistic American owners who had put them under a now-bankrupt lease-management firm. "Blown sails," Barr murmured reminiscently, "halyard splices all meat-hooked, clapped-out engines, galleys infested with roaches—"

"And heads that only work backward. I see you remember," Jolly laughed. "That was some voyage."

Her deep, slightly hoarse voice was made for laughter, Barr reflected, as he found himself grinning. "It was the worst passage I've ever made," he corrected her. "You drive a boat too hard, Jolly."

"But you got her home, Jeremy," she replied. "Which is why I'm asking you again. I've got to get the three of 'em up to goddamn Jersey or someplace by the end of July."

"Sorry, but we're chartering Glory back in New England," Gillian put in. "As soon as we get home."

"Just thought I'd check." Jolly glanced from Barr to Gillian and back, arched an eyebrow in an unspoken question Barr chose to ignore. "But I see it's not to be." She hoisted herself to her feet. She was not really overweight, Barr decided. Just well upholstered. "Come over and have a drink with my gang. Both of you."

"Thanks. Maybe later," Gillian replied. She was making an effort, and it showed. "Good to see you, Jolly."

"Whatever," Jolly said, and winked over Gillian's head as she swung away.

He finished his rum swizzle and motioned for a refill; as he lit a Camel he saw Gillian's expression through the smoke. "Okay: What is it?" he said.

"I was just wondering how a person gets to call you by your front name," she answered. "She's the only one I ever heard do it. I figured there must be a reason."

Barr loathed his first name and never used it. That Jolly did was something which had annoyed him for years, but never enough to make an issue of. "She just does," he replied. "It's not what you think. She's not my type—as you said yourself—and she never was."

He realized before the words were out of his mouth that she'd take the opening. "Brings us back to the previous question, doesn't it?" she said. She leaned forward, driving her words at him: "Just what is your type? Or, to be blunt about it, why not me? I'm better than she is. In every way."

The conversation had already gone too far, but he had just enough rum in him to reject a diplomatic retreat. "That's a dumb thing to say," he snapped.

"What's the matter, Barr? I'm smart, I'm a good sailor, I've got a better body than she does—not as much of it, for sure, but what there is ain't so bad." Her eyes were glistening, and she shook her head angrily. "God, I've done everything but throw myself in your lap. Don't you know how I feel?"

Barr was on his feet, his glass knocked over in his haste. "You remember what we said—what *you* said—at the beginning of the season? 'No lust in the fo'c'sle,' right? 'If we stay professional, we stay friends.' We did and we have. I like you a lot, Gillian. But that's where it stops. I'm sorry. I really am."

"Oh, go to hell," she said, her voice low and furious. "Or go play with Captain Jolly, if that's what turns you on. I don't need fake sympathy from some clapped-out sailor who couldn't even keep his own boat off the rocks."

He had already turned on his heel, away from her. Behind him, he heard her say "Wait, Barr," and then what might have been "I didn't mean it." Captain Jolly, grinning, was holding out her arms to him, a drink in either hand.

Barr came back aboard *Glory* well before dawn (Jolly was not fond of morning-afters) and dropped silently down the forward hatch into the fo'c'sle. The other berth was empty, but he put no meaning to it until, half an hour later, he heard a door somewhere aft open and close, and a moment afterward Patrick, carrying his shirt and deck shoes, stepped quietly.

Glory sailed north the next morning, prematurely, with a hungover, resentful skipper, a hungover, angry owner, and a hungover, lovelorn mate. The hangovers were all they had in common. The passage which might have brought them together seemed only to lock them into mutual isolation. And now Barr was reduced to solitary smoking in the increasingly chilly cockpit, while Patrick and Gillian smoldered silently in the cabin below, surrounded by a different kind of chill entirely.

A scraping footstep on the pier alongside yanked Barr out of his sour reverie. "Excuse me," said a hesitant, very New York voice. "This is the yacht *Glory*, please?"

The speaker was short and bald and nearly globular, his shape emphasized by a khaki leisure suit that outlined him far too plainly. Since he was standing directly in front of a life ring that had GLORY painted on it in three-inch letters, Barr wondered if he were not quite bright. He had, however, long since become used to the obtuseness of landlubbers. "That's right," he said.

"Is Miss Verdean—what do you say?—on board?"

No one who knew Gillian for more than five minutes called her that. "You a friend of hers?" Barr asked.

"Since she was a girl," the round man said, smiling earnestly. "Actually, the father of a friend. Sarah Farber—maybe Gillian's mentioned her? Sometimes she calls herself Farmer. Look, I wouldn't bother you so late, but it's very important."

The little man's anxiety was making him lean forward, as if he were pressing into a high wind. Barr suddenly realized how churlish he had been sounding. And the name Sarah Farber did ring a distant bell. "Sure," he said. "Come aboard. Gillian's down below."

The visitor eyed *Glory*'s gunwale, a good three feet above the pier, with deep apprehension. "Maybe my shoes aren't right," he said. "City shoes."

"That's okay," said Barr. "We've got carpeting on the side deck. Let me give you a hand." The little man managed to raise one elegantly shod foot to the gunwale, and Barr heaved him aboard.

"Thank you," he said, puffing slightly. He felt in a pocket and extracted a small leather case. "My card." Barr accepted it gingerly. Across it, in hyperactive type, sprawled the words CALICO JACK ACTIVEWEAR, and below, almost too small to read in the dim light from the pier, *Sol Farber, President*.

"That's me: Sol Farber."

"Right," Barr replied.

"I meant not Calico Jack," Farber added. "That's just some kind of name from Down Below—Australia, you know?" He paused expectantly. "And you?"

"Oh. My name's Barr. I work for Gillian."

"Not a boyfriend? Too bad." Barr's head snapped around, and the round man patted him on the arm. "Don't mind me. I can't help it. Tillie—that's my late wife—she used to tell me, 'Sol, someday you're going to say the wrong thing to the wrong guy and he'll break your head for you.' Nobody has, yet."

"Right this way, Mr. Farber," said Barr evenly. "Maybe I'd better go down the ladder first." The nearly vertical companionway dropped six and a half feet into a narrow passageway that was lit only by a dim red bulb at ankle height. Slipping easily down the ladder, Barr flicked on the gooseneck lamp over the waist-high table to starboard, on which was spread a chart of Western Long Island Sound. Below the table's surface were six deep drawers filled with charts of the entire East Coast and all the islands of the Caribbean— Greater Antilles, Virgins, Windwards and Leewards—while above was a double row of bookshelves with safety rails and, in fitted racks cushioned with green felt, the navigator's tools, dominated by *Glory*'s ancient, perfect Plath sextant, the property of the great-uncle from whom Gillian had inherited the yacht. Across the passage was a toilet compartment and the smallest of *Glory*'s guest cabins, used by Gillian when no charterers were aboard; aft, behind a varnished mahogany door, lay the so-called ladies' cabin, a U-shaped chamber dominated by a huge double bunk.

Farber lost his footing four steps from the bottom of the companion ladder and half-fell, half-slid the rest of the way. Barr, who had been expecting it, caught him easily and propelled him forward, toward another narrow doorway through which came the buttery yellow glow of oil lamps. The cabin beyond, unquestionably the center of *Glory*'s accommodation, was about fifteen feet on a side. It was paneled in carved mahogany, in the fashion of a half century earlier, and contained four curtained sleeping alcoves, two on each side, above and outboard of settees upholstered (by Gillian) in deep blue plush. The settee to starboard had an extension at right angles, along the forward bulkhead, and in the L thus formed sat a huge gimballed table which Barr had spent three months taking down to bare wood and refinishing. The deck underfoot consisted of varnished teak planking the color of maple syrup, with inlaid strips of blond holly, and the overhead was ash, almost the same color and a pleasing contrast to the glowing mahogany of the bulkheads and lockers. The deckhouse, with its small, old-fashioned rectangular windows, raised the headroom to seven feet—even more under the skylight in the center. The whole cabin was dominated by a heavy-breathing oil of *Glory*, under her original gaff rig, that hung on the starboard side of the forward bulkhead. The yacht had been painted shouldering her way through a preposterously fake tempest, and the ornate gold frame, which had originally surrounded a near-life-size nude, had been liberated by Patrick from a condemned saloon.

Farber paused on the threshold, taking in the scene. He nodded his approval. "A nice place you got here," he said. "I like it." Gillian was not to be seen, but the unfamiliar sound of hard-soled shoes on the companionway ladder's treads had brought Patrick to his feet. Farber's gaze went from the cabin to *Glory*'s mate, six feet of pure physique encased in khaki shirt and trousers that looked as if they had been starched and ironed five minutes before. Farber turned to Barr, a knowing expression lighting up his round face. "So *he's* the boyfriend?"

Patrick's easy, polite smile erased itself, and he stared as if he couldn't believe his ears. Barr, with an effort that cost him dearly, managed to keep his voice level. "Not exactly. This is our—*Glory*'s—mate. Mr. O'Mara."

"I said something wrong again?" Farber asked, a certain satisfaction in his voice. He turned to Patrick, who was watching him the way a bird watches a snake. "How do you do, young man: Sol Farber. You ever think of being a model?"

Barr had yet to see Patrick completely taken aback, and this was not to be the time. "Patrick O'Mara," he replied, baring his perfect teeth and extending a powerful, well-manicured hand. "Pleased to meet you, sir."

"You know, it's a good thing you broke your nose once," Farber continued, inspecting him with friendly interest. "You could be too handsome, otherwise."

Patrick's grin was getting a little rigid at the corners, and his color had heightened by two shades. Barr decided it was time to let him off the hook: "Mr. Farber's come to see Gillian," he explained. "A friend of hers."

"Oh. She's in the . . . she'll be right back," said Patrick, with a quick glance at the forward bulkhead. "Why don't you sit down, Mr. Farber. Make yourself at home."

As he spoke, a series of dull, metallic clunks and the gurgle of water sounded through the thin planking. Farber looked alarmed: "What's happening? Is the ship sinking?"

"It's all right," said Patrick reassuringly. "It's just a sort of . . ." His voice trailed off in a mumble.

"Toilet," Barr snapped. For some reason the mate, a sometime paratroop sergeant who could burn the ears off a mule in three languages, froze completely when he had to refer publicly to certain bodily functions or the apparatus accompanying them. Barr privately put it down to a blue-collar upbringing on the South Shore of Long Island, but had never quite had the nerve to say so.

Just then, a door in the forward bulkhead opened, and Gillian appeared. She had changed into the flannel nightshirt she customarily wore to bed, and as she stood blinking in the cabin lights she looked to Barr no more than fifteen years old. She stared at the little man, cried "Uncle Sol!," and swept him into her arms.

After a minute he held her away from him, shaking his head in wonder. "More beautiful than ever," he said. "Such perfect skin, even with all that sun." He glanced pointedly at her left hand. "Still not married. But at least you got two young men here to choose from."

Given the past two weeks, Barr thought, it was probably the most disastrous remark Farber could have made. Gillian's jaw dropped, and then she burst into helpless laughter.

"You're incorrigible, Uncle Sol." Her face suddenly softened, and her eyes became too bright. "I forgot: Sarah. I was so sorry to hear about her."

In Barr's mind the relay closed at last: This must be the father of Gillian's college roommate, lost at sea ten months before, when her boat sank returning from the Bermuda Race. When Gillian had heard the news she'd been numb with grief for days.

"I still have the letter you wrote," Farber was saying. "It was the nicest of all. Just like you." He was, Barr saw, clearly touched by Gillian's sympathy—but, oddly, not sorrowful. Excited, if anything. Barr looked across at Patrick, whose raised eyebrow said that he'd noticed the same thing.

Farber eased himself onto one of the settees. Low as it was, his feet barely reached the deck. "That's what I came to see you about, Gillian: Sarah."

She dropped gracefully to the seat beside him. "A memorial service? I'll be proud to help."

To Barr's astonishment, Farber laughed aloud. "No," he said, "not a memorial. Because my Sarah isn't dead."

GILLIAN

For a moment she thought she'd misheard. "Not dead? But Uncle Sol, it was in all the papers." Still unable to absorb the news completely, she managed to catch herself: "I mean, it's wonderful, of course. But when did she turn up?"

"She hasn't," Uncle Sol said. From a pocket he drew a large envelope and fumbled in its contents. "This turned up," he said triumphantly. "Last week."

It was, she saw, an ordinary picture postcard, scuffed along the edges and curved in a way that suggested it might have spent some time in a back pocket. She recognized without difficulty the familiar scene on the front—the flag-festooned lighthouse on Bermuda's Gibbs Hill.

"What does it say?" Patrick asked.

"Come here and see," Gillian replied.

He didn't need to be invited twice. He positioned himself carefully on the settee beside her, his leg just barely not touching hers. "Not mailed from Bermuda," he offered, after a minute.

"Can you read that postmark? I can't," Gillian said.

"Well, it's a U.S. stamp," he explained. "Postmark might be St. Thomas."

Gillian tilted the card an inch from her nose, scanning the inky blur from a different angle. "It might," she conceded. "Might just as easily be St. Louis."

" 'Don't worry Daddy I'm all right love Sarah,' " Patrick read aloud, slowly and without inflection. "Well, she didn't waste words."

"Sarah always hated to write," Uncle Sol put in. "Even in college, Gillian used to answer her letters for her."

Patrick looked a question, and Gillian explained. "In New London: Connecticut College. We were roommates."

"The twins, people called them," Farber said. "They went everywhere together. On dates, everything. They even dressed alike."

Memory warmed her spirit. "Courtesy of you, Uncle Sol." She gave his arm a squeeze. "If I'd had to pay for my own clothes, it would've been potato sacks, all the way."

"So that's how come I thought of you," Uncle Sol said, abruptly businesslike. "Her best friend. I know she's alive—this is her writing, nobody else. But they're trying to talk me out of it."

"They?" Gillian said. "Maybe you'd better tell me about it." She wondered if she sounded as wary as she felt. Sarah had always moved through life inside a cloud of dippy chaos, but what was charming in a girl of seventeen had become very tiresome in a woman of twenty-five. Come on, she admonished herself, think of everything Uncle Sol's done for you—practically a father to you all through college. "Start from the beginning," she said.

"The card came while I was away," Uncle Sol said. "At a convention. It was mailed to Scarsdale, where I live. I'm alone now, so it just sat till I came back. When I read it, I went first thing to where Sarah worked."

The New Federalist? Gillian asked.

"That silly magazine," he agreed, nodding. "I remember exactly what you said about it: 'Mildly left-wing and basically harmless.' " He looked at Barr. "As WASP as you," he added. "But without a sting, if you know what I mean."

Barr's faint grin ticked Gillian's heartstrings, the way it always did. But he said nothing, and his eyes were watchful.

"Anyway," Uncle Sol went on, "I thought it was the best place to start. The boat she was on—the one that sank—it belonged to a man from there. He was supposed to have drowned, too, so I was sure they would know at the magazine what happened."

"And didn't they?" Gillian asked.

"Nothing," he replied. "What was even more strange to me, they didn't want to know." He addressed the disbelief on Gillian's face. "I know it sounds crazy, but that was what I was feeling. I talked first to this woman—she's the office manager—and then to Sarah's boss: it was his brother who owned the boat. His own brother, maybe not drowned after all, and he didn't want to talk with me about it."

"You mean it was too hard for him to talk about?" Patrick asked, looking puzzled. "Think he'd get over it in a year."

"No, no," Uncle Sol said impatiently. "It was all sympathy running out his mouth, but like he was watching me from behind his eyes, if you know what I mean."

Patrick clearly didn't. "Well, that's pretty strange," he allowed.

"You're telling me? A strange fellow altogether." He turned to Gillian. "I could feel it, he wanted me out of there. And he wanted Sarah to stay dead."

"Explain," Gillian said.

"It was the postcard. He spent this whole time telling me why it didn't mean anything. Sailors give other sailors letters to mail, he said. And they carry them around for months before they drop them in the box. He's a sailor himself, he told me. Maybe you know him: Winthrop Huddleston." He rolled his eyes. "What a name—a real Mayflower ascendant."

Patrick looked startled, but Gillian was familiar with Uncle Sol's adjustments to the language. "Name means nothing to me. How about you, Barr?"

"I heard of him, back in City Island," Barr replied slowly. "Never met him, though. Old money, old boat, as I recall. But he did have a point about the postcard, Mr. Farber. Your daughter could've given it to a friend to mail, and he—or she—could've forgotten it for months. It happens."

"Not this card," Uncle Sol said firmly. "This one she wanted to get to me. I'm sure of it."

Barr's shrug was almost imperceptible, but Gillian could feel he had written Uncle Sol off as a nice old guy chasing rainbows. He was probably right, too. But loyalty and affection spoke for her. "So what do you want me to do?"

"Find her for me. Whatever it costs, don't worry." He enclosed her hands in both of his, forcing her to look into his faded eyes.

"Sarah's my only child, the only family I've got left now that Tillie's gone."

"But Uncle Sol," she objected, hearing—and hating—the bleat in her tone. "I don't know anything about finding people. You want professionals—police, the FBI, the Coast Guard, an *agency*."

"Gillian, listen to me," he said. "I've already been to agencies. I'm up to here with agencies. Cossacks and commissars, all of them. But you know sailing places, where she might be. You've got I'm sure hundreds of sailing friends. You know my Sarah, what she'd do."

Do? she thought angrily. Something looney and self-destructive, the way Sarah always had. Then she saw the naked anguish in his face and heard herself saying, "Well, maybe . . ."

"Hey, just a minute," Patrick interrupted. "I'm sorry for your trouble, Mr. Farber, but we've got a living to make. We've got a schedule to keep . . . customers." He pulled at the sleeve of Gillian's nightshirt. "You know that, Gillian," he pleaded.

"It's not as if the customers were beating on the hull," she said, not meeting his eye. "I'd have to look at the datebook to be sure, but we really don't have anything except a couple of daysailing parties till after the Fourth of July."

"Which is three weeks—three and a half—away," Uncle Sol put in quickly. "So you cancel your appointments, whatever you call them, and I'll rent your boat *and* you for the whole time."

"But Mr. Farber," Patrick objected. "That's five thousand a week. Nearly twenty thousand dollars."

"So what? My Sarah's worth a lot more than that to me. And I've got it, young man. You tell him, Gillian."

Before she could agree that twenty thousand was indeed peanuts for Sol Farber, Barr pushed himself away from the table he'd been leaning against. The light from the oil lamps glanced off his bony forehead and his prominent cheekbones, leaving his eyes in shadow. "Money's not the point," he said, irritation plain in his voice. "The whole idea is silly. *Glory*'s a sixty-five-foot ketch, not the Missing Persons Bureau. And even if we did know where and how to look for your daughter . . ." He pulled himself up short, shaking his head.

"You were going to say?" Uncle Sol asked quickly.

"It doesn't matter," Barr replied, reddening.

"Maybe my Sarah doesn't want to be found?" the old man suggested. Barr's expression remained blankly polite, but Gillian could feel his surprise. "You think that didn't occur to me?" Uncle Sol went on. "I love my baby, but she doesn't fool me." A warm, disarming smile—right on cue, Gillian thought. "At least not much."

Barr was not going to be charmed, she saw. "If she doesn't want to be found," he said, "it just makes finding her that much harder. Assuming she's still alive at all."

Gillian glared at him, but Uncle Sol seemed not to notice. "You have an advantage those big bureaucrats don't have, Mr. Barr. You're a sailor. Maybe it takes one to find one."

"A sailor?" Barr, clearly puzzled, looked to Gillian. "I thought you said your friend Sarah was something in a department store. Before she went to work for that magazine."

"A buyer," Gillian agreed. "In Bloomie's, I think."

"Assistant buyer, in Alexander's," Uncle Sol corrected her automatically. "I got her the job, I should know. But since she met this Roger Huddleston, she's a sailor. Twenty-five hours a day—you remember how she is, Gillian?"

Do I ever, Gillian thought. A girl of enthusiasms, our Sarah. And, remembering, she found herself grinning.

Barr was shaking his head. "Even so—" he began.

"And this Roger of hers," Uncle Sol said. "Was *he* a sailor!"

"That's the brother?" Patrick put in. "Of the guy who owns the magazine?"

"Who else?" said Uncle Sol. "Him you could find easily, Mr. Barr. Sailing is his life, Sarah said."

"Chartering is ours," Barr replied. "Anyway, it's supposed to be."

"But we'd *be* chartered," said Patrick suddenly. "You heard what Mr. Farber said: He'll hire us for a solid four weeks, full rate."

"This could drag on for months." Barr's face had closed, in a way Gillian knew all too well. "And the other point remains. We don't know how to do this kind of job. We'd be taking Mr. Farber's money for nothing."

"That's my chance to worry about," Uncle Sol said. He pushed himself to his feet. "Look, you want to talk this over without me? I can understand." He took the fat envelope and set it on the table. "I put this together myself. The stories that came out last year. Pictures of Sarah. Letters I sent and replies I got. Everything. You read it, please, and then you call me tomorrow. First thing in the morning."

Sorting the contents of Uncle Sol's envelope on *Glory*'s big main cabin table, Gillian managed a surreptitious glance at Patrick, standing beside her. But not surreptitious enough, she realized, as his gaze locked onto hers. She looked quickly away, angry with herself all over again. What a disaster that night in Antigua had been—she'd made a fool of herself with Patrick, and hadn't even made Barr jealous. Up on deck, Barr was trying to help Uncle Sol regain the pier, under a drumfire of personal questions. She couldn't hear Barr's answers, but none of them went beyond a syllable. Still, he sounded good-humored, which was more than he did with her these days. Ever since that awful night she'd felt him slipping away, the relationship they'd built over the winter shattered in a few thoughtless minutes.

It was no better with Patrick. Even before Antigua, she'd suspected how he felt about her, but she'd been so busy stalking Barr that she paid no attention, just kept herself out of reach and let him build up pressure. It'd been lazy and selfish of her, she knew that now, but how many girls would turn off a hunk like Patrick? Once she'd allowed him—be honest, Gillian: encouraged him—to make his move, no more evasion was possible. And when she turned him down, he simply couldn't understand what was happening. It wasn't so much ego as precedent. He'd never got that far with a woman and finished the night with his pants on. Under other circumstances Gillian would have found the result funny, but she liked Patrick, had no problem with his open sensuality, felt like a teasing bitch for taking advantage of him.

Barr came back down the companionway, and the faint smile vanished from his angular face when he saw her expression. Damn, she thought, here it comes: the unavoidable argument. Now we find out how much we really share. At least, with Barr in the cabin, she didn't have to avoid looking at Patrick. His big hands were folded on the table in front of him, and whatever it was wouldn't melt in his mouth; any acting school in the country would give him top marks for his version of Politely Attentive Concentration.

Barr wasn't buying it, to judge by the twist of his wide, thin-lipped mouth. The skipper's clear distaste had halted him at the after end of the cabin, propped against the bulkhead and ready for instant flight. She made herself ignore the man at her elbow and addressed Barr evenly: "You think this is a mistake."

"A *big* mistake," he agreed. "Aside from us not being competent for the job, there's plenty to do aboard *Glory* before the season begins—all the refitting we didn't finish before we sailed from Antigua, plus a few new deficiencies . . ." He let his voice trail off, but he didn't have to finish the sentence. If Gillian hadn't insisted on setting sail three days early, *Glory* would've been far better prepared, and the toll for the homeward bash across the Gulf Stream would have been a lot lower.

"So the job doesn't thrill you. Think of the money."

"Twenty thousand dollars," Patrick said, his voice caressing the words.

"We could make all this year's loan payments, and have enough left over for that new diesel we've been putting off." Some of the glow faded from Patrick's face, but he nodded agreement. Barr, however, remained visibly unmoved. "What is it you want, anyway?" she demanded. "I would've thought Uncle Sol's offer was perfect for you—all the cash for a full month's charter, and no charterers underfoot."

Barr's grin was quick and, she saw, involuntary. "That part's fine. I just don't like taking Mr. Farber's money under false pretenses."

Gillian realized her temper was close to snapping. She made herself speak coldly: "There was one thing I didn't want to say in front of Uncle Sol . . ."

His mouth worked itself into a wry attempt at a smile. "I could hear you not saying it. *Glory* belongs to you. Point taken."

Was this it, then—the moment her carefully assembled dream came apart? *Glory* was, quite simply, her life. But *Glory* without Barr was unthinkable. He knew the boat's weaknesses and strengths as no other person could; his skills and devotion were what kept *Glory* alive, kept her from becoming just another old hulk. And there was still, in the back of her mind, the hope that his feelings for *Glory* might transfer, at least a little, to *Glory*'s owner. At the same time, Gillian's affection for Uncle Sol and her friendship with Sarah were the deepest relationships from a lonely girlhood. It wasn't fair, being torn apart by the people and things you loved. She realized she had been holding her breath in the silence. Patrick was immobile except for his eyes, which flicked back and forth between Barr and Gillian. "Then you know what my decision is," she said, amazed at how calm she sounded.

"I think so. And it's the wrong one." His quiet words hung in the air. She waited for him to stalk out, and then she saw that his hand, dangling at his side, was trembling almost imperceptibly. He's wound as tight as I am, she thought. He may not love me, but he loves *Glory* enough to stay. I hope.

"You don't have to be involved," she offered. "I can set things up so Patrick and I work around you."

"No," he said flatly. "That won't fly, and you know it." He paused, and it seemed to her as if *Glory* herself were waiting for his next words. "Since we don't know what we're doing, we'd at least better be working together at it. As far as I'm concerned, Mr. Farber's hired the whole *équipe*: horse, foot, and guns."

"But you still don't think it'll work," she said. And immediately thought, Why can't I ever leave well enough alone?

Patrick surprised them both by breaking in. "Look," he said, obviously feeling his way as he spoke, "this could be someplace where the regular experts don't know any more than we do. Like Mr. Farber said, we—you two, anyway—know sailing places and sailing people. I bet that kind of thing's more important here than official police procedure. Anyway, all we have to do is the best we can; we haven't got anything to prove."

"Nothing to prove?" said Barr, his eyebrows shooting up. "I thought Farber hired us to find his daughter, alive. That sounds to me like a good deal to prove."

"You really don't think she's alive, then," Gillian said.

"Christ, Gillian—I don't know, any more than you do," Barr snapped. "Look, there's two possibilities. First and most likely is just what her boss Huddleston said: She died when the boat sank, but she'd already given that postcard to somebody to mail; it spent several months in his duffel bag or back pocket before he remembered it. Or maybe some post office in the islands let it age for a while before they got around to sending it on."

"And the other possibility is that she's alive but doesn't want to be found?" Gillian asked. She could feel the tension slackening.

"Why wouldn't she?" Patrick demanded.

"Maybe she's in some kind of trouble," Barr said, with a shrug. "Or she did something she's afraid to face her father with. Or she just decided to head out for Oz. Result's the same either way. And it's been almost a year since the sinking. If she doesn't want to be found, she could be anywhere by now." He hesitated. "Farber's a nice old guy. I like him, too. But maybe he'd be happier in the long run not finding her."

"What I think," Patrick put in, the self-conscious peacemaker, "is that we ought to look at these papers before we start making theories."

"It's okay with me," Barr answered. "Gillian, suppose you tell us what all that stuff is."

"Right," she said briskly. As she sorted, she tried to ignore the small voice that kept reminding her of the dozens of things Sarah had done in just four years of college that she hadn't dared confess to her parents. "This bunch is biographical material about Sarah: pictures, yearbook entries, résumés. This one is Uncle Sol's correspondence about her disappearance. Letters to the Coast Guard, Bermuda Harbour Radio, the Navy—on and on. And this third bunch is news stories about the sinking. I think we might as well begin with those." She picked a clipping up from the small pile. "*Soundings*, last September, 'Yacht Sinks Returning from Bermuda. All Four Aboard Feared Lost.'" She held the newsprint cutting, already yellow around the edges, under the nearer oil lamp, and began to read aloud.

"'A 35-foot yawl, less than a day out of Bermuda on its way to New York, sank on June 29th under unexplained circumstances, with the apparent loss of its four-person crew. The Alberg-35 Sea Horse, owned and skippered by Manhattan publishing executive Roger Huddleston, went down before the eyes of the crew of the yacht Aggressive, which, like the Sea Horse, was returning to the United States after competing in the biennial Marion–Bermuda Race. The Aggressive's crew observed no one aboard the Sea Horse, which had cleared from St. George, Bermuda, only hours earlier, with a four-person complement: her 38-year-old owner; his friend and business colleague Sarah Farmer, 27, also of New York; André Corduan, 31, of France; and . . . Dawnstar Perigee, 23, of Montecito, Calif.' "

Gillian raised her eyes to find Barr and Patrick looking equally stunned. "I didn't make it up," she protested. "That's what it says right here, Dawnstar Perigee."

"From California," Patrick added, as if that explained everything.

"Go on," said Barr.

" 'Corduan and Perigee had replaced members of the Sea Horse's Marion–Bermuda crew who had flown home earlier.

" 'According to the Aggressive's skipper, Gould Richardson of Westerly, R.I., he sighted the Sea Horse just after dawn, 20 miles northwest of Bermuda. Her sails were furled, and she was in sinking condition. Weather conditions—a 25-knot westerly and seas of four to six feet—made it too risky for the Aggressive's crew to attempt to board, but Richardson said he put his 39-foot wooden boat close enough alongside the Sea Horse to be certain that no one was aboard. The sinking yacht's six-man life raft, carried in a canister on the cabin top, was missing, and her mizzenmast had apparently gone over the side. Alerted by radio, rescue units based at the U.S. Naval Air Station Bermuda and at Hamilton conducted an air and sea search of the area, but no trace of survivors was found.

" 'A spokesperson for the Marion–Bermuda Race Committee expressed surprise and regret, but noted that the Sea Horse had passed her prerace safety inspection "with flying colors." In addition to her inflatable raft, the yacht carried a VHF-FM transmitter, an Emergency Position-Indicating Radio Beacon (EPIRB), and a flare pistol with both meteor and parachute flares.

" 'Huddleston, who had skippered yachts in four Newport–Bermuda races as well as the two previous Marion–Bermuda events, was regarded as an exceptionally experienced sailor. Farmer had done several months' racing and cruising in coastal waters, mostly aboard the Sea Horse. According to acquaintances, Huddleston planned to sail back to the United States with only Farmer as crew, but an intestinal ailment had made him change his mind and take on two additional hands. Corduan, a professional deep-water racer, had competed in a number of ocean races in Europe, as well as the recent Transatlantic. Perigee's qualifications were unknown. According to knowledgeable Bermuda yachtsmen, the weather, while uncomfortable, posed no danger to a well-found 35-footer.' And that," Gillian concluded, "is about it."

She glanced around the cabin. Patrick's face wore a thoughtful expression, but he had nothing to say. Barr had withdrawn into himself, and she guessed that he had summoned up, from twenty years' offshore experience in three oceans, a mental picture of the boat, the crew, and the weather, and was trying to fit it to the circumstances of the newspaper story.

"What's that other clipping?" asked Patrick at last.

"From *The New York Times*," Gillian replied. She scanned it quickly. "Pretty much the same as the *Soundings* story, plus a sketch of Roger Huddleston: 'Business manager of *The New Federalist*' . . . 'ardent sailor' . . . 'Vietnam veteran.' Unmarried, no children. And this: 'Ms. Farmer, the daughter of Solomon Farber, president of the men's clothing firm of Calico Jack Activewear, is an editorial assistant at *The New Federalist*, which she joined six months before the race.' "

"I don't get this Farmer-Farber stuff," Patrick complained. "Was she married to some guy named Farmer?"

"No, she wasn't married," Gillian said; having to make this explanation always annoyed her. "Sarah went through a period of sticking it to her parents, and changing her name was part of it. She didn't want to be rich, boring Sarah Farber from Roslyn, Long Island, anymore. She wanted to be . . ." What? Gillian doubted that Sarah ever really knew.

"Wild and free, and not Jewish," Barr suggested, not quite under his breath.

He was probably right, though she was damned if she'd admit it. She went on as if she hadn't heard him. "It happened a couple of years ago. She was doing real well as assistant buyer in Alexander's or wherever, but she was just burned out. Went down to Caneel Bay to lie in the sun, and came back a different person, with a new name." A different person with a taste for cocaine and a mayfly tattooed on the inside of her thigh, Gillian might have added. "She tried social work, but it was all just reports in triplicate. Wrote short stories, but nobody bought them. Finally did a nonfiction article about homeless women in New York, and sold it to *The New Federalist*. They hired her two weeks later."

"I thought you said you'd lost touch with her," Barr said.

"One lunch," Gillian replied quickly. "Two hours of high-velocity girl talk." Uncle Sol had pushed her into that meeting—Sarah would listen to her old roommate, he said. Tell Sarah her mother's dying, and couldn't she come home, just till it was over? The reunion had ended in tears and refusal, just as Gillian knew it would.

"This looks like another story from *Soundings*," Patrick said, snapping her back to the present.

"You read it," she said.

"Um . . . 'No New Clues in Bermuda Yacht Sinking.' That's the headline." He glanced at the top of the page. "Last October. Okay, here goes." He read in a loud, tense, artificial tone that reminded Gillian he was not by inclination a reader: "'Investigations in the United States and Bermuda have unearthed no additional clues to the sinking on June 29th of the yacht Sea Horse and the disappearance of her four-person crew. The yacht's life raft remains missing, and no derbis has been . . .'"

"No what?" said Barr.

"Oh. Day-bree," said Patrick, pronouncing it with exaggerated care. "That's what I should've said. 'No debris has been found that would give investigators any clue to the cause of the sinking. Bermuda Harbour Radio, the island's official station monitoring ship and boat traffic, stated that a woman, presumably crewmember Sarah Farmer, had checked the Sea Horse out with them over VHF-FM at about eleven P.M. local time on the 28th. The boat's position was given as being off Kitchen Shoal, two miles from the entrance to the harbor of St. George. At that time, according to the duty operator at Harbour Radio, the signal from the Sea Horse was loud and clear, and there was no indication of any trouble aboard.' Hey, listen to this: 'One of the last-minute additions to the yacht's crew, André Corduan, had been "assisting H.M. Customs authorities" in an investigation of alleged violations, but no charges had been made. Corduan was put ashore in Bermuda from the French yacht Ouragan, under obscure circumstances, and given an air ticket back to France.

"'The other crewmember taken on in Bermuda, Californian Dawnstar Perigee, had arrived on the American cruising yacht Shadowfax, whose skipper, Lawrence Wurling of Bennington, Vt., said he was unaware she had sailed aboard the Sea Horse. During the week before the Sea Horse's departure, Perigee and Corduan had frequently been seen together and with other sailors in bars and restaurants around Hamilton and St. George. Bermuda police emphasized, however, that there was no evidence to support a rumor that the two had attempted to hijack the Sea Horse, sinking her in the process.'" Patrick set down the clipping with a dissatisfied air.

"It's the *Marie Celeste* all over again, except that it sank," Gillian said.

"*Mary*," Barr said absently. "*Mary Celeste* was the ship's name. Not *Marie*."

"Fabulously helpful," Gillian replied. "But that does seem to be all of it."

"Is that a picture," asked Barr, from his position across the cabin. "With the second *Soundings* piece?"

" 'The bow of the sloop Sea Horse, moments before she sank,' " Gillian read. " 'Photo taken by Gould Richardson, skipper of the yacht Aggressive.' Here. You want to look?"

Barr took five reluctant steps across the cabin and accepted the clipping, as Patrick asked, "Any chance they'd raise the boat? None of the stories say anything about that."

"Not a prayer," Barr replied, without looking up from the blurry photograph. "Water's a thousand fathoms deep where she went down. Maybe more." He handed the clipping back to Gillian and turned as if to leave.

"Where're you going?" she demanded.

"Thought I'd start end-for-ending the anchor rode," he said. "That way, at least one of us'll get something useful done tonight." She forced her mouth to stay shut, was still clamping her jaw when he stuck his head back through the cabin doorway: "By the way, you might try to get hold of the original pictures that guy Richardson took. There's something funny about the way *Sea Horse* looks, but the newsprint makes it too blurry to be sure."

He would stay, then. She had won the first round. She felt a nearly overpowering urge to laugh or cry or maybe both; and she also felt the faintest pressure of Patrick's muscular thigh against her own. Damn.

The wind off Fisher's Island Sound was a gentle southwesterly, blowing across the ebb tide just strongly enough to kick up a thousand tiny ripples, each one flecked with a glitter of afternoon sunlight. The outline of Fisher's Island itself, five miles away, was as sharp as an engraving hung at arm's length. The feeling of futility Gillian had carried up seventy-five miles of I-95 couldn't withstand the beneficent gleam. She smiled at the launch boy, whom she had sweet-talked into running her out into the yacht club anchorage, and he grinned conspiratorially back at her. "That's *Aggressive* right over there," he said, above the hoarse rumble of the launch's engine. "The yawl with the mahogany brightwork."

"She's beautiful," Gillian said.

"She is, too," the boy agreed. "Fifty years old, and looks like they drove the last screw yesterday. Old Poppa Richardson, he spends all his spare time on her, just about every day but Sunday." He throttled back and lowered his voice. "Just remember what I said: You told me you were a friend of his. I could get in a lot of trouble otherwise."

"Count on me," Gillian replied. She handed him the tightly rolled ten-dollar bill he had been eyeing for the past several minutes; as the launch swung alongside the old yawl, she reached for the main shrouds and stepped easily aboard.

Her weight caused the yacht to heel slightly, and the man on his knees in the cockpit looked up in surprised annoyance. Under a breeze-blown mop of white hair, his gnarled face was the same deep red-brown as the wood he was varnishing. He was wearing paint-spotted khakis and a grubby navy blue sweatshirt with YALE '35 in discreet lettering on the breast. "Who in heaven's name are you?" he asked. As Gillian saw his face darken, she gave him her most dazzling smile.

"Mr. Richardson?" she said. "My name's Gillian Verdean, and I'm terribly sorry to interrupt you, especially on such a perfect varnishing day. But it really is a matter of life and death, and you're the only one who can help me."

"Well," he said, carefully setting down the varnish brush on top of the open tin. He rocked back on his heels and studied her with sharp, faded-blue eyes. "Life and death," he repeated. He glanced quickly at her feet, and she knew it had been worth the effort to clean her Top-Siders before setting out that morning. For the rest, her preppy-lady-sailor's disguise—a modestly loose polo shirt and faded Breton red slacks—had walked her through the yacht club without question.

"Really," she said. He was clearly a tough, scraggy bird, and her imagination had no trouble supplying his background: a retired industrialist, without a doubt; probably turfed out of his boardroom by a coven of yuppies. He was the kind of old man she liked, and she let her approval show.

"Well," he said again, getting to his feet a little stiffly. "I guess you'd better tell me about it, Miss Verdean." He slid back the companionway hatch. "Come below?"

"Thank you," she said. "This may take a few minutes—want me to cap the varnish can?"

"Oh, sure," he answered. His amused expression took ten years off his age and made her wonder, momentarily, if the cabin were such a good idea. "Any excuse to stop working," he added, and she realized that his smile was as much for himself as for her.

Stepping carefully down the narrow ladder, Gillian found herself struck, for the twentieth time at least, by how tiny the cabins of older yachts could be. This one was dominated by its four bunks— pilot berths against the yacht's white-painted sides, and transoms below and inboard of them—but it was clean and bright, and everything in sight spoke to her experienced eye of little money, spent with painful care. "Drink?" Richardson asked. "All we have is water from the ship's tank and cocoa—*not* made with water from the ship's tank."

She matched his grin, to show she appreciated the distinction, and accepted cocoa gratefully. When they were seated on the transom berths, facing each other and almost knee to knee, she began: "It's about *Sea Horse*, the boat you saw sink last summer." His lips pursed, but he didn't interrupt. "A friend of mine was in her crew. Her father asked me to see if there was any chance she might have survived."

"I see," Richardson said, in a tone that indicated his puzzlement. "You got my name from *Soundings*, I suppose? Their story was complete, at least as far as we were concerned. We didn't see a soul aboard, and we came right alongside." He paused. "I guess we should've tried to lash *Aggressive* to her, put someone aboard, but the old girl"—he reached out to touch one of the yacht's white-painted frames affectionately—"isn't up to rough stuff. Come to mention it, neither's the crew," he added.

She smiled back at him. "Racing across the Gulf Stream's not for sissies," she said. "Six-foot seas and a twenty-five-knot wind . . . I wouldn't have laid *Glory* alongside, either."

"Your boat?" he asked politely.

"A ketch. A big old Herreshoff. We keep her down in East Norwalk."

Richardson's bushy eyebrows shot up. "Not *the Glory?*" he said. When she nodded, her pride showing, he said, "Most beautiful yacht on the East Coast. Next to this one. My word, imagine a child like you owning *Glory.*" Mock apprehension, and then: "I do beg your pardon, but everyone under fifty looks fresh out of the cradle to me these days."

A likely story, Gillian thought. She prided herself on reading character, especially in men. This one had upended his share of secretaries, and there were a few gropes left in those big, liver-spotted hands. "My great-uncle left her to me," she said, filling in the sudden silence. "I run her for charter, with a skipper and mate. It's the only way I can afford to keep her."

"Of course," Richardson replied. Her explanation made perfect sense to him, she saw, and wondered how he'd have handled the truth about her and Barr and Patrick. "But I've taken you off the subject," he said. "What can I tell you about *Sea Horse* that wasn't in the article?"

"You're absolutely sure she was *Sea Horse*—you saw the name?"

"No doubt at all, I'm afraid," he replied. "It was on the transom, in one of those big, tasteless modern designs. What do they call them? Hull graphics." He reached behind him without looking, and plucked a pencil and pad from a small locker. "I remember distinctly," he said, drawing carefully and slowly. "It looked like this." Head on one side, he scrutinized his drawing. "No, not quite like that," he said, holding it out to her. "I'm no artist, but perhaps you get the idea—both the esses in 'Sea Horse' were cartoons of the creature itself."

It was crude but perfectly plain. "I see," she said slowly, deciding how to phrase the next question. "The paper quoted you as saying there wasn't anyone aboard. How could you be positive?"

"You're right, of course," he agreed quickly, as if he had been waiting for it. "Realized the minute I saw my words in print. What I should have said—meant to say—was that there couldn't have been anyone aboard who was conscious." He grimaced. "That still bothers me, to tell you the truth. There might have been someone below, someone who needed help but couldn't get out of the cabin."

"One, maybe," Gillian said. "But surely not four."

"My wife's very words," he said, smiling at her. "I dare say both of you are right."

"You're being awfully helpful," she said. "Just two more questions, and I'll be out of your hair."

"It's no trouble at all, Gillian," Richardson replied. "I haven't had so attractive an interruption in a long time."

Oh, *that* kind, Gillian thought. Once he'd told you he was married he felt free to make a pass. She batted her lashes at him, wishing they were longer and the eyes behind them any color but brown. "You're obviously an old salt, Mr. Richardson," she said, leaning just faintly on *old*. "Have you any idea why *Sea Horse* was sinking when you found her?"

"Not really," he said. "We could see she had a problem—aside from being nearly awash, that is. But it wasn't anything that would've put her under."

"A problem? I don't remember anything in the article about that."

"I expect I forgot to mention it. They did the interview over ship-to-shore, you know. It makes for a rather choppy conversation."

"I know what you mean," she said, happy to steer him into safer waters. "But what was it about *Sea Horse* that bothered you? Was it the mizzen being down?"

"I didn't even know she was a yawl till I saw the newspaper story. What I noticed was her main boom, actually. It was detached from the gooseneck, with the sail furled loosely around it, and the whole thing sort of jammed down the companionway hatch."

"You think the gooseneck might've broken?" she asked.

"That was my first thought, of course. We couldn't see any signs of damage at the fitting, but something quite small could've let go. Anyway, it wouldn't have affected her ability to stay afloat."

"Nor her ability to send a distress call," Gillian reflected aloud.

"I've thought about it, of course," Richardson continued. "Especially on the voyage home. The crew and I talked it over; they're even older than I am, if you can believe it, and with much more experience among the five of them. The consensus was that there'd been some sort of accident on *Sea Horse*, and it caused her crew to panic. A broken seacock no one could close off, perhaps—something like that could be quite terrifying. So they abandon ship, forgetting to send a distress call or trigger the emergency transmitter . . . she did have one, as I recall."

"An EPIRB? Yes."

"They're in the raft, and it deflates somehow. And they drown. *Finita la commedia.*" He suddenly focused on Gillian's face. "Oh, dear. That was thoughtless of me. Anyway, it's a *very* feeble theory."

"It covers the bases," she said. "But don't worry about sparing my feelings. Everything you've said has already occurred to my skipper." *My skipper:* That was what attracted her—this old guy was Barr, forty years down the road. Unnerved, she pulled her mind back to the situation at hand. "One other thing. *Soundings* said you sent them a roll of slide film, which they processed. They converted the best shot of the sinking to black-and-white and sent the slides back to you. Do you still have them?"

"Of course." He looked momentarily embarrassed. "It sounds heartless, but I just couldn't seem to stop shooting. We had fourteen or fifteen that came out. . . . Anyway, I'll be happy to lend them to you; if you can stop by the rectory, you can have them now."

"The rectory?" she asked warily.

"Where I live, you know. Didn't mention it to the *Soundings* reporter. It always looks so odd in print, a priest owning a yacht."

Was he putting her on? "You're a priest," she said, handling the word with exaggerated care.

His smile told her he was toying with her, at least a little. "Episcopalian, my dear. Can't let the Romanists snaffle off all the good job titles. Now, why don't you hail the launch for us, while I still have a shred of reputation left?"

PATRICK:

SUNDAY AFTERNOON,

NEW YORK CITY

Standing on the upper deck of the Coast Guard ferry, he glanced at his watch and wondered how Gillian was making out up in Rhode Island. Three o'clock: She'd be done by this time, and on her way back to Norwalk. Hell, the way she pushes that little red Mazda, she's probably halfway home already. The vibration of the ferry's engines, turning over slowly, had been coming up through the steel plating under Patrick's feet, and now he felt the beat pick up as it prepared to leave the slip on the Manhattan side for the five-minute voyage across the channel. Spread in front of him, New York Harbor gleamed in the afternoon sun—to his left, up the East River, the classic stonework and spider-web cables of the Brooklyn Bridge and, just to the south of it, the masts and yards of the square-riggers at South Street Seaport; to his right, the broad sweep of the Upper Bay, with a big orange Staten Island ferry sliding easily across it; directly ahead, less than half a mile away, the mellow red brick of the Governors Island Coast Guard base, dominated by a tall, narrow concrete structure that looked like a windowless building but was in fact the ventilating tower for the car tunnel between Manhattan and Brooklyn.

A sailing vessel, crammed with tourists and pushed by the strong ebb tide, whipped past the ferry slip, and he mentally registered it as a gaff-rigged schooner. A year ago, before he'd met Barr and Gillian, he wouldn't have known a schooner from a catboat. The two of them had given him that, and so much more: a whole new world still opening before him. One he had to understand, if he was to have a chance with Gillian.

She had everything he liked in a woman: looks, passion, brains, and nerve. Too much of the last for her own good, sometimes, but it only made him want her more. What he felt was deeper than just wanting, though. Almost tasting the word, he let it form: okay, *love*. But not the kind he was used to. When it came to love, Patrick considered himself an expert; he'd been in love dozens of times, sometimes with two girls at once. He knew all the stages—the first tingle, the hot pursuit, the way it took over your head. . . . Sure, it wore off after a while, but while it lasted there was nothing like it.

With Gillian everything was different, and no fun at all. She liked him—he was sure of that—but for the first time in his life he wasn't able to push a woman's liking over the edge and make her fall for him. Every time he'd thought he had her set up, she slipped through his fingers. The worst moment, though, had been that night back in Antigua, when everything had gone exactly according to plan, only to blow up in his face at the end. He'd been completely thrown then, and all he really knew now was that he'd somehow blown the chance he'd been waiting for all winter.

When he'd glanced up from the guitar and seen her sitting there alone, her face like stone and Barr across the room with that big blonde, Patrick had felt his heart leap. He hit three fast, hard chords, drawing every eye in the place, and was halfway into the pounding beat of "Why Have You Left the One You Left Me For?" when he saw the trap in the words and skidded into "Good-Hearted Woman," realized it wasn't what he wanted either, and segued into a messy bridge to nowhere, his brain spinning its wheels all the while. He saw Gillian get up, moving toward the exit, and the answer came to him. Barely louder than the noise of the crowd, he slid into the melody of the Mozart duet the two of them had been fooling around with all winter, in spare moments between charters. She paused, clearly not sure of what she was hearing, and he began to sing: "*La ci darem la mano*. . . ."

He knew she couldn't refuse a challenge, and he was right. She turned, gave him a sweeping, exaggerated curtsey, picked up her cue, and sent the music right back at him. They'd never sung in public before, and to Patrick's delight they were damned good—

her pure, slight voice just the right size for the little space, and his easy, untrained baritone the perfect complement for her. By the end of it, she had worked her way to his side, and in the raucously sincere applause, her lips formed the two words *why not.*

They'd sung some more—an old Ian and Sylvia piece as a duet, and "Wolf Creek Pass," with Gillian humming the backup—and then she wanted to dance, but on a real floor, so they took a cab to a nice little hotel on the south coast. After a while, with their temperatures rising all the time, they both felt a need to get lost in a crowd, which meant another jolting ride, this time to a big touristy place up by St. John's, full of sweaty people off a cruise ship. Without a word between them, both knew the way the evening was going to end. Usually at this stage Patrick liked to play it cool for a little, let the pressure inside himself and his partner build slowly, but Gillian would have none of it. Every look was an open demand, every sentence vibrated with double meanings; by the end of the evening, he hardly dared to go out on the dance floor with her.

The ride back to English Harbour was torture. They had to share the only remaining cab, make dumb conversation with a couple they didn't even know, while Gillian clutched his hand so hard her nails drew blood. People were still hooting and singing aboard the other boats in the anchorage, but *Glory,* riding stern to the stone wharf, lay silent and empty. Gillian had dragged him into the after cabin, with the big double bunk, and their first embrace ought to have singed all the paint from the bulkheads. She stepped back, her hands trembling as they worked at his shirt buttons, and he tilted her head back so he could look into her face. In the cabin's dim light he wasn't sure what he saw there, but she shook her head sharply. He could have—should have—just taken her then, hard and fast. Instead he said "I love you," and felt her go rigid.

"Jesus, O'Mara, why'd you have to wreck it." She sounded, all of a sudden, angry and disgusted and tired to death. He didn't get it. Women *always* wanted to hear *I love you* just at that moment, and he'd never wanted to say it more. Later, he was able to admit what the back of his mind had known all along—it'd been Barr she was clutching, and Barr she would've been in bed with, given the choice. The knowledge stung, but somehow it didn't turn him off. The opposite, if anything. What he didn't know was how to change her mind.

The ferry's engines raced; it scraped out of its slip and began to thump its way across the sunlit water. The harbor smelled hot and oily, the way it always did on bright days. Being under way jolted him out of his gloomy daydream. Maybe this Farber thing would give him the chance to show her what he could do. Show her he was as good a man as Barr, even if he'd never be as good a sailor. The trouble was, he liked Barr. Admired the hell out of him, though he hadn't a clue what Barr thought of him. Or what Barr thought of anything, for that matter.

Before joining *Glory*'s crew, Patrick had spent nearly seven years in two armies—surrounded by other men, in barracks and tents on three continents—and he figured he'd hit every type by now, from the silent smolderer who wound up going berserk in the mess hall to the eager puppy who couldn't wait to tell you about his old lady's favorite position. Barr was something else, though. Not that he was hard to live with; even if he usually looked as if he'd slept in his clothes, his half of their tiny cabin was just as neat as Patrick's. He didn't snore, he smoked only on deck or in the main cabin, and personally he was as clean as a cat. The only weird thing about him was the books. Above each of their berths ran a long, narrow shelf; Patrick used half of his for socks and underwear, neatly folded and held in place with netting strung from the overhead, and the half up by his head for his cassette player and the collection of tapes he listened to on headphones. Barr's shelf, by contrast, was a head-to-foot row of paperback books, most of them so old they were held together with silver tape, so you couldn't even see the names. Not that it mattered to Barr, who was as likely as not to pick one without looking and start reading it in the middle.

In six months, they'd had exactly one personal conversation. At least Patrick thought it had been personal; he still wasn't positive. It'd been early in the season, and *Glory* was at anchor off Mustique; the charterers had drunk themselves to bed early, and Barr was reading as usual. Patrick, instead of listening to Crystal Gale or C. W. McCall, was brooding about his afternoon encounter with Mrs. Wilkes. Ginnie. The thirty-year-old wife of a fifty-year-old high roller from Greenwich, Connecticut, and not bad-looking in a tennis-playing kind of way. He'd been flirting with her, the same as he did with all the lady customers. Part of his job, after all, was being friendly to the guests, and it was up to him how he defined friendly. In Ginnie's case, since her husband seemed interested in every other female in the world but her, Patrick had turned the heat up a notch or two more than usual. She had responded so fast and so strong that he'd backed off in a hurry—Mr. Wilkes was the one writing the checks, and Ginnie wasn't *that* good-looking.

But such things had happened before, and Patrick knew how to disengage painlessly. He'd been surprised and annoyed when Ginnie, with a couple of extra rum swizzles under her belt, had begun needling him: "Here he is, folks!" she'd called out. "Mr. Patrick O'Mara, who can make the unexamined life really sit up and work." The other people in her party, all college types, seemed to think it was pretty funny. And though he'd pretended not to hear her, it was still pissing him off.

Finally, he couldn't stand it anymore. "Barr, can I ask you a question?"

He didn't look up. "Sure."

"What's the unexamined life?"

Barr didn't need more explanation. He'd been there, and Patrick had seen his private smile flick on and off, as it did again now. "Well," he said slowly, putting the book down on his chest. "Have you ever wondered why you're here?"

"On *Glory*, you mean?"

"On the earth, actually. Why you were born."

"Hell, they taught us that at school." He closed his eyes and rattled off the familiar words without thinking, the way he'd done a thousand times for Sister Mary Charles: " 'God created me to show forth His goodness and to share everlasting happiness with me in heaven.' But what does that have to do with anything?"

"It depends. But the next time Mrs. Wilkes gives you any crap about the unexamined life, you lay that line on her. I guarantee it'll stop her in her tracks."

From the deck below came the clash of metal gates, signaling the ferry's arrival and jarring Patrick back to the present. He looked down at the crowd waiting on the pier, mostly libertymen going across to Manhattan. Coast Guardsmen in civilian clothes stuck out just as much as any other military out of uniform, Patrick reflected, though Coasties in uniform had, to an ex–Regular Army NCO, the unconvinced look of people wearing rented costumes. He was trying to pin down why that was so, when he saw Will Evans, looming over everybody around him. Evans was in the electric blue trousers, light-blue short-sleeved shirt and white-topped garrison cap that Patrick figured must be the Coast Guard's Class A uniform. Aside from the different clothes, though, Will looked exactly the same as the moment he and Patrick had said good-bye, three years before, at the main gate of Fort Dix.

"Hey, you old son of a bitch!" Evans roared up at him, turning heads throughout the crowd. As Patrick stepped ashore he was folded in a massive bear hug that lifted him clear off the ground. "Damn, you look just the same, khakis and everything," Evans bellowed. He was a huge, hairy man with a voice that made windowpanes rattle and a face that looked as if he had stopped a runaway train with it. He set Patrick down gently, like a china doll, and took a step back. "Damn," he said again.

"You look pretty healthy yourself," Patrick said, when he had got his breath back. "What's the collar pin mean? They let you pick up your Army grade?"

"Hell, no—I had to earn this," Evans rumbled. He grabbed Patrick by the arm and pulled him toward a low brick building. "C'mon. I got my car back here." As they turned the corner the sharp spring wind, booming up New York Harbor, almost snatched Evans's flying-saucer cap from his head. "I'm a bosun second," he said, his confidential rumble sending half a dozen herring gulls into terrified flight. "It's just an E-5, but a whole lot better'n buck sergeant. I got my own forty-one-footer to skipper." His explanation carried them to his car, a VW convertible with a cancerous top, and he wedged himself behind the wheel, like a grizzly in a phone booth. "It's only half a mile, but we might as well drive."

Sliding into the other seat, and ignoring the pile of smelly laundry in back, Patrick said, "Looks like the Coast Guard agrees with you, Will. Didn't you like it outside?"

Evans turned the key and tramped the engine into shrieking life.

"Tell you the truth," he laughed, "outside wasn't like I thought it'd be." He shot the little car backward, stabbed it to a halt, and screamed out of the parking lot in first. "This suits me. Lots to do, low chickenshit index, good people—a third of us've been in other services before." He looked quickly at Patrick. "You'd like it."

"Probably would." He grabbed at the door as the VW careened around a corner. Along the street ahead of them, a row of comfortably shabby two-story brick homes fronted the whitecapped harbor. "You know what this looks like?" Patrick said. "Not counting the water, I mean? Officers' country on an old army post."

"You're not as dumb as you look, boy," Evans chortled. "That's what it used to be—headquarters of First U.S. Army, till about twenty years ago, when they moved us in. A damn good base: all the fun of New York without the muggings." He downshifted for a corner, and Patrick could almost hear the gears in his head shift, too. "So what do you think of civilian life?"

For a second, Patrick considered the triangle aboard *Glory*. "It's different," he allowed.

"I could get you back in," Evans said, looking at him from the corner of his eye.

"Back to taking orders from candyassed college kids? Come off it, Will," Patrick replied, but he was surprised at the momentary temptation he felt. He pushed it down. "On the phone you told me you found someone who could help with what I'm looking for."

"No problem," Evans replied. "Turned out I knew her already. She's a QM 1, working SAR in Station New York."

"I don't do alphabet soup anymore," Patrick said. "What's QM— a rank? And what's SAR?"

"Search and Rescue. QM's a quartermaster, mostly admin work; she stands duty P.O. here, kind of like a dispatcher. But she was working in the RCC—the Atlantic Area Rescue Coordination Center—when that sailboat sunk last year."

"She got a name, this SAR QM?"

"Susan. Susan Grover. Married to some guy used to be a Coastie. Now he's in the Merchant Marine, ships out for three months at a time. I figured I'd introduce you two and then clear out." Evans darted a quick look at Patrick, who ignored it. He tried again: "She's not bad-looking, Susan. And real, *real* lonely."

"Is that so?"

" 'S what they tell me." He paused. "You get married or something? You didn't use to be such a stiff."

Patrick forced a grin. "Must be getting old."

"Bullshit. You're just out of practice—I remember how they used to fall over when they saw you coming, with their little legs all spread. Christ, you must've screwed the entire female half of Salvador, and most of south Jersey after we got home. You just need to be back in a uniform."

"Hey, give it a rest, will you? This is business."

"Oh, *business*," said Evans. "That's different." He braked the car hard, the way he always did, and yanked it over to the curb. "Okay, here we are."

"Will Evans makes you out a real romantic character," she was saying. They were seated across from each other at the base's Burger King—like every other Burger King Patrick had ever seen, except for half of its customers being in uniform.

"Romantic?" said Patrick. "How so?" Knowing Evans's taste in women, Patrick had expected someone loud, big-breasted and low-slung, but Susan Grover reminded him of a greyhound—slender and nervous, with tight, fine-boned features. Her accent was mid-South, and from the way it came and went Patrick guessed she'd spent some time trying to erase it.

"Well, he told me you two were advisors together in Central America, and when your hitch was up you signed with mercenaries in Africa, like these guys you read about in *Soldier of Fortune* . . ."

Patrick snorted, wishing Evans had kept his mouth shut. "It reads a lot better than it lives, believe me."

". . . And then last year you got yourself shot, fighting some kind of gang in Brooklyn, and ran a big sailboat through Fire Island Inlet in a hurricane." Her eyes were an unbelievable deep violet that could come only from tinted contact lenses, and she was watching him with either fascination or complete disbelief.

"Was that before or after Will had me leaping tall buildings at a single bound?" he said, feeling more uncomfortable by the second.

"Well, maybe it wasn't a hurricane," she said, allowing her half-smile to broaden and warm. "But I did check with Station Fire Island,

and they surely do remember y'all coming over the bar in a full easterly gale. You scared the daylights out of them."

"They weren't the only ones," he replied. "Listen, did Will . . ."

"He told me about the case you're workin'," she said. She leaned forward, lowering her voice. "So what are you now, a private eye?"

It was a fair question, and he was still short of an answer when she continued: "I dug the Sitreps out of the file. Situation reports," she added, seeing his expression. "I didn't have time to make copies, and I can't give you the originals. In fact . . ." She glanced around the low-ceilinged room, empty except for half a dozen schoolkids and as many off-duty Coasties, all resolutely ignoring them. "In fact, I shouldn't be showing these to you, except that Will said you're okay."

"Would it be better if we went someplace else?" he asked. Her eyes widened and a wave of pink rose from her collar. "To look at the reports, I meant," he added quickly.

"Oh," she said; her blush deepened, but to Patrick's tuned ear she sounded almost disappointed. The violet eyes broke free from his. "That won't be necessary." Suddenly, she was all efficiency. She opened her purse and extracted several folded sheets. "Have y'all ever read one of these?"

"No. Let's have a shot." After a minute, he looked up at her, watching him expectantly. "I get about one word in three," he confessed, and risked a grin. "Guess maybe I need a translator."

"It's kind of like shorthand," she agreed, smiling again. She got up and moved to his side of the table, pulling her chair close to his. She was wearing just a trace of some perfume Patrick almost remembered the name of. Whatever it was called, he knew it was expensive. Her fingers were long and slender, the clear-polished nails cut short. She wore no ring on either hand. "Okay, this is the first one. From *Resourceful*. She was on LE—law enforcement—patrol about a hundred miles northwest of Bermuda. Anyway, she was the nearest unit, so she became on-scene commander. This American yacht, the *Aggressive*, turned up just in time to watch the *Sea Horse* sink, so the case went right into distress phase." Her finger traced the steps, point by point down the typed page, and with each explanation, the meaning behind the Coast Guard's private language became clearer to him. "They really pulled out all the stops: *Resourceful* put up her helo, the Bermudians sent out their own SAR boat—it doubles as the St. George pilot boat—plus a couple of tugs, and the Navy launched a P-3 from the Bermuda air station. And of course there were yachts all over the area . . ."

"Those were heading home from the race?" Patrick interrupted.

"Most of 'em," Susan agreed. "There must've been something like a hundred and fifty sailboats in that fleet. But there's always yachts coming into Bermuda or leaving. I think they get like a thousand a year—it's the only place to stop between the Azores and the Eastern Seaboard."

"And nobody saw anything? No wreckage, no empty raft?"

She shrugged. "No wreckage. Empty raft, that can be a tough one. You know what one of those things costs? Some fisherman finds it floating around, he might just take it home and then not have the nerve to admit what happened." She paused until he looked her in the eyes. "This what you need? You just tell me what you want."

"Susan, you're an ace," he replied, putting a little extra warmth behind it. "A real ace." He let his eyes stray down. The uniform— blue skirt and jacket, with her three chevrons on the sleeve in red— suited her slender figure perfectly, but then she had the kind of shape that anything would look great on. "So tell me about the search," he said, aware that the silence between them had stretched out too long.

"It was really two searches at once," she said. "Because they had so many facilities available. *Resourceful*'s helo did an expanding square, from the datum of the sinking . . ." Seeing Patrick's slightly glazed expression she said: "When you have a known starting point—where the *Sea Horse* sank, in this case—you can search outward from there, flying straight legs at right angles to each other, each leg a little longer than the last. That's an expanding square. But we also had a pretty sure course for her, from Kitchen Shoal, where she checked out by radio, to the sinking point, so the Bermuda SAR boat ran a track line pattern along that heading."

"And nobody saw a thing," said Patrick. "How long did they look?"

"They had eight hours of daylight, plenty of time," she replied. "And because *Resourceful*'s skipper figured there might be people in the water, he had everybody search at quarter-mile intervals. Patrick, what they did was like a full-court press," she said earnestly, putting her slender, white hand on the back of his square, tanned one, then quickly pulling it away as if his skin had burnt her fingers. "If it was just heads in the water, they still could've missed them, but it's unlikely they'd miss all four."

"I see what you mean."

"Lots of those racing sailors wear personal strobe lights," she went on, sounding a little breathless. "In case they go over the side. So we searched through the night, too; and all the next day. *Nada.*"

"Could they maybe have drifted . . ."

She was shaking her head. "We're not amateurs. There's a circular current runs clockwise around Bermuda; they plotted it into the search patterns. The search aircraft even queried the yachts in the area, by radio. Talked to nearly every one of them, and no one saw anything."

"What about a hijack attempt?" he asked. "The newspapers said something about that, as a rumor."

"They always do," she said. "We'll never know for sure, but it doesn't fit the scenario."

"Even so, wasn't one of *Sea Horse's* crew—that French guy—in trouble with the Bermuda police?"

"My goodness, you *have* done your homework," she said approvingly. "Our people checked that out, too, and he was a possibility, a real love-'em-and-leave-'em creep. Just like a Frenchman, wouldn't you know? But it was all small stuff: a handful of funny cigarettes, a case of booze. No heavy stuff, no violence . . . just the other way, in fact: Even the smell of an angry husband and he'd be out the bedroom window like a shot." She darted a quick glance from under her lashes.

"A wise policy," Patrick replied, poker-faced. What else had Evans told her about him?

"And that California chickie he picked up, Dawnstar something— her real name's Willis, by the way—she'd been in trouble, too. Skipped probation for hit-and-run, back in Santa Barbara. Not a criminal, really, just an airhead."

"What about the owner of the boat?" Patrick asked. "And his girlfriend. She's who I'm looking for, the girlfriend."

"The owner was a Vietnam vet, Air Force officer . . . that was a little funny: The Air Force didn't like him much, but they wouldn't say why. Something he did back in the war, but never got charged for. But he was legit all the way—job in the family business, some little pinko magazine; never arrested, never even got a parking ticket. And his friend had her wild days, when she was in college, but she straightened out afterwards." She grinned. "God, I hope they never put the dogs on me . . . some of the things I did, I tell you."

"Same for all of us," said Patrick absently, thinking that it looked as if Barr had been right again. And disliking that almost as much as he hated going back to Gillian empty-handed.

Susan began putting the papers back in her handbag. "Will told me a little of what this is about. You're really acting for that girl's father, isn't that it? Why does he think his kid might still be alive?"

"Because last week he got a postcard from her, saying so." She started to speak, and Patrick put his hand up to stop her. "I know what you're going to tell me. Two people have already said it: the card was kicking around for months before it got mailed, right?"

"Probably." She considered for a long moment, very much the cool professional, before she went on: "Look, we never officially close out a case like this—it's suspended, pending further developments. But I can give you the unofficial scenario. *Sea Horse* starts taking on water; maybe she hit something. We know the skipper was too sick to stand when they cleared customs in Bermuda, so it's somebody else who goes to the radio—one of these digital jobs—and punches up the wrong channel. Sends a distress message out into the blue, and nobody hears it. The water gets deeper, and the pump can't stay ahead of it. They launch the raft and climb in, while the boat sails on by itself. Maybe the raft has a leak, or only inflates partway—that happens all the time. Or maybe it gets punctured or flips, and that's the ball game for them."

"And they forget to set off the emergency transmitter. The EPIRB," Patrick put in. "They leave it behind."

Susan pursed her lips. "Well, that's a puzzler. The EPIRB was packed inside the raft canister—we know that from the race inspection report. So if anybody got into the raft, the emergency transmitter was right there with them."

"Assuming they knew what it was."

"Shoot, if they could read the label, they'd know what it was," she said. "Like I told you, it's a puzzler. And so's that postcard. But you get used to that kind of thing in the SAR business."

He pushed his chair back. "Susan, I can't tell you how much help you've been. Really: I owe you for all this. And just to prove it, I'm going to ask another favor."

"You got it," she said quickly. And added, in a different tone, "Unless you want the keys to a forty-one-footer."

He felt the hairs on the back of his neck stiffen, but he said only, "Can you make me copies of these Sitreps? I'll be happy to pay for them."

"Forget it," she laughed. "That doesn't cost anything, 'less you're a taxpayer. You want me to mail 'em to you, or will you pick them up?"

Women or music, timing was everything. And he was enjoying himself. "Oh, I'll pick them up. And treat you to dinner."

"Isn't much of anyplace to go, here on the Island."

"I wasn't thinking of the Island," he replied. "I was thinking of a little place I know in Greenwich Village."

"Greenwich"—she pronounced it like the color—"Village? Hey, that'd be supercool. You know, I've been stationed here more'n a year, and I've never been there. Not a lot of fun you can have in New York on a QM's pay."

"Don't worry about it. We're on expenses." He felt her interest sharpen. "You know, if you had a chance to double-check the files, just in case there might be another of those Sitreps . . ." He looked deep into the fraudulent violet eyes.

"Never know," she said, matching his stare. "Might just be. Think you could read it yourself, now?"

"I think I'd still need an interpreter."

Suddenly, he realized he hadn't thought about Gillian for nearly an hour. On the other hand, she probably hadn't thought about Patrick O'Mara all day. Anyway, it had been months since he'd flirted with a young, attractive woman. And it felt as good as it ever had. He got to his feet, reluctant to leave, and Susan stood up facing him. In her low heels she was nearly as tall as he was. "You know," she said slowly, "you're not what I thought you'd be like."

"And what was that?"

"Well, from what Will Evans said, I knew you'd be a tough guy, and you are. But he also said you were the best NCO he ever knew."

"Did he?"

"You don't seem like a petty officer. At least I hope not."

She was getting at something, but he wasn't sure what. "What's a petty officer like?" he asked, looking pointedly at the chevrons on her sleeve.

"Oh, this is just my disguise," she smiled, covering the insignia with her long, slender hand. "Your real noncommissioned officer can make anything, fix anything, or do anything—all he needs is an officer to point him in the right direction."

It was near enough to draw blood. "You prefer the guy who does the pointing?" he said, keeping his voice even.

"Not for me. I like a guy who can point himself. Real few men can."

"Hope I won't disappoint you."

"I'm sorry," she said quickly. "I didn't mean to get personal." But she had, and each of them knew it.

Hunkered down on the floating pier alongside *Glory*, Barr was removing crusted grease from inside the drum of the starboard genoa winch, which lay disassembled on a doubled sheet of newspaper beside him. Humming under his breath, he poked into its corners with a retired toothbrush, pausing occasionally to clean the bristles in the coffee-can of gasoline at his elbow. There were plenty of other, more urgent jobs—three single-spaced pages of them in *Glory*'s Defect Book, down on the chart table—but none that allowed his hands to work independently of his racing mind.

Something was wrong with that photograph of the sinking *Sea Horse*. He was sure of it, but no nearer pinning down the problem than he'd been last night. The picture was underexposed and slightly out of focus, and being reproduced on newsprint didn't help. But there was something about that mainsail, bundled around its boom and rammed down the companionway, that kept tripping a tiny alarm in the back of his head.

"My God, Barr! What on earth . . ." Gillian was standing on the pier a few yards away, gaping at him. Following her eye, he looked down at himself.

"I was just cleaning the winches," he said.

"With your *nose*? Not to mention your hair and your toes." She began to giggle helplessly. "You're incredible. You must've given your mother fits." She put down the flat black box she'd been carrying and surveyed him more carefully. "Thank heaven you aren't wearing anything but shorts. You wait right there, and I'll get some clean rags and more gasoline. You're not coming aboard in that state."

"But I haven't finished."

She considered the pile of gleaming pieces laid out to dry, the far smaller group of parts yet to be cleaned. "How much longer?"

"Maybe ten minutes. And fifteen more to regrease and assemble the whole thing."

"Plus a couple of days to ungrease you." She gave a theatrical sigh. "What's the use?"

"None," he agreed. She was right, of course—he was a mess, as usual. But two days ago she would've been furious, and he made the obvious deduction: "You must've had a good afternoon."

"I got the slides," she replied. "And met a neat older man. Not bad for six hours' work."

"Not at all. What's that you're carrying?"

"Slide projector. I borrowed it from the Power Squadron classroom behind the chandlery. I figured we could hang a sheet or something in the main cabin, blow the pictures up to life-size."

"Good idea. Just let me finish this."

"And clean up," she warned, picking up the projector. She swung herself up over the gunwale and looked down at him. "In exactly thirty minutes, I'll have a double-strength dark-and-stormy on the cabin table."

"Sounds great," he said, rubbing furiously at a bit of dried grease.

"And if you're not right there, I'll dump it down the galley sink," she added, with a triumphant grin he had not seen in a month.

The sea had a metallic blue-gray look, ugly little waves with white tops. One of them was breaking over *Sea Horse*'s cockpit coaming in a flurry of spray.

"He was shooting at five hundred," Gillian said, from over Barr's shoulder. "That's why it's so dark."

"Uh-huh." He reached back to twist the projector's focus knob until each flying drop was distinct. *Sea Horse* was probably too far down to save even then, he reflected: at least three feet of water over the floorboards. They were right not to board her. The photographer must have been holding the camera low, shooting under his own boat's main boom. . . . Who was it said the quickest way to flatten a sea was point a camera at it? Hiscock? No, Chichester. The stern graphic with the sea horses was sharp enough, though. And ugly as hell. "Let's try the next one," he said.

As the projector clicked, he felt rather than heard someone step aboard, the minuscule change of *Glory's* trim. An instant later the image flashed on the screen: *Sea Horse* was sliding under on an almost even keel, everything forward of the doghouse already immersed. "Holy shit!" said Patrick's hushed voice, from the cabin entrance.

"Grab a chair," Gillian said. "We're almost done." And to Barr, "You want the next one? They're not in chronological order."

"Wait," he replied.

After a long moment, Patrick said, "That port. The after one in the doghouse. Is it busted?"

Barr shook his head silently, and Gillian said, "Just crazed. As if somebody hit it with an axe."

Or the butt end of a boom, Barr thought. But if you were going to take the boom off at the gooseneck and then ram it down the companionway, you wouldn't swing the end out over the side. Or would you? He shrugged. "Next."

In terms of composition the slide was a near-disaster; the horizon was cocked at an angle of twenty degrees, and the left-hand third of the frame was blocked by the blurred leech of *Aggressive's* mainsail. The photographer, standing on his own boat's cabin top, must have lost his balance as he shot down over *Sea Horse's* stern and across her empty cockpit, directly into the companionway. But all at once Barr knew what had been bothering him about the other pictures he'd seen.

Gillian must have felt him tense. "What is it?" she demanded.

"The mizzen's completely gone," he said. "Mast, boom, standing rigging, the works. But there's no sign of damage aft."

Gillian voiced the question that was on Patrick's face: "So what?"

"So a mast doesn't fall like that," he replied, and as he spoke the wrongness of it clarified in his mind. He'd witnessed three dismastings and, as a boatyard manager, seen the results of a dozen more. "When a spar goes down it makes a mess—scars on the deck, dents in the pulpit, that kind of thing. Stays and shrouds trailing over the side, scraping the gelcoat. This—this is practically surgical."

"Well, it's gone just the same," Gillian objected. "I mean, you can see the fittings for a mizzen right in the picture." She pointed: "Mast step, just behind the cockpit. Chainplates for the backstays and lowers and . . ." She paused, at a loss.

"Split main backstay," he supplied.

"Right. She was set up to carry a mizzen, and she raced as a yawl—it's right here in the fleet roster: '*Sea Horse*, 34'9" yawl.'" A solution lit her face. "If the crew took the mizzen off for some reason, could they have struck it down below?"

Barr had already considered that. "Too long. The boom, sure; not the mast."

"But how—" Patrick began.

"You're sure that's only the main boom sticking out the hatch?" she asked.

"With the mainsail wrapped around it: yes," Barr replied.

"Well, she may have raced as a yawl, but she sank as a sloop," said Gillian, with a touch of impatience. "Another of those mysteries of the sea they're always talking about."

"I guess I'm dumb, but I don't get it," Patrick put in, sounding annoyed. "How can the same boat be a sloop *and* a yawl?" Barr hid his surprise: in less than a year aboard *Glory*, the mate had assimilated so much that you forgot he'd never even been on a sailboat until the previous spring. His appetite for information sometimes seemed insatiable, but like so many other fact-eaters he felt betrayed when data shifted underfoot.

"A boat can't carry two rigs at the same time," Barr assured him. "Of course not. But you can take one rig off a hull and replace it with another. Some owners do it to make a dog sail better; others just like to experiment. It was a lot more common about twenty years ago—several boatbuilders came out with models you could order as sloop *or* yawl. The people who built the Alberg thirty-fives were big on that: they had three or four stock boats you could buy rigged either way. It wasn't a big deal for them—move the mainmast step and the chainplates, cut the sails a little differently."

"But those are like factory modifications," Patrick objected, and Barr nodded. "Could you just pull a mast off and still have the thing sail?"

"Sure, if it was the mizzen on a yawl. Or even on a ketch. Oh, you'd have a few balance problems, but she'd sail well enough." The answer clearly left Patrick dissatisfied; he was happier with things that either worked or didn't. Barr also knew that this wasn't the moment for a dissertation on center of effort in a sail plan.

"So what does it mean, Barr?" said Gillian, after a moment. "You're the expert, you tell us."

"You've got it wrong," Barr replied, with a wry grin. "What we experts do is take complex problems and make them insoluble. Frankly, I haven't a clue what the mizzen is about. Probably there's a perfectly obvious answer, once you talk to somebody who sailed with Roger Huddleston."

No one seemed to have anything else to contribute, and at last Patrick broke the impasse: "I don't know about you two, but I'm starved. What's for supper?"

"Whatever you're making," Gillian replied. Barr felt her glance over at him. "I'll give you a hand in the galley, while the great mind broods out here."

He sat alone, flicking from slide to slide as he tried to assemble a coherent theory from what the pictures told him, but the information refused to coalesce. What am I sure of? he asked himself. Start with the basic details: seas about four feet, wind—a northeast wind, from the way the watery morning sunlight lit the waves— about fifteen or twenty knots. Enough of each to make a seasick, inexperienced crew scared and miserable, maybe; but this was not an inexperienced crew.

Nothing visible wrong with the mainmast gooseneck, or nothing major anyway. A pin might have let go, but they could've improvised a repair. The same went for the mizzen, assuming they'd sailed with it rigged in the first place. Anyway, he reminded himself, they could simply have turned around and powered the few miles back into St. George. The crazed doghouse window? Definitely a blow, and from something blunt, not sharp. But again, not a crippling defect, certainly not in those conditions.

She had sunk on an even keel, or nearly so. That needn't necessarily mean much, but it argued against a big hole in the bow, say from a collision. Maybe a hose had come off a galley seacock—but that was what seacocks were for: close the damn thing, and the leak stopped. Or say the seacock broke off. You could still plug it, if you got to it in time. If you didn't panic.

That was still the most logical explanation: They'd suddenly discovered the cabin full of water, lost their heads, tossed the raft
canister over the side, pulled the string that inflated it, and got in.
People were goddamn stupid about life rafts, maybe because of the
name. A raft was just a smaller boat than the one you were leaving.
And one that could be punctured or leak or flip over.

But why the boom and sail in the companionway? It was easy
enough to assemble a theory, until you got to those intractable
pieces of aluminum and sailcloth.

What about the sails? He flipped back through the slides until he
got one that had been taken over the sinking boat's bow. Not a
particularly good or informative shot, but it did show a furled jib,
still hanked to the forestay and crudely lashed to the lifelines. One
sail accounted for. And the fabric wrapped loosely around the main
boom was the mainsail—he could see a batten pocket, with the
batten still in it, and what might have been a sail number on the
cloth. Staring at it again, he wasn't so sure. Maybe not a number,
maybe a stain. Or just a shadow. He leaned forward, his frustration
finding its own voice: "What the hell *is* it?"

"Pork vindaloo," said Gillian, sounding surprised. He straightened
up to see her standing at his elbow, holding a steaming kettle that
had already filled the cabin with an almost explosive concentration
of garlic. "You liked it the last time Patrick made it," she said. "Why
don't you shut the projector off before it burns a hole in the sheet?"

Barr built himself another forkful of pork and rice, wondering if
what he had already eaten was really dissolving his fillings or if it
just felt that way. Across the table Gillian's face glowed moist in
the lamplight, and he felt the drops of sweat on his own forehead
gathering for a renewed descent. Patrick, of course, showed no hint
of the volcanic effects of his own cooking, but then he never did.
He was sitting back now, sipping his second beer and outlining the
results of his foray onto Governors Island. He sounded pleased with
himself, which was fair enough, but Barr had the faint, nagging
feeling that he was holding something back.

". . . So you see," he concluded, "it was a regular full-court press,
what they did to find *Sea Horse*'s crew."

"Certainly sounds that way," Barr observed. He helped himself to another frosted bottle from the ice-filled bucket on the deck at his feet. "Good thing that cutter happened to be around. What was she doing in Bermuda?" he asked idly. "Part of the offshore drug patrol, I suppose."

"Some kind of law enforcement," Patrick replied. "I didn't . . ." he paused. "Somebody outside on the pier. I'll go see who it is."

"It should be Uncle Sol," said Gillian. She slipped from behind the table and began stacking the dishes as she talked. "When I called him to say we'd take the job, he told me he'd get us a deposit right away. It's like him to bring it around himself."

Reluctantly, Barr watched the remains of his dinner vanish into the galley. He lit a Camel and puffed a cloud of garlic-flavored smoke at one of the oil lamps, whose flame reeled back for a moment and then burned more brightly than before. Patrick's cuisine, picked up God knew where, relied on a kinetic variety of sauces and sea-sonings, no combination ever exactly repeated. His ability to mask third-rate meat and dead vegetables within a cloud of spice had been a godsend in the West Indies, where most of the available provisions were best not seen, let alone eaten, in their natural state.

Clumsy steps on the companionway ladder, and Sol Farber stood in the doorway, sniffing the atmosphere, which would have toppled a miner's canary. "A little accident in the kitchen?" he said. "Never mind—it could happen to anyone." His smile, a weak imitation of what Barr recalled from his first visit, flashed and as quickly vanished.

"What's the matter, Uncle Sol?" said Gillian, reappearing from the galley.

"Matter? What should be the matter?" He attempted another smile, even feebler than the first, then slumped on the settee across the cabin from the big table. Glory's crew watched him in silence, and after a minute he shrugged. "So okay," he said, his voice flat. "I had a call today. From Sarah."

"That's wonderful!" Gillian exclaimed automatically. Clearly it was not, and Farber shook his head.

"What did she say?" asked Patrick, still standing in the main cabin doorway.

"She was—you know the word *meshugge?*" Farber asked. "Crazy. She was like crazy, crying and yelling at me." He was staring at the deck as he spoke, his thick, short-fingered hands locked together in front of him. " 'Don't rock the boat,' she said. 'You got to stop rocking the boat.' "

"Rocking what boat?" Patrick demanded.

" 'They'll kill me otherwise,' " Farber went on, as if he hadn't heard. "That's what she said. 'If you want me alive, don't rock the boat.' "

"But she is alive," said Gillian. "That's the important thing. I guess we can call off—"

"*No!*" Farber shouted. He looked around him at the three startled faces. "Sorry. I didn't mean to yell. But I don't want to call anything off." His voice was trembling with intensity. "*I want you should find my Sarah.*"

"Look," said Barr. "From what you've just said, your daughter doesn't want to be found. Just poking around could be dangerous for her." It was strange, he thought: A part of him was delighted at the chance of escaping from this absurd business, just as another part was being drawn into it.

"Don't you see," Farber was saying earnestly. "That's all the more why you should keep looking. If she's with people who might kill her, you think they're going to change their spots because we back off?" He paused, and a look of calculated cunning altered his cherubic, old man's face. "Anyway, I decided. It's going to seem like we're doing what she said. I'm going to stop looking. . . ."

". . . But we're not. Is that what you mean, Uncle Sol?"

"Exactly on the head," said Farber with satisfaction. "Whatever it was made Sarah call, it must be connected with me, when I went to the magazine."

"Just a minute," Patrick interrupted. "When did she call you, Mr. Farber?"

"When?" He and Gillian seemed to be holding their breath, as Farber considered the question. "Just after I got to the office. Maybe nine-thirty in the morning. Why?"

"Then it wasn't us," Gillian said, relaxing visibly. Quickly she explained what she and Patrick had been doing, but Farber was shaking her off even before she'd finished.

"No, no," he said. "It comes from that magazine, those new federals. I'm sure."

"Looks as though you may be right," Barr agreed slowly. "When was it you went to see them?"

"Three days—no, four days ago." Comprehension unwrinkled his forehead. "I see what you're thinking: It took a while for them to get hold of her. So maybe she's far away." His lips pursed. "You know, the call sounded like it might be coming from another country—lots of crackles and little foreigners talking in back."

Patrick, whose gaze had been moving from speaker to speaker, piped up: "Any chance you were followed here, Mr. Farber?"

The old man's mouth fell open. He seemed about to deny the possibility, and then visibly reconsidered. "I don't know, Mr. Patrick. Could be—this isn't the kind of thing I'm used to."

Patrick was already opening the foul-weather gear locker. He pulled out a nondescript navy blue jacket and wool watch cap. "Maybe I'll have a little look around," he said.

"But they'll see you coming up the pier," Gillian objected. "If there's anyone there, which I doubt."

"No, they won't. I'll take the dinghy—it's tied alongside—and paddle over to the gas dock." His eyes were glittering with the prospect of physical action. He shrugged on the jacket and zipped it up. "Be back in a few minutes," he said, and was gone.

"But if there *is* someone out there," Farber began. "Maybe armed with a weapon, you know?"

"All he has to do is breathe on them," said Barr.

Gillian darted a poisonous look at him, but her voice was firm and confident: "Patrick can handle himself, Uncle Sol."

"If you say so." The old man subsided unhappily. "I don't want to bring my troubles on you, that's all."

"We can deal with it," she said, her tone ending discussion.

What you mean *we*, white woman? Barr thought. Aloud, he asked: "You've got no idea where your daughter might've been when she called?" Overhead, Patrick's rubber soles squeaked faintly, as he moved forward along the side deck.

Farber shook his head. "It happened so fast. One minute I'm reading the paper, not a thought in my head, and the next my Sarah's screaming at me from maybe a million miles away. Before I could even think, she hung up."

The dinghy's padded bow thumped faintly against *Glory's* side; through the open port over Barr's head came an irregular *plash* as the little boat shifted to Patrick's weight. Gillian seemed not to have heard, her mind on the main problem. "Uncle Sol's absolutely right about where to start," she said. "*The New Federalist*. I'll call them first thing in the morning."

"*Call* them?" said Barr and Farber together.

"For a job." She looked at the two of them impatiently. "Well, it's the obvious thing to do. I can't just waltz in there and start asking questions."

"But it could be dangerous," Farber objected.

Farber was right, of course, but Gillian was wearing her mind-made-up look. She reined herself in with visible effort. "Which of us has the best chance of getting inside?" she said to Barr. "Seriously. Remember, I've worked in an office—hell, I've *run* an office."

It was true. In her first year with a small sailmaking firm, Gillian had gone from secretary to office manager. By the time she left she'd been completely in charge. "But what do you know about magazines?" Barr asked. "Or politics?"

"What did I know about sailmaking? I can type a streak; I'm good on the phone; I have an organized mind," she said. "Everything else is detail."

"I don't like it. . . ." Farber was saying, but Barr cut him off.

"She's right, you know. It makes sense." Gillian rewarded him with a flashing, unexpected grin; he felt it run right down his backbone and back up again.

She turned to Farber, whose protests had subsided to a rumble. "I'll need a place to stay, Uncle Sol. Somewhere in Manhattan. I can't use *Glory* as a home address."

"No," Sol agreed. "That could start them thinking. Listen, I have just the place for you—Mrs. Boyd, she works for me in shipping. A widow, very sweet, like somebody's mother."

"She has an apartment?" Gillian asked, sounding dubious.

"An extra room, actually. But it's a big place, on the West Side. Gillian, you'll love it: so clean you wouldn't believe, with white lace on everything, even the back of the chairs. And she could use the extra money."

"That's taken care of, then," Gillian said.

"Assuming you can get the job," Barr put in.

"Oh, I'll get the job," said Gillian, and to Farber: "I'll call you as soon as I do."

"Better not," Barr said. "Why doesn't Mr. Farber call you here tomorrow night—from a pay phone."

Farber, who had been writing something in a leather-bound notebook, gave him a frankly appraising stare. "You've got a very intriguing mind, Mr. Barr. But maybe that's not so bad, in this case. You want Gillian and I should communicate through you?"

"I think you should communicate as little as possible, both of you," Barr replied. "You won't be able to work through me, though. I'll be in Bermuda."

Gillian's eyes widened in surprise, but before she could speak Farber nodded heavily. "You think something got overlooked down there?"

"Could be. Look, whatever happened to Sarah seems to have roots in New York, where she worked. But *Sea Horse* actually sank off Bermuda, and when she went down everyone's attention was focused offshore. No reason to look anywhere else. Now that we know at least one person survived, it seems worthwhile to check out the islands themselves. Maybe somebody saw her, or Huddleston, or the other two." And maybe somebody helped Sarah get wherever she is now, he thought. Small as Bermuda was, it was nearly all waterfront; there were dozens of places to look—boatyards, bars, stores—and hundreds of people who might remember.

"Agreed," said Gillian. "But one of us has to hold the fort back here. There's still a lot of items in the Defect Book to be cleared before the season starts."

They heard a step on the side deck, followed by the familiar sound of Patrick catapulting down the companionway three steps at a time. When he appeared in the doorway, his face was pink from the chill night air. "Nothing," he said. "Mr. Farber's Caddy is the only strange car in the marina lot. Nobody's parked outside the gate at all." He stopped. "What's going on?"

"We've been deciding how to handle this job," Gillian said, avoiding his eye.

"And I'm not going to like it," the mate replied, lowering himself onto the settee. "Tell me."

GILLIAN:
MANHATTAN,
MONDAY MORNING

She glanced down for the second time at the scrap of paper in her hand, comparing the scribbled address on it with the shiny brass numbers on the door of the brownstone in front of her. Could I have made a mistake? This place looks more like somebody's house than a magazine office.

From the lead-colored sky came a rumble of not-so-distant thunder. Rain any minute now, a real spring downpour by the look of it; time to get inside. Gillian opened the door and found herself in a small vestibule, facing a second door that had a half-length mirror set into it, above a polished brass plaque:

TNF FOUNDATION
Press buzzer

As she reached to push the worn black button she heard an asthmatic whir from over and behind the second door, and realized someone must have been sizing her up through one-way glass. Bristling slightly, she pushed the door open and stepped into what must once have been a quietly genteel entrance hallway, before the addition of the grotesque fluorescent overhead light and a gray steel desk that faced the door and nearly blocked the passage. Most of the desk's surface was occupied by stacks of typewritten manuscript, and a small, old-fashioned telephone switchboard took up the rest of the space. From behind the barricade a gray-haired, horse-faced woman regarded Gillian coldly. "Yes?" she said.

Gillian had devoted some care that morning to achieving what she thought of as a New York office look—discreet blue jacket with padded shoulders and a nipped waist, over a two-piece print—but the woman at the desk (a surprisingly young woman, despite the hair) had been working from a different concept: a New York Mets cap perched sideways on her steel-wool frizz, and her upper body was engulfed by a drab gray sweatshirt at least four sizes too large. When she straightened up for a closer, clearly disbelieving look at Gillian, the white lettering across the shirt's front stretched into legibility: *Fuck Authority*. "Well?" she said.

"I have an appointment with Miss Carew. I'm Gillian Verdean." As her name echoed momentarily in the stuffy air, Gillian felt a touch of apprehension. Not until breakfast had it occurred to her that Sarah might have spoken of her to the staff at the magazine. Gillian's first, panicky reaction had been to invent a pseudonym, but Barr squelched the idea: "It's an unnecessary complication. You don't have any papers to back it up. And even if your friend did talk about you, nobody remembers the names in anecdotes."

Not a trace of recognition brushed the receptionist's wooden features. "You can sit there," she said ungraciously, indicating a backless bench just inside the door. She picked up the phone, rammed a plug into a socket. "Hi. Did you have an appointment with a Ms. Verdean?" The face remained expressionless, but Gillian sensed disappointment. "Oh. Well, she's here." The receptionist hung up. Pointedly ignoring Gillian, she picked up a handful of typescript and began to scan it with exaggerated interest.

From outside came a shattering peal of thunder, followed by a sudden fusillade of rain against the outer door. Gillian thought gloomily of her lack of a raincoat or umbrella, of the certain wreckage of her borrowed high heels, which had already pinched off all blood flow to her toes. She wiggled them and, to distract herself from the agonizing tingle of returning circulation, looked past the receptionist into the relative darkness of the hallway. Along the wall to the right, a carpeted staircase climbed unlit toward the second floor; to its left, the passage ended in a once-ornate wooden door, which flew open, framing a sturdy female figure in jeans and a sweater.

The woman bustled forward into the unflattering light which made her puglike nose look broader than perhaps it was, and emphasized the bulge of her large, intelligent eyes and the spray of freckles nearly covering the upper half of her face. A pair of oversize glasses were cocked up above her forehead, the earpieces wedged into the mouse-colored hair drawn tightly back at her temples. It was, Gillian thought, a face that ought to have been severe, even forbidding, but it was transfigured by a welcoming grin even the slightly discolored teeth couldn't spoil. The grin drew Gillian to her feet, smiling, before the woman said a word. When she did speak, the words came in a high-pitched rush: "You're Gillian. Super. I'm Kimberly Carew: I run this place—or it runs me: I'm not sure which. Anyway, call me K.C., everyone does. And you're right on time, which practically nobody here ever is, though not"—she patted the stone-faced receptionist's arm—"not you, Ursula dear." She took Gillian by the elbow, steered her past the steel desk and its guardian. "No coat? You might be marooned here for days. Come on inside where we can talk."

The door at the end of the hall opened into another hall, its walls painted ballpark-mustard yellow. From behind pressed-wood partitions that jarred with the building's original plasterwork came a multiple tapping, like a dozen shoemaking elves working overtime. K.C., holding the door open, caught Gillian's glance. "Great second thoughts of Western Man. That's Arts—they go to press at three, so they're all rushing like mad." She darted past Gillian into a doorway that opened off to the left. "Here, this is my office; it used to be a bathroom."

Bathrooms must have been a lot bigger then, Gillian thought, as she eased herself carefully into a wobbly, ancient chair in front of a desk that was twin to the one in the outer hall. The room was windowless, but as if in compensation had two doors. The walls were nearly hidden by banks of ancient wooden filing cabinets, with magazines tossed carelessly on top of them and cartoons and faded newspaper photographs taped to the yellow plaster above. The effect of layered shambles was intensely claustrophobic, even to someone whose life was spent in yacht cabins.

The desktop, in contrast to the disarray surrounding it, looked like an illustration from an office manual—IN and OUT boxes with their contents in preternaturally neat stacks; stapler, Rolodex, three sharp pencils and notepad in a rigid line; telephone to the right and, on a portable typing table to the left, the flattened keyboard and screen of a laptop computer.

K.C. had thrown herself into a large desk chair and was watching Gillian with barely contained amusement. "The decor's not my idea," she said. "I inherited it."

Gillian mumbled something sympathetic, then remembered why she was there. "Here's my résumé," she said, extending a single sheet hammered out that morning on *Glory's* battered portable.

"Right," said K.C. She tugged the glasses down and began to scan the paper, then looked up. "Oh, and I ought to apologize for Ursula. She's just not a happy camper, I'm afraid, but then she's a legacy— her uncle's Books, you see—and being a nepot seems to bring out the worst in people."

Taken flat aback by this incomprehensible wave of confidence, Gillian could only blink, but K.C. was already immersed in the résumé. "Conn College," she said to herself. "We're the same age. Don't you have a classmate at *The New Republic?* Or is it *The New Leader?* I still can't keep them separate." Gillian, deciding an answer wasn't required, kept her silence. "Constable Sails, office manager," K.C. murmured, then looked up: "Do they make, you know, sails for *boats?*" A pugnosed grimace: "God, what a dumb question."

"I wasn't a sailmaker," Gillian said quickly. "I was just in the front office, and it was like any small business."

"Not like this one, sweetheart," K.C. replied, with a short laugh, still looking at the paper in her hands. "Holy smoke, do you *really* type seventy-five words a minute?"

"Without errors," said Gillian flatly. "Guaranteed. And I can do Lotus and WordStar."

"Fantastic. Super." She set the sheet down on the desk, aligning it carefully with the edge of the blotter while she composed the question Gillian had been dreading: "If you're all that good, how come you're cold-calling places like this? Sorry to be so blunt, but it doesn't figure."

Gillian had prepared a meticulous little speech about her lifelong obsession with politics, but instinct told her it would be a mistake.

Instead, she heard herself say, "Because I got fired and I don't have a reference. And I really need work."

K.C. pushed the glasses back up on her forehead. Unshielded, her eyes seemed to lose their cheerfulness. For a long minute she eyed Gillian thoughtfully. "Go on."

Gillian looked down at her lap, improvising desperately. "In a small place, sometimes, you have to make nice with the boss. I overdid it."

"You had an affair with your employer?" K.C. said.

Gillian nodded. Thus far, the story was true enough, she reflected. "But I'd worked my way up to office manager before it started," she said.

"That does make a difference." Gillian risked a look. K.C.'s expression was unreadable. "He found someone he liked better, I suppose. They always do."

Not true. But the real ending had to be changed, for effect. Ugh. "One of the girls on the cutting floor," she agreed. A small, choked sob wouldn't hurt, she thought, but it was beyond her powers.

"I don't suppose you drop this on just anyone," K.C. observed. Her eyes were suddenly far too sharp, and Gillian forced herself not to look away.

"You're the first," she said. "And I don't know why I told you."

To her relief, K.C.'s grin reappeared. "Everybody does. I'm the universal aunt, I guess—secondhand tribulation our specialty. But I hope you learned something."

The twinkle in K.C.'s eye said that sackcloth and ashes weren't mandatory. "I learned to keep my pants on in the office, if that's what you mean."

"An expensive lesson." K.C. tapped the résumé's edge against the surface of her desk. "We're not looking for anyone right now," she said slowly, and Gillian felt her heart sink, before the other woman continued. "But we're not exactly at full strength, either. You're the best thing to come through that door since me, and I'm damned if I'll let you get away without a struggle. Would you be willing to start at Ursula's desk?"

"If that's all there is. Do I get paid, too?"

"Sporadically." K.C.'s laugh was not entirely genuine. "You think

I'm kidding, but I'm not. This time of year it's pretty slim pickings
for us, but it'll pick up in . . . a little while. Right now, the best I
can do is two hundred a week. No medical, no dental, no retire-
ment—and if you think of any other benefits, we don't have those,
either."

To agree without a fight would, Gillian judged, be too suspicious;
it was worth the risk of losing the job. "I don't think I'm quite that
desperate yet," she said, starting to rise. She stopped halfway up as
her toes gave a collective shriek of agony and looked K.C. directly
in the eye. "Tell you what: Make it two-fifty and you've got a
receptionist, plus whatever else she is."

"I'll make it two-twenty-five, and guarantee you a promotion
within the week," K.C. replied. "*If* you promise never to tell Ursula."

"Done," said Gillian, dropping thankfully back into the chair. She
wondered if the blood had soaked through her shoes yet.

"I take it you can start right away?"

"Is after lunch right away enough?"

"Lunch is included," said K.C., and added, "I'm buying, of course."
She glanced at her watch. "We've even got time for the tour before
we eat."

"That's great," said Gillian, forcing a smile. "But don't feel you
have to—"

"No imposition at all," K.C. replied, getting to her feet. She took
a step toward the door to her left, then paused. "No. We'll start
where we came in; it'll be easier for you to remember the layout
that way." In the awful yellow hallway, she indicated the door they
had originally come through. "That's the original front door, when
this was an apartment. The building used to be two duplexes, one
on top of the other. The magazine has the bottom two floors. Now
we'll go back this way."

Ahead of them, past the pressed-wood partition, the narrow corridor went by three open-fronted cubicles on the right and another
temporary-looking wall on the left, to end at a glass-paned door.
The rain had stopped, Gillian saw, and a garden gleamed wet in the
sun. "We eat out there sometimes. All this in here, what used to be
a dining room and a nice big living room, is Arts. Theater, Books—
Ursula's uncle; his name's Simmons. And Cinema. Don't ever call it
movies."

"I won't." As K.C. hurried past, Gillian looked into one of the openings. The space inside was barely large enough for a small bookcase, a medium-sized desk, and a large, mournful-looking man, with a telephone handset wedged between shoulder and ear, who was typing furiously on a laptop word-processor.

"That's Mr. Tangvald," K.C. whispered, once they were past. "He's UN, so he should be upstairs in World, but this was the only office available. Turn left."

Beyond the garden door, on Gillian's right, another cubicle. K.C. looked in and gave an exaggerated sigh of relief. "He's out, thank God. That's Science: Dr. Horsch. He ought to be in World, too, but they can't stand him. And never forget, it's *Doctor* Horsch."

"Got it."

They rounded a corner, heading back the way they had come. "Art and Books," K.C. said again, waving at two open doors from which more typing sounds emerged.

The next office had a single empty desk and an abandoned air. A neatly lettered sign on the half-open door read *Ms. Carew*. "Used to be mine," K.C. said. "Before I got promoted. The door on the far side of it leads back into the office I'm in now."

"How come it's empty?" asked Gillian.

"Office politics," K.C. replied. "There's a lot of it around here— gets into the blood, I guess. That spot is for the assistant to the business manager, and I'll be damned if I'll give it up to Editorial." She gestured toward a narrow, sagging staircase that clung insecurely to the right-hand wall. "That goes up to World and Nation. And Production and the bathrooms, which may be more important. Win's apartment is on the floor above that, but you have to use the hall staircase." She gestured toward a closed swinging door ahead of them. "Used to be the kitchen. We've come back around to the front of the house, you see."

"Oh," said Gillian. Under the staircase to their right were high, leaning stacks of cardboard cartons. The upper layers were gradually crushing the ones below, and the cartons on the bottom had split, to reveal yellowing, tightly packed magazines. "Overruns," said K.C. On the left was another swinging door, this one open. Through it she caught a glimpse of a small, book-lined chamber with an austerely elegant wooden desk in the middle. A thin man in shirtsleeves sat behind the desk, reading. As the two women passed he looked up, and his eyes met Gillian's. They were dark, deep-set eyes that seemed to have the pain of ages reflected in them. But before she could ask K.C. who the man was, she found herself hustled forward into a room no bigger than a closet, with a second door at its far end.

"Teletype and fax machines," said K.C., waving at a table on which squatted the devices in question. "And through here's Research."

K.C. flipped a switch by the door, and a single ceiling bulb came on. The room was exactly like the library in Gillian's elementary school, a low-ceilinged dusty expanse with metal bookshelves along the near wall and standing in the middle, and a small desk facing the door. "Mrs. Bookhouser—isn't it a perfect name?—must be out to lunch already," said K.C. She snapped a second switch, and another light came on over to the left, illuminating more gaunt metal shelving, packed with thin magazines. "Those are the competition. The whole gamut, from *National Review* to *Masses and Mainstream;* there must be a dozen different ones. And next to them are our videotapes. Famous speeches, mostly. We're really proud of our collection: it goes back to Tricky Dicky and Checkers, and we've got Dr. King's 'I've got a dream,' and LBJ refusing to run again—a couple of hundred at least. And what's not on video is on cassette: those little boxes have the exact words of every significant political statement in every national campaign since 1932." She looked sidelong at Gillian. "Why do I have the feeling you're not impressed?"

"Oh, I am," said Gillian, who had been thinking about her feet. "It's a remarkable collection. I guess there's nothing else like it."

"Christ, no—who else would bother?" said K.C., with a whoop of laughter. "Do you suppose I could talk you out of the rest of the tour, in favor of a bite to eat?"

"I think you just might," Gillian replied.

The restaurant, El Sombrero, was a shabby, noisy place, already half full a few minutes after noon. K.C. was clearly a favored habitué, and she and Gillian were quickly bowed to a corner table, from which they could watch the freed office workers surging past on Third Avenue. "Two frozen margaritas, please," said K.C., as her rump hit the chair. "And extra chips," she called, to the waiter's retreating back. "I hope a margarita's okay for you," she said to

Gillian. "You have to get your drink order in right away, before they lose interest."

"A margarita's fine, thanks," Gillian replied, thinking that she might just pour half of it into each smoldering shoe.

"The thing is," K.C. said, "*TNF*'s been around nearly forever. . . ." She saw Gillian's expression and pulled up. "Sorry. I do that a lot. *TNF*'s what we always call the magazine. Roger used to say"— Gillian's ears pricked up, but Roger was not to be explained, not yet, anyway—"that we used the abbreviation because the full name was nonsense. I mean, we certainly aren't new, and I bet not five people on the staff even know what a Federalist is. *TNF* is just one more basic left-wing political journal, like half a dozen others, except that we've never been tied down to any party, and the only national candidate we've ever endorsed was Henry Wallace."

"The governor of Alabama?" asked Gillian, surprised out of silence. "The one who was shot?"

K.C. regarded her for a long moment. "Not exactly. No." She seemed to be on the verge of explanation, then shook her head. "Never mind. The point is, we've never been co-opted, not by any-body." The waiter reappeared with the two drinks and an immense wicker basket of tortilla chips. "*Gracias*," said K.C. "*Dos otros, por favor*." And to Gillian: "You've got to *re*order right away, too. Very short attention spans in here." She lifted her glass to Gillian. "Wel-come aboard. I have the feeling you may be just what we need."

"Thanks," Gillian replied, ignoring a tiny pang of guilt. She clicked her glass against K.C.'s. "Husbands and sweethearts: may they never meet."

"And to hell with all of them anyway," K.C. said, emphasizing her approval with a healthy swallow. "Not that I have any experience in the first category. Sometimes I think I'm the only person I know who's never been married." She dipped a corn chip in the smoky red salsa and looked over it at Gillian, clearly waiting for her con-fidence to be returned.

"Now you know two." Gillian took an appreciative sip of her own drink, remembering what Barr had said: Don't give away any more about yourself than you have to; that way you won't have to keep track of a lot of extra lies. "So tell me about the magazine," Gillian asked. "What do I have to know to get by at Ursula's desk?"

"Not a hell of a lot," said K.C., chuckling. She pushed the empty glass to one side just as a full one appeared to replace it. The waiter, a slender man with moist, reproachful eyes and a cross tattooed between his thumb and forefinger, set Gillian's second drink alongside her half-full first. "You wanta order now, Miss?"

"In a minute." K.C. picked up her glass in both hands and stared into it as if it were a crystal ball. "What does she need to know?" she asked it. "Well, the office is officially open from nine to five-thirty, but only the Production guys get here before ten, and both of them have keys to the front door. So do all the regulars, so your first job is screening calls and weirdos. Just use your good judgment, and if in doubt call me."

Gillian nodded comprehension, as K.C. paused for a restorative swallow before continuing: "The editors may hit on you to read the slush—the unsolicited manuscripts—but that's up to you. Your biggest chore is the switchboard: Roger got us a fancy direct-dial system, but the Luddites in Editorial won't use it, and nine tenths of the calls still come through you." She rattled on, as half of Gillian's mind took in details. Roger again. Next time his name came up, she had to be quicker. "And that's the routine," K.C. concluded, a few minutes later. "Pretty elementary, and you won't be doing it for long. Any questions so far?"

"How come the one-way glass door?" Gillian asked. "The neighborhood doesn't look that bad, or am I missing something?"

"The door's another of Roger's brainstorms," K.C. said; she raised her hand to forestall Gillian's question. "I'll explain about Roger in a minute. But the door can be useful—we get the occasional dangerous loony, and it's a lot easier dealing with them before they're inside."

"Sounds reasonable," said Gillian. "But how do you tell the crazies from . . . from people like me?"

"One basic rule: Don't let in anybody who claims to hold public office."

K.C.'s deliberate pause made Gillian realize she was supposed to supply the straight man's question: "Why not?"

"Well, chances are they're hallucinating. But if they really *are* politicians, they probably want to pick a fight with one of the editors.

We denounce absolutely everybody in both parties, and a lot of them have thinner skins than you might think."

"Both parties? *TNF* doesn't like anybody?"

"Not anybody who's alive at the moment," K.C. replied. "Say, are you going to let that poor margarita dilute itself to nothing? I'll be happy to take it off your hands." She pushed her own empty glass to one side and moved Gillian's into the damp ring it had occupied. "You like *fajitas*? Good. Hey, Miguelito: *dos fajitas*." From halfway across the room the waiter waved an acknowledgment. "History lesson: the only way you can understand us," K.C. continued, putting her elbows on the table. "*The New Federalist* was founded by a New England bleeding heart named Elbert Huddleston, mostly so he could tell people what a rotten con game the Spanish-American War was. Luckily for Elbert, he was a very rich man, or he might have got himself lynched."

"Because he—"

"Because it was yet another popular war. As Win says, war is America's favorite outdoor sport. *TNF*'s opposed them all, and we've mostly been proven right, which is the quickest way there is to become unpopular. In 1898, we said the battleship *Maine* blew up by accident, which it did, and in 1983, we said Reagan's invasion of Grenada was theatrical nonsense, which it was—did you know the American military gave themselves more medals for Grenada than there were troops involved?"

"Not really. I—"

"Between wars, we sharpen our teeth on big business. *TNF*'s exposed every major American corporation, from Johns-Manville to Ford, and every crooked president, which is to say all of them. *Gracias*, Miguelito. Just put the dishes in the middle—we'll help ourselves. We've been taken to court I don't know how many times, and we've never lost. Not once." As K.C. spoke, her hands nimbly constructed a *fajita*, laying on a tortilla the strips of beef, onions, and peppers; splashing dollops of salsa, guacamole, and sour cream; and then rolling the steaming mess into a drooping, dripping cylinder.

"You're very good at this," said Gillian, after her first attempt self-destructed halfway to her face.

"Just practice," K.C. mumbled, around a huge mouthful. " 'S no harder than rolling a joint. Messier, but no more difficult."

"Well, it's been a long time since I did grass," Gillian replied. "Not since college." Unrolling her now limp tortilla, she attacked its remaining contents with knife and fork. "Tastes fine anyway. Go on about the magazine."

"Where was I? Elbert. He won every battle and lost every war, but he never lost heart. He left *TNF* to his son, Owen, right after the First World War. Owen managed to hold things together through the Depression, and then he checked out, and his daughter, Ida, took over in 1939. She was only twenty-five, and a tiny little thing—under five feet tall—but just as tough as her grandfather. And just as contrary: Day after Pearl Harbor, *TNF* came out against World War Two. If the magazine had been more important, it probably would've been closed down. But Ida kept it going, using the family fortune, and even took time to have two sons—without benefit of official father. When Ida talked about feminism, she wasn't kidding."

"I guess not," Gillian said. "She still around?"

K.C. shook her head. "Went to her grave back in 1970—Say, you want a beer to wash that down? Probably not a good idea. Anyway, her sons were Winthrop and Roger, which brings us up to the present."

"Roger being the one who installed the direct lines and the one-way glass." K.C. nodded. "And he's the editor?" Gillian added innocently.

"No, Win's the editor. Roger's—Roger *was* the business manager. He died just about a year ago, in a boating accident."

"Oh. And he was your boss."

"Right. A great guy." K.C.'s plain face was again transformed by her sudden smile. "I guess we were the only two at *TNF* who didn't give a shit—pardon my *français*—about politics. That's why I was so glad to see you don't care about it, either. All that righteousness can make the atmosphere pretty heavy."

"But if you don't care about politics, why're you there?" Gillian asked. "Why was Roger there, for that matter?"

"Oh, Roger was there because of Win," K.C. replied. "That was his mission—taking care of his older brother."

"And you?"

"Me?" To Gillian's surprise she seemed to be taking the question seriously. "I'm a fixer," she said after a moment. "I can make things work. Anything." She grinned. "And there never was a place that needed someone like me more than *TNF* does."

"So you didn't get Roger's mission when you got Roger's job?"

K.C. looked startled. "Well, maybe I did, a little," she replied slowly. "I never thought of it that way."

"I don't know anything about missions," said Gillian apologetically. "It takes some getting used to."

"For sure." K.C.'s eyes seemed to be on something in the middle distance, over Gillian's shoulder; her expression had slowly changed from reminiscent to warmly understanding, and now to what looked like mischievous. "A mission is only something you believe in. Or some*one*, in my case."

"Win Huddleston must be a considerable someone."

"Oh, he is." K.C.'s tone was matter-of-fact. "Win Huddleston is a saint."

K.C.'s calm certainty was as unnerving as her words. "A saint," Gillian repeated, trying to sound neutral.

"Not in a religious sense, of course," K.C. added, apparently to herself. "Win's a guy who's willing to make these tremendous sac-rifices—everything he owns, if necessary—for what he believes in. But he isn't a wimp about it, and he doesn't mind if you don't see things his way." She paused, considering what she had said. "Pretty limp definition, I know. You'll have to meet him yourself."

"I can hardly wait."

"You won't have to. He just came in the door." She called past Gillian, pitching her voice over the crowd noise: "C'mon over and join us, Win. Someone here I really want you to meet."

It was the thin man who had been reading alone in the wood-paneled office. Now that he was standing he looked to be about middle height and might have gained another inch by straightening his rounded shoulders. His long face, from a few feet away, looked as smooth as a boy's, but as he came up to the table Gillian realized he was considerably older than she'd thought: his dry, fine-grained skin was etched in a pattern of tiny lines, and his brown hair was wispy thin on top. He was wearing an obviously expensive, obviously antique tweed jacket over his white shirt, frayed at collar and cuffs; his narrow, striped tie had a faded ink stain halfway down.

"Hello," he said to Gillian, extending a thin hand. His wide mouth, belying his eyes, looked to be on the verge of a crooked smile. "Don't look so startled. The introduction from ambush is K.C.'s favorite social strategy."

Whatever K.C.'s intention, it was quickly frustrated by the arrival of Huddleston's luncheon guest, a pompous-looking man in an expensive suit. "Foundation," breathed K.C., signing the check with a flourish. As she led Gillian to the door she added, "You can smell the money fifty feet off."

For the rest of the afternoon, Gillian sat at Ursula's side, learning very little about her duties and more than she needed to know about how *TNF*'s newest editorial assistant planned to revolutionize journalism. When Win Huddleston returned from his lunch, he bestowed an absent-minded smile on Gillian and Ursula, but whether he actually saw them was an unanswered question.

By the end of Gillian's third day at *TNF*, she was able to identify about a dozen of the faces that regularly passed her desk. Most were senior writers from the first floor: Mr. Tangvald, who spent three hours a day listening to the phone but never spoke into it; Mrs. Hastie—Theater—who arrived at noon barely sober enough to stand, and left at six in exactly the same condition; Dr. Horsch, who acted and looked like a movie Nazi, right down to the monocle; Mr. Simmons of Books, who must have got in and out of his office by magic, since he was far too wide to fit through the narrow door. If they had a common denominator, it seemed to be booze. None of them was expected to wobble back from lunch before three, and Ms. Littleyard—Music—was said to be still drying out somewhere in Connecticut after the rigors of the opera season.

The people from the second floor were quite different. "Production" was two elderly men who had worked together for so long that they were nearly twins. One, Gillian knew, was Jake, and the other she nicknamed Not Jake, but she wasn't sure which was which. The Politicals, as the staffs of Nation and World referred to themselves, were for some reason as young and hyperactive as the personnel of Arts were aged and somnolent. Whenever they talked politics, which was all the time, their eyes glittered with anger and their voices seemed about to crack with outrage. Though they varied in appearance, from the five-foot-square Ms. Klein, who bore the imposing title of World Editor, to a junior Nation writer named Wolters who was tall and angular enough to snag low-hanging clouds, they seemed to Gillian essentially similar. "We're all wall-flowers," Ms. Klein remarked, toward the end of Gillian's official welcoming lunch at El Sombrero. "That's how we wound up at *TNF*. And why we all try too hard."

The lunch, which Gillian had hoped would give her the oppor-tunity to put some discreet questions about Roger and Sarah, was a dead loss. All the others present except for K.C. were furiously preoccupied by a Supreme Court decision announced that morning, and could scarcely wait to denounce it. As a result, conversation around the table was a series of white-hot monologues, with Gillian the only audience. At the end, exhausted by secondhand passion and still lacking the remotest idea of what her colleagues had been talking about, she went ruefully back to her desk.

It was maddening, she reflected. Everyone (Dr. Horsch excepted) was as friendly as could be, yet in three whole days she had found out next to nothing about Sarah. The only trace of her friend's six-month tenure was an unexpunged listing in the house phone direc-tory. When Gillian had asked offhandedly who Sarah Farmer might be, it became apparent that practically no one remembered her, except as the silly child (First Floor) or little *bourgeoise* (Second Floor) who had vanished with poor Roger. And when Gillian asked K.C. point-blank, all she got was an offhand "Oh, she hasn't been here for ages." No reference to her tragic disappearance at all—though, admittedly, K.C. was at that moment beset by *TNF*'s creditors, threat-ening to confiscate the current issue.

About Roger, on the other hand, there were plenty of opinions, most of them in the form of allusion. "The house Don Juan," wheezed Mr. Simmons. "Our own Alcibiades," Mrs. Bookhouser offered, and then blushed clear down to her collar. Mrs. Hastie got tangled in a long, complicated quotation from which Gillian got the confused impression that the late Roger had been either Oberon or Robin Goodfellow, or perhaps both.

The Second Floor's reactions, though less literary, were equally

baffling. Mr. Ringgold, the Nation Editor, had dragged Gillian physically into his office. "You see those?" he said, indicating an entire
wall full of journalistic citations. "Roger got us those. He was Our
Man in Saigon."

"Roger? He made this place *fly*," said Jake (or maybe Not Jake).
"I remember when he first came here, in 'sixty-eight, wasn't it? Man,
he was a ball of fire. It all changed after 'Nam, though. He lost
something over there. Not that he still wasn't a big one for fun and
games, but there was something missing, you know?"

"He was a sexist pig," snapped Ms. Klein.

Her assistant, a softly blowsy girl named Dorrian, completely
disagreed: "Roger was so great—he used to take everybody out
sailing on his boats. He was always buying these old sailboats, must
have had a different one every year."

That night, alone in her dreadful ladylike room on West Thirty-
third Street, Gillian tried to ignore the whine of a television preacher
boring through the partition, and wrote down everything she had
learned about *TNF* and Roger and Sarah, wondering if it was ever
going to start forming a coherent picture. What made her task more
difficult, she decided, was that the magazine itself remained a mystery to her: what made it work (beyond the most basic mechanical
routines), what paid for it, why it even existed. Gillian knew well
enough that part of her problem was political illiteracy—though
maybe, as K.C. had laughingly suggested, it was political tone deaf-
ness. Another part was simply the nature of her job—she saw everybody come and go, but never had the chance to share the daily bits
and pieces that created friendships and led to confidences. She felt
like a waterbug, skating across a pond's surface without being able
to break through to the world beneath.

When she checked in with Patrick (phoning *Glory* from Mrs.
Boyd's apartment), she tried to explain it to him, but he was still
sulking over being left out of the excitement, and nuance wasn't his
strong suit anyway. She had the feeling that Barr would have understood, though from what Patrick told her, he seemed to be running
up against his own blank walls down in Bermuda.

Barr had certainly left for the islands eagerly enough—without
even saying good-bye, which still rankled absurdly. Maybe he'd been
right in the first place: maybe there wasn't anything to find, beyond

some private disaster that Sarah wanted to hide from Uncle Sol. Gillian set the steno pad she'd been using down on the doily-covered night table beside her bed, clicked off the forty-watt bulb that grew out of Saint Christopher's ceramic skull, and lay back for what she expected to be a long night. Tomorrow was Thursday. She'd give it till the end of the week.

At two minutes to five the next afternoon, the switchboard at her elbow buzzed twice: an inside call. She picked up the handset. "Front desk."

"I'm sorry I missed your lunch Tuesday." The quiet, well-educated voice was familiar, but she couldn't immediately put a face to it.

"Oh, that's okay," she replied and then, realizing who it was, added a "Sir," which sounded so wrong that she heard herself tack on an awkward "Mr. Huddleston." The ghost of a chuckle at the other end made her ears go hot.

"I'll make a deal with you," he said. "If you'll scrap the honorifics, I'll buy you a belated welcoming drink."

This is it, she told herself—or it could be: the break she'd been waiting for. She forced herself to take a breath before replying, "That would be very nice," in a tone so demure it surprised her.

"Excellent," said Win. "Why don't you close down the switch-board. I'll be right out."

It was more like ten minutes before he appeared, muttering something that sounded like ". . . learn to wipe their own behinds." Seeing her raised eyebrow, he colored slightly. "Sorry for the delay. It's damned hard to get out of this place sometimes."

Gillian picked up the coat she'd tossed on her chair. "Then let's run for it before you have to wipe . . . before someone else turns up."

The abstracted look he'd been wearing congealed on his face, then transmuted to a slow, incredulous grin that was so infectious Gillian felt her face stretch to match it. His eyes held hers, and in that instant the distance between them telescoped to nothing, as if they had known each other for years.

"Yes," he said.

"Yes what?" she managed. For some reason she seemed to be short of breath.

His grin widened. "Yes, K.C. was right. You *are* what this place needs."

A perfectly ordinary compliment, she told herself. Nice, but hardly original. So why did she feel as if God had just given her His autograph? She was still wondering when Win took her arm and led her up the dusty, carpeted stairway to his apartment. At the top the landing widened out into what had once been an elegant little foyer, dominated by an age-darkened oil portrait of a thin-lipped man with worried eyes and, under it, a scarred half-oval mahogany table. The portrait looked as if it should have been labeled *Our Founder*, and the resemblance to Win was striking, even under the dirt of decades.

Win apparently had no trouble reading her expression. "Great-grandfather Elbert. Who else?" He took a handful of loose keys from his jacket pocket and selected one. The solid-looking door with its ornate molding would have been impressive if someone hadn't painted it the same institutional green as the walls. Win unlocked it and motioned her in. "I'm afraid it's pretty squalid, but come in anyway: I want to hear all about you."

She'd been keeping a meticulous log of everything that caught her attention at *TNF*—several pages in her private shorthand for each day, scribbled down the moment she returned to Mrs. Boyd's after work. The latest entry was headed *Thursday, 6/17*.

The rest of the page was blank.

PATRICK:
EAST NORWALK,
FRIDAY MORNING

By ten-thirty, the southwesterly breeze had freshened enough so that Patrick, wedged uncomfortably in *Glory*'s engine compartment, could hear the water slapping against the hull by his head and feel the boat's small movements against her dock lines. His immediate attention was absorbed by the delicate job of resoldering a wire into the back of the tachometer, a task made more demanding by the need to lie on his side while manipulating the hot iron and the coil of solder. But part of his mind was replaying his phone conversation, the night before, with Sol Farber. Patrick had called the old man with a report on the investigation's progress—or lack of it—and had let slip his own feeling of frustration at being left out of things.

"I see what you mean," Farber said. "There isn't anything left for you to check out on." He paused. "Unless . . . no, that would be silly."

"What? What would be silly, Mr. Farber?"

"I was just thinking about that *Sea Horse* boat. Maybe it sank because there was something wrong with it, something those race committee people missed."

"Well, there's no way to find out now," Patrick said. "Not with *Sea Horse* sunk three miles deep."

"What if somebody knew the boat was bad before it sailed to Bermuda?" Farber persisted. "Somebody where this Roger Huddleston kept it—the marine, or whatever it is."

Talk about a long shot. Patrick said as much, and could almost

hear Farber's shrug at the other end of the line. "Just trying to help.
I figured, what could it hurt to ask?"

And what was a little extra effort worth, to keep the client happy?
"Okay, Mr. Farber: I'll check it out first thing tomorrow."

While he ate breakfast Patrick looked through all the papers Farber
had given them, but no mention of a marina or yacht club could
he find. The obvious place to ask was at *The New Federalist;* Gillian
could find out in a minute. Of course, they'd agreed he should call
her only at Mrs. Boyd's, but if he waited till the evening, it meant
letting a whole day slip by.

By eleven, he knew that if he spent another day in *Glory's* bilges,
bent up like a pretzel, he'd probably go nuts. He gave the tachometer
wire a careful tug, decided the soldered joint was okay, and began
to worm his way backward toward the engine hatch, holding the
hot iron away from himself. After all, he told himself, Gillian fields
the incoming calls. Nobody can eavesdrop on her. Even if Farber's
idea wasn't all that great, it deserved a look.

"*New Federalist.* G'morning." Prepared to hear Gillian, he was caught
off guard by the sullen female voice at the other end.

"Uh, is Miss Verdean there?"

The voice, already cold, iced by ten degrees. "Wait a minute."

A series of loud clicks resounded in Patrick's ear, followed by an
exasperated, sotto voce "Shit!" and then Gillian's clear, impatient
tones: "Yes? Hello?"

"It's me. Aren't you on the switchboard?"

"I got promoted. Is something wrong?"

"No, everything's okay. I just needed some information fast."

"Well, be careful what you say." She was definitely annoyed, but
that was just too bad; he was part of this team, too.

"Can you tell me where you-know-who used to keep his boat?"

"Who? . . . Oh." He heard what sounded like paper rustling. "Why
do you want to know?"

"Your uncle"—leaning on the word—"said maybe there'd been
something wrong with it, something the race people didn't know
about. He thought I should check it out."

"Oh, for God's sake." Not just annoyed; really pissed. "All right.
He kept it on City Island: the North City Y.C. You know it?"

"Brown building halfway down the west side? Looks like a condo?"

"That's the one. And listen." She paused, and he got the idea she was assembling her next sentence with care. "Are you going there today?"

Now she sounded hesitant; what was going on? "Hadn't decided. Is it a problem?"

"No, I just wanted to make sure we wouldn't run into each other tomorrow." He was still sorting it out when she went on: "His brother keeps a boat there, too. I'm going sailing with him."

"Oh." He heard his own disappointment. "I thought you were coming back up here for the weekend."

"Patrick, this is part of the job. We don't have forever."

"Sure," he said. "Of course. I just wanted to show you the new wiring, some other jobs I did. But it'll keep for a day."

"I may not be up Sunday, either," she said. "Looks like things may be starting to move. I can't talk anymore."

"Okay. I understand. I'll call you tonight," he replied, and hung up. Damn: he'd been counting on having this weekend alone with her. It'd be—would've been—the first time in almost a year. And she was going sailing with some forty-five-year-old wimp instead.

No, that was unfair. She was going sailing with Win Huddleston so she could talk to him about his brother. Maybe she'd be able to learn something from him, some information she hadn't been able to dig up in the office—and something Barr couldn't find in Bermuda, either. Not that Barr seemed to be getting anyplace, judging by his last call.

But what if I was the one who broke this open? Suddenly the idea of driving down to City Island—it was only half an hour away—made a lot more sense.

Gillian's car was in the boatyard parking lot, and the keys were hanging over *Glory*'s chart table. Patrick's hand was on them, when it suddenly occurred to him that he couldn't just walk into a yacht club and start asking questions about one of the members, especially one who'd been dead a year. He had to have a reason, or be somebody who had a reason.

The answer, when it came to him, was right in front of his face, in the form of a business card taped to the bulkhead: *Rory Soderstrom*, it said. *Claims Investigator*. The real Soderstrom was trying to weasel his company out of paying for an ugly scar someone had made down the side of Gillian's scarlet RX7, but he could just as well be following up on an insurance claim made by the family of that California ding-a-ling, Dawnstar Whatever-her-name-was, who'd drowned—or was supposed to have drowned—aboard *Sea Horse*. It was a perfect cover.

An hour later, the new, improved Rory Soderstrom sat comfortably behind the wheel of Gillian's Mazda, doing seventy down the fast lane of I-95 and feeling better than he had all week. By way of costume for his role Patrick had put on a sportcoat and the less frayed of Barr's two neckties, a navy blue number with little red and white lighthouses on it. Under each lighthouse the numerals 1984 appeared in white stitching. Patrick had once asked what 1984 stood for, but the reply—"Four days wringing saltwater out of my socks"— hadn't told him much.

At the City Island exit, he dropped the RX7 back to thirty-five— a speed that seemed right for an insurance adjuster—and began trying to think himself into the part. Back in Bay Shore High, where Patrick had been an enthusiastic member of the Drama Club, his faculty coach had always said that real acting wasn't costumes and makeup but getting inside the skin of your character. After a couple of false starts, Patrick found he could do it—in front of an audience of one or two; but when he was confronted by a murmuring sea of faces he simply locked up. This time, he reminded himself firmly, he only had to convince one person at a time, someone who had no reason to believe he wasn't talking to the real Rory Soderstrom.

As he tooled the Mazda down City Island Avenue, though, Patrick found his concentration broken by familiar sights. For almost a year after he'd left the military, he had been the paid captain of a big power yacht that seldom left its City Island slip, and in off hours the designated lover of the owner's insatiable daughter; a lot of the guys he'd grown up with would've said he had it made. He'd thought so himself, for a while, and it certainly beat soldiering. Then he'd met Gillian, and everything had changed. Looking back at it now was like staring down the wrong end of a telescope: a tiny life full of tiny people.

He swung down a bumpy side street lined with small, neat houses that still had front lawns and dusty trees. This neighborhood was the old City Island, before condos and marina developments; it wouldn't last much longer. The end of the street was marked by a chain-link fence with an open gate, and a board with the faded name *North City Yacht Club*. Patrick pulled over to the curbless edge of the pavement and parked. Think the way an insurance adjuster thinks, he told himself as he locked the car, but when he tried his mind produced nothing but a blur.

Without the sign on the gate, the North City Y.C. could have been mistaken for an oversize parking lot with a grubby motel along one side. Here and there on the potholed asphalt a few boats sat propped on cinderblocks; some displayed FOR SALE BY OWNER signs that looked as if they had been in place through the winter. To Patrick's eye the rundown, neglected look of the place seemed over-done, as if the members had gone to a lot of trouble to achieve it. At first glance the clubhouse seemed deserted, but then he saw movement in one of the ground-floor windows and headed toward it.

From behind a warped plywood door labeled *Members Only* came the sound of angry voices, male and female. He knocked twice with no result and pushed it open. The room was wide and long, its walls hung with meaningless strings of international code flags. Several of the acoustical tiles were missing from the low ceiling, and the linoleum floor badly needed waxing. The voices were coming from a big TV set in the corner around which half a dozen overstuffed chairs—the room's only furniture—were huddled. "Hello?" Patrick called. "Anybody home?"

A gnome's face, brown and wrinkled as tree bark, appeared from behind one of the chair backs. "Who you lookin' for?" the old man asked, over the TV voices. "Nobody here but me. Not till after work."

"Well, maybe you can help me," Patrick said.

The wrinkled face suddenly assumed a sly expression. "You wanta be a member, that it?"

"No, no," Patrick replied quickly. "I'm looking for information *about* a member. A former member."

"We ain't responsible," the old man snapped back. "You got to collect from him."

"That's not it," Patrick said. He had continued to move forward during the exchange and now found himself towering over the chair. "The gentleman in question is deceased," he continued. "I'm from the insurance company." The gnome gaped up at him. "You must've known him—Roger Huddleston?"

"Hu'leston—sure," the old man cackled. "I know Hu'leston. Only he ain't dead. His boat's right out in the anchorage. *Kassandra.*"

Patrick lowered himself cautiously onto the arm of the neighboring chair. "Not that Huddleston," he said. "His brother Roger. Owned an Alberg thirty-five called *Sea Horse.*"

"*Sea Horse?*" the old man repeated dubiously.

"He was a member here," Patrick insisted, speaking very slowly. "He was lost at sea about a year ago, coming back from Bermuda."

The old man's small, bright eyes lit with comprehension. "Oh, you mean *Sea Horse,*" he said. "Ol' Roger's boat. But she didn't berth here."

"She didn't?"

"Just sometimes. Roger, he kept her at Hutchinson River Boatworks."

"How come?"

"Christ, *I* don' know," the old man replied. "He just did."

"Hutchinson River Boatworks," Patrick said. From its name the place had to be in the Bronx, but he was sure he had never heard of it. "You know where it is?"

"On the Hutchinson River," the old man said, with a malicious twinkle. Patrick resisted the urge to pick him up and shake him, but the struggle must have showed on his face because the old man quickly added, "You can see it from the Parkway, goin' south. Two more exits, then go over the river and back north. You can't miss it."

Pulling his mouth into a smile, Patrick got to his feet. "Thanks a lot," he said. "You've been a big help."

" 'S okay," the old man answered. His gaze had returned to the TV, but he suddenly looked back up at his questioner. "You're no insurance man," he said, with heavy scorn. "You're a cop—I can spot 'em a mile off."

If the North City Yacht Club was a gloomy dump—and it was— the Hutchinson River Boatworks was ten times grimmer, two or three acres of cinderblock storage buildings and mangled fiberglass hulls, all of it encircled by an eight-foot chain-link fence topped with coils of murderous-looking barbed wire. Three sides were edged by gray marsh that gave off a combined odor of dead marine life, rotting plants, and stale diesel. On the fourth side lay the Hutchinson River itself, a narrow, mud-banked stream that seemed, from its color and smell, to have its source in a giant crankcase somewhere upstream.

When Patrick got his first full look at the place, his immediate impulse was to turn around and go kill the old troll whose twisted sense of humor had sent him to this abandoned junkyard. But the gate hung open, and the sign on it looked relatively new:

HUTCHINSON RIVER BOATWORKS
Hull-Engine Repairs
Salvage
Slips

He drove in, the RX7 jouncing hard over the bare, rutted ground, and parked next to the least forbidding of the buildings, alongside a shiny new Porsche whose New York plate read NIKIWI. Seen from inside, the yard seemed less of a shambles. While the view from the approach road was blocked by the low hill of unidentifiable plastic fragments, behind it hulls of abandoned boats lay in orderly rows— sailboats on one side, power cruisers on the other—with access paths between them for a mobile crane. Three blue-coveralled men, armed with power-driven screwdrivers, were removing the stainless steel deck fittings from a big sailboat. They worked silently and fast, and never even glanced up at Patrick.

As he stood bemused, a voice called out, "Hoy! C'n oi 'elp yer, mite?"

Whatever he might have expected to hear, it was not Cockney, and his brain took a couple of seconds to make the translation. By then he could see the voice's owner, a stocky, muscular man about his own age, dressed only in very short shorts and ankle-high work shoes, with a mane of straight blond hair to his shoulders. He approached Patrick with a bouncy stride, one grimy paw extended. "G'day," he said. "I'm Nico Butler."

Automatically, Patrick took the other's hand. It was as strong and nearly as large as his own. As he groped for his pseudonym, he was aware of two very sharp blue eyes appraising him. "Soderstrom," he remembered at last. "Rory Soderstrom."

"Good-oh, Rory. Now, what can I do for you?"

"I'm hoping you can give me some information."

Butler's eyes narrowed momentarily, but his quick grin was disarming. "Give it me best shot."

"I'm in insurance," Patrick began, extending his fraudulent calling card, "but I'm not going to sell you any. Actually, I'm checking out a claim." He had roughed out his speech on the way from City Island, and found himself agreeably surprised at how easily it flowed. Butler nodded, turning the card over in his hands, as Patrick explained that he was helping out a firm in California, running a final check on the disappearance at sea of a young woman. . . .

"Oh, I get it," Butler interrupted. "You mean the bird who was on poor Roger's boat, comin' back from Bermuda. Don't recall the name, except it was somethin' weird."

"Dawnstar Perigee. That's the one."

"Dawnstar fuckin' Perigee," Butler agreed, shaking his head. "Don't know which'd be worse: drownin', or livin' with a name like that."

Patrick shrugged. "Anyway, her parents insured her life for a lot of money."

"And your company's not too keen on shelling it out, right?"

The real Soderstrom, confronted with the same question by a furious Gillian, had puffed up with a starchy resentment Patrick did his best to imitate: "We're happy to pay legitimate claims, Mr. Butler. But we have to be absolutely certain—"

"Hey, no offense, mate. And you can scrap the *Mister.* Nico's me name—short for Nicholas."

"Nico from New Zealand," said Patrick agreeably.

Butler grinned. "You picked up on the accent."

"I picked up on your advertisement," Patrick replied, nodding at the Porsche.

"Oh, that." Nico shrugged. "It's a rebuilt. Nothin' much under the hood except wishful thinking. Now," his voice was abruptly businesslike, "why don't we go into the office, and do this sitting down?"

He led the way past a building that seemed to be leaning away from the wind, saw Patrick's quick look through the dusty windows.

"All that in there's engines," Nico said. "Everything from one-lung Palmers to a V-twelve come out of God knows what. We pull 'em out of the junkers, oil 'em up nice and shiny, squirt a little ether in the air intake. We got masts, winches, cleats, stoves—you name it, if it comes off a boat, it's in here someplace."

Patrick stepped into the sudden gloom of a windowless cinder-block bunker. The smell of badly cured resin stung his nostrils, and he felt more than saw great, shrouded shapes looming over his head. Before his eyes had adjusted to the darkness, his host opened a narrow door and motioned him into a cluttered office. Nico dropped into a swivel chair behind a desk piled high with papers and indicated the room's only other chair, whose seat was occupied by a complex-looking chunk of machinery. "Just toss whatever that is on the deck," he said cheerfully. "Now, how can I help you screw the helpless survivors? Just a joke—sorry."

"What I've been looking for is someone who knew *Sea Horse* really well," Patrick began, choosing his words with care. "Since Roger Huddleston kept her here, and you obviously know boats inside and out, I thought you . . ."

"I'm it, all right," Nico said. "I even sailed to Bermuda on her. You didn't know that, I see."

"No, I didn't," Patrick agreed, tamping down a sudden warm glow of excitement. "You must've been a good friend of his."

"And he was a good customer of mine. Sorry to lose him either way," Nico replied. "I was watch captain for the Marion–Bermuda," he continued. "Like most Kiwi sailors, I race a good bit, and Roger needed all the help he could get."

"Oh?"

"Now, don't make too much of that," Nico objected, rocking forward in his chair. "I can see I've got to watch me tongue with you. Roger was a first-class sailor, very conservative. It was the boat was the problem."

"Something wrong with *Sea Horse?*" Patrick asked, feeling the glow heat up.

"I'll tell the world," Nico replied feelingly. "Bloody cart horse she was. Couldn't get out of her own way."

"Unseaworthy, you mean?"

"Lord, no," Nico laughed. "Just the opposite. Heavy as my office safe, and just as tough. Underrigged and badly tuned, and those sails he had were a joke."

Up the wrong creek without a paddle, Patrick thought. But to nail it down he said, "She'd have been a good boat in heavy weather, then?"

"Mate, she needed all the heavy weather she could get. Laughed at typhoons, she did. We even built a mizzen for her, to put a little spring in her step."

"Did it help?"

Nico shrugged. "On reaches, maybe—and in Roger's head. He loved it."

Patrick heaved himself out of the chair, whose sagging bottom nearly touched the floor. "Funny he took it out, then," he said casually.

From the corner of his eye he saw Nico freeze, halfway up. "Out? He never did."

Now *that* touched a nerve, Patrick thought. Trying not to betray too much interest, he said, "Maybe not, but when she sank, she had one mast—didn't you see the picture in *Soundings*?"

"Picture?" Nico looked surprised and annoyed. "What d'yer mean?" Silently Patrick took out a copy of the newspaper page and passed it over. Nico accepted the sheet reluctantly, turning it one way and then the other as if a different angle of light might change the photograph. "Come to think of it," he said after a long minute, "I think I do recall Roger saying something about striking the mizzen for the voyage home. Because of all the downwind work, you know."

"Oh?" Patrick said, thinking: God, I wish Barr was asking these questions.

"Well, that's how it is on a dead run," said Nico, watching Patrick from the corner of his eye. "Bleeding mizzen just cuts the air to the chute. 'Course, I wasn't there meself—flew back even before the last boat crossed the line. Kind of a shame to miss the parties and all," he added chummily, "but some poor sod's got to mind the store, and around here I'm the only one speaks English."

Don't try to sidetrack me, sport. "There's that much running, coming back from Bermuda?" he asked. "Enough so you'd take down a mast?"

"That's what it says on the Pilot Chart," Nico replied, with a shrug. "Roger was the kind who took that bumf like it was Holy Writ. Someone like you'd know better, of course."

"I would?" Patrick tried hard not to look as wary as he felt.

"Well, sure," Nico said, looking pointedly toward Patrick's throat. "Havin' sailed in a Bermuda yourself, I mean. I was in the '84 race, too—aboard *Timberwolf*," he added. He paused, waiting for Patrick's response.

"That must've been wild," Patrick managed. Why couldn't Barr just have said right out what the goddamn tie meant?

"That it was," Nico agreed. He held the door open for Patrick. "And how did your boat do?"

"Just one of the pack," said Patrick, stepping into the big, dimly lit room. "Are those repair jobs?" he added, before Nico could throw in another question.

Nico patted the big hull nearest him. "This one is," he said. "Most of 'em are too far gone to repair. We get 'em from people like you—insurance companies—as total losses."

"And you strip the good stuff off them for resale," said Patrick. "Winches and engines."

"Don't forget the lead from the keels," Nico agreed. "That's a big item these days. What we can't sell we chop up for landfill. Bloody glass-fiber hulls last forever, otherwise."

The sunlight, when they emerged, seemed brighter than ever. "I never thought of that," Patrick said. "Sounds like an interesting job."

"Only if you've got vulture blood," said Nico. "Anything else you need to know?"

"Nope. This should wrap it up," Patrick replied. He had the key in the Mazda's door lock when one of the hulls caught his eye. It had a deep, jagged gash at the junction of the plastic hull and the lead keel, and the aftermost three feet of its topsides had been badly scorched from deck to waterline, but by comparison with its torn, gaping neighbors it appeared relatively intact. "That one looks like she might be a fixer-upper," he said idly. "An Alberg thirty-five, isn't she?"

Once again, Patrick had the sense of Nico pausing in midmovement. "Her? Not a bit of it," said the New Zealander. "She *was* a Vanguard—close to the same size, and built by the same company.

Deceivin' appearances, that's what she is, inside and out. Her whole interior's gutted—you could put your foot through the hull."

"Too bad," Patrick said, sliding behind the wheel. "Galley fire?"

"Right-oh. Crew panicked and jumped overboard, and she sailed herself onto a rock."

"Too bad: She still looks repairable. Well, thanks a lot, Nico. You've been a big help."

"It makes a nice break from crunchin' boats," he said, thrusting his hand into the Mazda's open window. "Mind how you go."

After three wrong turns Patrick finally located the eastbound I-95. Once he had slipped the RX7 into the traffic stream, he let his reflexes do the driving while he considered the conversation with Mr. Nico Butler. *Did I make an asshole of myself?* More important, *did I make him suspicious?* On balance, he had to admit, the answers were *yes* and *maybe,* in that order. To make it worse, his memory kicked up Barr's warning to Gillian about the dangers of false identities.

So was the whole trip a total loss, as his brain kept telling him? He slowed for the tollgate at Mamaroneck, fished the correct change from his shirt pocket, and passed it over. "Not yet," he heard himself say. "I'm not through yet, dammit." The tollbooth attendant, a hefty young woman, seemed to shrink back in her plastic enclosure and looked out at him nervously. He gave her a broad wink and floored the accelerator.

When all else fails, ask Mrs. Mulvey: It was something Barr said often. People might refer to Mrs. Mulvey, the bookkeeper at *Glory's* boat-yard, as The Gorgon, but she knew absolutely everything about the Norwalk waterfront and a surprising number of other facts besides. And she had a soft spot for Patrick, thanks to his policy of being especially attentive to plain, older women. He dropped the Mazda neatly into its assigned space outside the Carey & Willard office and stepped into the cool interior that always seemed to smell of wood chips and diesel oil. On a high shelf behind the counter the VHF radio—Mrs. Mulvey's own party line—blinked its single red eye as it scanned back and forth across the channels. She was sitting at her scarred rolltop desk and, as she looked up, gave the long handle of her old-fashioned adding machine a vicious yank. "Afternoon, Patrick. I haven't seen your friends lately."

"They're out of town, Mrs. M," he said. To avoid the inevitable next questions, he added, "Barr's down in Bermuda and Gillian's in the city. Your hair looks nice." In fact, it looked like old rope that had been spliced, coiled, and then varnished, but it must've taken a lot of work.

Mrs. Mulvey's long face cracked in a narrow smile, as her hand went up to touch one of the stiff-looking coils. "It's just the same old thing," she said. "What can I do for you?"

"Do we have any Alberg thirty-fives in the yard, Mrs. M?"

"Alberg thirty-fives." He could almost hear her memory whir. "Not for years. Mr. Hopkins had the last one, *Eleuthera*, her name was. Back in '76."

"Oh." Well, it'd been worth a try. Suddenly, the other name popped into his head. "How about a Vanguard?"

"Well, of course we do," she said. "You walk past it every day. The sloop with the name."

He knew instantly which one she meant: there was only one boat named *The Agony and the Ecstasy* at Carey & Willard, and maybe, with luck, in the whole world. "Mrs. M, you're wonderful," Patrick said. Before she could move, he bent over the counter and kissed her full on the lips.

"Patrick O'Mara!" she gasped. A slow smile lit her face more brightly than he would have thought possible. "You're dreadful," she said. He blew her a second kiss on the way out the door.

The Vanguard was in its slip, only two down from *Glory*, and Patrick looked it over with growing satisfaction. Well, he thought, I may not know as much about sailboats as Barr or Gillian, but this baby is absolutely not the same as the hulk Nico Butler said was a Vanguard. The doghouse isn't as round, the ports are different, and the hull's got much more—what's the word?—sheer to it. He turned on his heel and walked quickly back toward Gillian's car. Mrs. Mulvey was standing in the office doorway, waving what looked like a thick, dog-eared magazine at him. "They're in here," she called. "Both of them."

What the hell was she talking about? "I remembered we had a

stack of these," she was saying, as he approached. "Old Mr. Carey used to buy a new one every year." Now he could see the printing on the cover: *1969 Sailboat & Sailboat Equipment Directory*. He took the book—more like a catalog—from her. It was full of writeups of stock sailboats, one to a page, with photo and sail plan for each, and he flipped the pages over until he came to the Alberg 35.

"That's it!" he exclaimed. "That's the one." He turned to Mrs. Mulvey and enfolded her in his arms, lifting her off the ground. "I just may elope with you," he said to her scarlet, breathless face. "But right now I've got to run." He set her down with exaggerated care and vaulted over the stair rail. Two men he knew by sight—powerboat owners, he thought—were standing in the parking lot, staring at him with their mouths open. As the RX7 shot out of the yard, scattering gravel, their heads turned in unison to follow him.

The gate was closed when the Mazda pulled up in front of it. Closed and secured with a huge chain and the biggest padlock Patrick had ever seen. He got out of the car and surveyed the huge mound of boat fragments, but there was no sign of life, aside from a gray rat the size of a small dog that watched him fearlessly from its perch on what had once been a sailboat transom. From where Patrick stood little of the yard's interior was visible; he stepped cautiously off the pounded dirt of the entrance road, his feet sinking almost at once into oily brown mud that smelled of death and bilge. Edging his way along the chain-link fence, where the ground was not quite liquid, he reached a point from which he could see the main building and, parked in front of a pair of huge steel doors, the square frame of a Travelift crane. Slung from it, in a pair of wide canvas straps, was a scorched and battered sailboat hull. Its lead keel had been removed, as had its cockpit winches, its propeller, and its rudder, but it was without doubt the boat Patrick had last seen lying on its side, a hundred yards away; the boat Nico Butler had insisted was a Vanguard and which was unquestionably an Alberg 35.

Patrick worked his way farther around the yard's perimeter, ignoring the mud that squelched around his nearly new deck shoes. He caught a glimpse of something hairy scurrying through the weeds, nearly stepped on a dead gull that was lying on its back with its wings spread. At last he was as close to the Travelift as he could get—maybe twenty yards off. Close enough to see that the Alberg's keel had been ripped free from the hull, leaving a border of shredded fiberglass. Fast work, he thought. Looks like the chain saws are next.

But why? Why tell a stupid lie and why, now, this rush to chop up a particular boat? What was the point? Maybe Gillian would have a clue; he glanced down at his watch: She'd be back in her rented room by the time he got back to East Norwalk.

"No, she already left," said the piping, old woman's voice of Gillian's landlady, Mrs. Boyd. "She couldn't have been here for more than five minutes, and then her gentleman arrived to pick her up."

"Oh," Patrick said.

"I never knew a girl to dress so fast," Mrs. Boyd continued cheerily. "She's a real bolt of fire, your friend."

Maybe if you worked for Sol Farber long enough you started to talk like him. "Did she say when she'd be back?"

"No, but her gentleman was talking about taking her to a show, so it'll probably be late. And she's going away for the weekend, too."

"She told me." Well, to hell with it, he thought, as another idea occurred to him. "Would you ask her to give me a call in the morning, before she leaves? My name's O'Mara; she has the number."

"I'll write her a note," said Mrs. Boyd. "Put it on her night table."

"That's great, Mrs. Boyd. I really appreciate it," he said, but his mind was already racing ahead: The Coast Guard kept reports of marine accidents, he knew. Anything where the damage was more than a couple hundred dollars. Maybe they'd have something on a sailboat that was gutted by a galley fire, and then hit a rock.

And besides, it was a perfect excuse to call Susan Grover. As he unfolded the slip of paper on which she'd written her home phone number, the ghost of her perfume wafted up from it; for a moment he could see her plainly, and not in a uniform.

The square tower housing Bermuda Harbour Radio sat on top of an abandoned nineteenth-century fort that was tucked into the crown of a hill overlooking the town of St. George and its nearly landlocked harbor. The station itself occupied a large room full of modern communications equipment, and from two hundred and fifty feet above the water provided a godlike perspective not only of the island-studded anchorage and its narrow entrance but also, by radar, of the ocean around the archipelago.

"It *is* a good view, isn't it," agreed the station watchstander Barr had been talking to. "A regular panorama." He stared out at the harbor as if he had never seen it before, a slender man with receding hair and paler skin than most Bermudians had. In a more businesslike tone he added: "Were there any other questions you wanted to ask? I'm afraid I haven't been very helpful."

He hadn't, but not for lack of trying. "Can't think of any," Barr replied. "You know more about the *Sea Horse* sinking than anyone else I've talked to. And right off the top of your head, at that."

"Well, it was so unusual. Not the fact of a boat sinking within sight of the islands—that's happened hundreds of times, what with the reefs and all. But finding no survivors, nor even bodies, when the searchers should've had everything on their side . . ."

At his elbow, a radio suddenly crackled and spoke: "Bermuda Harbour Radio, yacht *Silkie*."

"Excuse me," the man said to Barr. He picked up the microphone and keyed it. "*Silkie*, Bermuda Harbour. Switch six-eight."

An American yacht inbound, with questions about customs procedures. The conversation, made clumsy by the constraints of two-way radio, seemed likely to go on for some time. Barr waved farewell and stepped from the shaded office into the blinding sunlight of midmorning. Up here on the hilltop the northeast wind was strong and hot, tugging at his damp shirt. Off to the north towering gray clouds were ranking themselves along the horizon, and the atmosphere was already soggy and leaden; it would probably rain by lunchtime. As Barr started down the steep hill toward the town below he was more than a little tempted to shortcut his schedule for the morning and go directly to the White Horse to see if a couple of rum swizzles could wash away his frustration.

He had deliberately saved St. George for last, telling himself that Hamilton, the colony's capital and center of activity, was the logical place to start looking for recollections of the year-old sinking. The islands' two biggest yacht clubs were there, and Barr could count informed acquaintances in each. Not to mention the police and Customs and the Tourist Bureau, each of which required a visit. The city itself had no attraction for him, however. Over the years that Barr had been sailing to and from Bermuda, he had watched Hamilton selling more and more of its soul to the tourists; on his last three passages, he had moored out at the east end of the colony and not made the long haul around South Channel into Hamilton Harbour at all. The big cruise liners tied up bow to stern along the waterfront now seemed to dominate the whole town, and the shoals of bewildered, tottery ancients who wandered in and out of the overpriced stores that lined Front Street had no connection to the Bermuda he remembered from his youth—not all that long ago, he told himself—when he had first come ashore after a bruising passage down from New England. Maybe Hamilton could still remake itself into a sailor's town when the racing fleet was in, from Newport or Marion, but the rest of the time it seemed almost as freeze-dried as Nassau.

St. George, on the other hand, still had some of the feel of old Bermuda, even though a black-hulled cruise ship was lying up against the wharf on Ordnance Island, the sound of her dinner gongs and P.A. system wafting over the town. St. George's shops were more chi-chi every year—branches of the big Hamilton stores for the most part—but there was still economic room for the steamy laundromat the sailors used, and the minuscule supermarket where cruising yachtsmen went to get ice, and bars like the White Horse, where late at night you could hear sailors expanding on the truth in three or four languages. But St. George's biggest appeal remained its harbor, where close to a hundred sailing yachts were tugging at their anchors, with room for an easy two or three hundred more. From their sterns the flags of half a dozen nations snapped and popped in the breeze, and even if most of the boats were flying the familiar American yacht ensign, you could still count on more than a few Red Dusters, a couple of Canadian maple leaves, a French tricolor or two, and the black, red, and yellow of Germany. When Barr had set out from his guest cottage that morning, his feet had automatically directed his track out of the straight way and down to the waterfront. Looking across the anchorage, he had felt himself at home, felt his heart lift (though he would never have said so) at the sight of so many other wanderers.

Breakfast was three cups of coffee and a truly revolting pastry, wolfed down in a tiny shop that catered to early-rising fishermen; as he tried to ignore the sugar clawing at his tooth enamel, he picked up one of Bermuda's several newspapers, captivated by its front-page headline: EAST END SOOT FURY. The story, disappointingly, had to do with the irritation of Bermudians whose cars had been dusted with cruise-ship stack exhaust, but the wonderfully lunatic words stuck in his head like an omen, and as he had trudged up the hill to Harbour Radio he could almost convince himself that his luck had turned.

Now, as he walked back down, the sniveling undertone of reason, which had insisted all along that a breakthrough was too much to hope for, was too loud to ignore. After nearly a week of failure, this last blow had struck with more force than he'd expected. Of course, the money he was spending was Sol Farber's, but Barr found himself more anxious then ever for the old man to get something for it. Anyway, the next stop on his list was almost in front of him, a boatyard at the end of the harbor, much patronized by delivery skippers and other sailing professionals.

The yard's only building lay twenty yards or so beyond the end of the paved side street. A sportfishing powerboat was hauled on the slipway, half her bottom gleaming with fresh antifouling paint; a center-cockpit ketch was tied up to the bulkheading. The yard office was the obvious place to begin, but he had to have a cigarette before he could bear talking to another stranger. Lighting up, he pulled the smoke into his lungs and wandered over to the bulkhead. The ketch lying alongside was a type familiar to him from the Caribbean—a fat, shoal-draft clunker with far too little sail and far too much ambitious accommodation. An ex-bareboat almost certainly, headed back to her Stateside owner after serving out her indenture.

That unknown owner was in for a shock, Barr reflected. Savage tropical sun had reduced the now-furled sails to stiffly feeble caricatures of their original shape, while burning the life out of the teakwood trim. Jolly charter parties had bent three of the lifeline stanchions inward and dinged the rubrail in a dozen places, besides cracking the binnacle compass like an eggshell, while even jollier Caribbean mechanics had doubtless wreaked their happy-go-lucky repairs on engine and water system. He didn't envy the sailors who had brought the sad old tub this far, and who still had the Gulf Stream to cross.

Heat on his fingertips reminded him his cigarette had diminished to nearly nothing. Reluctantly he ground it into the crushed shells at his feet and was turning toward the yard office, when the sailboat's companionway hatch slid open and a familiar mop of coarse blond hair appeared. "I thought you were supposed to be chartering in New England," said Captain Jolly. Before he could answer she continued, "Me and my frog crew can't seem to bleed the fuel line so it stays clear. You want to take a look?"

Barr lifted himself out of the engine compartment. "Okay," he called, over the level, unmuffled roar. "You can shut her down." The shattering noise dropped to an asthmatic stutter, the engine gave three barking coughs and died. In the ringing silence, the only remaining sound was the whine of the blower.

"It's fixed now?" asked Jolly's crew, a young man named Jean-Paul Aubier. He was lean and angular, with a hawk's nose and a mass of curly black hair. And, like most of the French professional sailors

Barr had met, a bikini so small and form-fitting that it was more advertisement than garment.

"It should get you home," Barr replied. He looked up at Jolly, who had been operating the throttle from the cockpit and was now crouched in the companionway. "Your battery's about had it, you know. What happened to the number two?"

"It died on the way up from St. Thomas," she replied. "They didn't have the right size replacement in stock here, so they're sending one over from Hamilton. It's still too small, but I'm sailing tomorrow, no matter what."

That was typical of Jolly, Barr thought. But it was her voyage, not his. Aubier, to judge by his sober expression, was less than delighted by the situation, but he was probably too young and certainly too macho to overrule his female skipper on the grounds of mere safety.

"We owe you a drink, Barr," said Jolly. "There's rum in the locker behind the stove, and ginger beer and limes in the icebox." She leaned forward for a closer look. "I think we owe you a new shirt, too, but the drink comes first."

Fifteen minutes later, his tongue loosened by four ounces of Gosling's Black Seal, Barr was finishing a slightly edited version of the *Sea Horse* saga: ". . . sunk without a trace. And I do mean without a trace."

Jolly, who was still on her first drink, looked puzzled. "So you flew all the way down here on the strength of a postcard, Barr? Anybody else, I'd say he was just ripping off the client, but I know you better'n that."

He had already made up his mind to take Jolly a bit further into his confidence. "More than a postcard. We know the girl's alive, but I can't tell you why we know."

Jolly shrugged. "If you say so. But I still think the Coast Guard's right about the sinking: *Sea Horse* sprang a leak, started going down, and the crew panicked."

"*Non.*" Jean-Paul, sitting curled up like a cat in a corner of the cockpit, had been so silent they'd forgotten he was there.

"What d'you mean, *non?*" Jolly demanded.

The young man was obviously constructing his reply with difficulty, and Barr realized that Aubier's command of English wasn't as complete as his lack of accent made it seem. He put his hand on Jolly's arm to silence her. "Not *panique*," he said after a moment. "Not André Corduan."

"You know him?" Barr snapped.

Jean-Paul shook his head. "Not to say hello with. But by . . ." he groped for the word, pounced on it: "Reputation. There are not so many of us who follow the sea in yachts, *n'est-ce pas?* Corduan was well known in the *cercle nautique*." Jolly leaned forward as if to say something, but Barr squeezed her other arm and she sat back. "He was not to say famous," Jean-Paul continued. "No Tabarly, no Marc Pajot. But a sailor of skill and courage. He had been already in a boat wreck, I know; a sprung leak would not trouble him."

"If he was so good and so well known," Barr said, speaking slowly and carefully, "why was he put ashore from *Ouragan?* Why did he take a last-minute berth, without pay?"

Jean-Paul's shrug was a minor Gallic masterpiece. "Perhaps the girl . . . who can say for certain? But Corduan was . . . *comment dit-on méchant en anglais?*"

"Naughty," said Jolly, at the same instant that Barr replied, "Troublemaker."

"Yes, yes," said Jean-Paul delightedly. "Both things. But look— there is a French yacht here in St. George now, *Jacques Coeur*. Her skipper sailed the Route du Rhum in *Ouragan*, and he is old friend of mine. Maybe he can tell you something."

"We'll take him to the White Horse and ply him with your client's booze," Jolly suggested. "Jean-Paul can translate from the French, and I'll translate from the Jean-Paul."

"Sounds to me like everybody's going to get plied," said Barr. "Well, what have I got to lose?"

A westerly puff raced over the water toward *Kassandra*, ruffling the surface as it came. Gillian, who was handling the yawl's mainsheet, glanced toward Win and realized he hadn't noticed it, absorbed as he was in the sheer beauty of the day. She eased the main a few inches just as the gust struck, and instead of staggering the boat leaped ahead, heeling slightly as she did so. From the leeward side of the cockpit, the elderly, apelike man whom Win called Otley caught Gillian's eye and winked.

"What do you think of her—*Kassandra*?" he asked. Even before they'd left the mooring, almost eight hours earlier, she'd been able to tell that he was a more-than-competent sailor who'd come to terms with age by substituting timing for muscle. Otley, she gathered, had sailed with Win in this same boat for twenty years, and she worded her answer accordingly.

"A real lady. Stiffer than I would've thought." Gillian's boarding-school upbringing made her feel awkward without the lubricant of a *Mister*, but she still didn't know if Otley was his first name or last, or a nickname. So far she'd managed to avoid calling him anything.

He beamed at her. "That's the Concordias, all right. Ladies every one. It's the hull shape: hard bilges." Win was watching the two of them with a proprietary air that Gillian might have found annoying in anyone else; with him, though, it seemed somehow right that his friends should give him pleasure. Out here on the water, he seemed to have shed ten years. "Win said you'd been a sailmaker," Otley observed. "What d'you think of the sails?" His gap-toothed smile had gone suddenly crafty, and she had the feeling the question wasn't really aimed at her.

"I *worked* for sailmakers," she said. "I wasn't one myself." She scanned the sails with narrowed eyes, just as if she hadn't already noticed they were blown almost completely out of shape, the jib missing a snap and the mizzen marred by ugly black streaks where it had chafed against its upper shrouds. "They look okay for cruising."

"How about for racing?" Otley insisted, glancing at Win.

"Go ahead, Gillian—tell him they're awful," Win said. "Otley's been at me about them for three seasons."

"Well," she said cautiously, "I don't think I'd use them for *serious* racing."

The two men burst into delighted laughter. "A diplomat," Otley crowed. "If I hadn't been watching her face, I'd almost say she meant it."

"You should see her at the magazine," said Win. "Less than a week, and she's got them all eating out of her hand." Almost all, she corrected silently: Ursula, abruptly retranslated to the reception desk, had not yet stopped smoldering; and K.C.—to Gillian's surprise and disappointment—seemed less than overjoyed at being provided with the assistant she'd been demanding for so long.

She did not, she found, want to talk about the office, not out here, with the wind ruffling her hair and the sun warm on her skin. It was possible—more than possible—that a year of sailing *Glory* had ruined her permanently for offices.

Win was watching her, she saw. He was able to read on her face too damn much of what she was thinking. She grabbed more or less at random for a safe subject: "You told me you don't race *Kassandra*."

"We haven't raced her much, that's true," he agreed. A dollop of spray struck his face, red from the sun and breeze. "But this summer we have a grandiose plan."

"Grandiose is the word," Otley muttered in a stage whisper, and to Gillian: "You've heard of the Bermuda Race? Of course you have. Well, we're in it, up to our . . . ears."

She was frankly amazed. *Kassandra* scarcely seemed ready for a friendly overnighter, never mind a 650-mile thrash across the Gulf Stream. "That's wild," she said, and then added, "But doesn't the race start the end of next week, up in Newport?"

"Right," Win said, and his amused expression said that once again he'd picked up the meaning behind her words. "We're not in as bad shape as we look, though. The boat's going into intensive care, you might say. Tomorrow morning. I've got an expert who'll overhaul her—"

"You got Nico?" asked Otley, looking as if he were impressed despite himself.

"The very man. He's my starboard watch captain, Gillian: I hope you'll meet him soon. And we'll have a brand-new main and genoa, delivered Tuesday. . . ." Win rattled on, clearly pleased both by Otley's grudging approval and his own efficiency.

Gillian suspected that most of Win's performance was for her ears—like much of what he'd been saying to Otley all day. It was crazy, of course: how could this knowledgeable, sophisticated shaper of the world's opinion be playing up to her, like a teenager on his first date? Just the same, she was almost ready to admit that this man who was so incredibly assured when it came to dissecting world events needed her approval, felt unsure of himself talking to her. The idea was a heady novelty, and she found herself at a loss to deal with it. Win's behavior made her feel almost motherly, which was crazy, too—he was at least twenty years her senior. Maternal was a new and peculiar sensation and, she decided, not necessarily a pleasant one.

"Unless you're planning to sail all the way to Rhode Island to-night," Otley interrupted, "maybe we'd better head back now."

"Oh," said Win, cut off in full spate. He looked absurdly crestfallen for a moment, then saw Gillian watching him and grinned at her. "That's why I keep Otley around," he said. "To take me down a peg, when I get unbearable."

"And it's a full-time job," Otley added, but she saw the flash of deep affection in his old eyes.

"I like him: Mr. Otley," she said, as the taxi rounded the corner of First Avenue. "You must've known him forever."

"Can't remember when I didn't," Win agreed. He leaned forward in the seat. "Right up ahead, driver. Just beyond the little tree." As the taxi coasted to a stop, he was groping in his hip pocket.

"Can't we split this?" Gillian asked, then realized how out of her supposed character the remark had been.

Win appeared not to notice. He counted the bills from his wallet— scuffed and worn, but Mark Cross just the same—and she couldn't help seeing the solitary ten that remained. "Certainly not," he said. "For one thing, I'm the boss, and for another, I happen to know you weren't paid yesterday."

"Nobody was," said Gillian, opening the cab's door and stepping out. "K.C. said the cupboard was bare."

"God, how I hate that phrase." He shut the door a little more firmly than necessary. "But not as much as I hate it's being true."

"K.C. said it was just temporary," Gillian offered, feeling as if it were somehow her fault. "Just a matter of waiting till our ship comes in."

"Did she say that, too?" Win's voice was acid. "I'll have to have a word with her about clichés."

"Everybody seemed to take it very well," Gillian said. Why am I soothing him? she asked herself. I'm the one who didn't get paid.

"I don't know why you're being so reasonable," Win remarked, unlocking the front door. "You're the one who didn't get paid."

"Well, I can hold on a little longer," she said, thinking of the fifty dollars in her wallet and the five hundred tucked under her panties in Mrs. Boyd's dresser.

"Only a couple of weeks," Win said, his tone defensive. "Three at the outside."

They were standing in the entrance hall, silent now and dark except for the glow from the single bulb on the second-floor landing. "K.C. said it had to do with the way *TNF* was funded. Something about foundations."

"Fiscal years," Win replied gloomily. "We get a lump sum at the beginning of their fiscal year, but it always runs out toward the end."

"Foundations all have the same fiscal?" asked Gillian in surprise. "Like an industry standard?"

"Damned if I know. Probably has to do with taxes—Roger used to handle all that, and now K.C. does. Thank God." She was about to reply when he held up his hand. "Someone's in the office."

She strained her ears, but the only sound was the horn-streaked murmur of traffic from outside. Suddenly the door at the end of the hall opened. It was K.C., and instead of her usual jeans and sweater she was wearing a modish jacket with fullback shoulders and rolled-up sleeves, and a pair of baggy trousers. "How was sailing?" she asked.

"Perfect," said Gillian, realizing as she spoke that she actually meant it, that she had gone nearly eight hours without brooding about Barr. Or about why she was here.

"What're you up to, K.C.?" Win asked. "I hope you aren't wasting your weekend trying to find an extra dollar in the exchequer."

"Not likely. I know what's there—what's *not* there—better than anybody. I've just been straightening up the paperwork for the Clam and Foot's fund-raiser. On Wednesday," she added pointedly.

"I'll be there, never fear."

He sounded resigned, Gillian thought, and K.C. seemed to hear it, too: "You won't have to stay long. We've got Broadway Rose to hype it up, but they do expect you to make an appearance."

"I know, I know." To Gillian: "Has K.C. told you about the Clam and Foot?"

"Just that it's short for Young Publishers' Chowder and Marching Association," Gillian replied. Some kind of social trade group—it took up a good deal of K.C.'s telephone day, and from the giggling and whispering that wafted to Gillian, at her new desk in K.C.'s outer office, she suspected chowder and marching were only code words for matchmaking and gossip.

"Roger founded it," said Win, breaking into her thoughts. "Like so many things my brother started, K.C.'s been stuck with carrying it on."

"The Clam and Foot's been damn helpful," K.C. said. "Very supportive, and right now *TNF* can use all the support it can get."

"Of course," Win replied. "You're quite right, and I'm an ungrateful roach. Why don't you come upstairs and join us for a drink?"

Oh, hell, Gillian thought. And just when I had the chance to pump Win about his brother. In the event, though, it was K.C. who brought up the subject, once the two women were settled in Win's dim, shabby living room, and their host was making drinks in the kitchen.

"The Clam and Foot's really slid downhill without Roger," K.C. said, lighting herself a cigarette. "All the spirit's gone out of it, damned if I know why."

Win, reappearing from the kitchen, picked it up: "He just radiated enthusiasm; carried everyone along with him, whatever he was up to." In one hand he was carrying a silver wine cooler filled with chopped ice and slender bottles of Mexican beer. The thumb of his other hand was thrust through the handles of three ceramic mugs. As he set the cooler down on the coffee table, Gillian realized it must be an antique, the crest engraved on its side nearly worn away by decades of use. The mugs had a less exalted provenance, though: one bore the red-and-white Harvard seal, one a cartoon dog in primary colors, and one a cloven skull over the motto *Kill them all and let God sort them out.*

"Roger sent me that one, from Saigon," Win said. He kept it for himself and gave K.C. the dog and Gillian the Harvard seal.

"You went to Harvard?" Gillian asked, pouring her beer carefully down the inner side of the mug.

"It's in the bloodstream by now, like a virus," Win said. "Mother was Radcliffe, of course. And Roger dropped out."

"Equally of course," K.C. put in. "Dropped out and joined the Air Force."

"Youthful rebellion?" said Gillian. Her eyes had become accustomed to the gloom, created by heavy drapes that muffled the street noise. The walls were hung with the portraits of determined-looking people in heavy oval frames, alternating with cheaply mounted posters from past presidential campaigns. The whole room had the same schizoid air: costly, age-worn furniture garnished with dime-store ashtrays and bargain-basement lamps.

"Rebellion?" Win seemed to be considering her offhand question with great seriousness. "Maybe. But I remember what he said when Mother tried to stop him enlisting: 'It's not much of a war, but it's the only one going.' Adventure was what intrigued him. Excitement."

"Not patriotism?" Gillian offered.

"Good God, no!" Win groped for adequate words to counter the allegation. "My brother was flighty, yes. Impulsive, yes. Immature, absolutely. But he wasn't a fool."

"You two must've been quite a pair when you were kids," said
K.C. lazily. She drank in the same unobtrusive way Barr did: her
first beer had simply evaporated, and she was halfway through her
second. "Total opposites; like night and day."

Win gave her a sharp glance. "I suppose you could say so. He
was very good with money. Not," he added quickly, "that it mattered
to him as *money*, you understand. It's—it was the mathematics that
intrigued him."

Win was staring intently into Gillian's eyes, but not so intently
that she missed K.C.'s lips moving silently: *Sure it was.*

"Within a week after he came back from Asia he was running
TNF's whole business department. Brought in the switchboard, the
word processors, a dozen things. We're going to have a computer
link to our Washington office, as soon as we have a Washington
office. So many other improvements to make, as soon as we have
the money."

"And if Roger hadn't drowned," K.C. said harshly.

Win looked startled. "That goes without saying, of course."

"Roger *was* pretty good at the financial side," K.C. said, as much
to Win as to Gillian. "Especially the fund-raising."

"Which, as Gillian knows by now, is at once our lifeblood and
our shame."

"Shame's a pretty strong word," she observed, into the silence.

"I cringe every time I sign one of those damned begging letters,"
said Win, staring into his beer mug. "And oiling my way up to those
foundation representatives . . ."

"Come on, Win," K.C. objected. "They're not so bad. In fact, some
of them are nice guys."

"I'm sure they are," he replied. "Let's talk about something less
distasteful. Let's talk about sailing." The word alone seemed to
brighten him. "K.C., I can't tell you what fun I've had today. Gillian's
a superb sailor—far better than I am. And so self-effacing: She almost
made me believe I was in charge of *Kassandra.*"

"Oh, really?" K.C. grinned at Gillian. "How'd you like Otley?"

"I thought he was a teddy bear," said Gillian. And then, "What's
so funny?"

"Teddy bear?" gasped K.C. "This is old cactus-mouth Otley we're
talking about? I went out on Win's boat just once, and it was 'get

off that goddamn line' or 'get the hell out of the way' all day long.
You must be some sailor, Gillian."

This was getting a little too close for comfort, she thought. "Maybe
he's mellowed," she said defensively. "He seemed like an old sweetie
to me." She looked meaningfully at Win and pushed back her cuff
to expose her watch. "My God, I didn't realize it was so late. I've
got to get back to the apartment and change."

"You're right," K.C. agreed. "It is late. I'll split a cab with you."

"You're sure it won't be out of your way?"

"No." K.C. laughed. "It'll be out of *your* way. But I don't mind."

The taxi had gone two long blocks west before K.C. spoke: "You're
good for him, you know. I haven't seen him so up since Roger died."

If there was any trace of jealousy in K.C.'s tone Gillian couldn't
hear it. "He's a nice man," she said. "We did have fun today."

"He could use more of that kind of thing. He's very lonely—but
you could see that from the apartment."

"It's an unusual place," Gillian said, to keep K.C. talking.

"It's like geology," K.C. replied. "The underneath layer—the furniture, the portraits, the silver—that's all family. Most of it's inherited
stuff: the bucket he put the beer in, that goes back to the eighteenth
century. The decor, what's left of it, was Kitty's. She was his wife,
came from a rich family in Chicago; she bought his clothes, kept
his hair cut, treated him like a fancy doll. The cheap junk is Win's
own. It looks like he's got no taste, but the truth is, he's got no
patience for mundane things like shopping."

Not impatience, Gillian reflected. Win just has more important
concerns than groceries. He's like Barr that way, but Barr with a
mission. "What happened to Kitty?" she asked.

"Oh, she drifted off. After a while, she got a divorce. I heard she'd
remarried." K.C. paused, her head to one side as if she were listening
to the echoes of her own words. "People around *TNF* make her
sound like a soulless twit. I do myself, sometimes. But she wasn't.
She just finally saw there wasn't anything for her in that marriage."
She gave a short, humorless laugh. "Sleeping with Win must've been
like bedding down with last year's snakeskin—it looks lifelike as
hell, but there's nobody home." She darted one of her too-intelligent
looks at Gillian. "It's something to bear in mind."

Is that the impression I'm giving her? Gillian wondered. "I take your point," she replied.

"I'm not trying to chase you off," K.C. insisted. "When I said he needs somebody who can help him relax, I meant it. *TNF*'s killing him by inches. *TNF* and the I've-got-mine society. Just don't expect too much in return: with Win, the magazine will always come first."

"The slave of duty."

"Kind of like that," K.C. nodded.

"Roger sounds like he was very different," Gillian observed, trying not to seem too interested. "But he did have two things in common with Win—the magazine and sailing." She waited for K.C.'s response and, receiving none, said, "You don't agree."

"I know it looks that way," said K.C. slowly. "But the similarities just point up how different they were."

"How?"

"To begin with, Roger wasn't really interested in *TNF* in its own terms. He got involved because of Win, and he stuck with it because . . . well, I don't know exactly why. I guess he just hated to admit he couldn't make it work."

"Make it work?" Gillian asked.

"Show a profit, I should've said. That's—that *was* Roger's definition of function."

"And sailing? How were they different there?"

"You could probably define it a lot better than I can," said K.C. "But Win's had that same antique boat for God knows how long. Same antique crew, too—you haven't met Paul Marsh, but he's even older'n Otley. Now Roger, he had a different boat every year, and a different crew nearly every weekend. Nearly always girls, except for when he raced." The cab eased to a halt in front of a grim four-story building with a steel front door, a rusted fire escape down the front and three stone-faced young blacks squatting on the stoop. "Welcome to Hell's Kitchen," said K.C. "It's not much, but it's home." She fumbled in her purse and passed over three singles. "This should cover my half."

It did, precisely. "We'd better wait till you're inside." Though the cab door was still closed, Gillian realized she had lowered her voice.

"The three stooges? Don't give them a thought," K.C. replied. "This time of day it's all they can do to sit up straight. Besides," she added, with a quick glance at the back of the driver's head, "I give them a little smoke once in a while. Keeps them sweet." She opened the door and stepped out onto the curb, as the young men looked up at her, dimly expectant.

"Have a nice evening," Gillian called. "See you Monday."

"Same to you. And, Gillian"—K.C.'s mischievous grin lit up her plain face—"for God's sake, make Win take you someplace nice for dinner."

"So you're back at last," Mrs. Boyd cried, as she bustled around Gillian, her hands beating the air like small, fat wings. "I saw you drowned in the sea ten times already."

Any minute she'll start to cluck, Gillian thought. "Not a chance, Mrs. Boyd," she said firmly. "I've got to scramble. I'm expecting a gentleman."

"He was calling you," said Mrs. Boyd. "Now where did I put the messages." The radius of her aimless fluttering suddenly increased to include the rest of the small, overcrowded living room. "I put them all in one place," she muttered, bobbing among the oversized pieces of furniture, automatically straightening the lace antimacassar on each as she passed it.

Why would Win have called? Was he canceling? Gillian felt an unexpectedly sharp sense of disappointment.

"Here they are!" Mrs. Boyd was waving a sheaf of papers. Each square was a different pastel shade, each bore a different flower badly rendered in genteel watercolor. But each also had the same name written in Mrs. Boyd's large, illiterate printing: Mr. O'Mara.

"Oh, him," said Gillian, at once relieved and guilty. "Well, I guess I'd better call."

PATRICK :

EAST NORWALK,

SATURDAY EVENING

"I expected to hear from you this morning," he said. "I asked Mrs. Boyd to leave you a message. Last night."

"Well, I didn't get it till now, Patrick." Gillian's tone told him she wasn't about to apologize. "I came in late and left early. And I'm going out again, in a few minutes."

"You must really be onto something." His words sounded more sarcastic than he'd meant them to, but there was no pulling them back.

The half-beat of silence from the other end told him she'd picked it up. "I'm getting closer," she said. "It's slow going, but they're beginning to trust me now. I haven't got anything definite yet, except I've got a real strong feeling that Roger may be alive, and they— Win and my new boss, K.C.—know it."

"How can you tell?"

"It's nothing you could use in a court," she replied, sounding defensive. "The way they talk: every once in a while, when they're talking about Roger, it's suddenly in the present tense. Not just the words—the thought, if you see what I mean."

He didn't, but he wasn't going to press her, not when she was in this prickly mood. "What about your friend Sarah?"

"That's different," Gillian said. "It's as if she didn't exist." She paused. "Hadn't existed, rather." This time he was about to ask what she meant when she spoke again, in a different tone. "Look, I have to run. Win'll be here any minute." Another pause, and he knew what the next question would be: "Have you talked to Barr?"

"He called from Bermuda this afternoon. Said he'd given up on Hamilton—he's moved to St. George."

"Should've started there," she said, as if she were speaking to Barr directly. "And?"

"He's got a lead—maybe—to somebody who knew the Frenchman, Corduan, who sailed with Roger. It didn't sound like a hell of a lot."

"No," she replied flatly. "The answer's at *TNF*. If Roger's alive and kicking, they'll know where he is—and where Sarah is, too."

Gillian's assurance annoyed him, though he wasn't sure why. "Look, I may be onto something," he said. "Something I ran across yesterday afternoon, at this dump up in the Bronx." The reproach in *yesterday* gave her no choice but to hear him out, and he could feel her resentment over the line, growing stronger as he fumbled through the story of his trip to the boat salvage yard. Her impatience crippled his account, blew the names of the yard and its manager out of his memory, so he felt even more like an unprepared student trying to fake it with his teacher.

"So did you go back there today?" she demanded, before he'd finished. "Had they chopped this boat up?"

"Drove down first thing this morning," he admitted. "The place was closed, and the hull was still hanging in the Travelift."

"Sounds like they weren't all that desperate to get rid of it," she said, letting him down—putting him down—gently. But he could tell she'd written off his work. She'd missed the point, though: she didn't see that the yard manager's lies were the important thing, not whether it was an Alberg or a Vanguard, a sloop or a yawl. Before he could tell her so she went on. "Look, Patrick, I really do have to run. If I play my cards right this evening, I'm sure I can get into *TNF*'s books." Perhaps she sensed him biting back the obvious crack, because she continued immediately. "Roger was *TNF*'s money man: he's gone and the magazine is broke—but they're expecting a transfusion. I don't know why, and maybe the answer's in the files."

Well, probably she was right, Patrick thought; probably he was headed up a blind alley. But anger and frustration triggered the

words he'd promised himself he wouldn't say: "You'll never guess
who Barr's run into, down in Bermuda."

When the phone rang again, moments after he had slammed it
down, he could only stare at it. Then it occurred to him that Gillian
must be calling to apologize. Let her go to hell, he thought, but his
hand—shaking a little—reached out by itself. "Yes?"

"Patrick? Is that you?" The Southern accent was stronger than he
remembered it and she sounded excited. Patrick felt his wilted spirit
begin to revive.

"Hi, Susan. What's up?"

"I've been trying to get you, but first you were out and then the
phone was busy. Listen, Patrick, I've got something for you, but I
don't know what it means."

His head was still so full of Gillian he had no idea what she was
talking about. "Something for me?"

"About that accident, the one you asked me to check on."

Suddenly it clicked into place. "The sailboat that hit something
and caught fire at the same time?"

"Right. There wasn't anything in the accident reports, but things
were slow today, so I went through the assist reports, too—had to
go back almost a year, but there it was: July tenth, a thirty-five-foot
sailboat went hard aground on one of the Stepping Stones—"

"The rocks south of City Island?"

"The same. There was a boat on patrol in the area, Coast Guard
Auxiliary—"

"Auxiliary?" he interrupted. "Aren't they civilians?"

"Civilian volunteers," she agreed. "Like the C.A.P. is to the Air
Force. Anyway, he saw it happen. The sailboat was dragging ass
toward the Throgs Neck Bridge, just about dusk, and she hit real
hard. Our Auxiliarist helped pull her off, but she was low in the
water and he was sure she must be holed. Then some commercial
towboat showed up, and one guy got into a fight with him. While
they were calling each other bad names, the sailboat limped off the
way he'd been going."

She stopped for breath, and Patrick asked: "What about the fire?
The boat I saw in the scrap yard, her whole aft end was scorched
black."

"No, there wasn't anything in the report about a fire." He was sure she was waiting for his next question, but for the life of him he couldn't see why she was so excited. Boats ran aground all the time, and a lot of them did it on the Stepping Stones, a mostly submerged reef that lay across the direct line from the Sound to Throgs Neck. What made the boat in Nico Butler's yard different and traceable was the combination of collision and fire.

"Then what—" he began, and she cut him off.

"The name, Patrick. The name on that sailboat was *Sea Horse.*"

On I-95 ahead of him, the New York-bound traffic had slowed to a crawl, but Patrick barely noticed it. Roger Huddleston's *Sea Horse* had sunk like a stone in front of a camera and half a dozen witnesses. A full week later and seven hundred miles away, another *Sea Horse* spears herself on a rock, gets pulled free, and motors off into the blue. What in hell did it mean? At first he had told himself that the whole thing must be a coincidence: God knew how many thirty-five-foot sailboats were on Long Island Sound, and *Sea Horse* had to be one of the more popular boat names. There wasn't a word in the assist report about a fire, nor—Susan had checked—was there any mention in that week's accident reports or Sitreps of a sailboat burning.

A coincidence, he told himself again. So how come he was sitting in Gillian's car, dressed like a cat burglar in dark sweater, jeans, and boots? And why was there a pair of wire cutters and his miniature flash on the passenger seat beside him? He'd barely taken the time to thank Susan for what must've been a long day's work—in fact, he'd given her another job, to look up the name and address of the Auxiliarist who'd come to the assistance of the stranded *Sea Horse.* She'd jumped at it, though; her life must be a lot more boring than he'd thought. And of course she likes me—no point pretending she doesn't. A sharp girl, too. And a looker. Even if this lead didn't work out he'd pay her back, he resolved. And he had a growing idea what currency would be most acceptable.

An I-95 traffic jam couldn't last forever, though it might seem so if you were caught in it. Patrick's watch, which he'd turned so it lay on the inside of his wrist, read nine-thirty when he rolled the Mazda to a silent, lightless halt a hundred yards down the dirt road that led to the Hutchinson River Boatworks. Less than a mile away the massed towers of Co-Op City lit the overcast sky, and off to his right the steady rumble of traffic from the Parkway drowned the whispering of wind in the head-high reeds all around him. The tide was high now, and the smell from the marsh mud was not nearly as strong as it had been earlier in the day.

He detached the car key from Gillian's key case, which he tossed onto the floor on the passenger side. His wallet he slid under the driver's seat. Getting out, he locked the RX7, and stood silently beside it for several minutes, staring into the vegetation while his senses tuned themselves to his surroundings. As soon as his eyes could distinguish the individual reeds, swaying gently, he pocketed the car key and pulled the navy watch cap down to cover his blond hair. Moving slowly, he sidled along the edge of the dirt road, his shoulder brushing the reeds, until he was outside the chain-link fence. From where he stood the parked Travelift was screened by a building. Sodium-vapor floodlights on the roofs lit up most of the salvage yard, but as always there were plenty of corners and dead spots the lights missed; a careful, trained man would have no trouble moving from shadow to shadow. Not that there seemed to be anyone around. No watchman, no dogs—and why should there be?

This was always the moment he found himself wishing he had a gun. But guns, in Patrick's experience, tended to take charge of events. Too often you found yourself letting them decide what was going to happen instead of making the decisions yourself. And to-night there was no reason to think he'd need anything beyond the wire cutters.

They, at least, were required. The fence, when he'd inspected it up close, was a professional job—more so than a pile of marine junk would seem to call for, but probably the bare minimum in security for this part of the Bronx. Patrick squatted next to the chain-link and ran his fingertips along the bottom of the fence. He had half-expected an alarm wire, too, but there was none. Deeply ingrained training made him scoop up a dollop of sticky mud and, holding his breath, smear it over his face and neck, and across the backs of his hands.

The chain-link cut slowly, but after five minutes he had opened enough of a hole to slide through, and he allowed five more minutes for a cautious reconnaissance of the yard's perimeter. When he slipped around the last corner and had a clear view of the Travelift, he bit back a curse. The rolling hoist was in the same place it'd been that morning, but its heavy, canvas-covered slings hung empty: the boat was gone.

The sheet-metal sliding door of the building was padlocked: no chance of entry that way, not without a hell of a racket. But there were windows, small ones, a little above eye height. In a place like this it was no trouble finding something to stand on—six fiberglass lazaret hatches, already neatly stacked—and minutes later he was on tiptoe with his face against the dirty glass, staring into absolute blackness. He pressed the little flashlight against the pane. The small, powerful beam was soaked up by the sheer size of the room on the other side of the pane. Nothing for it but to go in blind.

The window, he discovered, wasn't designed to be opened at all, but its frame had only been wedged into the wall with thin wood shims. Remove two of them, and the whole thing came free, to be dropped quietly into the weeds below. Pulling himself up, he quickly panned the flash down onto the floor just inside; a six-foot drop to clear concrete. At the cost of a few splinters he wriggled over the sill and slid head-downward, landing on his outstretched hands and somersaulting to break the impact. The *whump* of rubber boot soles against cement echoed up against the metal roof. Not another sound, though, except for his own quick, hoarse breathing.

The flashlight was just too small to show him anything but huge, anonymous shapes. He pointed the light upward, and it reflected off a bare bulb set in the ceiling, high above. There was probably a wall switch someplace, but on second thought he didn't dare risk it. With the flash focused on the ground right in front of him, he paced toward the main door, its edges outlined by the glow of the lights on the building outside. There was something on the floor between himself and the door, but it wasn't boat-shaped, just a sort of low heap. Even when he was standing by it, playing the beam of the flashlight back and forth, he didn't realize at first what he was looking at. Then the light glanced off a familiar shape at his feet; he bent to pick up the heavy, triangular chunk of fiberglass: the stemhead of a sailboat, with the stainless steel fittings still bolted and glassed in place.

It was like a jigsaw: once you knew the overall design, the individual pieces began to make sense. The torch beam picked out a familiar curved section he recognized as the forward edge of the doghouse, lying against a sharply angled piece that had been blackened by flames. One corner of the transom, his eye told him, and he took a half-step forward.

As he did so, he felt rather than heard the soft footfall at his back, threw himself instinctively to one side. He saw a flash of movement past his head and, as he hit the cement rolling, heard the hollow clang of metal beside him and a deep bellow of rage and pain. Patrick's flash, knocked from his hand, rolled across the floor, illuminating a four-foot length of pipe that had been bent to a right angle by the force of its impact against the ground. Looming over the dropped weapon was a big, indistinct form—his assailant.

For the space of a few gasping breaths the two faced each other without moving. In the small flashlight's diffused glow, Patrick's attacker stood slightly crouched, his feet well apart. He was a massive man, broad as well as tall; the lack of light made it impossible to see his face clearly, but his features seemed flattened and blurry. His gloved hands, outstretched to grasp, opened and closed repeatedly. He had swung to kill, and he must still be feeling the jarring shock of iron against concrete right up to his elbows.

Without warning he sprang at Patrick, a flat-footed leap that brought him within hitting range. Patrick's left hand lashed out, two quick, hard jabs to straighten his opponent up for the classic right-hand smash. The big man dropped his head and took the blows on his skull. He was wearing some kind of thick cloth cap, which spared Patrick a couple of broken knuckles, but he heard his own gasp of pain just as the big man brought his palm down with a meaty slap on the back of Patrick's neck, pulling him forward into a bearlike embrace that reeked of stale sweat and damp wool.

In eight years of boxing, starting as a high school middleweight and working his way up to cruiserweight champion of his airborne division, Patrick had never met a man his own size who could stand toe-to-toe against him; outside the ring, the dirtywork picked up in barrooms on two continents had taught him how to handle brawlers of almost any weight or style. As the big man's arms engulfed him, Patrick snapped his head forward into the other's face and brought his right knee up fast and hard. By rights the fight should have ended then. His opponent only grunted and held on.

Held on and then lifted Patrick's hundred and eighty pounds clear off the floor, while his arms—as big around as *Glory's* fenders—squeezed. Patrick felt the bones in his chest creak with the pressure. His arms were locked helplessly at his sides. He was aware of a vast, dim, onion-scented grimace just visible through the mesh of a stocking mask. As the breath was pressed inexorably out of him, he kicked at shins the size of fire hydrants, to no avail. There was only one thing left to do and, baring his teeth, he did it.

The noise, somewhere between a snort and a squeal, didn't bear thinking about. Still, the tactic worked; released, Patrick landed on the balls of his feet. His legs nearly folded under him, and he staggered desperately backward out of the light. The big man was screaming wordlessly, pure rage converted directly to decibels. From the direction of the sound he seemed to have lost Patrick, who bounced off a smooth, curving surface and then paused for a second to take a tentative deep breath.

It hurt, but the second breath hurt less; he had just about decided that his ribs were intact when the overhead lights came on, flooding the room. At the far wall, fifty feet away, Patrick's opponent stood with his hand on an oversize knife switch. Fully illuminated, he was even bigger than he'd seemed in the half-light, an immense nightmare in a turtleneck jersey and what looked like tights tucked into high-topped black sneakers. He was still wearing his cap, and blood welled through the stocking mask and down his face. As he caught sight of Patrick, his roar rose to a shriek, and he leaped forward, his hands extended.

Patrick felt adrenaline knife through him. He feinted and dodged to one side, and the grasping hands caught air. He grabbed one wrist and twisted with all his strength; the other man seemed to read his mind, and spun away from the hammerlock with contemptuous ease, his free hand again reaching for the back of Patrick's neck.

A wrestler, Patrick realized. And three hundred pounds if he was an ounce. His own right fist shot out, and this time he didn't miss. The other man's already bloody nose squelched flat. It didn't matter: he kept right on coming. Patrick danced backward, feinted another right and slashed a left just below the big man's rib cage. His fist sank into a thick barrier of flab, but the punch seemed to have no effect, and it put him far too close to those oversize paws. The clumsy, open-handed slap across Patrick's jaw looked like slow-motion, but it felt like being hit with five pounds of frozen meat.

Patrick reeled backward, his feet skidding on a length of heavy chain lying loose on the floor. The big man paused long enough to snatch it up and came on again, swinging it like a whip. Patrick kept moving back, his eyes searching desperately for a weapon of his own; what he saw instead was a door. Time to get the hell out of here, he told himself. Fight again another day. He dodged to his left, felt the breeze of the chain as it missed his face by an inch and clashed against the floor. Feinted a second time, taking the opportunity to edge toward the door. The big man's breath was coming in whooping gasps, but Patrick had never gotten his own wind back, and if that length of chain ever landed, his brains would be all over the concrete.

Another swing, and Patrick darted forward to slam the left-right-left combination that had got him the division title. He might as well have hit his enemy with a balloon. The chain, swung short, lashed across his shoulder, bruising and knocking the wind out of him. Patrick reeled away, then slammed his shoulder into the closed door, which buckled open under his weight.

Shit: this isn't outside! The room he was in was stacked to the ceiling with open-topped cardboard cartons from which spilled ripped life jackets, flattened fenders, rusty fire extinguishers. Patrick's enemy loomed in the narrow doorway. His steam-whistle shrieking—how did he keep it up?—had a triumphant note. He lurched forward, pulverizing a box of seat cushions with his flailing chain. Patrick darted back, his shins colliding painfully with a heavy white plastic cylinder about three feet in diameter.

I've seen one of those before. What . . . there was no time to think: his enemy was on him, and the chain gouged a long strip from the wall next to Patrick's head. The cylinder was on the floor between them, and they moved cautiously around it, in a deadly kind of musical chairs. The big man swung again, and his weapon bounded up off the plastic shell, just as Patrick remembered what it contained.

He let himself be herded around once again before he saw what he was looking for—the length of braided nylon cord that hung from the cylinder's end. He would have to fall on his knees to grab it. If he missed he was dead. If it didn't work he was dead. If he didn't do something damn quick he'd be dead anyway.

Patrick dropped, snatched at the cord, and yanked with every ounce of strength that remained to him. The big man paused, baffled, and raised the chain whip for the killing stroke. From inside the cylinder came a sharp *pop*, and it split in half. For an instant Patrick saw his opponent full face, astonishment showing dimly through the bloody nylon. Then the face vanished, as compressed gas exploded into the inflatable life raft and it leaped out of the two halves of its container, writhing and squirming like a living thing—and slamming the big man against the far wall.

Not till Gillian's Mazda slid off I-95 onto the East Avenue exit could Patrick begin to accept that he was safe. He scarcely noticed the streets of East Norwalk sliding by, but the whirling of his brain slowed at last and stopped, and he saw he'd parked the RX7 in its usual space, outside the Carey & Willard office.

He didn't get out right away. The questions were ricocheting around in his head, just as they'd been doing since he'd scrambled behind the wheel, thirty miles and half a lifetime ago: Why a guard for a pile of ground-up fiberglass? And why a homicidal maniac for a guard? He had to ask somebody, and Barr was out of reach. Gillian? He looked at his watch: eleven o'clock. She'd still be out. God, between the three of them they'd really fucked up the communications on this operation. Well, what about the man who was paying the freight? Under the funny accent, Uncle Sol was a smart guy. Patrick got out of the Mazda, his legs like rubber, and walked slowly toward the pier.

BARR:

ST. GEORGE;

LATE SATURDAY NIGHT

The dapper, middle-aged Frenchman whose name Barr had never caught leaned across the table, his forehead corrugated with the strain of expressing his thoughts in an unfamiliar tongue. On his left, Jean-Paul Aubier watched anxiously, like the parent of a talented but unpredictable child. "Corduan was a good sailor, *n'est-ce pas?*" said the older Frenchman. "Not to panic, never. Just the opposite." He paused, clearly wanting to add something, then turned to Jean-Paul instead. "*J'voudrais dire qu'il . . .*" The rest of the sentence disappeared in a machine-gun burst of consonants. Jean-Paul nodded comprehension.

"Interfere," he said to Barr. "This Corduan was greatly given to interfere. That was why M'sieur"—again, the uncatchable name— "let him go. That and the chickies." Seeing Barr's expression, Jean-Paul glanced meaningfully toward the dapper Frenchman's companion, a fleshy young woman with a round face, whose gleaming scarlet mouth appeared to have been cast into a permanent pout.

"Oh," said Barr. "*Monsieur, savez-vous comment ce Corduan a . . .*" The prep-school French that had carried him unscathed through Molière, Corneille, and most of Racine was hopeless for a real conversation, and he collapsed back into carefully enunciated English: "How did Corduan find—obtain—the berth aboard *Sea Horse?*"

The dapper Frenchman considered a moment, then fired off another volley at Jean-Paul, whose lips moved silently as he framed his translation. Barr managed to sit quietly until at last he spoke: "Corduan met a man. Here, in the White Horse."

That must have been Roger, Barr thought—but why not ask and be positive? *"Savez-vous le nom de cet homme, monsieur?"* he asked.

The dapper Frenchman shrugged, lifted a conspiratorial eyebrow, and rapped out something from which Barr picked up only the words *là-bas,* as he inclined his head toward the bar, where Jolly was deep in conversation with a short, ugly man in Bermuda shorts and a T-shirt that said KISS A FISHERMAN across the chest. Jean Paul's eyes widened, and he turned quickly to Barr.

"He doesn't know the name," Jean-Paul said quietly, keeping his face turned away from Jolly and her companion. "But he thinks it was that one who talks to *la capitaine.*"

The one in question, invited over to join the group at the table, said he was called Toddy and was a shark fisherman by trade. Up close, his clothes gave off a smell strong enough to make the dapper Frenchman knock back his Campari-and-soda in a single swallow and then quickly remember an engagement elsewhere. Toddy, whose battered face looked like the record of a hundred lost battles, watched with a wry smile as the French couple hurried away. "Funny, the effect I seem to have on company," he said. His voice was deep and slightly hoarse, and his skin was the color and texture of a dried-out boot. When his drink arrived—the innocuous-looking rum and ginger beer combination that is the national drink of Bermuda—he raised his glass in Barr's direction. "Cheers." As he drank, he watched Barr over the rim of the glass. He set the drink down, his small bright eyes unwinking. "So you want to know about this Corduan."

"I want to know how he got aboard *Sea Horse,*" Barr corrected him. "The gentleman who was just here said you'd told him about the berth."

Toddy's face—square like the rest of him—wrinkled in what seemed to Barr a very humorless smile. "Wasn't like I was recruiting or anything," he said.

"Just doing a fellow sailor a favor?" Barr offered.

"Some fellow sailor," Toddy replied. His smile no longer looked connected to the rest of his face. "A prick with ears. Sorry, love," he said to Jolly, who had dropped into the seat beside him.

"I've always wanted to see one," she said, her voice dreamy. Barr suddenly realized she was very drunk indeed and, now that he thought about it, Toddy wasn't far behind her.

"See what, love?" Toddy asked. His wooden leer stretched to expose preposterously white, even teeth.

Before Jolly could offer the reply Toddy was clearly expecting, Barr put in: "If you weren't recruiting for *Sea Horse*, what were you doing?"

"Paying the bugger back," said Toddy absently, his eyes still on Jolly. "Listen, love—"

"Paying him back for what?" Barr interrupted. Then, thinking of Corduan's reputation: "Something to do with a girl?"

"That's right," Toddy said. He put his arm around Jolly, whose too-wide grin had been replaced by a fixed and glassy stare. "It was the girl doin' the recruiting."

Jolted, Barr said, "Recruiting? Dawnstar Perigee? I thought she was with Corduan."

"Well, for Chrissake, of course she was," said Toddy. "But she started off with me. It was the other gal, the crazy one, was lookin' for crew . . ." His voice trailed off, and his face clouded as the memory returned: "Dawnstar would've stayed with me, too, the little twit, except for that greasy frog—"

Barr heard Jean-Paul, beside him, shove his chair away from the table. Without taking his eyes off Toddy, he put his hand on the young man's shoulder, pressing him back into his seat. "*Restez tranquille,*" he said quietly. To Toddy, who had missed the exchange completely, he said, "The girl who was recruiting: Was she dark-haired, thin, middle twenties?"

"That's the one."

Barr released Jean-Paul and felt in his shirt pocket for the envelope with the four photographs. "This her?"

Toddy took the snapshot in both hands, held it nearly at arm's length as he stared hazily at it. "Maybe," he said after a moment. "Sure. Li'l heavier, but that's her all right."

"You're positive? It was almost a year ago."

"Oh, I'm pos'tive," Toddy said, still looking at the photo. "Abs'lutely pos'tive. She tried to get me on that goddamn boat."

"Asked you to crew for her on *Sea Horse*?" Toddy had begun to sweat, and his face looked greenish under the tan.

" 'S what I said, didn't I?" Toddy pushed his chair back and tried to get up. "I don' feel so good."

Barr put the shark fisherman's heavy arm over his own shoulder and levered him upright. "You need a little air," he said. The smell of long-dead fish and unwashed man was like a blow to the stomach. "So do I. Let's go outside." He glanced down at Jolly and then to Jean-Paul, who nodded.

The breeze had dropped with sunset, and the air was warm and moist. The nearly full moon overhead was carving sharp edges on the towering clouds off to the northeast, and the glittering cabin lights aboard the cruise ship at the wharf made a travel-poster picture. "Gorgeous, innit?" Toddy said. And then, "Gotta throw up."

Alternately pushing and dragging, Barr managed to propel Toddy up the main street's narrow sidewalk, past the post office and a shop with an incongruous display of heavy Scottish tweeds and sweaters, and then down a deliberately picturesque alley that wound through a cluster of tourist shops, shut at this hour, to a wooden walkway, beyond which was a stretch of concrete bulkheading where cruising yachts were tied up two and three abreast. The walkway was partly rotted out at one end, and this less desirable berth was occupied by a single sailboat, her cabin dark. Gasping with the effort, Barr heaved his companion's nearly dead weight across the treacherous boards and propped him over the bulkhead's concrete lip. Five excruciating minutes later, Toddy was sitting on the planks, his back against the concrete. "Sleep now," he said, and his head slumped forward.

Barr grasped a handful of slimy wet hair and pulled him back to a sitting position. "Not yet, friend." The moonlight showed Toddy's eyes tightly shut. Barr bumped the man's head, not too gently, against the bulkhead until one eye opened. "A little talk, and then you can cork off."

Encouraged from time to time by repeated head thumps and once by a slap across the face, Toddy slowly disgorged his story. He and Dawnstar had been drinking in the bar across the square from the White Horse, when they were approached by Sarah, who offered to stand them a round. Toddy had immediately jumped to the conclusion that a threesome was in the offing, and accepted eagerly. By the time he realized that sex was the last thing Sarah had in mind, the two of them were in a car, which she was driving, fast and badly. Dawnstar had somehow disappeared, but Toddy had the dim notion she was still back in the waterfront bar. He wanted to go back and get her, but Sarah would have none of it.

"Where'd she take you?" Barr asked.

Out of St. George, Toddy told him; past the Air Station and over the causeway. Then Sarah had pulled the car over to the side of the road. Again the prospect of sex loomed in Toddy's fogged brain, and again he was disappointed. A year later, he was still brooding about it. "Something wrong with her," he complained. "One fucked-up lady." They had sat side by side in the car, Toddy groping and Sarah fending off, until they were interrupted by headlights and the imperious hooting of a bus horn from behind them. "Silly bitch was parked at a bus shelter," said Toddy. She pulled clear to let the bus drop off a passenger, and when it started up again so did she.

"Down to Flatt's we went, trailin' along behind that bloody bus," muttered Toddy. At that point, apparently, he had passed out, because the next thing he remembered was the crunch of tires on sand, as Sarah pulled off the pavement and stopped in front of a coral-block wall overgrown with creepers. The night was black as ink, no moon at all, "and blowin' like hell," Toddy recalled. "Wind right off the ocean: I could hear the waves breakin' right close by."

"Nor'easter?" Barr asked.

"Oh, sure," Toddy agreed. "Unless it changed while I was out, you know."

But that, Barr knew, was unlikely. "What happened to the bus?"

The bus was gone—no, now that he put his mind to it, maybe he'd seen its taillights diminishing up the road beyond their turnoff.

Barr summoned up a mental silhouette of Bermuda: a narrow, fishhook-shaped string of islands knitted together by bridges and causeways, with St. George up where the hook's eye would be, Hamilton Harbour forming the bight, and the old Royal Navy base the barb. Sarah, who presumably didn't know Bermuda, had obviously been using the bus as a guide, so her destination must have been right along its route, somewhere between the small town called Flatts and the bus terminal in downtown Hamilton. And if Toddy could hear the sound of breakers carried on a northeasterly breeze, it narrowed the possible locations to a two-mile stretch of the north shore route.

Barr's attention was drawn by a rasping snore. Toddy's head had fallen forward again, and this time he seemed well and truly out. But some passerby had left a half-full glass—scotch by the smell—balanced on the concrete bulkhead, and the contents, thrown into Toddy's face, brought him spluttering up to the surface of consciousness. "Fuck you do that for?" Toddy snarled. Barr caught his slow-motion punch in midair.

"Just a couple more questions, Toddy."

"Goddamned if I will," Toddy replied, struggling feebly. "I'll call a cop. You can't do this to me."

With his free hand, Barr smashed the empty glass against the concrete and, as Toddy watched owlishly, picked from among the pieces a dagger-shaped shard. The bright moonlight winked off the damp glass as Barr held it a few inches in front of Toddy's bulging eyes. "Now, which side of the road did the car pull off—left or right?"

"Right," Toddy croaked, not taking his eyes from the glittering fragment. "Sea side, for sure."

"Good," said Barr softly. "Then what happened?"

They got out, Toddy replied. There was a door in the wall, and a man was waiting for them. A big, mean-looking man. He led them across a wide lawn, into a house. No lights, Toddy recalled—the man lit their way with a flash. They went to a bedroom on the ground floor, also dark. There was a man in the bed.

"You couldn't see him at all?" Barr asked. "Not even with the flashlight?"

"Didn't want to," Toddy said firmly. "Didn't want to see his face, hear his voice, anythin'."

Releasing Toddy's arm, Barr took him by the throat and slammed him back against the wall, knocking the breath out of him. "Why not?" Barr said. "Why were you so scared?"

Toddy shook his head, his eyes tightly shut. Barr laid the cold, sharp edge of the glass against his cheek and repeated the question, but Toddy only whimpered. "Please," he moaned.

Barr released his grasp on Toddy's throat and rocked back on his heels to consider his sweating victim. "All right," he said. "So you couldn't see what he looked like. He wanted you to crew for him?" Toddy nodded, his eyes still closed. "To the States," Barr added, and received just the trace of another nod. "What'd you tell him?"

Toddy's eyes popped open. "Not a sailor, that's what I said. A fisherman." To Barr's surprise, an expression of pleased cunning lit the other man's face. "He told me to get out. Said he'd get somebody else. Chewed the gal up real bad for even bringin' me—he was so mad at her he was shakin'."

"And he told you to forget you'd been there."

"Not him, the big guy," Toddy replied quickly, and then looked appalled.

"Don't worry," said Barr. "Your secret's safe with me. What happened after that?"

Sarah had taken Toddy back to St. George. She was sobbing, and the car kept edging over to the right side of the road so that Toddy thought for sure they'd be killed by oncoming traffic. She'd dropped him on the edge of town and sped off into the night, and he'd returned to the bar to pick up with Dawnstar where he'd left off, only to discover his place had been preempted by the Frenchman Corduan. "But I fixed him good," said Toddy venomously. "Put a spoke in his wheel, didn't I?"

"How'd you do that?" Barr asked.

"Told him about the gal who was lookin' for crew."

"But she'd driven away," Barr objected. "You just said so."

"No problem. I told him where the house was. Told him how he could get there on the bus."

"And now," said Barr gently, "you can tell me."

It was the wall surrounding the house that had stuck in Toddy's memory, and it was the wall that betrayed the place to Barr. From behind it came the overamplified menace of a heavy-metal band, and an angry wailing that was presumably a vocalist. As Barr stood by the road, considering what to do next, a three-taxi convoy pulled up and disgorged a round dozen boisterous people who seemed to know each other only vaguely. By the time they had paid off their respective drivers and sorted themselves out, their number had increased by one.

Within the wall, the lawn Toddy had stumbled across now shimmered in the varicolored glow from a network of lights strung overhead, and the gloomy, unlit house Toddy had entered was throbbing with life. Barr's offhand estimate put the surging, sweating crowd at well over a hundred, nearly all of them at a talkative stage; the band, its backs to the coral blocks, was red-faced with the effort of drowning out so much conversation. Over many years, Barr had perfected his own system of social invisibility, which consisted in tenuously attaching himself to the outer fringe of a group, nodding and smiling appreciatively, but never offering a competing anecdote. While he listened—or appeared to—he allowed the party's slowly gyrating interior current to swirl him toward its center, where a tall, fat man in a white dinner jacket was holding court. "Who's he?" Barr asked a girl at his elbow.

She stared at him incredulously. "Frannie? You don't know Frannie X?" She was thin almost to emaciation, with an exploded mane of blond hair and desperately eager eyes.

"Not to talk to," Barr replied. "We haven't met."

"Oh, *well*," she said, her face lighting up. "That's what I do." She looked him over carefully, then apparently decided he was acceptable. "I'm Erin," she announced.

"How do you do?" Barr said.

"I mean, what's your name?"

"Franklin Pierce," he said. "I'm in politics."

"That doesn't matter, love," Erin said, touching his arm in reassurance.

She led him slowly forward, through the crowd that surrounded the man called Frannie X. From his fellow guests' behavior Barr gathered he was expected to trot up for presentation, smarm for a moment or two, and then retreat, effusing gratefully. It was a performance the host seemed thoroughly at ease with, so much so that Barr found himself wondering how the oddly named Mr. X would react to a deviation from the script.

And as he was wondering, he found himself in the Presence. "Frannie," said Erin, "this is Mr. Pierce. He's—"

"An old friend of Roger Huddleston," Barr interrupted, stepping forward with his hand extended.

Frannie's reactions were very fast. "Roger who?" he asked politely, allowing his soft paw to be engulfed in Barr's calloused hand. But there had been an instant's hesitation, a flash of raw fear in the deeply recessed eyes. "I don't know anybody by that name."

"Oh, really?" Barr replied. "How about André Corduan? Or Dawnstar Perigee—now, *that's* not an easy name to forget."

With a moment to prepare, Frannie registered stony disinterest. "I think you've got the wrong house, Mr. Pierce." He fired a quick, imperative look past Barr's head. "Leo here will show you how to find the way out."

Leo was large and silent and disapproving. He held Barr by the elbow as he guided him across the lawn and through the gate. "You got a car out here, or a moped?" he demanded.

"No. I came by bus," Barr said.

"Ain't no more buses tonight." What might have been a smile of satisfaction creased his flat face. "Hamilton's. two miles that way. Enjoy the walk."

Barr waited until the gate had closed behind his escort before he set out in the direction indicated. Not that he had any intention of going to Hamilton, but it seemed a good idea not to rattle the cage any more than he had already. A couple of hundred yards took him around a slight curve and out of sight of the walled house; he was about to cross the road and hitch a ride back to St. George when he heard the eggbeater buzz of a moped approaching around the bend. He stepped back off the pavement to let it go by, but its single bright eye followed his movement and kept on coming. A drunk? A fool? A deliberate attack? As Barr crouched ready to jump aside, the moped's engine died to a splutter, and it rolled to a halt a few feet away. "Mr. Pierce!" a girl's voice called from behind the headlight. "Can I give you a lift?"

The outside of Erin's cottage was standard Bermudian: pastel pink stucco under a whitewashed raincatcher roof; it was one of a cluster set on a gentle slope across Hamilton Harbour from the city. Inside, the ambience was that of vacation rentals around the world—fussy draperies and cheap watercolor prints of what you could see by looking out the window. The furnishings had clearly survived a wealth of bad experiences: woven mat rugs that smelled of mildew and spilled drinks, a rattan coffee table whose original glass top had been replaced with a badly fitting sheet of painted plywood, heavy overstuffed chairs with cigarette burns on the arms. It was the kind of accommodation, in Barr's experience, that the owner of a Bermuda-bound racer rented for his crew, while he rioted in luxury at Glencoe or Grotto Bay.

Half a dozen Jacks ashore could make a pigsty of such a place: the too-small sink filled up with unwashed dishes, while scraps of food and dead drinks accumulated on every horizontal surface, and damp clothing hung in festoons from doorknobs and bedposts. Erin had managed the same general effect, and added to it a few personal touches—a huge makeup kit with a mirror built into the lid and its contents spilling across a table by the front window; a tabloid newspaper named *Show Business* whose pages, annotated in lipstick, had been spread over half the floor; a blue felt dragon with a cigarette wedged in a corner of its scarlet mouth. The whole place seemed impregnated with the burnt-garbage smell of old pot smoke, although the cigarette in the dragon's mouth was only a very stale Marlboro.

Erin had already established, in a series of shouts over her shoulder as the moped hurtled down the unlit side roads, that (a) she'd suddenly got bored with the party, (b) she felt bad about the way Mr. Pierce had been thrown out by Leo, who was a shit, (c) she was sure Frannie X didn't mean it, only so *many* people crashed his parties, (d) she kind of liked older men, and (e) since all the bars were closed, the only place they could get a drink was hers. Barr, hanging on for his life, was still able to dismiss (a) through (d) as nonsense. It was clear that Erin was prepared to play unguided missile until the moped's gas ran out or she hit something, which gave (e) a force it might not otherwise have had.

Besides, he reflected, as he rinsed out a couple of glasses in her kitchenette sink, it was the only way to find out what she was up to. From the bathroom, to which she had immediately retreated, he heard running water and the clash of glass against porcelain, followed by a low cry that sounded like dismay.

The refrigerator contained three kinds of beer and a package of processed cheese with a possibly therapeutic green mold over most of its surface. The ice in the ice trays looked none too clean, but he filled the glasses with it anyway. A bottle of vodka, half full, was on the kitchen counter, and he poured some into each glass just as Erin emerged.

"Ta-ta!" she cried from the doorway, dropping into a model's pose, hip thrown out and arms extended. "How do I look?"

Her hair, tamped down by the moped helmet, had been rewhipped into a furious cloud above and around her white marmoset's face, whiter still against the wet-looking, nearly black smear of lipstick. She had discarded the fashionably baggy sweater she'd been wearing in favor of an even more fashionable top that looked to Barr like a man's undershirt, circa 1925; the ribbed white fabric clung to her small, pointed breasts. She still wore the same trousers, loosely cut from some mealy gray fabric and fastened with straps and buckles in a dozen improbable places. Without the sweater's immense shoulderpads her whole frame seemed to have shrunk.

"Just fine," he replied, trying to sound as if he meant it.

Something in his tone must have given him away: her determinedly bright smile vanished. Without a word, she turned quickly and led him into the living room, where she flung herself into one of the armchairs. "So what brings you to Bermuda, Mr. Pierce?" she asked. Before he could frame a reply, she added, in a more natural voice, "Say, what was your first name again?"

"Just call me Pierce," he replied. "Everybody does."

"Pierce," she said, tasting the sound of it. "That's okay. Not exactly gnarly, but okay." She grinned, uncrossed her legs, and swung them up and under her. All at once, her eyes seemed to be sparkling with barely contained humor. "So why *are* you here?" she asked again, reaching for the glass on her side of the coffee table.

"Looking for someone," he said, not taking his eyes off her face.

She set the vodka down after only a taste. "Who?"

"For starters, a man named Corduan. A French sailor."

She nodded attentively. Unless she was a far better actress than he thought, the name itself meant nothing to her. "That wasn't the first guy you asked Frannie about," she said. Suddenly, she sprang to her feet. "Jesus! Aren't those ships something!" she exclaimed, staring out the front window.

Barr followed her look. Across the harbor three cruise liners lay berthed head to tail. Nearly all the cabin lights were off now, but the ships' yellow deck lights still gleamed across the water, as did the strings of bulbs that looped between their radio masts. For a silent minute Erin seemed transfixed by them, then spun away from the window and grabbed up her glass. "Never been on a ship. I flew down here," she confided. "Frannie flew me." She giggled. "But not the way you're thinking."

"You're a friend of his?" Barr asked.

She hurled herself back into her chair; for a long minute she sat with eyes closed while she weighed his question. "I am an employee," she answered finally. "A valued employee."

"Oh? What do you do for Mr. X?"

She did a quick double-take and burst into shrill squeals. "Mr. X!" she gasped. "Oh, shit!" She pounded her small hand against the stained upholstery. "Mister fuckin' X!" At last, just as Barr was beginning to think she might slide completely into hysteria, the waves of manic laughter subsided into choked giggles. "You really never heard of Frannie X, did you?" she managed.

"I'm afraid not." Barr wanted to ask her what was so funny, but was afraid of tipping her into a new outbreak.

"That's wild. That's in-fuckin'-credible."

"He's pretty famous?"

"Famous?" She was obviously groping for an explanation of just how famous her employer was. Finally, as if to a three-year-old, she said, "Like, Frannie X owns Utopia Parkway." She waited for his reaction. "You must've heard of Utopia Parkway, right? I mean, you're not from Mars or something."

"Sorry, Erin—the only Utopia Parkway I know is a road in Queens," he said.

She regarded him with grave amazement. "Sheesh. I mean, Frannie was on *Lifestyles of the Rich and Famous. Twice.* People know Utopia Parkway in . . . in *Idaho,* for Chrissake." Without warning, a shy, little-girl's smile lit her face. "That's where I'm from," she confided. "Coeur d'Alene."

Her mind had hopped away from Utopia Parkway, whatever that might be, but Idaho was not a subject Barr wanted to explore. Trying for a question that would head her off, he asked, "Have you been to Bermuda before?"

Watching him narrowly, she licked spilled vodka off her wrist. "Before what?" she finally asked.

"Before this time, that's all," he said. "Were you down here last year, for instance."

"Nope." Her face wrinkled in a parody of deep thought and then brightened, as if she had remembered something. "This guy you're trying to find—what do you want him for?" she demanded.

"I don't want him *for* anything," Barr said. "Just want to make sure he's still alive. He disappeared down here, about a year ago."

She seemed to be concentrating on her next question as she nodded her way impatiently through the first part of Barr's reply. About two beats after *disappeared*, her blankly intent face came alive. Surprise, confusion, and fear registered one after the other, like still pictures in an album. "Disappeared?" she whispered.

"With three other people," Barr confirmed. "Two women and a man; their boat sank a few miles offshore."

It meant something to her, he was certain of it. But she turned her face away as she scrabbled among the odds and ends on the wicker table beside her chair. "Say, you got a smoke?" she asked, her head still averted.

Barr took out his pack of Camels and shook one free. "Here."

"No, a *smoke*," she said, continuing to sift through cheap jewelry, matchbooks, and crumpled balls of paper. "As in toke. A joint— Christ, I forgot: you're not of this earth."

"How about another drink," he offered. "You seem a little jumpy."

"No, thanks." To show him how calm she was she sat back in the chair and crossed her skinny legs with elaborate care. It was quite effective, he thought, except that her hands were clutching the wicker arms so hard that her fingertips had gone white. The rest of her skin, where the makeup failed to cover it, was pale gray. "I just have a headache, is all."

"I'm sorry," Barr said. He made as if to get up. "I'd better go."

"No, don't!" she cried. "Please! I've got to—I'll be okay." Inspiration lit the pointed face. "I just have to go to the john. You stay right there."

Before he could reply, she had bounded to her feet and shot across the room. The door slammed behind her, followed immediately by the sound of running water.

Barr eased himself back in the chair, noticed he was still holding the pack of Camels. He nearly missed his own mouth with the extended cigarette, scorched his cupped hand with the match. "A little too much rum, perhaps," he announced to the room at large. But the old brain's still working: this kid was briefed by the mysterious Mr. X, all right. And in a hurry. If she can just remember the rest of what she was supposed to ask, it might tell me something. He took a deep drag, poked a space for the cigarette in an ashtray already filled to overflowing, and settled back to wait. After several minutes, he realized the water was still running in the bathroom. It sounded, through the closed door, as if the faucet was going full blast. He could feel the annoyance growing in him—wasting freshwater was one of the few cardinal sins he recognized, as heinous as missing a tide or anchoring too close to another boat; he could never reconcile himself to the way landsmen took freshwater for granted.

But fatigue and alcohol were stronger than annoyance. He felt himself slipping away, and forced himself to wobble to his feet. When he could stand the sound no longer, he knocked on the bathroom door, then called to Erin: "You okay in there?"

No answer, just the rushing noise. The bathroom was locked, but the wood and the lock were so feeble he barely had to put his shoulder to the door to spring it open. Erin, fully clothed, was sitting on the toilet seat with her head down and her elbows braced on her knees. Her left sleeve was rolled up, and an angry-looking constriction mark circled her thin little arm just below the bicep. The inside of her forearm was a maze of bruised puncture marks, one of which was still oozing blood. As he reached automatically across her to shut off the faucet, she raised her head and regarded him with curiosity. "What?" she said, quite clearly, and a sweetly magical smile lit her face.

Barr knew what that expression meant—he'd seen it before, a dozen times, on his own wife's face. Scooping Erin up in his arms, he lurched out to the living room and laid her down on the couch. "Sleep tight, kid," he said. "We'll talk some more later."

Her face had become nearly incandescent, but her eyes were closed. He eased himself quietly into the creaking armchair, though he knew that nothing short of the Second Coming would wake the girl for at least three hours. Glancing at his watch, he set his mental alarm for five-thirty and allowed sleep to claim him.

He came awake all at once, out of a vaguely disturbing dream that was only sounds, no images: whispering voices, and a door softly closing. He was alone in Erin's living room, which looked, in the early morning light, even more squalid than it had the night before. He pulled himself out of the chair, his locked muscles fighting him, and stared around the room. No Erin, but the bathroom door was closed, and he was sure he'd left it open. He stood irresolute for a moment, then decided the first order of business was to quell the awful taste in his mouth. He lit his last Camel and drew in on it deeply, but it failed to mask the cigarettes and booze of the night before, and he stubbed it out on a dirty saucer.

Now that he was standing he could see the door to the bathroom wasn't fully closed, and as he took a step toward it he saw why. A small, bare foot, filthy on the bottom and with its nails painted gold, was sticking through the opening. Apprehension struck his stomach a blow, and he had to force himself to cross the room.

She was lying on her back, naked, with one leg straight and the other crossed under it. Her arms were at her sides, and a piece of surgical rubber was still tight around the left one. Her head had fallen to one side, and her face was hidden, for which he was profoundly grateful. He knelt to feel for the artery in her ankle, but even before he touched her cold skin, he knew.

He stood too quickly, felt his head spin. Looking around for her clothes, he saw them rolled in a ball beneath the sink, next to a hypodermic with a bent needle. He went into the small bedroom and tore a stained sheet off the bed. Leaning over to cover her scrawny, pathetic form he saw a tattoo on her left breast, above the tiny nipple. It was a scarlet heart, edged in blue, and lopsided, as if it had been drawn freehand by a child. For a long moment he stood, bent awkwardly, staring; then, slowly, he lifted his eyes to the dead girl's shadowed face. Her own eyes were wide and blank, her mouth agape, but what caught his intent gaze were two tiny feathers—one that seemed to be stuck to her smeared lipstick and another just visible in the corner of her mouth.

As he spread the sheet gently over the small body, recollection tugged at his numbed brain. He dropped quickly to one knee and turned back a corner to uncover her left arm, with the rubber tourniquet still pulled tight and held fast in a clove hitch. The bruise from the earlier tie still showed beneath the surgical tubing. Suddenly, his mind kicked into gear. He jumped up and ran into the living room. Next to the chair where he'd been sleeping was a shapeless sofa pillow. From where he stood he could see the reddish smear and the small tear in the cover.

If this is what I think it is . . . he heard the siren in the distance, cut off quickly, and knew he was right. He darted back into the bedroom, pried open the window, and was about to slide out when he remembered. Moving fast, he retrieved the key to Erin's moped from the dresser where she'd tossed it, and climbed out the window. It was only five feet to the ground, but he sprawled clumsily as he hit. The scooter was lying on its side next to the house. He heaved it upright and was wrestling its dead weight over to the pavement when he heard tires squeal just around the corner. Shoving the moped behind a thick rosebush, he threw himself on top of it just as the police cruiser skidded around the curve and pulled up outside the row of cottages. Two large constables, one black and one white, climbed slowly out. The white one consulted a scrap of paper and pointed to Erin's cottage. Hitching up their belts, the two walked around the side of the building, toward the front door.

The instant they were out of sight Barr was on his feet, pulling the moped up. The thing seemed to weigh a ton, and its wide footrest kept jabbing at his ankles as he pushed it desperately down the road. Once around the corner and, he hoped, out of hearing, he climbed aboard. Mercifully, the engine kicked in on the first try. He was about to drive off when he noticed the helmet hanging from the handlebar and jammed it on, pulling the sun visor down over his eyes.

Barr had no illusions about his driving abilities, on four wheels or two, and for the first few minutes of mindless flight it took all his concentration to keep the moped on the road and vertical. Without a map he had only the most general idea where he was, and when he came at last to a main road running east and west, instinct pointed the scooter toward the morning sun. After a mile or so the road angled northward, and he was just looking for a turnoff that would take him back to the east when he found himself in the familiar pastel village of Flatts. *I have to think, and I can't think and drive this goddamn thing at the same time.* He pulled the scooter off to the side of the road and killed the engine.

Had he been wrong to run? On balance, he thought not. Someone had murdered Erin—smothered her, he guessed—and set him up as the fall guy. The dope paraphernalia had probably been tossed in for atmosphere and to piss off the Bermudian police, who went crazy about that kind of thing. To Barr the frame looked obvious, but would the island cops see it the same way? Barr's long-standing distrust of officialdom in all its forms was almost as ingrained as his habit of handling things by himself. And, he reflected, once the cops got their hands on him, the only way to get free would be to tell them—and anybody else who was plugged into their offices— the truth about why he was there. Might as well put a gun to Sarah Farmer's head and pull the trigger. No, what he had to do was get clear as quickly and quietly as possible.

His memory flashed on the clove hitch around Erin's arm, and he realized that some level of his brain had been puzzling about it; a sailor's knot, and one she couldn't have tied one-handed, even if she knew how. At first he'd thought it was part of the frame—but how would Erin's killer have known Barr was a sailor? It was a fact, and maybe important; right now, all he could do was make a mental note of it.

The police had been tipped, so they probably had a description of him. What they didn't have was a name—not one that would do them any good, anyway. The big question was how long it would take them to connect the party-crashing Franklin Pierce with the Captain Jeremy Barr who'd been making a nuisance of himself throughout Hamilton, asking questions about the *Sea Horse* sinking.

Still, why should they instantly connect the two? The link was *Sea Horse* and her crew, but Barr had the feeling that Frannie X wasn't about to provide them with that information. Toddy would know, but he didn't strike Barr as the kind of man who'd go to the police of his own volition. Fingerprints? Barr's were all over the apartment—

but they weren't on file here in the colony. Conclusion: he had a few hours, but not a whole lot more. It was definitely time to get the hell out of Bermuda. Which raised a whole other set of problems. The airport would certainly be watched, and the cruise liners would probably get a good going-over before they were allowed to sail; short of hijacking a Navy P-3, there was only one other way off.

He pushed the kickstand back up and squeezed the accelerator, roared onto the road toward St. George's without looking and nearly ended the story under the wheels of a cream-colored truck with a burgundy-faced driver. He zoomed over the causeway, reined himself in and chugged sedately past Kindley Field and over the bridge to St. George's Island. It was still early on a summer Sunday; even the churchgoers weren't out yet. He felt his confidence swelling as he swung the scooter down the unpaved road into the boatyard, where his breath locked in his throat. The ketch was gone—not at dockside, and not visible on a mooring, either. Jolly must have got her battery or decided to sail without it.

Despair blanked his mind. If a police car had rolled up at that moment he would have surrendered without a word. Up on the slipway, a man was slapping paint on the sportfishing boat's bottom. He saw Barr, waved a cheery good-morning, and called something that didn't sound like a greeting.

With the moped's echo still in his ears, Barr shook his head. "What'd you say?"

"I said, were you looking for your friends? On the ketch." He pulled a pair of plastic goggles up on his head; his eyes were ringed with clean white skin, but the rest of his face was dappled with brick-red drippings.

"I guess they sailed," Barr replied. He knew he shouldn't stand around talking, but what difference did it make now?

"This morning," the painted man called back. "They're sailing this morning. They're anchored over behind Smith's Island, waiting for the Customs boys to wake up, so they can clear."

For a moment the news didn't register, and when it did Barr almost fell off the scooter. "Well, I just wanted to wish them a good trip," he managed. "Too bad I missed them."

"Though if you ask me," the painted man continued, "they'll be lucky to sail today at all. What with the hangovers they brought aboard last night. You should've seen the little Frenchman carrying her."

"Wish I had," Barr replied. "Must've been a sight." He touched the moped's throttle and swung around in a wide circle, back out the dirt road. A reprieve, he thought. Just maybe, a reprieve.

GILLIAN:
SUNDAY MORNING,
MANHATTAN

If it's 8:00 A.M. in New York, she asked herself, what time is it in Bermuda? An hour later: nine—assuming the islands were on daylight saving, too. Or so she thought; Barr would've known. What was he doing now? she wondered; and why hadn't he checked in with Patrick?

As Gillian strode down Fifty-first Street, she tried to fix her mind on anything but what she was going to do. The impulse had surfaced while she was toying with the immense breakfast Mrs. Boyd had insisted on fixing her, and she had fled the claustrophobic apartment—sad-eyed Jesus staring down from every wall—without even finishing her coffee.

The morning coolness still hung in the air, but the sun was warm on her forehead, working into the small knot of hangover right behind her eyes. She was probably lucky to feel no worse from her night on the tiles with Win, but maybe the wine had just burnt off: Gillian hadn't danced so much in years, or talked with such feverish intensity. How had she ever thought of him as a dry stick? And how could one man amass so much information on so many subjects? She'd wanted to listen to him forever, while he—it was still hard to accept—he wanted only to talk about her: her feelings, her opinions, her experiences. He seemed entranced by her, and she in turn had been fired by his admiration, feeling herself witty and beautiful in his eyes.

In the prosaic sunlight, however, it was hard for her to see what she could have said to delight him so. The sweep of his knowledge had stunned her, and the depth of his vision . . . he'd made her laugh aloud and cry (actually weep in public: she could remember *that* clearly enough), but the few fragments that had stuck in her head sounded dull and flat when she replayed them. The magic had gone out of them, somehow. Or stayed with the magician.

How, she wondered, did real detectives manage to keep emotion and investigation separate? Not that Win Huddleston had any grip on her emotions, of course, but it was hard to observe a man coolly when he was burying you in compliments. Some of them might've been flattery—had to be—but when he said he'd never met anyone like her, he certainly sounded as if he was telling the truth. Probably that was what attracted him: the only woman he knew who didn't have a cast-iron political agenda to shove in his face. Still, he *was* attracted, and that made her feel queasy about spying on him. Last night she'd found herself toying with the idea of confessing why she was at *TNF*, to see if she might not get his cooperation with a direct appeal. Just about then Win had slid into a long anecdote about his brother, and it brought the scapegrace Roger to such vivid life that Gillian couldn't imagine Win was talking about a dead man.

If Roger wasn't dead, why did Win—and K.C.—pretend he was? More to the point, where had he gone? Because Roger was the key to what had happened aboard *Sea Horse*. And by extension he was probably the key to why Sarah was in hiding. Maybe the two of them were hiding together.

If Win was lying to protect Roger then it was okay, Gillian told herself, for her to deceive Win—especially if doing so might lead to Sarah. And that, in a nutshell, was why she was walking toward the *TNF* offices, so she could repay Win's friendliness and generosity by burglarizing his files. She couldn't see any better course of action, though. She seemed to be getting nowhere by asking questions, and who knew what might be found among Roger Huddleston's cartoned possessions, still cluttering K.C.'s office? Besides, Sunday morning was the perfect time to snoop—Gillian knew from the dreary Ursula that no New Federalist would put his nose through the front door till noon.

When *TNF*'s offices were officially closed, the street door was secured by three imposing locks in a vertical line; it was somehow typical of the place that the same key opened all three and that the inner door leading to Arts wasn't even locked. Gillian paused in the mustard-yellow passageway, straining her ears for any sound. All the lights were off, and the only illumination was a secondhand gleam of sunlight from the backyard, reflecting off the walls. For a moment she thought she heard a man's voice, muffled and far away, and then it was gone. She walked down the narrow hall toward the light, then turned left and left again; the squeak of her deck shoes on the bare wood floor seemed to ricochet off the partitions.

In the diffused light from the yard, now behind her, she could just make out the entrance to her own cubicle. Suddenly, she heard it again—a man's voice. Though the words were blurred, his message rode in the tone—harsh, aggrieved; a man who knew himself wronged. The sound seemed to be coming from her own cubbyhole, but after a second she realized the speaker was actually in K.C.'s office beyond. Gillian edged around the corner and saw the slit of light from K.C.'s nearly closed door. The speaker was momentarily audible: Gillian caught the phrase "fifteen million of your dollars," uttered with angry disbelief.

Silence, except for a quick, low whirring she could not quite place, and then the man's voice again. He was talking loudly about freedom—he was in favor of it, but didn't sound happy about the idea—and Gillian took three steps forward under cover of the sound. Through the door she could see K.C. sitting at her desk, staring fixedly ahead of her, presumably at the speaker. Suddenly her face creased with annoyance, and she reached forward. A sharp click cut the man's voice off in midsentence.

A radio? The whirring came again, and it dawned on Gillian that the sound was a tape recorder, in fast-forward or reverse. But K.C. was hardly the girl to spend Sunday morning listening to some clown haranguing her about freedom. So what was it all about?

The whirring had stopped and the man's voice was speaking— something about Russians, but Gillian was too busy edging forward for a better view to pay attention to what he was saying. At last she was in position, pressed uncomfortably between her chair and a filing cabinet, to see the surface of K.C.'s desk: lined yellow pad on the spotless green blotter, two yellower pencils beside it; a large, vaguely familiar green-covered paperback lying open between the pad and the black tape player—a perfectly ordinary cassette player, but something about it looked funny. . . .

At Gillian's back the phone on her desk rang. For an instant her heart stopped dead, then leaped ahead, hammering, as she instinctively grabbed for the receiver. "Hi," said Patrick's voice. "It's me." He's worried, she was thinking, when the door to K.C.'s office flew open.

"Who the hell . . . oh, it's you," K.C. said. With the light behind her it was impossible to see her expression.

"Gillian? You there?" She pressed the receiver hard against her ear, but Patrick's voice sounded loud enough to be heard all the way to Jersey.

"Hello, Mrs. Boyd," she said into the phone. "What's the matter?" Putting her palm over the mouthpiece, she said to K.C. "My landlady."

"What?" said Patrick. "Oh, you can't talk, right?"

"That's it," Gillian replied. "Is there some emergency?"

K.C. had stepped halfway back into her office, so the light fell full on Gillian's face. Her ears were on fire, and she wondered if she looked half as guilty as she felt.

"There is, but we can't do anything about it," Patrick was saying. "Barr called from St. George a half hour back. The cops are after him and he's trying to get off the island."

"Is that so," said Gillian. "You don't have to talk quite so loudly, Mrs. Boyd. I can hear you just fine." Don't react, don't let it sink in, she was thinking. Barr'll be all right. He can handle it—he always has.

"He was calling from a phone booth. Collect." Patrick seemed to be speaking even louder than before. "Didn't have time to say anything else."

"Then I guess there is nothing I can do about it, Mrs. Boyd," Gillian said, trying not to grind her teeth. "I just this minute got to work, and I'm going to be busy all day. Why don't we talk about it later?"

"What? Oh, okay. I'll hang around here in case Barr can make it to another phone or he needs bail or something."

"What a good idea," Gillian trilled. "Talk to you later, then. 'Bye." Her still-galloping heart had dropped out of her throat back to somewhere near its usual position. She didn't dare take the long, shuddering breath her lungs craved—not with K.C. watching so narrowly.

"Didn't hear you come in," K.C. offered. She spoke quietly, but Gillian could feel she was still as rigid as a cat about to pounce.

"Like I said to Mrs. Boyd, I just arrived. In fact, I was just coming around the corner when my phone rang." She clicked her desk lamp on and looked up at K.C. with what she hoped was ingenuous concern. "Hope I didn't scare you. Maybe I should've called out or something, but I didn't hear you, either."

Did K.C. relax just a millimeter? Gillian thought so, but knew she was still tiptoeing through a minefield. "That's all right." K.C., turning to go back in her office, spun back without warning. "Your landlady? What'd she want?"

"Mrs. Boyd?" she said, stalling desperately. You didn't talk to Patrick, she reminded herself. Don't think about Barr. "A nice old lady, but she . . ."—Gillian snatched an excuse from the air—"she worries too much. I left the heater in my room on, and she wanted to tell me how dangerous it was. One of those old-fashioned electric heaters?" she added, improvising on the theme. "The round ones, you know, with the screen over the front?"

"Oh." K.C.'s sudden grin lit her plain face. "Well, she was right." This time, she went all the way into her office before she turned and spoke again: "So what brings you to this dungeon on such a lovely day? I thought for sure you'd be out sailing with Win."

"Oh, I'm going to," Gillian replied. "But later. I had a little catching up to do."

It was a foolish lie, as she realized from K.C.'s expression. So far, Gillian's job as K.C.'s assistant consisted only in typing what K.C. called the Poor Pitiful Pearl Letters, soliciting contributions from foundations, companies, and wealthy individuals with a record of supporting liberal causes. Win, who composed the letters in pain, took an almost childlike pride in having each one unique, but they were in fact so nearly identical that Gillian had taken to typing them with her eyes closed. If she'd had a mail-merge program, she figured, the whole day's correspondence could be got out in a couple of hours; even doing the work by hand, she was finished by three in the afternoon, as K.C. well knew.

All of which flashed through Gillian's mind in the time it took K.C.'s eyebrows to climb a disbelieving quarter of an inch. Before *TNF*'s business manager could challenge her, Gillian hastily added, "Actually, what I wanted to do was weed the correspondence files. Half the stuff in there's a million years old. . . . Say,"—looking pointedly past K.C.—"is that a tape recorder? I kind of thought I heard a man's voice from outside, but I couldn't be sure."

Her question was intended only to defuse the subject, but K.C.'s puglike face flushed a blotchy scarlet, and she moved to block Gillian's line of sight. "That? It's a . . . it's just a cassette player. I had it on while I was working, but you know how it is"—an almost convincing laugh—"I wasn't really listening."

Instinct told Gillian to press her unexpected advantage. "Sounded like some guy making a speech," she observed. Seeing K.C.'s eyes go hard, she added carelessly, "But you probably tune out that kind of thing automatically."

"I probably do," K.C. agreed. She was still standing warily in the doorway, and seemed to Gillian ready to hold her ground indefinitely.

"Guess I'll get started," said Gillian. Still talking, she walked around her desk to the row of file cabinets that occupied one wall. "I'm just going to make a sort of survey and flag what looks as if it could go."

"Oh, that's fine." K.C. put her hand on the door as if to close it, then apparently changed her mind and sat down behind her desk. Gillian slid the file drawer open and began ostentatiously to riffle through the swollen, dusty manila folders. Miraculously, she had managed to will Barr from the front of her mind, but she knew that the slightest relaxation would bring him front and center again.

The correspondence *was* old as time, letters dated from ten years before, most of them dealing with *TNF*'s small classified advertising section. She dove gratefully into the morass of prehistoric trivia ("Bumper sticker bargains: No More Three Mile Islands, Qaddafi Sucks, others. $1 ea. or 12 for $10."), while forcing her memory to produce a picture of the cassette player as she'd seen it in the moment before the phone rang.

She remembered thinking, *something funny about the tape player*, but what? Wires, that was it: three wires emerging from the black case.

Not emerging, plugged into it, she thought, and saw them in her mind: red, black, and white plastic plugs, stuck into jacks at the unit's end. The wires seemed to run separately for a few inches, then dove inside a single insulated cover and ran—where? One wire might have gone to a power source, but K.C.'s office had no wall sockets at all; one might have been for headphones, but there were none in sight. And why three, anyway? Maybe another look would reveal the answer.

Gillian pulled a random letter from the folder she was holding and walked into K.C.'s office. "All of them are junk like this," she declared, tossing it on her boss's desk. "I haven't found a thing worth saving yet."

K.C. accepted the yellowing page reluctantly. As she read it over, Gillian glanced covertly at the cassette player, saw she had moved too slowly: its door gaped on an empty interior, and the triple wires were gone. K.C. looked up. "You're right," she said. "It's garbage, for sure. Tell you what," she went on, pushing her chair back, "why don't you check those folders against a current advertisers' list, just to be on the safe side. Monday—tomorrow—we'll have one of the mailroom boys cart away everything that doesn't match." K.C. smiled up at her assistant. "Just remember to save the folders themselves. We use 'em over again."

Gillian contemplated three hours of pointless, dust-impregnated effort and managed a complementary smile. "Right. Do you have an advertisers' list? I don't."

"Sure thing." There was, Gillian thought, just a trace of triumph behind those protuberant eyes. "In here," she said, pulling open her desk's middle drawer. She handed Gillian a single typewritten sheet, old and crumpled, with several of its entries lined out and a couple of new ones handwritten at the bottom. Gillian accepted the paper without really seeing it, her eyes on the small plastic box that was partly hidden under K.C.'s yellow pad. The container, about the size of a deck of cards, had a dirty white label across one end, and on it a name, WM. MILLER, in smudgy type.

At the filing cabinets, acutely conscious of K.C.'s watchful gaze on her back, Gillian tore through the ancient files like some avenging angel. As her efficient hands sorted, rejected, and (very rarely) set aside, her racing mind considered the unknown Mr. Miller and wondered why K.C. found his taped voice so interesting. Wondered, too, about the triple wire and its colored plugs. She had the strong feeling of having heard or read about just such a connector, and recently, but somehow she also knew that her usually excellent memory hadn't filed the information under tape recorders.

And what had happened to Barr?

BARR :

SUNDAY MIDMORNING,

ST. GEORGE HARBOUR

The breeze on his chest was cool, almost chill, but his back, beneath shirt and blazer, was running with sweat. Under him the moped puttered sedately along the road that paralleled the south side of the harbor. Barr's overheated imagination saw police everywhere—whizzing back and forth in their little white cars, on mopeds, standing watchfully at corners—but, thank God, the road was now filling up with ordinary Bermudians, on their way to wherever they went on a Sunday morning. Church, judging by their dress, and he allowed himself a small frisson of congratulation for the foresight that had made him risk going back to his rented room to change into city clothes. The room was paid up through tomorrow, so there was a reasonable chance his landlady would assume he was still there for another twenty-four hours at least.

The gear he'd left behind wouldn't, Barr thought, tell investigators much of anything—a small U.S. Army duffel with some unknown sergeant's name and serial number stenciled on it, a couple of cheap shirts and an extra pair of khakis, three sets of J.C. Penney underwear. None of it bore his name or even a laundry mark. Everything else he'd brought to Bermuda was on his back or wrapped in brown paper and strapped to the scooter's luggage rack. The return air ticket in his pocket was an open reservation, and his entry permit specified a two-week stay, so no ordinary document check was likely to ring a premature alarm.

Not bad, for a beginner, he thought—then remembered how he'd very nearly blown it all with the phone call to Patrick. Not that he'd meant to go near a telephone, but as he cut through the nearly deserted Market Square to get his bearings, he'd spotted the empty booth, and it'd seemed like too good a chance to pass up. Just as Patrick answered *Glory's* phone, though, Barr had noticed the police cruiser parked half a block up Water Street. He'd managed to stammer out some kind of message before hanging up; he couldn't recall a word of what he'd said, but he remembered perfectly the telephone handset gleaming with his own sweat.

Now, on the airfield runway off to Barr's right, a jet was running up its engines with a roar that drowned the scooter's ratcheting whine. On his other side, through the trees, he could catch the occasional glitter of sunlight on the harbor. At last he came to the narrow cross street he was looking for and turned sharply left. At the foot of the road a stone pier extended into a small-boat anchorage that was protected from winds and seas by a low, swampy, uninhabited island. Barr ran the moped right onto the pier before killing the engine. He pulled off the helmet—its interior was saturated with the smells of Erin's hairspray and perfume—and sat straddling the scooter, considering what to do next. Away to the left the anchorage widened out, and a quarter mile offshore Jolly's ketch rode at anchor by herself, not a sign of life on deck. He could just make out a swatch of red hanging limply from the starboard spreader: the Bermudian ensign, which meant that Jolly had not yet cleared the boat for departure.

A quarter of a mile of water between him and safety; a lousy five hundred yards. Put that way it didn't sound like much, but Barr's swimming consisted mostly of groping his way under *Glory's* hull to wipe off the early film of marine growth and the occasional dive for a fouled anchor—more occasional than ever, now that Gillian had decided diving was her job. She swam with the same determination she brought to everything, and for a moment he could picture her slight form cutting through the flat water, stroking with the neat precision that was peculiarly hers. What was she doing right now? Sailing on Long Island Sound with her new boss, if Patrick was to be believed; jealousy was silly, but the idea annoyed him just the same.

Behind him, he heard quiet footsteps on the concrete. He turned too fast, almost spilling himself and the scooter from the narrow pier. "Hey! Easy does it, son," said his observer, a tall, leathery figure in stained white trousers and T-shirt. The accent was American Middle West; the gray crewcut and stand-at-ease carriage said *military* as clearly as a uniform would have. He smiled at Barr. "Don't tell me, let me guess: You're a visitor and you're lost, right?"

"Actually, yes," Barr agreed quickly. "I was looking for a way to the other side . . ." He gestured across the harbor: "To the cruise liner over there."

The leathery American's smile widened. "Not a prayer, buddy; not unless you can walk on water. You gotta go back the way you came, past the main gate of the base and then hang your first right over the bridge. Right again'll take you into the middle of town." He paused expectantly, as if waiting for his listener to vanish in a cloud of dust.

"Thanks a lot," Barr replied. "I'm in no hurry, really—feels good, being in the sun."

"I'll bet," the leathery American agreed cheerfully. "You're from New England, right? I was stationed up there once. Didn't see the sun for three months. Place called Portsmouth, New Hampshire—you know it?"

Just what I needed, a goddamn friendly compatriot, Barr thought. And aloud: "Not really; I'm from farther north myself."

"That'd be Maine, wouldn't it?" His interlocutor beamed at his own cleverness. "Wouldn't it?" he repeated.

"I beg your pardon?" Barr said.

"You come from Maine," the leathery American said, speaking slowly and distinctly.

"Maine? No." There was, he realized, no way out except through the kind of rudeness that made him wince even to think about. When he spoke, nervousness gave his voice a distant chill that was unmistakable: "You know, I don't want to keep you from whatever you were doing."

The leathery American's face went blank. "Well, hell. Just trying to be friendly."

"Quite." The monosyllable was the coup de grace. The military man's deeply tanned face went three shades darker. Without a word he turned his back on Barr and began casting off a small dinghy whose stern was made fast to the pier. Swinging himself down into it, he pulled a sawed-off oar from under the seat and began to paddle furiously toward a power cruiser moored a dozen yards out. The words "Stuck-up shit" drifted back toward Barr through the heavy, breezeless air.

The cruiser's twin engines coughed, caught, and roared. The American went forward, released the mooring with the skill of long practice, and guided the boat down the channel and into the wider harbor, with never a backward look. His neck was still a deep purple. And his dinghy was still made fast to the mooring buoy a few yards from the pier.

"Well, we *were* going to sail this morning," Jolly was saying, over the bleat of dance music from the radio. "But I might wait a day. Tell you the truth, I'm a little under the weather." She looked up from her third cup of black coffee; the tracery of red veins across her eyeballs was quite visible, even in the semigloom of the ketch's main cabin. She seemed to notice his appearance for the first time: "You fall in the water, Jeremy? You're soaking wet."

"It was a longer jump to the dinghy than I thought," he replied. "Listen, Jolly, I'm in a real jam."

Now he had her attention. Her brow furrowed with concentration, or perhaps just pain. "That smelly creep you were with last night?" she said. "What'd you do, toss him in the harbor?"

"Don't I wish."

The radio music stopped, and an announcer promised the latest news. Barr reached out and turned the volume up, as a different mid-Atlantic voice came on: "A young American woman died last night in her Cobb's Hill cottage, under suspicious circumstances," the newscaster began, running his words together in his eagerness to trot out a purely local disaster. "Bermuda police are searching this morning for a man, presumably also a visitor, to help them in their inquiries."

"What the hell—" Jolly began, but Barr waved her into silence as the announcer went on: Miss Erin Rhodes, a vacationer from New York, had left a private party on the North Shore, shortly after a gate-crasher with whom she had been talking was ejected by the host. She had been seen on her rented moped, with another person seated behind her, riding back toward her cottage. Police, acting on what the announcer daintily called "information received," had entered the cottage this morning and found her dead. Both the unknown man and the moped were missing. There followed a description of the gate-crasher that knotted Barr's stomach with its accuracy, even as he sourly applauded Frannie X's powers of observation. When the announcer finally turned to another subject Jolly, whose face had been growing gradually paler, muttered "Wow" under her breath and turned the set off.

"I didn't do it," Barr said, breaking the silence.

"Of course you didn't," she replied impatiently. "What'd you do with the scooter?"

"Shoved it in the brush behind an empty building," he said.

"Near here?"

"By the pier up in the small-boat anchorage." He paused. "How'd you know I didn't kill her?"

"I know you, Jeremy." She took a sip of her coffee, grimaced, and leaned over to pour the rest down the galley sink. "Besides, if you'd killed her you wouldn't drag an old friend into it."

She was right, he realized—though he was surprised at her perceptiveness. "I was set up," he said. "It's connected to what I came down here for."

"Figures. You want to get out of Bermuda?"

"Yesterday, if possible."

She got to her feet, blinked, and winced. "Christ, what a head." As Barr watched, nonplussed, she opened the top-loading galley icebox and began to pull items from it—several loaves of bread, a frozen turkey, a canned ham, a case of beer—and set them on the counter. Each time she extracted something she had to reach deeper inside, until she was on tiptoe with her heavy rump in the air, her whole torso inside. Barr heard a muffled remark from inside the box.

"What was that?"

She pulled herself out with an effort. "Can't reach the goddamn things," she gasped.

"What things?"

"Ice: fifty-pound blocks. There's three hundred pounds of it down there. That crazy box must be four feet deep." Something in his expression made her grin. "You're kind of slow this morning, Jeremy."

"Well, it's been a long night." Suddenly he understood: "You're going to stash me in there?"

"With the food on top of you. It's just till we get out of the harbor."

"What about your ice?"

"Over the side. It'll drift to shore, if it doesn't melt first."

"That's a major sacrifice, three hundred pounds of ice. Not to mention who knows how many years in the Bermuda jail if you get caught."

"You'd better be worth it, that's all I can say. Now, climb inside and pass up the rest of the provisions. I'll go wake up Jean-Paul to help with the blocks."

The ice blocks had gone over the side, but they'd been in the box long enough to chill it off entirely too goddamn well, Barr reflected. He was lying curled in a tight ball at the very bottom of the deep chest, with a blanket and two foul-weather jackets between his shivering body and the uncompromising shapes of the food on top of him. His face was at the box's lowest point, where the drain-pipe into the bilge had been unscrewed to provide an inadequate supply of diesel-tainted air. Thanks to three inches of foam insu-lation, not to mention the food itself, the conversation between Jolly and two Bermuda Customs men, which had gone on for about a century, was nearly inaudible.

At last he heard the thud of shod feet on the floorboards. Thank God, he thought; they're going to leave. Instead, the lid of the icebox opened with a crash. Between the cases and plastic-wrapped packages above him he could see a gleam of light. He held his breath as a deep voice said, "Just food in here, is that it?"

"Food and booze," he heard Jolly reply. She sounded exactly right—still cooperative, but bored and impatient. "It's all itemized on the supplies list."

"We ought to have everything out of there," said another voice, higher and slightly anxious. The kind of thorough, dutiful son of a bitch I really don't need just now, Barr thought.

Rattle of paper. "Whole lot of stuff on this list," said Deep Voice. Barr felt something move several layers above him: The man was digging down; then he stopped, called out, "Say, this stuff's all frozen. Anybody down there, he's frozen, too."

He very nearly is, Barr agreed silently, bracing himself against the icebox's sides to control his shivering.

"You heard what they told us: Check every space," said Second Voice. "Right down to the bottom."

"All right, man—*you* check it. My fingers turning to Popsicles," Deep Voice complained.

Second Voice's response, clearly visceral, snapped right back: "That's not my job. My job's the forms, your—"

"You want to poke through this stuff, you do it yourself," Deep Voice interrupted. "Anyway, we still got five more boats to clear before lunch. God knows how many more this afternoon." A momentary silence, in which Barr felt himself willing Second Voice to see reason.

"Oh, well, I suppose . . ." he began, wavering.

"All right, skipper, close her up," Deep Voice said. "You're on your way."

GILLIAN:
MONDAY MORNING,
MANHATTAN

For most of the morning she shuttled between the filing cabinets and her desk, disposing of the Mickey Mouse project K.C. had dropped on her. Some of the advertising accounts hadn't had a new entry in three or four years, though Gillian could see no earthly reason why the companies involved had ever taken space in a magazine like *The New Federalist* in the first place.

The job occupied only the thinnest upper layer of her attention. Below, her mind was free to gnaw at the question of K.C.'s mysterious tape recording. *Wm. Miller:* she saw once again the fuzzily typed label on the cassette box; could even, with a little more effort, hear the man's angry voice whining away. The more she thought about it, the less reason she could find for K.C. to have reacted with near-panic when she realized the tape might have been overheard.

On Gillian's ten-thirty coffee break she dove into the Manhattan phone book, where she found an appalling three pages of Millers, of whom a whole column and a half were William, Bill, or just plain W. It would take a week to call all those numbers, even if she knew what to ask when they answered. And what if the particular Wm. didn't live in Manhattan at all?

As maddening as the tape recording itself was the three-pronged connector that K.C. had whisked so quickly out of sight. The strange-looking wire attachment had seemed somehow familiar— but where could she have seen it before? She replayed a week's crowded memories of *TNF* over and over with no result.

Okay, she told herself, look at the problem from another angle: what does the connector do? All of its three plugs socketed into K.C.'s tape player; they connected it, and by extension the voice of the unknown Miller, to what? Forget the plugs—what did the other end of the wire look like? If she could just visualize it, she was sure she'd be able to guess what it plugged into. Trouble was, she had an almost crystalline recollection of K.C.'s desktop as it had been the day before, and there wasn't a single electrically powered thing on it except the telephone and the tape player itself. Because the ex-bathroom had no wall sockets, the lamp was an overhead fixture, the same kind of ancient fluorescent that whirred and flickered over Gillian's own desk; even the laptop computer on K.C.'s typing stand ran on self-contained batteries.

The laptop computer. Maybe that held the answer. K.C.'s was a twin to the one on Gillian's own desk, and to a dozen more that were gathering dust in corners of *TNF*'s offices. Another of Roger's gadgetary follies, Gillian recalled: an eight-line screen no serious writer could work with, internal memory smaller than that of a Pekingese, utter incompatibility with any name-brand machine; as one of the politicals on the second floor had remarked to Gillian, the laptop was really just a five-hundred-dollar notepad.

The silly thing didn't even connect to a disk drive—but it did possess one old-fashioned attribute: it could store programs on cassette tape, as Gillian recalled from her reading of the *User's Guide* she'd found in her desk drawer. . . . That was it: she now remembered seeing, in that same green-covered paperback, a fuzzy, black-and-white photo of a funny-looking connector, with three plugs, that could join the laptop to a tape player. Suddenly she heard, as if he were kneeling beside her, Barr's amused, slightly hesitant voice: "One thing about you, you're the only woman I ever met who reads the directions." At the time he'd said it, she thought he was making fun of her obsessiveness; only later did she realize he'd meant it as a compliment.

Gillian's head was so awash with the possibilities of the laptop computer, so possessed by speculation about the tape of the mysterious Wm. Miller, that she didn't notice when she'd finished the job K.C. had given her. Only after she'd paged impatiently through two irrelevant folders did she realize that she'd moved into a different part of the files. She glanced back inside the drawer and saw where she'd gone wrong—the cardboard divider headed BREAD & BUTTER NOTES in red letters—and focused for the first time on the thin folder in her hand. The cryptic title turned out to be just what it claimed. The manila folder held copies of five letters, one each over the last five years, acknowledging receipt of annual donations to *TNF* of ten thousand dollars from something called the Akasta Fund. The texts were identical, the phrasing a stomach-turning combination of cringe and smarm; Gillian heard her own sigh of relief when she saw that the signatory for *TNF* wasn't Win but Roger Huddleston.

She had glanced idly through several other folders, all the same kind of thing, when K.C. stepped out of her office, locking the door behind her. "Why don't you call it a day, Gillian? I'll treat you to a drink—unless you're whooping it up with our Maximum Leader this evening."

For a moment K.C.'s remark made no sense at all. Then she remembered she did indeed have a date with Win. What she wanted to do was retreat to her tiny bedroom at Mrs. Boyd's and pore over the laptop *User's Guide*, but caution warned her that this was not the moment to back away from an already suspicious K.C. "Just a quick one," she said, as brightly as she could manage. "Win's taking me to the movies."

"Sounds like he's getting serious. What is it?" K.C. asked.

"The movie?" Gillian consulted the yellow pad on her desk. "*Cries and Whispers*. Does that mean something?"

K.C. looked amused. "A pretty kinky way to get next to a girl, that's all. You must've seen it, though—I mean, it's Ingmar *Bergman*, honey."

Gillian felt herself bristle at the other woman's patronizing tone. "The only Bergman I go for is Ingrid. And the movies I like are all oldies."

"Ducks, this is not a movie," K.C. said firmly. "This is a *film*."

"Oh, dear, that bad?"

"Maybe even *cinema*. Make sure you get at least two drinks before you go. Or better still, a couple of joints," said K.C. "Trust me."

He lowered the binoculars, blinking as his eyes adjusted to the light. The damn curtains made it impossible to be sure, but the little house certainly seemed empty, and Joanie's beat-up Plymouth wasn't parked in its usual spot in front. Patrick saw a small figure coming down the road toward him, stepping with care around the puddles, and he raised the glasses again, only to lower them in disappointment: a little girl, and the right age, but not his Tracy. She quickened her steps as she went past the little red sportscar, gave it a quick, sidelong glance that made Patrick feel more conspicuous than ever. He couldn't stay here much longer—shouldn't have come in the first place, but when he found himself with two spare hours and the keys to the Mazda he couldn't resist.

If Joanie saw him, lurking around like some kind of child molester, there'd be hell to pay. And she'd be right: Patrick had given his solemn word that he'd stay away from them, that he wouldn't try to see their daughter. Except for the one time, when he'd borrowed a friend's camera with a telephoto lens (surely a father was entitled to a picture of his own kid), Patrick had kept his promise. He'd sent money whenever he could, from wherever he happened to be, and Joanie put it in Tracy's college savings account, the way she'd agreed, and sent him the receipts. (It was like her to make a point of that, even though he'd told her not to bother.)

He hadn't wanted Tracy to be born—had lit out and joined the Army when Joanie insisted on having the baby out of wedlock. She was married now, and Patrick had heard (through his youngest sister, the only one in the family he stayed in touch with), that the guy was going to adopt Tracy. It was the best thing, no question; and every time Patrick agreed with himself a big empty hole seemed to open in his heart.

Another, older child was approaching. Tall and skinny, blond hair in a ponytail. Patrick had to look again before he was sure, and then it occurred to him that he hadn't seen her in nearly two years. She was about a hundred yards away, just turning up the path to the house, when the old Plymouth rattled around the corner and skidded to a halt. Joanie got out, calling to the kid; Joanie hadn't changed at all, he thought—still the same tall, sunlit girl she'd been eight years ago.

She threw a suspicious look toward the Mazda, but then Tracy was showing her something in a book, and she turned away. Before she could take another look, Patrick hung a sharp U in the muddy street and headed back toward the parkway.

Speeding north on the empty Sagtikos, past the nightmare towers of Pilgrim State Hospital, he wondered why he'd come: there was nothing for him there, and yet he couldn't let go completely.

Back to work, he ordered himself. Next stop, the Bronx. He tramped viciously on the gas pedal, and the car leaped ahead.

The house he was looking for turned out to be one of a dozen small, red-brick homes that lined one side of the quiet street. A pair of polished brass running lights, big enough to have come off an ocean liner, flanked the narrow front door, into which some amateur woodworker had scribed *The Harrigan's* with a router. Patrick parked behind a ten-year-old Ford with a shredding hardtop and sat for a minute, organizing his head for the interview to come. Even though Susan Grover, who'd dug up Harrigan's name and prepared Patrick's way with a phone call, had said there'd be no trouble, Patrick felt uneasy. Uneasy and frustrated, as he had ever since Barr's broken-off call from Bermuda, yesterday morning.

Get going, he told himself. Sitting here isn't solving anything. He hoisted himself out of the little car, locked it carefully behind him, and strode up the narrow path of stepping stones to the door. It opened almost before he'd had a chance to push the bell, and he found himself looking down at a wizened leprechaun, about five feet tall and bald as an egg, with a narrow, suspicious face and angry little eyes. "You O'Mara?" he demanded.

"Patrick O'Mara," he confirmed. "And you must be Andrew Harrigan. Pleased to meet you." He put out his hand, and Harrigan inspected it for several seconds before extending his own for a quick, reluctant squeeze.

"I guess you want to come inside," Harrigan said, not moving out of the doorway. He was wearing a navy blue jumpsuit with an American flag sewn to one sleeve and a fancy organizational patch on the chest. "Well, come on." He turned on his heel and led the way into a tiny, pitch-black vestibule.

Indicating a narrow stairway, he said, "My office is up here. All my files and stuff. Used to be the kid's room," he added over his shoulder. "He don't use it anymore."

At the top Harrigan pushed open a door. "In here." The room was tiny, with a steeply pitched ceiling that came right down to the floor on one side. A plain steel desk filled most of the space, and several blue uniforms, each in a dry cleaner's plastic envelope, hung from hooks along one wall. Most of the other wall was filled from a foot above the floor to the ceiling with what looked like diplomas, in dime-store plastic frames. Harrigan closed and—to Patrick's surprise—locked the door. Without a word he went to the room's only window and opened it all the way, then dropped into an office chair behind the desk and eyed his visitor angrily. "You smoke?" he demanded.

Deciding that friendliness, or even politeness, would get him nowhere, Patrick replied, "No."

"Some kind of health nut," Harrigan muttered. Apparently noticing for the first time that his guest was still standing, he said, "There's a folding chair in the closet."

The space was packed with still more uniforms on hangers. A white hard hat and two flying saucer caps with scrambled eggs on the visors occupied a shelf above; below, boots, sneakers, and three pairs of shiny black artificial-leather shoes took up most of the floor space. Patrick found the chair, extracted it with difficulty, and set it on the floor squarely in front of Harrigan's desk. The little man was in the act of unlocking a drawer from which he produced a half-filled pack of cigarettes, matches, and the sawed-off base of a 105 mm howitzer shell. He lit himself a cigarette, inhaled deeply, and eyed Patrick through the smoke. "You ain't Auxiliary," he said.

"No, I'm not," Patrick replied, and let the words lie on the desk between them.

Harrigan took another long, long drag on his cigarette, and the ash suddenly fell off onto the desktop. He scooped the feathery powder up in his hand and dropped it into the shell. He saw Patrick watching him. "It's the only place I can smoke, up here," he explained. "If she catches me . . ." He shook his head unhappily.

Patrick could feel the tide of the meeting turning, knew that silence was his ally. He sat back in the folding chair and waited.

After a long, squirming moment, Harrigan burst out: "You must be from Washington, then. I thought they said they were gonna forget the whole thing."

Now Patrick saw a course to follow. He leaned across the desk and fixed his host with his iciest top-sergeant glare: "Mr. Harrigan, you should know by now: Washington. Never. Forgets."

Harrigan shrank into his chair as if struck. "Okay," he said, the surliness vanished, replaced by something close to despair. "What do you want?"

"Just tell me the whole thing," Patrick replied. "From the beginning." He took a small notebook from his shirt pocket and poised his pencil over it.

"You must've seen the report . . ."

Patrick rode the objection down: "In your own words, please." Pointedly, he looked at his watch. The gesture seemed to hammer home the little man's surrender, and he began to talk. Somewhere he'd picked up what he obviously thought was a military style of speaking—inside-out sentences full of extra-long words that didn't quite mean what he wanted to say. For a couple of minutes Patrick could barely understand him, but as Harrigan warmed to his story, the stilted forms fell away.

On the day in question, just about a year ago, Harrigan had been on patrol in Long Island Sound, off City Island, in his OPFAC ("In your *what?*" "My Operational Facility—my boat"), when he'd seen, from about half a mile away, a sailboat running westward, under power. It was obvious to Harrigan that the skipper was making a beeline for the Throgs Neck Bridge, and that he was going to run his boat right over Stepping Stones Reef, which lay directly in his path. Harrigan had attempted to warn him, first by radio and then by loud-hailer, but it was no use.

"Dumb bastard piled her right up, like I knew he would. Typical ragman." A year ago I'd have said exactly the same thing, Patrick reflected. How times change; how *people* change. He realized Harrigan was getting to the meat of his story, and tuned back in.

Harrigan had run his boat over to the reef, while reporting the accident to the Coast Guard over his ship-to-shore. At this point, a private salvage operator had come on the air, claiming the tow for himself, and a three-cornered verbal fight erupted between Harrigan, the Coast Guard duty officer, and the towboat skipper. "That's when I lost my temper," said Harrigan, his voice hoarse with emotion. "Sure I called him a blue-balled bastard, but he called me a prick first."

"Is that so?" said Patrick. Harrigan was looking expectantly at Patrick's notebook, so he wrote *Called him a prick* in letters big enough to be read from across the desk. The little man nodded, satisfied.

"And a lot of other stuff besides, when we were both alongside the sailboat," Harrigan continued. "Only none of that was on the air."

"Just as well," said Patrick sternly. Harrigan, who had begun to fluff up like a small, scraggly rooster, sagged back in his chair. "Continue, please."

"Forgot where I was," Harrigan muttered.

"You were fighting over who was going to get the tow," Patrick prompted.

"After I already pulled him off the rocks," said Harrigan. "He was real down by the head, thought he was gonna sink on me."

"But the towboat muscled in on you." The sequence wasn't hard to guess, and Patrick saw he was right.

"Yeah, friggin' government policy. Auxiliary's not supposed to compete with private enterprise," snarled Harrigan, the veins on his skinny neck standing out like wires. "You can bet some Commie thought that one up."

Patrick blinked, decided to let it pass. "But neither of you got the tow," he said.

"That's right. The goddamn joke was on both of us," Harrigan flared. "While we was yellin' at each other, the bastard just sailed away." He paused, breathing hard. When he went on, his voice was unsteady. "Look, Mr. O'Mara, I never did anything like that before."

Patrick fixed Harrigan with a coldly doubting eye and said, "Never?"

"Absolutely never." Patrick saw with astonishment that the little man was on the verge of tears. "Twenty-five years in the Auxiliary, I never used obscene speech on the friggin' radio *once*. I mean, I'm a *Communicator*: can you believe I'd say obscene words on the airwaves if I wasn't fuckin' out of my wits?"

So that was it. Laughter welled up almost painfully at the back of Patrick's throat; somehow he managed to keep his face wooden, but speech was beyond him.

"Listen, Mr. O'Mara. Search and rescue's my life," Harrigan pleaded. "If you take my radio license, you might as well cut my throat."

A wave of sympathy swept Patrick's amusement away. "Mr. Harrigan," he said solemnly, "I can assure you that your work has been noticed."

"It has?" the little man said, his eyes widening.

"And appreciated. At the highest levels." For a moment Patrick was afraid he'd gone too far, but then he realized Harrigan had gone limp from relief, not coronary arrest. "Now, there are just a few more questions I have to ask."

"Sure. Anything. Hey, you want a cigarette? Oh, I forgot, you don't—"

"A few more questions," Patrick repeated. "You may not see why I'm asking them, but we have to round out the file."

"Round out the file, sure." Harrigan nodded through the smoke. "Ask away."

Harrigan, it turned out, had his own files, and now that he'd decided Patrick was on his side he was eager to show them off. Copies of his patrol logbooks, his radio logs, his fuel receipts, his orders from the Coast Guard—he had kept them all. Patrick had to nod his way appreciatively through most of an inch-thick folder labeled *Patrols-July* before reaching the information he wanted: "Pulled Alberg 35 sailboat *Sea Horse* off Stepping Stones. 2 POBs. Refused further assistance."

"Sloop or yawl?" Patrick asked.

"Say again?"

"One mast or two on the sailboat?"

He considered, lips pursed. "Two, I think. Definitely two."

"You're certain it was an Alberg thirty-five?" Patrick continued, keeping his tone casual.

"For sure. It was engraved on this brass plate at the aft end of the cockpit."

"And you're sure of the name: *Sea Horse?*"

"Hell, I wrote it down, didn't I?"

Fair enough: For a man like Harrigan, Patrick realized, writing something down was the same as carving it in stone, an act not to be performed lightly. "Did you notice anything funny about the name, when you looked at it?"

"Funny how?" asked Harrigan.

"Like the way it was written," Patrick said. He didn't want to feed the answer to the little man, who was far too eager to say anything he thought would please.

Harrigan wrinkled his brow until his eyebrows nearly met. Slowly his face brightened in recollection: "Oh, yeah. Right. The sea horses. There was pictures of sea horses on it someplace."

"Something like this?" From the back of his small notebook Patrick produced a copy of the sketch Father Richardson had done for Gillian.

"Yeah, like that." He paused. "At least I think it was. You got to remember it was a year ago."

"Right," said Patrick, replacing the drawing. From his shirt pocket he took a plain envelope with four photographs in it. "Now, what about the people on the sailboat? How many'd you say there were?"

Instant suspicion darkened Harrigan's face. "It's right there in front of you," he said, pointing to the logbook page. "See? *Two POBs.*"

"Of course. And POBs . . ."

"Persons on board."

"You're sure there were only two." Patrick held up his hand as he saw Harrigan start to bristle: "What I mean is, did you count them yourself, or was that what the skipper told you, or what?"

"Oh." Harrigan retreated back into thought. "Must've been what he told me. There was two of 'em on deck, a man and a woman— I do remember that."

Patrick handed over the four photographs. "Could they have been any of these?"

"Shit, man, I don't know," Harrigan protested. He looked help-lessly at the pictures. "Maybe this one was the Hispanic."

Patrick felt a stab of excitement. "Hispanic? Which one?"

"This one," said Harrigan doubtfully, pointing to the shot of Sarah Farmer. "Or maybe it wasn't. She was thin like this, and with black hair—but I sure wouldn't swear to the face."

"Could she've been speaking French, not Spanish?" Patrick asked.

"Naw, it was spick all right," Harrigan replied.

"You're positive?"

"Goddamn right." His face clouded again. "Didn't my own son marry one of them? After all we done for him? I heard enough of that jabber-jabber-jabber to last me a lifetime. She was speaking Espanyole, mister. Take my word for it." A thought widened his eyes. "Say, how come you're interested in these people? They aren't, you know, *perpetrators*, are they?"

"Well, I didn't know what to say to that, so I just winged it. Told him he knew too much already, but I was sure he'd keep it a secret." Patrick glanced up from his coffee for a reaction.

Sol Farber, who had followed the account without an interruption, seemed pleased. "And he gobbled it up, no?" Patrick grinned his answer, and Farber's smile widened to a paternal beam that seemed to light up the small, deserted restaurant. "Mr. O'Mara, I can see you handled this Harrigan with real kid gloves. You must have a talent for this kind of work."

"I could see he wanted to be important—on the inside of things, you know," Patrick replied, warming to Farber's open approval. "He threw it in my lap."

"Ah, yes. But you made him throw. That's the important thing."

Farber caught a passing waiter's eye. "I think just a small piece of cheesecake, please. And another coffee. For you, Mr. O'Mara?"

"Oh, no more, thanks." Patrick patted his shirtfront. "Another bite and I'll blow a button."

"Suit yourself, but I think you could stand a little more meat on your bones." With a clatter of china the waiter deposited the coffee and cheesecake; Farber helped himself to a forkful that reduced the slice by half. "So tell me something, Mr. O'Mara, where have we got to?"

"Sir?"

"You know what I'm saying. Your friend Barr is in Bermuda—at least we think he is, we aren't sure; Gillian is in with the new federals; you're running around the Bronx taking chances that make my stomach turn over. Where's it getting us? What do we know about my Sarah?"

"Well, it's a little hard—"

"Not that I mind spending the money," Farber interrupted, waving his fork at Patrick. "I want you should be sure of that. But we seem to know less than when we started."

The remark echoed Patrick's own estimate precisely. "Okay, there's not a whole lot we can say for sure," he began, feeling his way. "But all three of us seem to have some kind of action going. I mean, when we started I thought at least one of us was going to come up dry. Tell you the truth, I figured it'd be me—that idea of yours looked like a thousand-to-one shot at best, but it stirred something up."

"I never heard somebody sound grateful for almost getting killed," said Farber. "Sorry. Go ahead."

"I just don't like being left out. Anyhow, Gillian's positive that Roger's got himself stashed away somewhere, probably with Sarah, and that Roger's old secretary and his brother both know a lot more than they're telling. That's point one."

"Go on."

Farber was looking impressed, and Patrick continued more easily: "Point two, even though we don't know what happened in Bermuda, we do know that when Barr started asking questions about the *Sea Horse* sinking, it blew up in his face. We just have to wait till he surfaces to get the details."

"*If* he surfaces," Farber said. "And what about you? You found a boat with the same name—okay, but it's in little pieces and six hundred miles from the right place. That's progress?"

"Somebody tried to part my hair with a pipe when I got too curious," Patrick pointed out. "It's got to mean something."

"In the Bronx, I'm not so sure," said Farber gloomily. "But maybe you're right. What were you thinking to do next?"

Patrick had already worked that through. "Check out the Hutchinson River Boatworks—"

"You're not going back there," snapped Farber, with a forcefulness that rocked Patrick back in his seat. "I'm not willing you should be hurt or maybe killed on my account."

"I wasn't planning to go in person," Patrick replied. "Whatever that Alberg thirty-five used to be, it's a pile of fiberglass chips now. No, I was going to see what I can find out about the yard itself— how well they're doing, who their customers are, who that Kiwi is."

Farber eyed him with a respect Patrick found very pleasing. "How you going to do that? They won't be in Dun and Bradstreet."

"Friends," said Patrick, who had only the foggiest idea of where to look. "I was a paid skipper, working out of City Island, only a year ago. I got friends there I can ask, and they'll pass me on to other friends. That kind of thing." As he spoke, his words began to make his idea seem plausible. "And I've got a source inside the Coast Guard," he added. "We're having . . . going to have a meeting tonight."

"You already said about your friend in the Coast Guard." Farber's eyes were twinkling with amusement. "She's a nice girl?"

"And what did you tell him, Patrick?" Susan Grover's smile gave nothing away at all. "Am I a nice girl?"

"You're the most gorgeous woman I know," said Patrick, and realized it was no less than the truth. She was wearing a plain black dress, short enough to show off her legs, and no jewelry except small pearl earrings. When Patrick had led her into the restaurant the eyes of every man in the place, and half the women, had focused on her.

She twirled the champagne glass between her long fingers. "I have the strong impression that you're a scoundrel when it comes to women."

And you're just about ready for a scoundrel, he thought. But he heard himself ask, "What do *you* think about the two *Sea Horses*?"

Her lazy smile cooled. "Coincidence," she said. "I bet if you looked in a directory of boat names, you'd find a whole passel of boats called *Sea Horse*."

"Nine in the last edition of *Lloyd's Register*," he admitted.

"You see?" She tilted her head an inch or two, and the soft light silhouetted her perfect profile.

"Still doesn't say why that big ape tried to beat my head in. Nothing I could see in the Hutchinson River Boatworks was worth a manslaughter rap."

She sighed. "I thought this was supposed to be a date," she said. "You're beginning to sound like a Coast Guard inquiry, and I get enough of those during working hours. Which this definitely is not."

"Sorry. You're right." His own casual remark to Farber materialized in his head. "Look, Susan, if you'll do me one more favor, I promise not only to forget this project for the rest of the evening, but I'll take you to . . . to any night spot you want to name."

"Now that's more like it," she beamed, extending her hand to him. "You got yourself a deal, only it might be a longer evenin' than you bargained for."

Her hand was smooth and dry and warm, and it moved invitingly in his grasp. He felt his reluctance slipping away, made one final gesture toward duty: "This Hutchinson River place. I need to know all about it, and the Kiwi who runs it. Can you help?"

"Sure can. I've got some real good buddies over in Enforcement." She pulled her hand back, but so slowly it was a provocation, not a withdrawal. "I think this calls for another champagne."

"You got it. And then?"

"Oh, I kind of thought we'd let *then* take care of itself," she said; her violet eyes looked wide and deep enough to drown in.

B A R R :

M O N D A Y   E V E N I N G ,

33° 05′ N, 64° 58′ W

Just before sunset he handed the wheel over to Jean-Paul. The northeast wind was kicking up to twenty knots or so, and across the western horizon the backlit clouds towered like the battlements of a nightmare city. Jean-Paul had climbed into chest-high foul-weather trousers, and his jacket was wedged conveniently to hand between the mizzen shrouds and the lifelines. Before going below Barr observed him surreptitiously for a few minutes: The young Frenchman was still oversteering, but less than he had been earlier in the day—and, to do him justice, the ketch had turned hard-mouthed as the wind rose, staggering under too much sail. It was past time for a reef, but Barr knew he'd have to suggest it himself. Jolly would never think of reducing sail until the lee gunwale was underwater, and Jean-Paul, for whatever reason, was clearly deter-mined to fight the wheel until the steering cable snapped.

Barr could see they were in for a messy night, and the three-day high-seas forecast called for gales through the period. At least they'd be favoring gales, though when the boat was sheathed in rain and spray you got soaked no matter where the wind came from. Right now he felt tolerably dry, in Jolly's extra sweater and a peeling pair of foul weather pants they'd found at the back of a locker. His own shirt and trousers—the only ones he'd brought aboard—were stiff with saltwater; one splatter of spray or rain and they'd be sodden again. Even if he stayed below for the entire passage, his deck shoes

would still be squelching wet when they tied up inside Barnegat
Inlet, their destination. Once, not so long ago, he'd have shrugged
it off; now the prospect of wet feet for four days filled him with
gloom. Did that mean he was getting old? Maybe. But what it meant
for sure was that he planned to push this spavined old cow as fast
as she could go.

He swung down the companionway. Jolly was wedged behind
the small chart table, muttering under her breath as she stared at
the loran screen. "I don't suppose you can fix one of these, Jeremy,"
she said.

The screen was showing an error message he didn't recognize.
"What seems to be the problem?" he asked, as he grabbed a handful
of cookies from the snack locker, arranged them carefully in a shallow
plastic dish.

"Damned if I know. According to this"—she waved the instruction
book at him—"the set's not getting enough juice, but every once in
a while it settles down and locks on for a minute or two."

Rooting through the canned food supply under the sink he selected an oblong tin with a slotted key attached to its bottom.
"Sounds like an intermittent bad connection. But wait a minute till
I open this, and I'll have a look." He twisted the small, impractical
key until the flat tin's lid was rolled up into a tight metal cylinder,
poured the excess oil down the galley sink drain, and reached into
a drawer for a fork. "Maybe a cold-soldered wire at the plug," he
suggested, probing at the tin's contents. "Have we got a twelve-volt
soldering iron?"

"Don't be silly." Jolly snapped off the set and turned toward Barr
with a startled look. "What're you eating?"

"Anchovies, I think." He sniffed the open tin. "Right. Want one?"

"No, but what in Christ's name are you putting them on?" she
demanded.

"What? Oh, chocolate-chip somethings. Not bad: sure you
won't—"

"I won't," she said firmly, averting her eyes. "I'd forgotten what a
coarse feeder you are, Jeremy. Would you like to take those things
up on deck? Please."

"Sure. But listen, Jolly, we ought to take in a reef before it gets dark. This tub won't lose any speed now, and we won't have to sleep on our ear. Besides, that steering's got a lot of slop in it—I don't think you really want to load it up too much."

"Wait one," she said, closing her eyes and touching her fingertips to her forehead. "I forgot how damn diffident you are when you're not skipper. *Don't really want to load it up too much*: That means the whole thing could let go any minute, right?"

"Well . . ."

"Go tie in your reef. And take those things with you."

At midnight, Jolly came down the companionway scattering water from her foul-weather gear. "Not a fit night up there for man nor beast," she observed, peeling off her jacket and safety harness together. She hung them from the fire-extinguisher bracket next to the ladder, then braced herself against the galley counter and began tugging at a boot. Barr, who had been sitting at the navigator's desk, replaced the microphone he'd been holding.

"Hold your foot out." He wrestled first one damp boot and then the other off her feet and tossed them beneath the companion ladder.

"Thanks," Jolly gasped, as she began to writhe herself free of the clinging trousers. "Did you get through on the sideband?"

"No problem raising the high-seas operator," Barr replied. "But no answer on shore."

He felt the quick, appraising glance Jolly gave him from under her lashes. "Maybe Gillian's out on the town," she said. "Wish I was."

"No, it was Patrick I was trying to reach."

"Then he's definitely out on the town." Jolly leaned into the icebox and took out a half-full bottle of molasses-colored rum. "Slug?"

"Thanks." Barr tilted the bottle, handed it back. "I wanted to reassure him I'd got away. Maybe it wasn't necessary."

Jolly opened her throat and let two long swallows flow down. "I expect they just assumed you made it. Those two think you walk on water, you know." She held the bottle out to Barr and, when he shook his head, replaced the cap and wedged it back in the icebox.

"Well, I'm certainly out of my depth in this mess," he said feelingly. "Just hope they're doing better at their end."

Jolly unbuttoned her thick flannel shirt and pulled down her jeans. Under them, in the interest of water absorption, she was wearing lightweight long johns. Barr reflected that it would be hard to design less erotic garments, especially when they bagged at the knees and seat. She stood for a moment, balancing easily against the ketch's pitching, as she surveyed the available sleeping spaces. Barr had mentally earmarked the main cabin's only seaberth, a settee that was currently on the heeling yacht's low side; but Jolly winked at him, murmured "Skipper's privilege" and climbed into it. Pulling a blanket over herself, she said, "Pass me that paper I was reading, would you?"

He picked the crumpled sheets from where she had jammed them, between two volumes of the Sight Reduction Tables, and automatically smoothed them out. Jolly's reading habits hadn't changed, he saw: NIGHTCLUB GANG RAPE LEAVES TODDLER PREGNANT blared the headline. "Here you go: all the news that's fit to print."

"So what does Gillian read?" she replied, as she took the paper from him. It was a rhetorical question, but he was startled to realize he didn't know. And just as startled that he hadn't taken the trouble to find out. Jolly, clearly misconstruing his expression, said, "I just like to keep up with the jet set, that's all."

The jet set: he hadn't heard that term for a while, but it repelled him still. There were plenty of them around in the islands, if you looked. Not many in Bermuda, though. Except . . . "Jolly, does the name Frannie X mean anything to you?"

She glanced up in surprise. "The owner of Studio Fifty-four. No, another place—Utopia Parkway, that's it."

"What's the rest of his name, do you know?"

She pursed her lips, stared up at the cabin overhead. "Martini . . . Martelli . . . Martello: That's it, Martello. But he hardly ever uses it. Everybody knows him as Frannie X. Innkeeper to the Stars."

"What?"

"Innkeeper to the Stars. *People* or *Us* or one of those magazines called him that. You know him, Jeremy?"

"Not yet," said Barr. "But I will."

Three in the morning, or very nearly. He stood behind the ketch's wheel, feeling the chill from the stainless steel rim seeping up his hands to his wrists. The last rain squall had ended an hour before, and now the ketch was galloping lumpishly through a rising chop, pushed along by a strong nor'easter. Jean-Paul was asleep on the bridge deck at the cockpit's forward end, wrapped in a sleeping bag. Through the open companion Barr could hear Jolly's earth-shattering snores. *Another thing I forgot about her.*

He'd always enjoyed the night watches, especially when he could stand them alone, but for some reason this one seemed to drag on forever. His mind kept going back to Gillian, flashing glimpses of her that had registered over the past winter—her face lit with laughter at one of Patrick's songs; her sudden look of entranced discovery when her first star sights had worked out exactly right.

And then, without warning or transition, Gillian's face was replaced by another—equally young, but pinched and bloodless, wide-open eyes staring up at nothing.

Silly, harmless, helpless child, he thought. *Stiffened limbs jammed awkwardly between the toilet base and the wall; the picture was so clear he could see the pattern on the worn linoleum beneath her, the blue-edged scarlet heart amateurishly tattooed over her small, sagging breast. Poor, dead kid. . . .* He felt a hand on his shoulder, and snapped back from a dank, sour-smelling room to the clean chill of the open sea. "You okay, Jeremy?"

He looked down at the jury-rigged compass, lit by a red-lensed flashlight tied in place with elastic cord. He had to blink twice before he could see the card clearly enough to be sure he was still on course. "I'm all right. What's up?"

"It's half-past four. You let me sleep through my watch change." In the half-light from the flash he saw her head cocked quizzically. "You sure you're all right?"

"Of course I'm sure. Why?"

She hesitated, leaning closer. In the flashlight's glow he saw concern and curiosity in her face. "Nothing, except your cheeks are all wet."

All through the previous evening's dinner Win had seemed obsessed by the race to Bermuda. He'd never made such a long open-water passage as skipper, and Gillian could see that the reality of it, scary and exciting at the same time, was just coming home to him. It was a state she could empathize with; she herself had been bouncing off the bulkheads the previous October, before *Glory* had sailed south for the islands. Gillian had had Barr to lean on; Win, it was obvious, had an oracle, too. He started out with "Roger always relied on loran" and "Roger hated the Swedish watch system," and slid almost imperceptibly into "Roger swears by dry ice" and "Roger always tries to make landfall between midnight and dawn," until Gillian was tempted to ask if Win was getting his advice by Ouija board.

After the movie, a third drink—which by then Gillian badly needed—and to top the evening off a verbal, oddly chaste, completely unexpected pass in the back of the taxi. She found herself so rattled by the combination of Win Huddleston and sex that everything else flew out of her head. By the time she remembered the laptop owner's manual in her handbag she was in bed, exhausted by her own diplomacy.

When she slid upward into consciousness she carried with her a dream of Jeremy Barr, standing bare to the waist at *Glory*'s helm. Or maybe, she reflected lazily, it was a memory; she'd seen him that way often, though never naked—which said a lot about his instinct for privacy, considering the close quarters in which they lived. Holding the mental picture of him in focus, she pasted herself into it, wearing the pastel green bikini she'd bought in Fort-de-France, the one that always made the male charterers blink when they first saw it. For a few minutes she allowed herself to hover at the delicious edge of fantasy, before her bedside clock burred her back to the real world.

At breakfast she fielded Mrs. Boyd's seemingly innocent questions—Mrs. Boyd was gently, persistently worried about the state of Gillian's soul—while trying desperately to grasp the contents of the laptop *User's Guide*, propped against the coffee pot. The text, she decided, had been incompletely translated from the Japanese, and the result was maddening: the little computer could indeed exchange information with a cassette tape player, storing programs on tape and then calling them back into its own memory, but the instructions on how this was accomplished were to Gillian purest Samurai.

At last she cut heartlessly into Mrs. Boyd's monologue, something about the young adults' program in her church: "Do we have a Yellow Pages around here, Mrs. B?" She quickly located the American distributors of the laptop computer, but their address was way downtown, somewhere in the mazy heart of the West Village. She glanced at her watch: not nearly enough time now, but she could just fit it into an extended lunch hour, as long as she skipped eating.

She arrived at the magazine before K.C. did, and slipped the laptop machine from her own desk into the oversize bag she'd bought especially for the purpose. Then she settled down to wait out the morning, confident only that the next three hours would last for three days. In a little more than due course K.C. materialized, jumpy and hostile from what she said was a bad hangover. After emergency repairs—two mugs of black coffee the consistency of lubricating oil—she tossed a thick stack of files on Gillian's desk. "Lapsed donors," she announced.

Gillian contemplated the stack. "Means what?" she replied coolly.

K.C. looked suitably abashed. "Sorry. These are people and organizations that used to make regular contributions to *TNF*; to the foundation side, tax deductible. For whatever reason they dropped

away, and Win wants to go after them again. He's drafted a letter—
it's here on top—and you can see from the former correspondence
how he addresses each of the contacts."

Gillian had been leafing through the papers as K.C. spoke. "This
one's ten years old," she protested. "How do we know this Terrence
Amberson is even with the organization anymore?"

"Good thinking. We don't," said K.C. "You call first and double-
check. If there's a new name in the job, note it down and pass it to
me."

"After I write the letter?"

"No. With new names, don't send a letter at all," K.C. said. "Win
or I will make a personal approach first."

It was, Gillian saw, very much the usual sort of thing, the kind
of letter that Win said made drops of blood form on his forehead.
Genteel begging—how he hated it; and how he must love *TNF* to
force himself through it, year after year.

"Any problems?" K.C. was watching her intently.

"None at all," Gillian replied, pulling the stack toward her. "Do
the carbons go in the Bread and Butter file?"

K.C.'s head snapped around. "How d'you know—" She caught
herself, gave an exaggerated wince of agony. "Christ, what a head!
No, give them to me—I'll take care of it. You've got enough to do
before you leave for Bermuda."

Bermuda? Of course, the race—how could she have forgotten?
And why hadn't Barr called?

She hurled herself doggedly into the letters, which turned out to
be exactly the kind of tranquilizer her jumpy nerves required. By
the tenth repetition, she could have recited Win's dreary prose in
her sleep. She sandwiched carbon paper between another letterhead
and yet another onionskin and rolled the combination into her
typewriter. Her fingers batted out the date, hit the line advance
twice. Without really looking, she launched into the address.

And froze in midstroke, unbelieving:

Mr. Sol Farber, President
The Tillie Farber Fund
25 West 4

She turned back to the copy she was working from, a single-page letter contract between *TNF* and the contributor. Uncle Sol's signature was unmistakable, a series of huge loops and swirls. The date was a year before, when the Tillie Farber Fund had agreed to advance the goals of *The New Federalist* to the tune of five thousand dollars. Gillian lifted the page; under it were more carbon copies of contracts; clipped to each was a *TNF* interoffice memo authorizing deposit of the specified amount. The donations started four years earlier, a thousand dollars at first, then two, then the abrupt jump to five, then nothing.

What could it mean? Why hadn't Uncle Sol told her? More to the point, why hadn't he told Win when he'd come to *TNF*, asking about Sarah? There was, Gillian decided, no point in just wondering. When she finished the letter she slipped the carbon copy under her blotter. She had the sense of it smoldering there for the rest of the morning, ready to burst into accusing flame.

"I might be back a little late," she said, handing K.C. the completed letters. "There's only a dozen more to do."

"Take your time, kiddo," K.C. replied. She seemed to have recovered her usual bouncy friendliness. And her usual curiosity: "You're not doing a matinee with Win, by any chance?"

The idea of sneaking off with Win to some midtown hotel was too grotesque to take seriously, and she threw K.C. a glare of genuinely mock disdain: "My body is a temple, you rotten girl." But she could see that K.C. was waiting for a responsive answer, too: "Just some errands to run downtown."

First the Tillie Farber Fund, she decided. From a rank of pay phones in the lobby of a nearby office building she dialed Calico Jack Activewear. Uncle Sol, when she confronted him with his contributions, sounded baffled and defensive. "TNF Foundation, it's the same as the magazine? I never even knew. Look, Gillian, I set up the fund in Tillie's name when she got sick. She asked me to. I didn't want to do it, honest to God: it was like she was giving up on life. She made out the list of people and how much they should get, and I just sent the checks. I remember, now that you ask, she used to read the little magazine, but I never connected. Listen, you should

see some of the names on that list of hers—homes for homeless
kitties and retired rabbis and I couldn't tell you what . . ."

It was too much. Uncle Sol didn't have to snow her with all that
stuff. And at the same time, too little—like, why had he kept on
contributing after Aunt Tillie had died? In a flash of perception, she
saw an answer. "Uncle Sol, how did Sarah get her job at *TNF?*"

Silence. A long, long silence, followed by an embarrassed laugh.
"Serves me right," he said. "You see right through an old man like
me. Sure, it started like I said—one of Tillie's do-good things. Then
when Sarah decided she wanted to be a writer, I got to thinking.
So sue me."

"And once she was hired? . . ."

She could almost hear his shrug. "I figured I paid my due. From
what I saw of the magazine, Sarah wasn't any worse than what they
already had."

"Win—the editor—knew about this?"

"No, only his brother. The one Sarah sailed with. He hired her."

Full circle. Or was it full dead end? She left the booth feeling as
if the pavement under her feet had lost a little of its solidity.

East-West Computers was on the third floor of a lone office
building so narrow it looked as if it'd been squeezed upward by the
low warehouses flanking it. The lobby was a marble hallway that
smelled of disinfectant and urine, with an elevator that looked like
one of the steel-jawed traps in an animal-rights ad. The door to the
East-West office was blocked open by a carton, and the long, low-
ceilinged room seemed to be entirely filled with cardboard boxes,
except for a lone desk by the door. A youngish man in a glen plaid
suit a size too large for him looked up from his sandwich. He had
a dartboard complexion and bleak eyes that brightened when he
saw Gillian.

"Hi. You're the best thing that's walked in all week," he said,
getting to his feet. "You must be here by mistake."

"Not if you're East-West Computers."

"In person. Peter East. Honest, that's my real name." He put out
his hand, saw the mayonnaise on his fingers, and thrust it into his
pocket.

"Don't tell me your partner is West."

"Hashimura. His name's Wallace Hashimura," East replied. "He's not here."

"That's all right. You'll do fine." Gillian set her bag down on the desk and extracted the laptop computer. "This is yours, right?"

"Our Model A," Peter East agreed, eyeing it cautiously. "Ripped off from NEC, out of Radio Shack, but you probably already know that." He picked it up, clicked it on. "Seems to be working all right."

"Far as I know, it is," Gillian said. "I need a little explanation about the peripherals. The *User's Guide* . . ."

"Is shit. I know. The *Useless Guide*. If we'd only had a good writer, we might not be here in this dump." He set the machine down. "So what do you want to know?"

Peter East might look like the prototype computer nerd, but once he became absorbed in the subject he knew, he turned into a different person, caressing the little laptop as if it were a living thing; and in his hands it seemed almost alive. His partner had come across the machine in Japan, he told Gillian, learned it was being adapted for the American market by two big electronics firms, and instantly decided to piggyback on their investment. "We thought we were smarter than they were," East said. "They were stuffing the box with chips, but we decided that a cassette-tape memory was the way to go. Boy, were we wrong. It never flew." He looked down at his brainchild ruefully. "Hell, it never even flapped."

"How come?" Gillian asked.

"It just wasn't what people wanted," he shrugged. "And the cassette player didn't help, either: another bright idea that Wally picked up in his City College marketing class."

Gillian looked her question.

"An add-on purchase, you know? We couldn't get into the cassette market; too many people there already. So Wally decides we'll sell a special cassette recorder that connects to the Model A."

"Special how?"

"Special like we took the GE decal off and added our own," East confessed. "We got it from both sides: GE came down on us like a landslide, and people who owned the Model A figured out that any cassette machine would work, if you just twiddled the volume a little." He saw her brow furrow, and explained: "The computer sends the program to the tape recorder as a series of beeps and squeals; if you play the tape it sounds like mechanical nonsense. When it goes the other way—when the tape player is sending the program back into the computer—the volume has to be exactly right, or the computer can't hear it. It can be a real fiddly adjustment to make."

"I see, or at least I think I do," Gillian said slowly. "Could you show me how it works?"

"Sure. Easiest thing in the world," East replied. "Here, we'll use one of our special tape machines—you got a program?"

"Not with me."

" 'S okay. We'll use this sample." He picked up a small plastic box and tipped a cassette into the palm of his hand.

"Can you use any kind of tape?" Gillian asked. "It doesn't have to be special?"

"Hell, no," he replied, inserting the cassette in the player. "Oh, high-bias is best, but anything'll do in a pinch. Record right over old stuff if you want—the computer doesn't hear words, you understand, just its own language."

Now she had her answer, she was almost sure, but she asked the final question to nail it down: "What do I need to connect the tape machine to the laptop? Some kind of special plug, I suppose."

"I was just coming to that," he replied, fumbling in his desk drawer. "It's a standard cable. NEC makes them, so do a bunch of other folks. It's got three jacks—"

"Red, black, and white," she put in triumphantly.

"You got it: red goes in the mike jack, black in the remote, and white in the earphone."

"Then what?"

"Then it's simple." And to her surprise it was. All she had to do was have the computer search the cassette tape for the particular file she wanted it to send back to the laptop. The file would come over the wire into the computer, which would (once the volume control was set properly) memorize it. After that, she need only instruct the computer to display the file on its screen.

Gillian glanced back at her notes. "What happens if I don't know—" She caught herself: "—don't remember the code name for the file I want?"

Peter East opened his mouth as if to answer, and a sly, knowing grin lit his face. "Don't remember?" he echoed. "Could be a problem. But you named the file, right? And the computer accepted it, right?" She knew he was teasing her on but kept nodding agreement. "The computer only accepts four-letter words as file names, so you just make a list of the four-letter words that apply to the file's content. It'll fall in your lap sooner or later." He regarded her with ill-concealed amusement, and added, "After all, you made up the name yourself, didn't you?"

Shit, that's four letters, but it probably isn't the combination I want. "Let's say—just for the sake of argument, mind—that I can't come up with that code name. Does the information in the file sit there and rot? There must be a way to get at it."

"Might be," he allowed. He was enjoying himself, she saw— something he probably didn't get much opportunity to do. "I might be able to help you, but I'd have to be sure you weren't breaking into somebody else's files."

I'm letting him call the tune, she realized. Mistake number one with any man, especially a little creep like this. "Well, of course it's somebody else's file," she said wearily. "Now, can you tell me how to get into it, or do I find somebody who really knows these machines?"

He bridled instantly. "There's nobody knows the Model A better'n me. But—"

"Probably Radio Shack would be the place to go," she went on, ignoring him. "One of their back-room guys could pull this little toy apart in five minutes, especially for a couple of hundred dollars." She saw his eyes widen, and added: "Of course, I'd rather do business at the source, with a friend."

"I'm a hacker, not a cracker," he said. "I don't plant viruses in other people's stuff or steal calls from the phone company." He was going to give in, she saw, but he had to run through his justifications first. She let him talk, waiting silently, and was duly rewarded: "The file you want is on a tape with a bunch of others?" he asked, not meeting her eye.

"I don't know. I mean, there's other stuff on the tape, but it's a regular voice recording, and the file I need has probably been laid over it, someplace in the middle."

The expressions marched across his unguarded face: surprise, puzzlement, dawning comprehension. "Hidden?" She nodded. "If you were going to hide something that way," he went on, as much to himself as to Gillian, "you'd have to be sure to choose a recording nobody's likely to play. . . ."

She thought of the dogged, whining voice, lecturing an unknown hearer about freedom and money. "It is."

"Could be tricky getting the computer to pick it back up, though," he continued. "It's only a matter of finding the exact pitch on the cassette player, but it could take time, especially if you hadn't preset the machine." He paused, as if to consider a new line of thought. "I suppose the original file got wiped out of the Model A it was sent from," he said.

"If she's got any sense, it was," Gillian muttered.

"But you don't know what it was about."

"No."

"More than one file?"

"Beats me."

"Well, you can get the first file back, anyway. After that there could be a problem," he said.

"Explain."

"When you set the computer up to request a taped file, the program asks you to supply the file's code name," he said. "That command's there because most cassettes have half a dozen files on them. But if you don't specify a file, the program doesn't loop you back. What it does," he continued, observing that she was still following him, "it automatically selects the first file that's in computer language and recalls that."

"So no matter what, I can get into one of the computer-language files on that tape," said Gillian triumphantly. "Thanks a lot, Peter."

"Now, wait," he replied in alarm. "I didn't say that. Could be lots of other problems."

"I'll call you if there are," she said, taking out her wallet. "Here's the two hundred I promised, and I'll buy one of those special tape players of yours, and a three-plug cord, too."

"But you don't have to," he said earnestly. "You can get the same thing at Radio Shack for probably half—"

"Shut up, Peter." She counted out the bills. "Keep the change."

"Gee, that's great," he said, stuffing the money, uncounted, into his pocket. "You know, I don't even know your name."

"No, you don't," she replied, and saw the light go abruptly out of his eyes. "Look. I really appreciate your taking all this time with me."

"It was a pleasure," he said. "You're the only person to come in here all month. Except the guy from the bankruptcy court."

She stood swaying to the uneven rhythm of the IRT, her back against the smooth, cold door. Now I know what K.C. was up to Sunday morning, she told herself. I even know how to get at whatever she was listening to.

If I can get my hands on that tape.

The telephone caught him on the upstroke of his fifty-first pushup, and he was so ready for the call that he bounced right to his feet and picked up the phone before it could ring a second time. "Sure, I'll accept," he said eagerly, and then: "Where are you? What's happening?"

Barr's voice sounded surprisingly clear, but an indistinct surge of sound rose and fell behind it. "I'm on my way back to you, should be home in two-three days. Over."

His tone warned Patrick not to ask for details, but he couldn't restrain his curiosity completely: "You're okay? No problem getting away?" After a second, feeling slightly foolish, he added "Over."

"I got a lift from an old pal," Barr replied. "But I had to leave in my socks, you might say. Ran head-on into part of what we're looking for. It got pretty rough. I think you and our friend had better play it safe till we can sort this all out. Over."

"It's been kind of bumpy back here, too," said Patrick. "I got a lead on the boat—or some boat—and damn near got my head beat in. These people seem to be in two places at once." He paused, and Barr's voice broke in.

"—just a big party line," he was saying. Even over the background noise he sounded tense. "You don't know who might be listening. Over."

"Okay, okay. I get it." How could I forget? Patrick thought. "The thing is, we can't pull back now. Both of us are onto leads that we've got to follow up. Over."

There was a long silence, and Patrick wondered if the connection had been broken. The background noise surged up again, louder than before, with Barr's voice cutting thinly through it. "All right," he said reluctantly. "But be careful. Both of you." Pause. "How is she? Over."

It was not *Glory* Barr was referring to, though a month ago it would've been. "Full of beans when I talked to her last. That was Sunday, after you called from—" He caught himself. "From back where you were. She's hard to stay in touch with. Over."

"Well, *stay* with her," Barr said. "Even if she tells you not to. It's important." A fuzzy crash cut him off, and the sounds of other voices in the background. "I've got to run. We're having a gale, and the damn boat's trying to come apart. I'll call you when I get to shore. And be careful."

Careful of what? Patrick asked himself. Or whom? He thought about another bowl of shredded wheat, decided against it, checked his watch for the fourth time, and dialed Mrs. Boyd's apartment. Though it was only seven-thirty, Gillian had already left. But she'd left a message for him, if he was Mr. O'Mara: He should call her as soon after eight as possible. At work, on her direct line. Mrs. Boyd gave him the number, an unfamiliar one, and he hung up.

What was she up to now? he wondered. First she gets mad at me for calling her, now she wants me to. Well, I've got to talk to somebody or burst.

The voice that answered was male, upper-class, and startled. Almost sure he'd dialed the wrong number, Patrick found himself apologizing: "I'm sorry. I was trying to reach Gillian Verdean."

"She just came in," the voice said. "Hold on, please."

He was clicked onto hold, and then he heard her. She sounded excited, determined, and just a little out of breath—what Barr called her bit-between-the-teeth voice. "Hi, did you get my message?"

"If I'm who you think I am, the answer is *yes*," he said, trying to sound severe, and failing. Gillian in this mood was irresistible, at least to him.

"I tried to call you first thing this morning, but your line was busy. Any word from the front?"

"He's on his way back." A sound that might have been Gillian releasing her held breath. "Expects to be home by the end of the week. Who was it I just talked to? You got a secretary already?"

She laughed. "That was my boss, Mr. Huddleston"—a barely perceptible emphasis on the name—"He got in early today."

"Your boss? I thought you worked for that woman."

Another silvery laugh, and this time he realized she was laying it on deliberately. "I did, till yesterday afternoon. Now I'm assistant to the editor."

"Well, congratulations. I guess."

"Definitely," she said; too definitely. "But I won't be here that long. I'm sailing to Bermuda Saturday morning, in the race."

He was stunned. "You're sailing where? Listen, you can't do that, Gillian—"

"Oh, yes I can," she trilled. "Why not?"

He hadn't the beginning of a reason, but every fiber of him knew it was a mistake. "Listen, we have to talk. How about lunchtime."

"No. Sorry, but today's the editorial staff lunch. I really have to go."

"Well, drinks after work. Or dinner. Whatever you like. But we have to sit down and figure out where we're at."

"That's fine," she replied. "Because I've got a lot to tell you. Wait a minute: I know how we'll handle it. Have you got a pencil?" Gillian had slipped imperceptibly into command mode, and he knew her well enough to accept that there was nothing to do but go along.

"Shoot."

"You know my sailing gear, the stuff you've been holding for me? Bring all of it—boots, foulies, two sweaters, jeans, extra socks—and drop it off at Mrs. Boyd's. She gets home around six; I'll tell her to expect you at six-fifteen. Then you meet me at Utopia Parkway, the nightclub on Fifty-second Street, at seven."

"Utopia Parkway?" he repeated. "I never knew you liked that kind of place. Besides, will they let us in?"

"The magazine's running a fund-raiser there tonight. Just say you're coming to the *TNF* party; mention my name or K.C. Carew if there's a problem. I don't know when I can get away, but we'll go have a drink or something afterward and get all our ducks in a row."

He felt out of breath just listening to her. And some of Barr's nervousness had transferred to him. He didn't like the whole setup, but he couldn't think of anything to offer in its place. "Well, okay," he said slowly. "I still don't know if this is such a red-hot idea."

"It'll be fine, you'll see. And I can hardly wait—"Her voice went suddenly girlish again, and he guessed that someone might be standing over her"—I'm just *dying* to hear about the part you got in the show. Baritone lead: That's just *super*. So long, now."

He stared at the handset in bewilderment. Part? Show? He was a baritone, of course, but what the hell was she talking about? Gradually it sank in: she had thrown him, in half a dozen words, the identity he was supposed to assume for the night. Now all he had to do was flesh it out, and hope it matched whatever she was telling her buddies.

"I don't think I'm ready for this kind of thing," he said to the dead telephone in his hand. What he really needed was action, like a face to punch or a woman to make love to. Susan Grover. He could see her hair on the pillow beside him, her sleepily satisfied face. She'd be at work by now. He started to dial, replaced the phone. When they'd talked yesterday, he could tell from her voice she was ready for more; but if he called her so soon it'd be a step down a road he wasn't sure he wanted to travel. At least not yet. Besides, he didn't want to get her any deeper into all this until he could see where it led. He had to talk to somebody, though. . . . Of course: there *was* a person he could call, someone who was already involved—no one more so—and who always seemed to have a good idea or two. Patrick picked up the phone and dialed Sol Farber's number.

For a certified watering hole of the rich and famous, she thought, Utopia Parkway looked pretty drab: a plain, four-story brownstone not much different on the outside from the *TNF* office, except for a blue-and-white-striped awning with the club's name on it in gold letters. It was just six o'clock when Gillian and Win arrived, having walked across town through rush-hour traffic, but already a scattering of celebrity-watchers huddled on either side of the entrance. Most of them were young—paper-white faces and stiffly spiked hair in colors seldom seen by daylight—but here and there among the gargoyles were middle-aged women who looked as though they might have come in from Tenafly, say, or Port Chester. A ripple of expectation brushed across them as they caught sight of Win's slightly mildewed dinner jacket and Gillian's black cocktail dress, bought for the occasion.

"Trying to decide who we are," Win remarked. "They stand here for hours, waiting for a two-second glimpse of someone whose picture they've seen on TV. It's pitiful."

"Uh-huh," Gillian murmured, squirming inwardly under the avid, devouring eyes.

From a few feet away the club's door looked as ordinary as the rest of it; only when Win knocked did she realize there was no knob on the outside. "They're a commentary on America," he continued, at conversational volume. "Don't you wonder what they do when they're not standing here?"

She felt herself cringe at his words, darted a sidelong glance to either flank; the staring faces registered no emotion, though they must've heard what he said. "I feel like the rare lesser grosbeak or something," she muttered. "Can't we go inside?"

"Oh, of course," Win replied, raising his hand to knock again. As he did, the door swung silently inward.

The figure looming in front of them was about the same dimensions as the door itself, but a lot less decorative. Even for so large a body his head was outsize, with heavy, brooding features that suddenly twisted into a manic grin. He was wearing black tuxedo trousers, an oatmeal-colored sports jacket over a maroon turtleneck, and a flesh-colored adhesive bandage across the bridge of his nose. On his lapel was a stick-on label that had HI! MY NAME'S printed on it, and GOLEM in purple ink beneath.

The giant spoke, in a high, almost childlike voice: "Welcome to Utopia Parkway, Mr. Huddleston. Good to see you again, sir." He stood aside, and Win stepped through the opening. As Gillian hesitated, a hand with fingers the size of hot dogs took her gently but irresistibly by the arm. "Come on in, sweetie," he squeaked, and apparently without moving her feet she found herself inside. The noise alone was like being slapped in the face, a couple of hundred voices straining to make themselves heard over the thumping bellow of rock music coming from speakers embedded in every plush-covered wall. The dim, high-ceilinged room was lit by varicolored spotlights that panned over the audience in random patterns, carving paths through the already dense clouds of smoke. Some perverse genius had turned up the heat, and every smell—tobacco mostly, streaked with perfume, whiskey, and food—was intensified by a factor of two.

Win was instantly seized by Simon Ringgold, the gray, intense editor of the Nation section, and Gillian found herself outside their whispered tête-à-tête, alone in a crowd that seemed comprised of two utterly disparate elements. One consisted mostly of taut men with blow-dried hair and expensive suits, who juggled cigarettes, cocktail glasses, and dishes of ominously colored hors d'oeuvres with practiced ease. The other type, which tended to coalesce around nuclei of TNF staffers, was younger, modishly disheveled, far noisier, and already more than half stoned—the membership, Gillian assumed, of the Young Publishers' Chowder and Marching Association, a.k.a. the Clam & Foot.

A very tall, weedy figure loomed behind Win and Ringgold; he was mouthing a greeting at her, and after a third look she recognized Ringgold's assistant, Tryg Wolters, freshly divested of the awful beard that reminded her of kelp and draped in a jacket whose fabric was clearly derived from burlap. She felt oddly grateful to have someone to talk to, and she liked Tryg anyway. He was newly come to the big city, from a small, ultraliberal university in the Pacific Northwest, and prided himself on a languid iconoclasm. Just beneath the veneer and liable to break through at any moment was an unquenchable, puppylike enthusiasm that Gilliam warmed to even when she didn't know what he was talking about.

She moved to his side, accepted a tequila-scented smack on the cheek (still comradely, but closer to her mouth than usual) and a greasy meat patty from his heaped plate. She'd been thinking that Utopia Parkway seemed a strange place for a magazine like *TNF* to stage a fund-raising party, and because she didn't have to be diplomatic with him she said so.

"The whorehouse of the plutocracy, sure," Tryg agreed, a good deal more loudly than necessary. "But the Salvation Army soup kitchen probably wouldn't attract so many high rollers."

Win, standing with his back to them, stiffened as if he'd been goosed and spun around. "We really owe a lot to Mr. Martello," he said severely. "Frannie may be a social butterfly, but at least he doesn't do any harm to society—as if anything could harm *this* society."

"Writing your editorial, Win?" asked Ringgold, with a cynical grin. "You've got your Jahweh-sees-the-Golden-Calf look again."

Win's schoolmaster glare gave way to a self-deprecating smile that transfigured his careworn features. "Pompous, wasn't I? Sorry, Tryg." The young man, who'd looked crushed, was now visibly glowing, and Win continued: "Still, it's hard not to feel bitter sometimes. You saw what next fiscal's defense budget is, didn't you? Compared to HEW? Or education?"

Oh, God, thought Gillian. Here they go again. Her expression must have given her away, because Ringgold winked at her as he said, "Hey, lighten up, boss. You'll scare your new assistant right back to the business department. Save the fulminating for the foundation people: they eat it up."

"And we need all the fulminate we can get," Tryg put in. "If you know what I mean."

It seemed an innocent enough remark to Gillian, but this time both Ringgold and Win turned angrily on the gangling young man, who took an involuntary step backward. At that moment K.C. hove into view. She was wearing a scarlet dress with a black sash circling her middle a bit below where her waist should have been, and a hemline high enough to provide a glimpse of powerful thighs; she looked to Gillian like a longshoreman in drag. Her fixed smile—hostess on autopilot—changed to dismay as she saw Win. "My God, you're so *early!*" she cried, waving a clipboard at him as if she could fan him back out the door.

"You said six," Win replied, crestfallen. "And it's five past."

"Oh, don't worry," she said. "I just don't want to waste you on this two-bit crowd. Go practice your speech till the real money people get here." She took him by one elbow and Gillian by the other and led them toward the check room. "Here, give the lady your coats and we'll get you something to drink. You've got a busy evening ahead of you." She blew a kiss past Gillian, toward the immense man who had opened the door to them. His vast face lit up in a parody of joy, and he pursed his rubbery lips back at her.

"Who *is* that monster?" Gillian whispered into Win's ear. "Golem can't be his real name."

Win seemed amused. "It's not, of course. His real name is Tadeuzs Krips, I think. He's a professional wrestler, and Golem is his stage—or is it ring?—name."

"He's the bouncer," K.C. put in. "All the nightclubs have them. Golem's become kind of a celebrity since he started working for Frannie X."

"And Frannie X is who? The owner?" said Gillian.

"Martello. That's right," said Tryg, from over her shoulder. "Innkeeper to the Stars."

K.C. disappeared with Win and returned alone almost immediately, carrying two tall drinks. She thrust one of them at Gillian. "Take a slug, kid, and then step into my office over here behind the plant," she said. Obediently, Gillian swallowed a mouthful of margarita and allowed herself to be dragged into semiseclusion behind a bedraggled palm that was growing from a solid bed of cigarette butts. "Listen," K.C. continued urgently, "I've got a big job for you: I want you to be in charge of Win tonight."

She felt a sharp stab of uneasiness. "But—"

"You can do it, Gillian. In fact, you're the only one of our so-called colleagues I'd trust in a social situation."

"Thanks, but I've got another—" Before Gillian could finish K.C. rode her down again.

"Come on, kiddo, you're not on that boat to Bermuda yet. This is work, and damned important work. If *TNF* doesn't get heavy pledges from these people, we don't eat. And I'm sure"—heavy emphasis—"you're interested in our future." Gillian had become used to K.C.'s good-natured bullying, but this had an altogether different edge to it, almost a command.

"Of course I am," Gillian replied, keeping her voice light. "I'm happy to do anything I can, but you didn't warn me about this, and I'm expecting a date to pick me up later."

"A date." K.C. turned an appraising gaze on her. "Well, we'll work it out somehow. I can look after him."

Not bloody likely, Gillian thought, suddenly appalled. "Listen, why don't you tell me what I'm supposed to do?"

"Right," K.C. agreed. "Win's in Frannie X's office, looking over his speech. He likes to memorize it, though I wish he wouldn't. We'll give him half an hour, then pry him out and make him meet people. That'll take both of us: I'll bring around the folks he has to make nice to, and you get them offstage after they've kissed his ring or whatever."

"Offstage where?" Gillian asked, looking around her.

"That's a manner of speaking. You just dump them back in the crowd, but gracefully. Oh, by the way—some of 'em will probably try to cop a feel. They know we need their money, and they take advantage of it. Be nice to them anyway."

No different from working in a sail loft, thought Gillian. "I'm surprised Win would sit still for that kind of thing."

K.C. laughed. "He wouldn't. Christ, no—if he knew about it. It's our job to see that he doesn't. Now, after Win makes his speech, he may try to sneak out, but a lot of the heavy hitters will want to press the flesh with him. Just make sure he stays until Frannie and Broadway Rose start the auction: That'll distract the crowd and he can vanish."

"Broadway Rose?" said Gillian uncertainly. "The name sounds familiar, but I don't . . ."

"I thought you lived in New York," K.C. said. Was that suspicion in her eyes? "You're more out of it than I thought. Broadway *Rose*, kiddo: our very own borough president. The sometime belle of the White Way and probably the next mayor."

"A politician?" Gillian was flabbergasted. "I thought you said *TNF* never supported—"

"*Almost* never," K.C. corrected her. "Broadway Rose is the exception to my rule. When she gets to be mayor we'll probably chew her ass like we do everybody else's. But all a borough president does is think pure thoughts."

"I see," Gillian replied uncertainly. It sounded very unlike what she'd learned of the magazine's way of working, but K.C. knew what she was talking about.

"Enough," K.C. said. "Let's snag us a couple more bad drinks and circulate. There's people I want you to meet before we unleash the dog-and-pony show."

Squinting through the glow induced by a warm margarita and two watery rum and Cokes, Gillian had to admire K.C.'s social sleight of hand: She produced the foundation types, who seemed essentially interchangeable, at precise intervals, like targets in a shooting gallery. Gillian in turn presented them to Win, who bestowed a few trenchant observations on each, fielded the inevitable compliment about his struggle for universal peace and justice, and shot back a well-rehearsed pitch for the dollars they controlled. Just as he was concluding, Gillian would see K.C. approaching with the next candidate; her own function was to cut off the interview as quickly as possible and ditch the guest back in the crowd, before returning to be introduced all over again. The operation ran as smoothly as an assembly line, though after a while it occurred to her that the foundation representatives might be performing, too. After all, there was no

logical reason for them to interrupt their drinking so Win could tell
them about the decay of the West.

The man she was easing away from Win was tall, fattish, and so
smoothly contoured that he reminded Gillian of a gigantic egg—
except for his roving hands, one of which, on the small of her back,
was working slowly downward. He tilted himself over her and she
braced for the proposition she knew was coming. "I trust the meeting
won't run so late this year," he confided.

"The meeting?" she asked, taken quite aback.

"After the auction," he said, with a touch of impatience. "If it gets
through early enough, perhaps you and I could—"

But Gillian was never to know exactly what the egg had in mind;
the room's babel was shattered by one of the loudest unamplified
human voices she'd ever heard.

"Darlings!" it trumpeted. "I'm here!" Everyone whirled toward the
door. At first Gillian saw nothing but backs, and then the crowd
split apart. Her first impressions were of clothing—wide-brimmed
hat whose plume reminded her of Cyrano de Bergerac, floor-length
cape in dramatic Mexican stripes, heavy boots that crashed against
the bare wood floor. "Win! *Salvator mundi!* Embrace me." The deep,
gravelly voice belonged to a supremely ugly woman with a face like
an intelligent frog's, all mouth and eyes and flat nose. She crossed
the room in five echoing strides and swept Win into her arms,
ignoring everyone else. His face, already high-colored from heat
and embarrassment, turned scarlet. The watchers erupted in applause,
and Gillian's companion turned to her. "Broadway Rose is here," he
said.

It was the voice that triggered Gillian's memory, which now supplied the same face, a lot younger, on black-and-white film. Of
course: back in the fifties, Rose Sadowa had been a famous come-
dienne, stage and screen both; the wisecracking ugly sister who told
Joan Blondell to stand by her guy. So this was what'd become of
her. Whatever Broadway Rose might feel about her new career, she
seemed to be in a celebratory mood. Standing with her arm around
Win, she surveyed the crowded room with delight. "A good house,"
she said. "Lots of deep pockets."

His look of embarrassment changed to something like alarm, and he motioned Gillian to him. "Rose, I'd like to introduce my new assistant, Gillian Verdean."

"Oh, yes," said the older woman, eyeing her with interest. "A pleasure."

Gillian had the feeling that a curtsey, or even a prostration, might not be out of order, so she only stood straighter. "How do you do?"

Up close Broadway Rose was even uglier than at a distance, but her overpowering personality made her looks irrelevant. Gillian received a smile that curled her toes and realized she was smiling back. At the same time, she was aware of being keenly if momentarily weighed and then discarded. Broadway Rose turned her attention to the next person in line, and Gillian saw, from the corner of her eye, K.C. beckoning across the room. What *now?* she wondered, her eyes drawn to the tall man standing next to *TNF's* business manager. My God, it was Patrick—but where had he gotten that butterscotch-colored corduroy jacket, that midnight blue shirt? And an ascot, for Christ's sake! Who did he think he was?

Well, of course, you dummy, he's just trying to do what you told him to—look like a New York actor, or what he thinks an actor looks like. And as she got nearer she decided the impersonation wasn't so bad. Patrick's powerful shoulders were emphasized by the jacket's nipped waist, and there was something about the way he was holding his head, as if positioning his profile . . . "Patrick!" she said. "Am I glad to see you."

He grinned at her, relief plain on his face, and folded her in a more than theatrical hug. "Patrick's only been here a few minutes," K.C. announced. "He's already charmed Doris practically out of her socks."

Doris? Gillian took in the woman at Patrick's left. It was none other than Mrs. Bookhouser, *TNF's* librarian; normally a colorless wraith, nearly invisible in direct sunlight, she was painted like a Kewpie doll and swathed in brightly colored shawls. She had yet to exchange more than daily hails and farewells with Gillian but now gave her cheek an echoing kiss, sticky with unblotted lipstick. "You look wonderful, dear," she fluttered. "Your young man is so sweet—he's been telling me all about his career in the theater."

"Well, you don't want to believe everything Patrick says, especially when he's telling it to a woman," Gillian replied absently. Something had given her memory a sharp tug, something connected to Mrs. Bookhouser. Now it was gone, but she knew it was important. If only she had a minute's quiet, she was sure she could capture it again—and at that moment Patrick took her arm.

"Say, who's that humongous guy on the door, the gorilla with the funny name?" he demanded, under his breath.

Gillian saw something almost like fear in the back of his eyes, and Patrick scared was enough to drive every other thought from her head. "He's just the bouncer," she said. "Maybe you've seen him on TV: Win says—"

"Duty calls, kiddo," K.C. interrupted. At the far end of the room, spotlights had focused on a small stage, and Broadway Rose was waving the crowd into silence, while Win stood behind her, shifting from foot to foot. "Come on," said K.C. impatiently, and to Patrick, "You stay right here, big guy. I want to hear more about that career of yours."

PATRICK

He was still watching Gillian move through the crowd in K.C.'s wake when he felt his elbow jogged from behind and turned to find himself facing a woman almost as tall as he was. Her bony face was handsome in a hawklike sort of way, blond hair pulled back so hard it slanted her gray eyes. "Sorry," she said, not meaning it. She stared Patrick up and down, taking her time. "Nobody who looks like you could possibly be with *TNF*."

Her kind of woman always put his back up, and he knew better than to give her an inch. "You're right. I'm not."

She wasn't to be put off, though: "I haven't seen you at the Clam and Foot, either."

The funny name barely registered: some club K.C. Carew belonged to. Gillian had mentioned it. "No."

"And you sure as hell aren't one of *them*," she went on, nodding contemptuously at a knot of suited figures a few feet away. "So what are you, anyway?"

"I'm just here," he replied, thinking that her gray suit and high-collared blouse made her look like a lawyer, and her snotty manners went a long way to confirm it.

He waited for her next question, but she only smiled—if that was what it was: hard to tell with somebody who had no lips—and said, "You're with the house? You look a lot less shopworn than most of them. My name's Sally Rail, by the way." Her eye went to his empty hands. "Don't they let you have a drink when you're working?"

Before he could answer the lights dimmed and a snare drum rolled for silence. The first speaker was the ugly dame Patrick had heard called Broadway Rose; she was up only long enough to introduce Utopia Parkway's owner, a deeply tanned sleazeball named Frannie something, who grabbed the mike as if he planned to take it home with him. He rattled off a couple of terrible jokes and launched into a rambling speech about *The New Federalist*. Frannie wanted the crowd to know that he admired both the institution and its leader very deeply and sincerely; he started to tell everybody why, and Patrick let the thread snap, his eye drawn to Gillian.

She was standing next to the small stage, with a thin, nothing-looking guy who must be Huddleston. He was whispering to her, and she strained upward to hear him. The look on her face was too close to worship for Patrick's peace of mind; if she'd gazed up at Patrick that way he knew damn well he'd have lost no time moving in, but Huddleston didn't seem to notice. Well, maybe he wasn't interested in women, though he didn't look all that old. Or maybe he was a fairy; in this kind of mob you couldn't be sure about anybody.

Across the packed room a single head stuck out above those around it. The bouncer: Golem or Goyim or whatever his name was. He, too, was listening intently—to someone who wasn't tall enough for Patrick to see from where he stood. The outsize bulk was certainly the same as the guy who'd jumped Patrick in the salvage yard shed, but the bandaged nose was what had set alarm bells ringing in Patrick's head—even though Golem had looked right through him when he'd opened the club door.

Of course, a bandaged nose wasn't a complete ID, but as Patrick studied Utopia Parkway's bouncer the doubts ebbed away; this was the man who'd tried to kill him. (He could still hear the length of chain hiss past his head and clash against the life-raft canister.) If that was so, then there had to be a connection between the two places—and probably a connection with *The New Federalist*, too. And if Barr was right, the connections extended all the way to Bermuda. A lot of people must be involved, people with money and clout, if they could get a high public official to turn up at a party like this. But what were they up to? What made it go? He had to get Gillian alone so they could compare notes.

The press of bodies between Patrick and Golem parted momentarily, giving him a glimpse of red dress and fluffed out, mouse-
brown hair: Gillian's boss. No, he remembered: since this morning,
her ex-boss. K.C. was on tiptoe, whispering up toward Golem's ear;
the crowd shifted and she was hidden. The bouncer's heavy face
remained in view; across the room his eyes met Patrick's and darted
away.

The audience was getting noisily restless. Beside Patrick, Sally
Rail growled, "I know Frannie's indispensable, but he's so goddamn
boring." She fumbled in her purse and took out a gold case; it contained three neat, obviously homemade cigarettes. "I don't suppose
they let you smoke on duty, either?" she said and then, seeing his
expression, added, "Oh, all right—I'll suffer in silence: I know the
rules." If the rules meant that pot smoking wasn't allowed in the
club, Patrick thought, there were people in the audience who didn't
know or care: The thick, heavy air had grabbed at his throat when
he'd come in; now the smoke felt like sandpaper in his nasal passages.

On the stage, Frannie had at last sensed the crowd's impatience;
he sawed his speech off short and turned the mike back over to
Broadway Rose, who came on like a tornado, tramping down the
babble with sheer volume and the raunchiest anecdote even Patrick
had ever heard. While her listeners were still torn between shock
and laughter, she segued into a mean, funny fantasy on bedroom
life in the White House, wound the routine up with a flourish and,
as the room shook with laughter, began again. This time her voice
was so quiet, even with the mike, that the crowd hushed itself to
hear her. It was a string of praises for somebody unnamed, a sequence
of "the man who . . ." sentences that made her subject into a star,
then a saint, and finally a savior.

To Patrick, who was cold sober, her speech sounded plain crazy
where it wasn't actually meaningless, but he had to admire the driving
rhythm that had the audience stamping its feet in time with her
gravelly voice, till even the smooth-faced, cold-eyed money men
were whistling and shouting. Now Huddleston was on the stage,
looking as if he didn't know what to do with his hands. Gillian, still
out of the spotlight, was beaming up at him like the pope's own
acolyte. The crowd was so wound up that even Broadway Rose was
drowned out, and as she turned toward Win, her arms outspread,

they gave one hoarse roar that shook loose a spatter of dust and something like a small bird's nest from the rafters.

Win embraced her, and stepped forward into complete silence; Patrick could hear Sally Rail's hoarse breathing, and a truck down-shifting in the street outside. "Listen to this," Sally whispered, her narrow face flushed. "He really is wonderful."

Win Huddleston had obviously learned his speech by heart, in-cluding the gestures, and for the first couple of minutes his awk-wardness was all Patrick noticed. As Huddleston warmed up, though, he quit straining to project; his voice dropped half an octave, his hands stopped jerking in the air, and he began to talk to his audience as if each of them were an old and valued friend.

If it was technique it was damn impressive, Patrick thought: he could feel that the younger half of the audience was already hooked. Gradually, though, as he began to take in what Huddleston was saying, he found himself moving from surprise to disbelief and finally to a baffled, smoldering anger. He'd never imagined that another American—a smart, educated, sincere guy—could believe his coun-try was not just sick but evil, and took it for granted that his audience agreed. But they did, the younger ones anyway. Patrick didn't think of himself as patriotic; he didn't think about it at all, but he himself saluted the flag and recited the Pledge of Allegiance as a matter of course; and when *Glory*, home from the islands, had passed close to the Statue of Liberty he'd felt his throat go tight as he stared up at the towering greenish figure. He knew that other people—Barr, for one—felt differently, and it didn't bother him. At least it never had till now.

At the end, the roaring applause lasted a full minute, long enough for Patrick to get hold of himself. "Listen, big boy," murmured Sally, "a few of us are moving to more private surroundings, after the auction. How late do you have to stay?"

"Right to the end," he said firmly, wishing she would vanish. It seemed a weak enough brush-off, but her eyes widened and she nodded.

"Of course: the meeting. I should've known you'd have to stay for that." He was wondering what the hell she meant, when she dropped her voice to a whisper. "Is it true what they say? That the whole year goes down in fifteen minutes? I heard . . ."

Her face went bloodless, and the whisper trailed off into nothing.
Patrick looked around, expecting Golem at least, but it was only
K. C. Carew, grinning up at him. Her face gleamed in the dim light;
heat and smoke had made it come out in blotches. She glanced at
Sally; it seemed to him that the grin, which never faded, hardened
momentarily. "Vanish. He's mine," she said, and the tall woman
disappeared quickly into the crowd. K.C. turned to Patrick: "There.
You're safe from the carnivorous Rail. But now you have to deal
with me."

"No offense," he replied, "but it was Gillian I was looking for."

"And find her you shall," K.C. beamed. "As soon as she's shep-
herded our Leader through the required gauntlet of interviews." She
flagged down a passing waiter and ordered a double margarita for
herself and a beer for Patrick. "Now. You were just about to tell me
how you met her. . . ." From behind the bottle-bottom lenses, her
eyes were unblinking.

"I like your young man," K.C. announced to the approaching
Gillian. "You didn't tell me he was a singer."

"I didn't tell you anything," Gillian replied, glancing quickly at
Patrick, who was beginning to feel like a squeezed orange. "I *did*
mention to Win that he'd just got a great part in a show. Baritone
lead."

He'd prepared himself for this one and was able to jump in on
cue: "That's right. Billy Bigelow, in—"

"*Carousel*," K.C. interrupted brightly. "Must be the Village Light
Opera production, right?"

Innocent question or trap? He saw what might be a frown on
Gillian's face. "Don't I wish," he said. "Didn't even know they were
doing it. We're the Pell Street Playmakers; d'you know us?" The
company was real, anyway; he'd noticed their shabby marquee only
two nights before, while barhopping the Village with Susan Grover.
But he'd completely forgotten the name of the show they were doing
and prayed they were as obscure as they'd seemed.

"I've heard the name," K.C. said, in a tone that clearly said she
hadn't. "Ah, here's our conquering hero."

Win Huddleston's approach was slowed by clusters of eager ad-
mirers. Who were they, anyway? Patrick wondered. Spoiled kids

and silly-looking women who couldn't imagine how lucky they were. Serve them right if they found themselves dropped down in Salvador or Chad for a couple of days—they'd be begging to get back to the U.S. of A. Huddleston was still flushed from his triumph, but he acknowledged Patrick's cool greeting with what sounded like genuine eagerness. "Did I do all right?" he asked. "I'd appreciate a professional opinion."

"I don't qualify as a professional," Patrick replied. "Semipro, maybe." He felt the others waiting, realized he was going to have to say something about Huddleston's speech. "That was quite something, what you said about America," he began. "I never heard anything like it. . . ." He trailed off, not trusting himself to be more specific, but Gillian was already speaking.

Not speaking; gushing: "It was fantastic, Win. I mean, I've sensed these awful problems, but I always thought we were going to solve them, as soon as the country came to its senses." She sounded nearly breathless, and Patrick couldn't tell whether she'd jumped in to rescue him or because she agreed with the garbage Huddleston was spouting.

"The country ran out of soluble problems twenty-five years ago," he was saying. "And of course it hasn't had any viable solutions since 1861."

What kind of asshole crack is that? Patrick thought, but the others—including Gillian, he saw from the corner of his eye—looked as if they might pass out. "It's so brave of you to speak out this way," said someone. "Aren't you afraid of reprisals?"

"From the administration? They've tried before, and we're still here," Win answered. "As for the great American public, they'll never hear of it. And if they did they'd forget by tomorrow." He paused, and Patrick sensed a pronouncement. "The real armor of America isn't righteousness, it's poor memory."

Win surveyed his audience, obviously expecting some reaction, and his eyes met Patrick's. "I never thought of it that way," Patrick said.

"I'm starved," said K.C. "Let's get out of this place."

"Is the show over?" Patrick asked. "Somebody said something about an auction and a meeting—don't you have to stay for those?"

"The auction? It's just the usual stuff," said K.C. with a laugh.

"Overpriced sets of books by the great socialist thinkers, albums of folk songs by real coal miners. Frannie and Broadway Rose handle it."

To Patrick's ear, K.C.'s brush-off sounded a little overdone, but he didn't know her well enough to be sure. "And the meeting?" he pressed.

"What meeting?" Gillian looked surprised and puzzled.

"We *definitely* don't want to be here for that," K.C. said. "It's when Rose and Frannie put the screws on the big contributors. Our presence would cramp things all to hell, take my word for it."

"You've got an answer for everything," Patrick said.

K.C.'s mouth opened to reply, but Huddleston spoke first: "What about a restaurant, K.C.? Have you got any ideas?"

"I have an inspiration," she replied, looking straight at Patrick.

He scanned the menu uneasily; the entrees looked like ordinary tourist Italian, but their names made him squirm—Veal Trovatore, Zuppa Aida, Antipasto Mefisto ("Develishly Hot"). As did the invitation across the top, in big black type: *Our Singing Waitpersons will be happy to Serenade you at your Table, or be a Star, and Sing Along with Maestro Bruno at the Steinway!*

"I knew you'd like this place," said K.C., not trying to hide the malice in her eyes.

"Oh, sure," Patrick replied. "Real fun."

Across the table, Gillian was the target of a long monologue that might as well, from what Patrick could make of it, have been in Chinese. It seemed to be an anecdote, and from the tone of Huddleston's voice the punchline was finally coming, after many side trips.

At Patrick's elbow K.C. was asking, "Do you have operatic ambitions? Seems as if most singers do."

"Not me," he answered easily. "What I really like to sing are old songs—I guess you'd call them folk songs."

Across the table, Huddleston paused expectantly. "And how did you answer him?" Gillian asked.

"I hope you don't go for that Joan Baez crap," said K.C. "Or what's-his-name Dylan, the sniveling millionaire."

"I told him," Huddleston continued, "the only thing you have to bear in mind is that Norman Mailer is"—two long beats—"a cryptofascist." He sat back, waiting.

"Oh," Gillian said. And then, slowly, "A cryptofascist? Really?"

"Irish," Patrick heard himself saying. "D'you know 'Legion of the Rearguard'?"

"Well, you have to have followed his work," Huddleston explained. He seemed disappointed. "Have you read *Armies of the Night*?"

"It's about this whale," K.C. announced, in a hollow tone. The other three froze in their seats, staring at her. "God, you should see yourselves," she gasped, and burst into helpless laughter.

I know that line, Patrick was thinking. "From 'Wonderful Town,'" he said to her. "The cocktail party scene."

Her eyebrows shot upward. "Good going, Patrick. You surprise me."

"And *you* surprise *me*," Huddleston added to K.C. He looks a little pissed off, Patrick thought. "You haven't had too much of anything, have you?"

"Hardly." K.C.'s voice was flat. "I think we'd better order. We can hardly expect Patrick to sing on an empty stomach."

So that was how it was going to be. He saw the dismay on Gillian's face, but a strange confidence was welling up inside him, bolstered by contempt and half a bottle of Orvieto.

The spumoni left a chalky aftertaste that even espresso couldn't cut through, and he didn't like the idea of warming up with "If I Loved You"—a choice K.C. insisted on. He sounded shaky to his own ear, and the final F was definitely strained, but he got a round of respectful applause from the other diners. Then, deciding to stick with Billy Bigelow, he launched a cappella into the far more difficult "Soliloquy," and almost lost his nerve. But the wine had eased both his vocal cords and his inhibitions, and he threw everything he had into the climax:

> I'll go out and make it,
> Or steal it, or take it . . .
> Or die.

The room was his—he could feel it. The audience simply erupted, and the house soprano, a heavyset lady with a mustache, swept him into a tearful embrace. Gillian's eyes were shining as she gave him a surreptitious thumbs-up, and he knew he was home free.

Walking back to the table, to which another customer had already sent a bottle of wine, he felt as if his feet were inches above the ground. Now all he had to do was get Gillian out of here, and they could sit down and wrap up this whole thing. But before Patrick could edge his way into a hint that they might call it a night, Huddleston had her ear again, talking about plans for the forthcoming race to Bermuda.

The goddamn race: Patrick groaned internally. He had completely forgotten that she was supposed to be sailing from Rhode Island on Saturday morning, and here it was an hour short of Thursday. He felt completely helpless—how could he object to her going, when as Patrick O'Mara the actor he couldn't even know what the Bermuda Race was? To make matters worse, K.C. had reopened her inquisition from his other side; her spatter of questions about his supposed career claimed just enough of his attention so he couldn't possibly eavesdrop on Huddleston and Gillian.

"Patrick: Guess what?" Gillian suddenly said, cutting across K.C. "Win's asked me to be one of his watch captains."

He had just enough presence of mind to look dumb. "Watch captain?" he asked, hoping Gillian alone would hear the warning.

Apparently she did: "Oh, I guess that doesn't mean much to you. But it's really exciting." She was laying it on too thick, Patrick thought, though Huddleston didn't seem to notice.

"My regular port watch man dropped out," he explained to the table at large. "Called late this afternoon. Gillian volunteered to fill in, and I'm sure she can handle it."

"That's nice," K.C. observed drily.

"And the starboard watch captain—there are two, you see, called port and starboard," he explained to Patrick, who felt as if he might explode. ". . . My other watch captain's a splendid young man. He's in the marine business, in fact. Nico Butler—perhaps you know him?"

The question was aimed at Gillian, but Patrick felt his own face freeze. Gillian brushed off the name without a blink; thank God he hadn't told her. Before he could recover, he saw K.C. watching him, through those thick, distorting lenses. "You okay, Patrick?" she asked. "You look a little sick, all of a sudden."

"I'm fine," he said, his voice a Death Valley croak.

"It *is* rather hot in here," Huddleston offered. "Why don't we all have another drink?"

"Well, I don't know about you people, but it's time for me to head for the barn," Gillian said, pointedly not looking at Patrick.

Win looked at his watch. "Shame to break up such a pleasant gathering, but I suppose you're right." He raised a hand. "I'll get the check."

At last, Patrick was thinking. At fucking last. Now all I have to do is talk Gillian out of this trip. But once I tell her about Golem and Nico Butler, even she'll have to agree I'm right. He realized K.C. had said something to him. "Beg pardon?"

"I was saying, I'm sure you won't mind seeing me home." He didn't quite absorb it, and she explained patiently: "Win can take a cab with Gillian, and you can share one with me."

"But I—"

"I'd really appreciate it," K.C. said. "The people in my neighborhood have been acting up a little."

"Please, Patrick," Gillian put in unexpectedly. "I've seen K.C.'s neighbors."

What could he say, except to throw a not-too-heavy look at Gillian and remark, "I'll be talking to you soon."

"I'll wait for your call," she promised.

As the taxi rolled west through Hell's Kitchen, Patrick found himself feeling more relaxed. The neighborhood *was* terrible, no doubt about it; maybe K.C.'s request had no strings attached. And when he saw the pair of blacks sprawled on the doorstep of her building, the rest of his doubts evaporated. "Christ, what a place," he said. "I'd better see you to your apartment."

"You don't have to do that," she laughed. "Once I'm inside the front door I'll be safe."

Patrick stepped gingerly over one of the figures, and then paused. "This guy didn't pass out," he said. "Somebody pushed his face in." He dropped to one knee for a closer look.

"I think you're right," K.C. agreed coolly. He was thinking that living in a place like this you must see a lot of violence, when something hard and cold slammed into his temple. As he crumpled helplessly to the pavement, he heard her voice, from far away: "Better pop him again, just to be safe."

B A R R :

T H U R S D A Y   E V E N I N G ,

M A N H A T T A N

"I thought you'd never get here," Gillian said, dragging him through the door. "Patrick's disappeared."

Barr was shaken by her obvious distress, the stains of worry under her eyes. He felt a sudden, urgent desire to take her in his arms— but paused to acknowledge the novel emotion, and the moment was past. "I tried to call *Glory* from offshore," he heard himself explain. "And then again after we got in. No answer either time." It had been a long day, and he was tired and waterlogged. Six hours hove-to off the rock-studded entrance to Barnegat Inlet in blinding sheets of rain, pitching and rolling until even Jolly's iron stomach failed her; not till midafternoon had he been able to bring the tubby ketch through into the bay and get her safely tied up at a marina, after which he still had to slip ashore unobserved and make his way, by taxi, bus, and train, into New York.

A small, round woman appeared behind Gillian. "Why, he's soaked!" she exclaimed, as if Barr were deaf or in the next room. "We have to get him dried off."

"He won't melt, Mrs. Boyd," Gillian replied wearily. But she allowed her landlady to lead him into a warm, soup-scented kitchen and place him in a ladder-backed chair. From the walls, pastel representations of the Savior looked on with resignation as the two women stripped off Barr's wet outer clothing and wrapped him in towels. Only after Mrs. Boyd had watched him ingest a bowl of chicken soup, a quarter of a pound of Swiss cheese, and four huge homemade brownies could she be convinced he wouldn't topple over where he sat.

As the kitchen door closed behind her, Barr put the last brownie down. "What d'you mean, *disappeared?*" he demanded. "What happened?"

She was on the verge of tears, he realized. Christ, I didn't have to snarl at her like that. "I don't know," she said helplessly. "I thought Patrick and I were about to break this thing wide open, and then he just vanished."

It unnerved him to see Gillian looking helpless; he forced an extra measure of calm into his voice: "Just take it slow. When did you see him last?"

She straightened her back, clearly ordering her thoughts before she answered. "A little after midnight, outside a terrible Village restaurant called the Dress Circle. We went there after the party— Win Huddleston, K.C., Patrick and I."

K.C.? Oh, yes—the woman Gillian worked for at Huddleston's magazine. *The party* sounded as if it might be significant; he put it on a back burner. He tilted the bowl and spooned up the last of the chicken soup. "What happened there, at the restaurant?" he asked.

"Nothing," she said. And then, reconsidering: "At least, I don't think so. We'd finished dinner, and Win was telling Patrick about me being his watch captain going to Bermuda—"

Astonishment blocked the last gulp of soup, just starting down his throat, into a choking gasp. "*What?*" he demanded, when he could speak again. "You must be out of your . . ." No. Stop right there, he ordered himself, seeing angry hurt light her wide eyes: "Wait a minute: You'd better drop back a bit," he said. "Let's see—today is Thursday. Why don't you begin on Monday?" He sat back in the uncomfortable chair and crossed his legs deliberately.

Her eyes are brown; funny I never noticed that.

He interrupted her only once during the next half hour: "What'd you say the name of the place was?" By then he was beyond surprise, and he sounded calm even to himself.

"The nightclub? Utopia Parkway. It's owned by a dreadful creep who calls himself Innkeeper to the Stars."

"Frannie X," Barr said without thinking.

Gillian was clearly surprised that he knew the name, but she pressed on: "Frannie X Martello. That's right. Why they chose that place for the magazine's fund-raiser I'll never know." She picked up her story, and Barr forced his exhausted brain in pursuit. When at last she fell silent, he was still sorting the details. "I hashed it up, didn't I?" she asked, after a minute or two.

"Hashed it up?" He recognized a favorite phrase of his own and smiled at her tired, anxious face. "You can't take solo credit for this one. It took three amateur cooks to make a hash this big."

She shook her head angrily, unwilling to be let off. "And what about Patrick?"

"I don't know." Meeting her eyes was as exactly as painful as he expected. "You say he left with this K.C. woman?"

"I saw them get into a cab together. Win brought me back here . . ." She paused, as if to allow Barr a question, then continued: "I expected Patrick to call; waited up till two. Then I figured, well, K.C.'s not exactly a beauty, but you know Patrick."

"And this morning K.C. told you Patrick dropped her at her place, and headed off in the same cab."

"That's right. She made a little joke about how fast he got out of there. Said he waited just till she unlocked the front door and then zoomed away into the night."

"It's possible," he said, but he was thinking that K.C.'s little joke was one touch too many.

"I didn't believe her, either," said Gillian. "But what could I say?"

"Exactly. What *did* you say?"

She shrugged miserably. "That I hoped he'd remember to call before I left town tomorrow."

"And that's another thing," he began firmly. "This voyage to Bermuda is just crazy, especially now."

"How can I know that?" she fired back. "You haven't told me what happened down there."

True, he hadn't. "Okay. Then you'll agree I'm right." But he didn't believe it for a moment.

• • •

"So part of the answer *is* in Bermuda, after all," she breathed, when he had done. "Roger and Sarah go there and disappear; Frannie X has a place there; now Win's sailing there."

Barr could see the way her mind was working. "Part of the answer's there, but a big part of it's here, too. Remember, Patrick was onto something, but he didn't have the chance to tell you all the details."

"I didn't give him the chance," Gillian corrected him bitterly.

"But there's someone who might be able to help," Barr said. "Patrick's contact at Governor's Island: the Coastie."

"The *lady* Coastie. Susan Grover." Gillian produced a wan but genuine grin. "I think that interview's a job for you, not me."

"First thing in the morning," he agreed. "I don't suppose your Mrs. Boyd keeps anything to drink in the house." He had another question to resolve with Gillian, but it was going to be tricky.

"The demon rum? Get real." This time she even laughed, and he felt his heart rise even as his hopes sank. "No, wait a minute," she corrected herself. "I just remembered: There's a little wine in an unmarked bottle in the fridge. She told me it was for a friend who needed the iron. Do you think you need iron, Barr?"

"Just now, I feel anemic as hell." Gillian went to the old-fashioned refrigerator and, after several seconds of clinking search, extracted an unlabeled bottle half full of suspicious vermilion fluid. "Never mind the glass," he said. He pulled the cork with his teeth, held the bottle to his nose, and took a wary sniff. From the walls, the eyes of the depressed Jesuses followed his movements.

"That bad?" asked Gillian, watching his face. He set the bottle down on the table and regarded its contents silently as he phrased his next question. But Gillian beat him to it: "I know what you're going to say," she blurted. "You're wondering if I can see things straight at *TNF*, on account of Win." She reached across, took the bottle from his hand, and swallowed a slug. "Oh, God!" she gasped. "What is it?"

"Rabbis drink it at communion," he replied. "To make them forget. You're right: that's exactly what I was wondering."

"Okay, here's where I am right now," she said, straightening her spine as if erect posture had something to do with self-perception. "First and foremost, Sarah's disappearance is only part of something else. Something that has to do with Roger's boat and K.C., and that tape recording. And maybe"—she was dragging it out of herself, he saw—"maybe Win's in it, too."

"Sarah's disappearance is the only problem we're being paid for," he reminded her.

"True—but misleading. We can't find Sarah until we can break open the rest of it."

"And how do you propose doing that?" he demanded. "You can't even define what *rest of it* is."

"You think I don't know?" Her voice caught, then steadied. "There's something else I can't pin down, and it has to do with *TNF*'s finances."

Damn, he thought: the one ingredient I really don't need. "Try telling me about it, in words of one syllable. You know how I am about money."

"Hopeless, like me about politics." She managed another uncertain smile. "Okay. What keeps *TNF* afloat is donations—maybe twenty, twenty-five big annual contributions."

"Totaling how much?" he asked warily. She always made it seem so simple, until about the third sentence.

"Last year, three and a half million."

Without thinking, Barr picked up the bottle and took another sip. Muscatel. And with something even sweeter added. "Three and a half million," he repeated. "You ought to be able to get your salaries on time. And bigger ones, too."

"Both of the above," she agreed. "But as of this week, the kitty's dead empty: no paychecks, till last night's pledges come in."

"So where'd it all go? I don't suppose K.C. lets you tiptoe through the books."

"Not hardly. They're in a locked filing cabinet, in her locked office. But I found a lead. You remember I told you about Uncle Sol's payoffs, to get Sarah hired?"

"I remember." And what else has Uncle Sol forgotten to tell us? he asked himself.

"Well, I had the carbons of his letter contracts, but I wasn't supposed to refile them after I wrote the new begging letter to him. K.C. made a real point of it." He nodded, to show he was following so far. "Okay, this morning K.C. didn't get in till late, and I was just sitting there going . . . crazy—" She blinked twice, and he pretended not to notice. "Anyway, I figured, just for the hell of it, I'd check the contracts against the Bread and Butter file. . . . I told you about the Bread and Butter file, right?"

"That's where you keep copies of the thank-you letters: I remember." He paused. "Maybe there's something about office procedure I'm not getting, Gillian, but why wouldn't everything—request, contract, acknowledgment—be in the same place? It'd seem a lot simpler."

She nodded emphatically. "You bet it would. And when I looked in Sol's Bread and Butter folder I found out why: According to the contracts and the interoffice memos, we were depositing just about half what Uncle Sol was giving us. I cross-checked the other lapsed contracts K.C. gave me, and it was the same."

"You think somebody was siphoning money off?" he asked. "But how could that work? I mean, those donations were in the form of checks—"

"Run them through a phony *TNF* account, then redeposit half in the real account," she whipped back.

"Somebody'd notice the discrepancies. Wouldn't they?"

"Sure—Roger and K.C. noticed. Maybe sooner or later the tax people would make the comparison, too. But it could be a long later. Another question: why are those foundations giving money to something like *The New Federalist* in the first place? I mean, these guys are real oppressors of the peasants, Barr. Why support a magazine devoted to putting you out of business?"

It was a point that hadn't occurred to him, but the answer wasn't that difficult: "They must be getting something for it."

"Well, of course they are. The question is *what?*"

"And you think the answer's in Bermuda?"

"Partly. And on that tape recording, if I can just get my hands on it."

The taped speech she'd overheard. Which might or might not have some kind of computer program recorded over it. "Maybe Roger's sending love notes to K.C.," he suggested. "Modem calls to modem, across the vasty deep."

She took his meaning, he saw, but shook her head: "Possible, but awfully risky. No, my guess is that K.C.'s got the operational plan on that tape, recorded by Roger for his own use before he disappeared."

"Only you don't know where the tape is," he reminded her. "Or how to get your hands on it if you find it."

"I'm sure K.C. keeps it stashed somewhere in the *TNF* offices," Gillian said. "And I finally figured out where. I think."

He could tell she wasn't ready to explain; knew there was nothing to gain by pressing her. "All the more reason for you to stay here in New York and find the damn thing," he said.

"If I find it at all, it'll be tomorrow morning," she said. "I'll get it to you, aboard *Glory*, before we sail."

"Sail? What in hell for? I need you here, to help look for Patrick," he said, playing the last card in his hand.

For half a second her stricken heart was in her face. "Do you think for a moment I don't want to?" she snapped. Her face was as hard as her voice, but her eyes were brimming. "Christ, I wish . . ." She shook her head. "If Patrick's dead, I helped kill him. I'll have to live with that." No longer able to hold the tears in, she whirled in the chair so he couldn't see her face.

Barr started to reach across the small table, then drew back. She might need consolation, but she wasn't likely to let herself accept it now.

After a long minute she straightened up, ignoring the tear tracks. "I've had a lot of time to think this evening, and here's how I figure it, Barr. If K.C. or Roger or . . ."

"Win Huddleston," he supplied gently.

"Or Win," she said firmly. "If any or all of them decided to kill Patrick, they'd have just done it. Made it look like a mugging or a stickup. Why bother kidnapping him, unless they wanted him alive?"

"For what?" he asked, though he could guess.

"Information, I think. Probably about me. Now, if I suddenly duck out of this Bermuda trip, won't it tell them what they want to know? Don't you see: there won't be any reason to keep Patrick alive. That's why I've got to go—and you've got to find Patrick."

Of course he saw. From the minute she'd begun talking he'd been wrestling with that hard truth, and the implications beyond it. "Damn it, Gillian, how can I let you go on that boat?" he burst out. "I just can't."

"Because you think Win's behind this," she replied. "Well, I don't. He knows something, but I think his guilty secret is Roger. I think I'll be as safe on *Kassandra* as here in Manhattan, and it'll give me time to get into Win's confidence. If I can do that, I bet he'll help me find Sarah."

"Because he's in love with you?" Barr heard himself say, and could have bitten his tongue.

But instead of bristling she laughed harshly: "The only thing Win's in love with is *The New Federalist*—that and saving the world from American greed. I never met a man with a mission before, Barr. It kind of takes your breath away."

Over the years, Barr had met several men with missions, a couple of whom wanted to save the world. The common denominator among them was a blind self-righteousness that could justify anything. The trouble was, Gillian would insist on learning that for herself, and the prospect scared him to death. "One thing," he offered, in his most diffident manner. "If what you say about Huddleston is true, just don't get between him and that cause of his."

"I'm not a child, Barr," she replied. "But Win is, in some ways. I can handle him."

Was she as confident as she sounded? He wished he knew. "I'd better get back to East Norwalk," he said at last. "Just in case Patrick should get away and try to call."

"Nine-oh-five from Grand Central," she replied immediately. "Track thirty-three, I think. You've got almost an hour to make it." She began picking his still-damp clothing from hangers. "I'll call you in the morning, if the coast is clear. And Barr . . ."

He looked up at her from the sock he was tugging onto his foot. She seemed to be searching for words, and her face was almost luminous. "Yes?" he prompted.

"Get him back. Please."

"I'll do my best." He wanted desperately to hold her, if only as reassurance, and he had the strongest sense of her wanting it, too. But what if he was wrong? What if she thought he was trying to take advantage of an emotional moment? He hesitated, and felt the spark between them break.

GILLIAN:
FRIDAY MORNING,
MANHATTAN

The New Federalist's library, in earlier days a generously proportioned ground-floor kitchen, had decorative iron bars on its two street windows, backed by solid wood shutters for privacy. The door that led into the main editorial area was sheet steel with a serious lock, installed at Roger Huddleston's instructions, to protect the teletype and fax machines just inside. The official extra key was kept, with all the other interior keys, on a ring that lived in K.C.'s top desk drawer. But since the *TNF* Editorial staff had a visceral reluctance to depend on someone in Business for emergency access to their offices, most of them had stashed backup keys in convenient crannies. Gillian counted on Mrs. Bookhouser's adherence to this custom, and she was not disappointed: the spare key, shiny under its coating of dust, lay exactly where Gillian had expected to find it, on the molding over the library door.

It was a little after seven, and the early-morning sun forced bright, narrow bars through gaps between the shutter slats, catching dust motes that floated in the silent air. Though the library was perfectly dry it smelled, as Gillian had remembered, of once-damp books. The smell was what had triggered her memory, as she sat brooding over Patrick's disappearance and waiting for Barr to arrive. At first she couldn't imagine why her mind should associate an odor of decaying paper and fish glue with a cassette tape, but she had learned to trust her senses and let them lead her on. The mental picture, when at last it came, clicked into focus so suddenly that she heard herself grunt "That's *it*." Mrs. Boyd, who had been observing her anxiously from behind a tract, blurted, "Are you all right, dear?"

"Fine, Mrs. B," she replied, holding the image firmly in her mind's eye: open metal shelves painted olive green, and on them rows of glass-fronted cases filled to capacity with boxed and labeled cassette tapes. She had seen the shelves just once before, on her first day's guided tour; what had K.C. said they were? Oh, yes—speeches from bygone presidential campaigns. What better hiding place than such a graveyard of broken promises?

Now, surveying the rows of cassettes, she found herself hard put to identify some of the labels. *Sargent Shriver* had something to do with the Kennedys, she thought, but *Cabot Lodge? Ed Muskie?* Who on earth could they have been? And then she saw what she was searching for, six small plastic boxes labeled *Wm. Miller*, one of which—if you looked very closely—was lacking the fine film of dust that shrouded the rest. She reached out to open the glass case, only to discover it was locked. Well, of course it would be.

She dropped to her knees, ignoring the dusty floor, to get a closer look. The glass-paned front of each case was hinged at the top, with a keyhole inset in its bottom frame. The lock was familiar to her, a type often used on boats. Any determined intruder over the age of six could pry the door open with a screwdriver, if he didn't mind leaving telltale scars on the door and frame.

Gillian very much minded. She rocked back on her heels and considered the possibilities. Given her only weapon, a Swiss Army knife, any assault on the glass-and-varnished-wood front of the case was going to make a mess. But what about the back of it? she asked herself, and moved around the steel shelves to the corresponding location in the next aisle, where she pulled free the books that concealed the rear of the case she wanted. Sure enough, its back, a single sheet of thin plywood, was held in place by only six screws.

Ten minutes later it was done—the empty tape case refilled with a dummy ("God Loves You, Sinner!", stolen from Mrs. Boyd's collection while her back was turned), the plywood back of the case screwed down, the books replaced in something like their original order, Mrs. Bookhouser's spare key back in its place over the locked library door.

But it was nearly eight. Time was beginning to press. In her own office, Gillian connected her laptop computer to the cassette recorder, into which she popped the stolen tape. Following the *User's Guide* step by step, she typed in the required sequence of instructions. To her gratified amazement, the tape player's wheels suddenly began to turn, but at normal speed; it could take an hour just to reach the momentary spurt of computer code she wanted, and she didn't have that much time.

She unplugged the tape recorder and began to fast-forward through the arid reaches of Wm. Miller's prose, stopping every few seconds to make sure she hadn't gone past the message she had to find. Even so, the tape seemed to crawl, as the minute hand of her watch picked up speed. Awful doubts surfaced: she'd picked the wrong tape box from the six in the case; she'd already overshot the brief stretch of computer language; she'd guessed wrong entirely, and there was no message on the tape at all—and then, blessedly, Miller was cut off in the midst of a sententious period. A moment of silence, broken by high-pitched gabble, like a henhouse conversation speeded up by a factor of ten. "All *right!*" she muttered, reversing back to Miller and replacing the computer plugs.

She wanted to race through the hookup sequence, but forced herself to recheck every step. The tape reeled, but the laptop's screen remained depressingly blank. Just as she was about to release her breath in despair, the words *Found LAST* appeared.

"Don't you mean *at last?*" she said to the machine, before she realized that LAST must be the name of the file. Last what? she wondered, and became aware of footsteps in the hall.

Both the laptop and the cassette player were battery-powered, so she simply scooped them up together and shoved the tangled mass, still running, into her desk's middle drawer, half an instant before K.C. rounded the corner. She eyed Gillian closely for a moment. "You look terrible, kiddo. What's the problem?" K.C.'s plain face mirrored nothing but concern, and her voice was so warm and friendly that Gillian had to remind herself of the coded tape transferring itself only inches away from her midsection.

"Didn't sleep too well," she replied. "Excited about the voyage, I guess."

K.C. was unlocking her office door. "Don't know that I'd find five straight days of throwing up all that exciting," she observed. "But maybe you have good—what's the word: sea feet? No, sea *legs*. Do you?"

By now Gillian was familiar with K.C.'s probing technique, and had her face arranged in a smile when the other woman darted a quick glance at her. "I'll let you know when I get there," she said.

"When are you and Win taking off? Noonish?"

Oh God, I forgot. He's giving me a ride up to Newport. She'd been supposed to bring her gear with her to the office, but it was still neatly stacked inside Mrs. Boyd's front door. "Well, I've got a last-minute errand to run," she improvised. "I may have to leave a little earlier than noon."

"I can't think why you came in at all, then," K.C. grumbled. "Just make sure you check off everything on Win's A-issue list before you go, okay?"

"Absolutely," Gillian agreed, while thinking: How the hell am I going to get all this computer stuff to Barr?

And from behind her came K.C.'s purr, dripping innocence: "By the way, is your actor friend still among the missing?"

Gillian's prepared defenses were all facing a different way, and the unexpected question caught her completely off guard. "Patrick?" His name tripped over the irresistibly rising lump in her throat, and she knew her next sound was going to be a gulping sob. I will not break down. I will not do it. Without turning, she managed a disdainful shrug and, from inner resources she hadn't known she had, summoned what sounded like someone else's voice: "Actors. What can you expect?"

She lifted the top file from her IN box and opened it. K.C. said, "Men in general. What can you expect?" and retreated into her office. Gillian stared down, unseeing, at the correspondence in front of her. *Oh God*, she thought, *let him be safe.*

At eleven, K.C. was summoned to Win's office for a financial meeting. As soon as her broad behind had vanished around the corner, Gillian pulled the laptop computer out of the desk drawer and consulted its main menu. The previously empty memory now contained a single file, LAST, which she called up to the eight-line screen. What she saw in the green-tinted window looked simple enough, and yet it made no immediate sense:

Lamprey
2 @ 150

7/15	rec 1st 150.	
7/24	.100	1.9
8/5	.050	1.85
8/15	.050	1.8
8/30	.075	1.725

She scrolled the text down, screen by screen, but it was just more of the same: dates separated by approximate two-week intervals; variable decimal fractions in the middle column; steadily decreasing numbers in the right-hand one. At December 13, the regular procession of figures was interrupted by an entry that read: *rec 2nd 150*. Then the format resumed again, ending finally at:

6/29	.060	−0.080

The next line signaled a new beginning, headed:

Horn
3 @ 145.

and followed by another progression of dates and numbers.

If I weren't so tired and jumpy, I could make some sense of this, she thought, scrolling the screens again, through half a dozen similar sequences, labeled *Queens, Uptown, Missouri, Hubcap, Easter Egg,* and *Tall Fox.* Impatiently, she skipped to the very end of the file, and the cryptic words *THIS next.*

From LAST to THIS? Another taped file, maybe. She pressed the cassette recorder's Play button, and was rewarded with a spurt of electronic birdsong. I should put this away before somebody catches me, she thought, even as her fingers were rippling through the hookup sequence.

THIS was a far simpler file than LAST, though its first two lines were nearly the same:

Lamprey
2.5 @ 153.

Immediately below was a third line:

6/13   50% dep OK.

And after that a space and a new entry:

Easter Egg
4 @ 150.
0 dep

No time for this, she admonished, jumping once more to the file's last line, the four capital letters *SFGB*. By now she had given herself so completely to the spirit of the hunt that she merely glanced toward the door before ordering the cassette recorder to disgorge SFGB. The laptop had barely announced *"Found SFGB"* when she heard cheerful whistling, punctuated by thumps, as *TNF*'s spastic mail-delivery cart groped its way down the corridor. Once again Gillian stuffed the still-running laptop into her desk drawer, cursing the mail boy under her breath. His visit was cut short by K.C.'s telephone, which Gillian finally picked up after a round dozen rings. Her mouth was shaped to say "Ms. Carew's wire," when she heard a heavy-breathing male voice at the other end: "K.C.? You there?"

My, but we're sounding tense this morning, Gillian thought. "She's away from her desk at the moment. Can I help you?"

"No," snapped the voice. Silence, except for the breathing and what sounded like heavy-machinery noises in the background. The voice was faintly familiar—probably *TNF*'s printer, except that he usually called one of the Jakes when he had a serious problem, and this man sounded too well educated.

"Well, in that case . . ." she began.

"Wait a moment. Please?" Another long pause. "Look, she *is* in the office, right?"

"She's in a meeting," Gillian replied, intrigued now.

"Oh God! D'you know when she'll be out?"

"Nope. Sorry." I've heard your voice before, my friend. And recently, only you were a lot calmer then.

"Well, tell her . . . tell her she's got to make a decision. *Today*. Have you got that?"

"She's got to make a decision," Gillian repeated slowly, as if writing it down. And then very quickly: "About what?"

"She'll know what it's about," the voice said.

She tried a different tack: "K.C. makes a lot of decisions. Would you like to leave a number? Or a name?"

Gillian could feel the man's reluctance oozing over the wire. "Easter," he said at last. "Tell her Mr. Easter called."

"Yes, sir," she said, in her best executary tone. "Mr. Easter called, to ask for a decision today."

"That's it, Miss . . ."

"Verdean," she supplied, and "Uh!" said Mr. Easter, the grunt of one who had just been slugged in the gut. He clicked off, and she was still staring at the receiver as K.C. reappeared, looking harried.

"Somebody called?" she asked, her eye going to Gillian's telephone console, on which the indicator light for K.C.'s line was blinking red.

"Just a minute ago. He sounded kind of upset. He said to tell you he had to have a decision today." She waited for the other woman's reaction, but K.C.'s face registered only blankness.

"What decision?" she said. "If it was the printer, their check is in the mail. Hell, pretty much no matter who it was"—she forced a laugh—"their check is in the mail."

"Not the printer," Gillian replied. "A Mr. Easter. As in egg. Oh." Her expression, she knew, was betraying the sudden, overwhelming recognition that swept through her. But K.C. didn't even see her.

"That asshole," she breathed. "That frigging *idiot*." She jammed the key into her office lock, wrenched the door open, slammed it behind her. On the phone console, K.C.'s direct line lit up. If I pick it up she'll hear the click, Gillian thought. Better leave well enough alone.

"There you are," said Win Huddleston, appearing without warning at her open door. He was dressed for the sea in khakis, a plaid wool shirt, and deck shoes, and he had a bulging duffel bag slung over one shoulder. "I hope you're not planning to go in that outfit," he added, taking in Gillian's neat tweed suit. "Unless you're going to change en route."

"No!" K.C.'s voice was clear through the closed door. "Not yet!"

Win looked startled. "Something wrong with our business manager?"

That's got to be real, Gillian thought. He can't be that good an actor. "It's some guy who called while you all were in the meeting," she said. "Man named Easter."

"As in egg?" he said, grinning innocently. "Well, let's leave all this behind us and hit the road for Newport. I'm picking the car up at Avis."

Her brain seemed to have gone into overdrive. "East Fifty-fourth? I'll meet you there, in about an hour. I've got two last-minute errands still on my list."

"I warned you to clear your decks early." A mock admonition only. She recognized the sailing-day excitement bubbling up from his soul. "That's not the superefficient Gillian I've come to know and love."

The word floated unclaimed for no more than half a second. "Get out of here," she said. "The quicker you vanish, the sooner I'll be ready."

"Your messengers go to Connecticut?" she asked the pimply young man behind the counter.

"If you've got the cash, they'll go to Patagonia," he said cheerfully. "Is that what you're sending?"

"Right. I didn't have time to wrap it." She set the laptop on the counter and flicked the On switch. The three files were in its memory: LAST, THIS, and SFGB. Would Barr have the smarts to get at them?

" 'S no problem," the counterman said. "I've gotta charge you for a padded envelope, though."

"Fine," she replied absently. She moved the main menu cursor to TEXT, hit the execute key. *File to open?* the screen demanded. She poised her hands, hesitated for a second, and typed BARR.

BARR:

FRIDAY EVENING,

EAST NORWALK

Spread before him, on top of a chart of Western Long Island Sound, were the sheets of lined notebook paper that summarized his afternoon on the telephone. Barr usually found himself able to think more clearly when standing at *Glory*'s chart table, but as he surveyed his own boldly scrawled notes all he could see was the dilemma he faced.

From the start he had been driven by a single, almost uncontrollable urge—somehow to get Gillian off Win Huddleston's boat—and at one point he'd snatched the keys to the Mazda from the hook next to the telephone and bounded up the companionway with some overheated notion of roaring off to Rhode Island and dragging her ashore. On deck, the crisp afternoon sou'wester blew the impulse to rags before he stepped off the boat. Even assuming he could find Huddleston's *Kassandra* in a Newport jammed with Bermuda-bound yachts and the spectator vessels assembled to see them off, how could he make Gillian come with him? And what would it achieve? Save her at the almost certain price of Patrick's life, not to mention her friend Sarah's. If they were alive.

Looked at rationally—he managed a wry smile—Gillian was probably safe for the time being: if Huddleston was guilty (But of what?), he would hardly want to attract the high-voltage attention that would come from losing a crewmember during the race. Once Gillian was in Bermuda, though, an arranged accident would be all too easy. With that thought came the momentary picture of a dead girl, wide-eyed and open-mouthed, jarring him again. Erin; he couldn't even remember her last name. He shook his head to get her out of his mind, but succeeded only in replacing her vacant, ashen face with Gillian's tanned, intent one.

Through the afternoon the two images slowly faded from Barr's head as he talked on the phone—to Sol Farber, to Patrick's former comrade Will Evans, to the smoky-voiced Susan Grover, to a cranky old lunatic named Andrew Harrigan. Thanks largely to Susan (yes, they had, he decided after thirty seconds' conversation) it was possible to track Patrick's footsteps and see what had been leading him forward. What Barr had learned in Bermuda and from Gillian, plus Patrick's discoveries, suggested a shape to the operation and, glimmering behind it, a motive.

At the same time, Barr's subconscious continued to brood about Gillian. He had come back from Bermuda eager to protect her, but now (and not for the first time) he realized she would never sit still to be protected. When he thought about her foolhardy stubbornness it drove him wild, until he gradually began to perceive that courage and intransigence were two of the things that made him feel the way he did about her.

And just how *did* he feel about her? "I don't know," he said to the blank face of the bulkhead chronometer. "I just don't know." No, that wasn't honest. He knew, all right. The real question was, could he go through all that again? Did he dare to expose his still-raw feelings to another searing?

As if it had been listening, the chronometer emitted a self-important whir followed by six measured tones. Six bells: 7:00 P.M.— I've been standing here too long. He reached out to the telephone and dialed. "Mr. Farber? Barr again. I need a hand."

Although Sol Farber behind the wheel of his Cadillac looked more than usually ineffectual, he handled the enormous vehicle with crisp precision. Even more impressive to Barr, he was able to conduct a coherent conversation while driving: "So you're sure that's where they have him?"

"It's handy and private," Barr replied, trying to override his own doubts. "They've got something going on there already, to judge by the reception Patrick got when he broke in."

"What makes you think they'll be too busy in this boat place to take care of you, too?" Farber said, sounding worried. "Patrick almost got himself killed, and—you should pardon my saying this—he's a lot bigger than you are. Unless you're one of those king fu people, of course."

"Not even Prince Fu, I'm afraid." If the masked giant in the shed was half as big as Susan Grover made him out to be, the fight would be over before it started. But Patrick would certainly have exaggerated, to impress her. I hope.

"You got maybe a gun?"

"Kind of," Barr agreed, thinking of the ancient Very pistol he'd tossed into the Cadillac's trunk.

"Maybe you should take mine. In the glove compartment." Barr took it out gingerly, a businesslike revolver with a very short barrel. "Don't worry. It's on the safety," Farber said, watching from the corner of his eye.

"Thanks, but I don't really get along with these," Barr said, replacing it. A sign at the side of the parkway caught his eye. "It's just around the next bend: the abandoned gas station."

Farber slid the big car into the right lane and then off the parkway. The headlights illuminated four vandalized gas pumps, a phoneless telephone booth, and a low fieldstone building whose windows were covered with sheet iron. Three solid lanes of Friday night traffic heading for Manhattan streamed past on their left; on the right, at the edge of the station's paved oval (grass already coming up through cracks in the asphalt), was a cobblestoned slope that went down to the sluggishly flowing Hutchinson River, here only a few yards across. Barr got out of the car, and Farber pressed the trunk release for him. "I hope you know what you're doing," he said.

So do I, Barr thought. It'd make a nice change.

From where he was crouched next to the noisome water he could look up to the orange-red evening sky and see Farber's silhouette, watching. He set down the bellowslike hand pump and pressed the inflatable dinghy's hull: hard enough. He checked that the wooden floorboards were tightly wedged in place, the oars and Very pistol lying on them, then waved up at Farber. The short man waved back and vanished. A moment later Barr heard the rasp and spatter of

gravel as the Cadillac pulled back onto the parkway, and then nothing but the undifferentiated rumble of vehicles.

He wrestled the inflatable over the rocks, slippery with some
unmentionable ooze, and into the oily water. At once the little boat
angled upstream, tugged by the invisible current—the tide was still
coming in, and all he would have to do was let it carry the dinghy
with it. He climbed in, soaking one foot in the process, and sank
to his knees on the floorboards, facing forward. He fitted the stubby
oars into the rubber rowlocks and gave an experimental thrust; the
boat moved farther away from the bank he had left, and now the
tidal current took a better grip on it, pushing it up the fetid creek.

He saw the boatyard's sheds, brightly lit against the black sky,
from two bends downstream. Stroking the dinghy in close to the
near shore, where the overhanging bank would put him in shadow,
he let the current carry him until the barrier fence was no more than
a hundred feet ahead. He reached for a handful of trailing reeds and
for several minutes knelt motionless, listening to the hum of the
traffic. The stream took an abrupt bend beyond the fence; presumably the boatyard's few piers were just around the corner. When he
was sure no one was patrolling the perimeter, he began edging the
rubber boat upstream again. Already the current's force was percep-
tibly less, which meant the top of the tide was approaching. The
ebb would—if all went well—carry him back down. And Patrick,
he reminded himself. Both of them. But he couldn't suppress the *if*
that kept rising to the surface of his thoughts.

A handful of boats sat disconsolately at the yard's floating piers.
Two of the vessels were deckless shells; another had clearly been
in a serious collision. To anyone ashore, blinded by the lights that
illuminated the sheds, the unlit floats would be in complete darkness.
He made the dinghy fast in a vacant slip and jammed the flare pistol
in his belt, then climbed slowly to the float on hands and knees,
feeling the narrow catwalk bob under him. His progress was in
relative shadow until the very top of the ramp that led from pier to
shore, where there was a wicket gate beneath a pool of yellow light
from an overhead lamp.

But no guard. Overconfidence? A trap? Or maybe there was simply
nothing left worth guarding. Still on hands and knees, Barr suddenly

saw the wire running along the underside of the gate. Was it an alarm? He had to assume so. The wicket was festooned with barbed wire, so swinging himself around the side was not a serious option. He was about to retreat down the ramp and reconsider his approach, when he saw headlights moving on the far side of the boatyard. No, he realized a moment later, they were coming from outside the perimeter fence. He shrank back into the shadows of the gate and watched.

The headlights, which had been flickering unsteadily up and down—a bumpy dirt road, presumably—steadied and stopped just beyond the main gate. Two figures materialized from the darkness and, after questions and answers that were too far away for Barr to overhear, swung the gate inward. The car was small and sporty, like Gillian's, and reminded him of some low-slung insect; it rumbled angrily into the yard and pulled up, and a woman got out. She seemed to be of middle height, overweight, reasonably young. The two guards were obviously used to her. They pushed the gate closed without a backward glance as she walked quickly to the smallest of the cinderblock buildings, opened a door, and stepped inside.

One of the guards got into the car and, revving the engine noisily, drove it to a parking slot while the other watched. The engine stopped and the first guard climbed out, but the second was already snarling at him, words that sounded as if they might be Spanish. He wants to play with it, too, thought Barr, as the second guard snatched at something in his companion's hand. Now or never. In plain view of the shore, he lowered himself from the ramp until his feet touched the rocky slope beneath, then scrambled up the incline, slipping and stumbling, pulling himself over the edge and onto the hard-packed earth beyond.

For several moments he lay gasping for breath, his body perfectly lit by the overhead lights, while the two guards squabbled over the car keys. The volume increased, and the two men were circling each other like cats, when a door slammed open and a deep voice bellowed "¡Basta!" As the guards turned to the new arrival and began to accuse each other, Barr scuttled into the shelter of the nearest building. Five minutes later peace of a sort had returned to the Hutchinson River Boatworks. The guards, grumbling audibly, were back at their post, the building door was shut, and Barr had moved from the first building, by way of a conveniently placed dumpster, to a position behind the smaller structure into which the woman had gone.

He had no further plan, though. No real idea what to do next. He could see light from windows set at least six and a half feet up from ground level, and occasional voices, both men's and women's, raised in what sounded like anger. Then a strange howling—did they have a dog in there?—that was broken off suddenly. Hours seemed to pass, and Barr's watch said it was only forty-five minutes; without warning the building's door opened and several people stepped out. The spotlight from directly above lit the tops of their heads brilliantly but left their faces in deep shadow. They all seemed to be talking at once, but three of them paused long enough to light cigarettes, and one of the remaining voices—a woman's—picked up volume and bore down the rest.

It was a trained voice, Barr decided, though not one he found particularly pleasant. Gravelly and insinuating at the same time, a woman who would wheedle or bully with equal ease. Bullying now: "I say *yes*. Don't wimp out, people. Get it over with."

" 'Twere well it were done quickly'? Is that it?" said someone else— male, educated, rather elderly.

"Don't *do* that!" snapped the woman. To Barr's surprise, fear put an edge to her tone.

"I apologize. I keep forgetting about your"—a half beat's pause— "professional superstitions," said the man, leaving no doubt that he hadn't forgotten at all.

Under the light, a heavy figure in a broad-brimmed hat pointedly turned its back on the others: the deep-voiced woman, Barr thought, just as another woman spoke—young, conciliatory, but firm: "Rose is right all the same. We don't have any choice. He's seen too much."

Barr's ears pricked up, and the next speaker, the educated man, only confirmed his suspicions. "That's murder, ladies and gentlemen. Murder one, if you want to be precise."

"Damn it," cried a new voice, shaking with emotion, "we're not criminals!"

"Have you looked at a statute book, darling?" The gravel-voiced woman again. "If what we've done ever gets out, none of us is likely to hear the birds sing again."

"But we just—"

"You knew—we all knew something like this might happen," said the young woman, cutting off the protest. "That's why Roger insisted on having this committee, to make the necessary decisions."

"But where does it stop?" demanded another, in rising panic. "You say we have to . . . dispose of this man. Maybe so. But according to what we heard inside, there's at least one more. And we don't even know who's behind them."

"But we *will* know," the young woman insisted. Good Eastern college, Barr thought; a sincere, reassuring, essentially friendly voice—which then uttered words that froze his backbone: "You weren't listening. Before we do what has to be done, this guy will spill his guts. I promise you that."

In the sudden silence, Barr heard the parkway traffic and a car horn, sounding twice, that cut through it. "Oh God, this is awful." A new speaker, joined by another: "I hate it. I didn't sign up for this kind of thing." And another: "Me either. This is the pits."

"Then go home and put a pillow over your head," said the gravel-voiced woman. "Because it took me a long time to get where I am, and I don't plan to run my next campaign from Dannemora."

Now a man who had not spoken before. Smooth, professionally agreeable, and—to Barr's amazement—familiar: "There's a compromise here, folks. We're just not seeing it." *Frannie X*, by God. He continued: "Just leave everything to the three of us. We'll take care of it, and you won't have to know."

"Ignorance won't be an excuse if it goes sour," objected the educated male, but he was drowned out by a chorus of tentative agreement.

"Then you agree," said the young woman. "Rose, Frannie, and I will take whatever action we feel is necessary."

"But we won't be part of it," said someone quickly.

"Exactly. Your hands are clean." Did he hear an edge of contempt in the young woman's pleasant voice?

"And what about the girl?" asked the educated man.

"Forget the girl. She's on ice for a while," said the young woman firmly. "Now, the rest of you get out of here."

"But before you go," Frannie put in, "I've got a little surprise. A *nice* surprise. Those of you who were on the committee last year remember we voted to keep back something for emergencies. Well, I think we can agree that this is an emergency. . . ."

"Fucking A," someone agreed loudly. "You bet," cried another, with an off-key, nervous laugh.

"Just come over to my car," said Frannie. He turned away, a dinner-jacketed shape whose glossy hair gleamed in the light, and like the rats of Hamelin the rest of the group scurried after him.

Their excited chatter faded. Quickly, before he could think about what he was doing, Barr moved from behind the dumpster, opened the door to the cinderblock building, and stepped inside.

PATRICK:

FRIDAY NIGHT,

THE BRONX

For a long time Patrick had fought the pain silently, his jaws clamped shut, but it got worse and worse until he heard himself whimpering like some kind of animal. At last he couldn't hold back anymore, and he screamed. The big kid who was holding his hips muttered "*Madre de Dios*," but Golem ignored him; his bare, sweaty torso loomed right over Patrick, and he smelled like a zoo. He held the two wires in his rubber-gloved hands, up where Patrick could see them, then brought them down again. This time the screaming went on and on, until it seemed to be coming from outside Patrick. Through it he was just aware of a door crashing open, and the gravel voice of Broadway Rose, low and furious, right next to his head: "For Christ's sake, shut him up. You're scaring the shit out of them in there."

All at once the pain was gone, but for some reason he couldn't stop screaming. A heavy blow just under his bruised ribs drove the breath out of him, and he felt himself swirl down into a soft gray haze, streaked with bright agony. Gillian, in her pastel bikini, floated past him; Sol Farber, shaking his head sadly; and Patrick's own daughter, Tracy, only in grainy black and white like the photo of her in his wallet. She'd been there for a few seconds, and now she was gone forever. Barr's face swam into focus, and Patrick knew he must be dying. He wasn't surprised, considering what they'd done to him over the past—what was it, now?—two days. Still, it seemed unfair that dying should hurt so much. He was still trying to say so when Barr put his finger to his lips, winked, and disappeared.

He heard other voices, echoing off the steel-beamed roof of the big shed. He turned his head, slowly because of the streak of pain just over his ear, and saw that the four of them had come back into the room, were standing a few feet away, next to the pyramid of empty resin drums. Golem's high, angry voice cut through the fog in Patrick's brain: "I told you: nothing. Not a word."

"What do you mean, *not a word?*" snarled Broadway Rose. "Christ, the way he was yelling we could hardly hear ourselves talk."

"Oh, yell—we can make him yell, all right," Golem agreed. "But he won't *say* anything."

"*Es verdad, señora,*" chimed in the big young Hispanic. His soft, gentle voice went with his doe's eyes and curly black hair. "Is no good, none of it."

"What about his wallet? Any clues there?" K.C.'s voice was as matter-of-fact as if she were buying a loaf of bread. From her tone, Patrick suddenly knew the real ordeal hadn't even begun, and felt a cold shiver of fear down his spine.

"Just the things you saw," Golem was saying. "Texaco credit card; old U.S. Army ID with his photo; New York driver's license, got an address on City Island—"

"A rooming house where he hasn't lived for a year," said K.C.

"Piece of paper with a phone number on it—"

"Right, we're following up on that."

"A hundred and fifty-seven bucks in cash," Golem continued doggedly. "And the kid's picture."

"A cute kid," said K.C. "A little girl, Patrick? Yours, maybe? I never thought of you as a daddy." She had come over to the big work table where they had him spreadeagled, was staring down at him with those smart, bulging eyes. She waited for him to say something, then shrugged. "No comment, is that it?"

Broadway Rose appeared at her side; her gaze traveled down his sweating, naked body with something like interest. "There's hardly a mark on him," she said. "What've you two been doing in here, anyway?"

"That was Easter Egg's idea," said Golem, sounding scornful. "In case we decided to let him go. We been working him over with these." He held up the two wires, and Patrick flinched at the sight.

A grimace wrinkled Broadway Rose's broad, flat face. "I see." And to Patrick, "We still could let you go. If you cooperate."

"No, dear," K.C. put in pleasantly. "It won't fly. Patrick's too smart to believe that." She leaned over the table; her voice was smoothly regretful, but some emotion he couldn't name flickered back in her eyes. "We can't let you go, and both of us know it, don't we? No point in waffling—we're going to kill you." She paused, waiting for a reaction. "You're a brave man. I can see that, even if I didn't already know."

He had no doubt that she meant every word. His brain knew he was as good as dead, but his gut hadn't accepted the news yet.

"The thing is," K.C. continued, as if talking to herself, "there are ways and ways of checking you out, and it doesn't much matter what you look like afterwards. What we're going to do, in case you're wondering, is put you in one of these barrels"—the empty drum gave a hollow *clunk* as she tapped it—"and fill it up with . . . what's that stuff, Luis?"

"Lead shot, *señora*, like what we pour in keel moulds," said the Hispanic kid, licking dry lips nervously. "Seal it off with the resin, drop it in the bay. *Vaya con Dios.*"

"Right. And we'll get away with it, Patrick."

They would, too. He'd just vanish for good—no bloated corpse bobbing up after a couple of weeks for the cops to find. He could almost feel the cold shot hard against his skin, and the resin—it'd be warm, then hot as it began to catalyze—oozing over his body.

K.C. was watching his face eagerly, and he knew she could read his expression. "Don't worry. By then you won't feel a thing." She leaned over him, and he caught a faint, acrid whiff of tension. "But what happens before that is up to you," she added. "If you cooperate, tell us what we have to know, it's a quick bang and lights out." As if to make her point, she held up a small automatic—a .32, his eye noted. "If you don't, it'll be a four-star bitch."

Again she waited for a reaction. Patrick forced himself to look anywhere but into her eyes. The other three stared at her; they seemed to be hypnotized. After a long moment she sighed. "Okay, here's how it's going to be, then. Nothing complicated, but it won't matter if you're the bravest man who ever lived. You see that heater over there? Golem, turn his head so he can see it." An ordinary, upright kerosene space heater, with a small bucket sitting on its top. His gaze went helplessly back to her.

"That bucket's full of water. Just plain water. Luis and Golem hold you so your hand is in it, up to the wrist. Then we light the flame and turn it all the way up. Takes about eight minutes to come to a boil. Takes about twenty minutes before . . . well, did you ever boil the meat off bones, to make soup?"

He had, and the mental picture, jumping out before he could stop it, was sickening. He looked quickly away from the innocent-seeming heater. Luis's mouth was tightly compressed, and he was shaking his head. "No, *señora*. The heater is no good."

"What's the matter, Luis? I thought you were a hard guy," K.C. said, lightly mocking.

"Is not that," he answered earnestly. "But the fire, the open flames . . ." He pointed to a large, red-lettered sign on the wall: ABSOLUTELY NO SMOKING. And to a row of drums below it: "These thing—acetone, toluene, resin. One spark and *whoof!*"

For the first time, K.C. let emotion creep into her voice. "Then you'd better make sure there aren't any sparks." He heard anger and, under it, a slight tremor; for no good reason it stiffened his spirit. She turned to Patrick. "This isn't going to be any fun for anybody. In fact, it's probably the worst thing in the world. And bear in mind," she added, as if it had just occurred to her, "you've got two hands and two feet. The feet take a lot longer."

Broadway Rose, whose face had slowly been turning a nasty yellow, gave a choking gargle and fled from the room, slamming the door behind her. K.C. shrugged. "Well, you know what they say: when the going gets tough, the tough go shopping. Let's do it, guys."

Knowing what was coming, Patrick had been gathering his energies, willing his strained muscles to obey him one last time. He knew he didn't have enough left in the tank to make a real fight of it, but he was grimly determined to make them kill him. First, though, he had to waste a little of the little strength he had, to put them off guard. Warily, Luis and Golem undid the knots that held him down to the worktable, but Patrick lay still, not tugging against the loosening rope. From half-closed eyes he saw Golem nod a warning to Luis. As the last knot came free, Patrick rolled to his left, feinting at Luis's face, and stabbed a hard right into his midsection.

Golem, who'd positioned himself where he couldn't be hit, dropped his three hundred pounds on top of the writhing Patrick, and improved the moment with a couple of savage jabs to the kidneys. Patrick gave a perfectly genuine moan and went limp, eyes closed. After a few seconds, Golem climbed off him and said to Luis, who was retching in the background, "I told you he was fast."

Something exploded across Patrick's face, but he allowed his head to roll loosely with the blow. "Hey! Enough!" called K.C., from a few yards away. "There's no point to this if he's out cold."

He felt Golem and Luis each seize an arm and drag him off the table. But a hundred and eighty sagging pounds of bone and muscle made an awkward load, and after a couple of tries at holding Patrick upright, Golem grumbled, "Let me do it, stupido."

Luis muttered something that ended in "su madre," but let go his grip on Patrick's arm. Golem was holding him up, groping for a fireman's carry, when K.C. said, "Just a sec till I get this going." The sharp tang of kerosene cut through the sweet, nutlike odor of resin that filled the air. A match scraped. Patrick, one arm draped over Golem's shoulder, could feel him tense at the sight of the flame. "Okay," said K.C.'s voice, hard now. "Bring him over here."

Golem bent forward and gave a preliminary heave that brought Patrick's torso up over his shoulder. Strong as the big man was, he lurched under the dead weight. Go, thought Patrick, and lashed out blindly with both feet.

One of them connected, a glancing blow. Luis shouted "Ay!" and reeled into a stack of square five-gallon cans, carrying them to the floor with him. Still draped over Golem's shoulder, Patrick pounded at his back with one hand, while he gripped the wrestler's belt with the other. Golem, squealing like a steam whistle, staggered around the room as Patrick's madly flailing knees and feet kept him off balance.

"I got him!" yelled Luis, just as K.C. cried, "Out of the way!" Deafening whack of a gunshot, and a searing flame cut across Patrick's bare buttock. But it was Luis who gave a loud groan and fell like a tree, blood streaming down the side of his head.

Patrick could feel his strength draining away. He managed a feeble jab at Golem's eye and was hurled to the concrete, the wind driven out of him. He lay completely helpless, with barely enough energy left to gasp for breath, as K.C. and Golem loomed over him. "Kick him in the balls," she said. "No—let me."

"What about Luis?" asked Golem, looking shocked.

"In a minute," she replied. "This is something I've always wanted to do."

"Freeze!" cried a voice from across the room. For an endless second all three of them were motionless—Patrick on his back, Golem standing over him in a half-crouch, K.C. poised to one side, looking past Patrick to the row of drums along the far wall.

She recovered first. "Well," she said slowly. "A new face."

Her words released Patrick; he turned his head toward the drums. Barr was standing behind one of them, his elbows propped on its lid, holding *Glory*'s big old flare pistol in both hands. His thin face was set like bronze. "Can you get up?" he said to Patrick.

On the floor, Luis gave a strangled moan and rolled partway over. Barr's eyes went to the injured man, and as they did K.C. brought up the pistol at her side. Patrick had just time to cry "Watch—" before she squeezed the trigger.

The first round scored a gash in the concrete and sang up into the cinderblock behind Barr, who dived to one side a half-second before three neat holes appeared in the drum in front of him. The echoes of the closely spaced shots were a continuous roar in Patrick's dazed ears, and he barely heard Golem's terrified squeal as he scuttled like a giant crab out of the line of fire.

Silence again, except for quick, harsh breathing and a liquid pattering sound Patrick couldn't identify until he noticed the three streams of purplish fluid spouting from the punctured drum; thinned resin, by the smell. K.C. stood calmly in the center of the room, holding the pistol in two-handed target-range style, panning it back and forth across the row of drums. Golem was braced with his back to the door, his eyes wide. "I better get help," he said to her.

"Sure," she agreed, never taking her eyes from the row of drums in front of her. Golem opened the door, Barr popped up from his hiding place, and K.C. fired by reflex. As he dropped back out of

sight the bullet slapped off the wall a foot over his head and ricocheted back across the room with an ugly whir that ended in a
sharp *clang*.

The door slammed shut behind Golem, and K.C. stood waiting.
Two more rounds, Patrick thought. Two more at the most. Did Barr
know? He must, or he'd have showed himself by now. The flare gun
held just one 25 mm shell. Phosphorus, Patrick thought; anyway,
something that burned like hell. Burned: of course—he was looking
right at the answer without seeing it. One of the five-gallon cans
that Luis had knocked over was lying on its side about two feet
from Patrick. The shock of hitting the concrete had sprung its seams,
and a small pool of colorless liquid was already spreading across the
floor. The can had no label, but the biting, too-sweet odor that
raked his nasal passages was unmistakable.

Slowly, slowly he reached out, his arm screened from K.C. by
the can itself. He grabbed the screw top, twisted. Nothing. Again,
but he knew his grip must be like a baby's. K.C., her eyes on the
far wall, had kicked off her high heels. She seemed unsure which
way to move, but all she had to do was hold the fort for two more
minutes and Golem would be back with the gate guards. Patrick
stretched his fingers around the can's top and twisted one last time.
Without a sound it backed off—one turn, then two, and he felt the
icy fluid running over his hand, the puddle spreading fast across the
floor.

K.C. looked down at her bare feet in surprise, then up at Patrick.
"What *is* that stuff?"

"Acetone," he replied, pitching his gasping whisper as loudly as
he could. "You're standing in acetone."

It was all the hint Barr needed: he appeared from behind a drum
at the far end of the line, and K.C. fired and missed. With painful
care she leveled the automatic again, just as Barr pulled the flare
gun's trigger. Patrick was already rolling, propelled by fear, across
the icy floor. He was aware of two explosions, the flare gun's shotgun
crash just ahead of the automatic's flat *crack*, followed by a hoarse
roar and an almost unbearable wave of heat. Now Barr was over
him, batting at flames that licked up Patrick's bare arm. He dragged
Patrick to a sitting position, and halted where he stood. A six-foot

sheet of fire stood between them and the door and from it, on hands and knees, crawled a living torch that sputtered and crackled as it came.

"Oh, Jesus," said Barr softly, taking a sleepwalker's step toward it.

"She's dead already," Patrick said, grasping Barr's arm. "And we are, too, if we don't get out of here." *Out of here:* Hope pulled him to his feet, dragging the paralyzed Barr back. The crawling figure, blackening as he watched, paused and then toppled gently to its side; the spreading lake of fire moved forward to surround it. "Come *on*, for Christ's sake," Patrick begged. "They'll be here any second." The door beyond the flames burst open, to a chorus of shouts, and slammed shut again.

As if awakened by the noise, Barr shook his head. "The window!" he yelled. "Let's go."

For as far back as Patrick could remember, he had been able to rely absolutely on his body—on its quickness, coordination, endurance and, above all, sheer strength. Now all of them were gone; he was helpless, propped naked against the gritty cinderblock wall while Barr, three inches shorter and forty pounds lighter, manhandled a fifty-gallon drum into position under the window. "Okay," Barr called to him, over the rising crackle of flames.

I can't. But he put one foot out and leaned into a tottering step. He lost his balance and started to fall; Barr was there in time, managed to push him back upright. Lifting his foot clear of the floor was more than Patrick could do, but he could shuffle, with Barr's big, hard hands supporting him. The drum seemed a hundred miles away, and the fire's crackling had deepened to a hungry roar. At last he was able to rest his elbows on the drum's lid, but he knew he could never pull himself up on it. He turned to Barr: "Can't do it," he croaked.

"What?" He could see Barr's mouth form the word, but could hear nothing over the flames. The heat on his back was nearly unbearable. He saw Barr's face harden, read his own death sentence there, and accepted it. One of them had to get away, save Gillian, get even with the bastards behind this. He tried to say something that would mean good-bye; Barr only shook his head impatiently and, with one awkward, grunting heave, boosted Patrick onto the drum. "Get up!" Barr roared in his ear. He put his shoulder under Patrick's butt and levered him to a standing position, belly level with the windowsill. The window was open, and Patrick slumped forward, half out of it. He felt Barr grab his ankles and lift, felt himself overbalance and begin to scrape painfully across the sill. All at once he caught a glimpse of the ground rushing up to meet him. It looked like sand, but when he hit, the impact was like rock.

His own shivering brought him back to consciousness, and the pulses of agony from his groin, his lacerated belly, his bruised head made him groan through clenched teeth. He was lying on smooth wood, but it was moving unsteadily beneath him. He tried to make sense of it, and became aware of the sound of lapping water, inches from his head. Above him, the night sky was clear except for thin, fast-moving clouds. Not clouds: smoke—he could smell it now and hear, not far away, the wail of sirens.

Then he heard other, nearer sounds: the slap of feet on wet rock; Barr's voice, from above and to one side: "The dinghy's right down here. You'll have to give me a hand with him, though. They damn near killed him."

"From the look of that fire over there," said Sol Farber's voice, between gasps, "the damage wasn't all on one side."

"No," Barr snapped. "It wasn't." He put one foot in the rubber dinghy and bent over, sliding his arm under Patrick's shoulders. Clinging to his shirt, his hair, his skin was the homely smell of broiled meat.

Patrick woke up once, hearing raised voices from the front seat. Barr was saying, "Why shouldn't we go to the police? We may not have an airtight case, but they'll have to listen to us."

"Why?" Farber demanded. "Tell me why they should listen to a couple of guys from nowhere like you? Besides, you killed that woman back there—"

"That was self-defense—"

"After she caught you breaking in? And look who you're going up against: a respectable magazine owner, you called him that yourself; a man who owns a big nightclub, he's probably paying off a

whole precinct full of cops; and if that shouldn't be enough," he
added, breathless but emphatic, "there's the borough president of
Manhattan."

"I didn't think of that. But—"

"Plus who knows how many bigwigs you don't even know about,"
Farber continued. "The U.S. Marines, could be."

"Okay. All right," Barr snapped. "The point is, what do we do
next?"

"I don't know," replied Farber. "I don't even know what this is all
about."

"Don't you?" Barr sounded surprised.

The next time Patrick surfaced he was slumped in one of the two-
wheeled carts that Carey & Willard provided for their customers to
wheel ice, groceries, and occasional drunken guests to and from their
docked boats. Patrick's upper half was more or less covered by
Farber's car coat, but a cool wind was chilling his bare legs, and his
feet were dragging on the pier's splintery planks. An hour's exhausted
sleep had put a small charge back into his batteries, and he was just
beginning to understand that he was going to live. Ahead of them
a telephone was ringing aboard one of the yachts—aboard *Glory*
herself, he realized, as they came abreast of her dark, silent shape.
The ringing stopped while Barr and Farber were heaving their nearly
helpless burden onto the deck, then began again just as the three
of them arrived in a tangled heap at the bottom of the companionway.

Leaving Farber and Patrick to untangle themselves, Barr struggled
to his feet and picked up the phone. "Yes?" he said. "Oh, hello, Miss
Grover." He looked down at Patrick with what seemed to be a thin
smile. "He's all right, but he can't come to the phone right now.
Yes, we found him, thanks to you." In the dim red nightlight over
the chart table, his bony face looked worried as he listened. "Who?
I see. No, no harm done, but I'm glad you called. We owe you a
good deal." Patrick could hear the sound of Susan's voice, but not
the words, and saw Barr smile again. "I'll see that he does. Yes, for
sure, and thanks again."

He hung up, and the smile was wiped from his face. He looked
down at Patrick, who had managed to sit up, his back against the

bulkhead. "She had visitors, just a few minutes ago. New York City cops, asking about you."

"Paper in my wallet," Patrick said slowly. "Had her number on it." Suddenly it dawned on him what Barr was leading up to: "Say, you don't suppose they'd—"

"They might," Barr interrupted. "D'you have a number for that other Coastie friend of yours, Evans?"

"Will?" He had to force himself to think. It seemed so long ago, part of another life. "Yeah—on the bulletin board over the phone."

Barr found it, started to dial, then paused and addressed Farber. "They'll be up here pretty soon," he said.

Farber nodded his agreement. "So what are you going to do?"

Barr's tiredness seemed to have dropped away from him like a ragged coat. "Well, I've got two phone calls to make: I want to ask Evans to keep an eye on Miss Grover, and there's a friend of mine up in Rhode Island who owes me a favor. After that, I think we'll go for a little sail."

"You're going *sailing?*" gasped Farber. "At a time like this?"

"I'm going hiding," Barr corrected him. "There's a string of islands just outside Norwalk Harbor, with a couple of nice little anchorages in them. Good places to tuck into while we figure out what to do next. But you can go ashore if you'd like. Might be the smart thing to do."

"Not on your life," said Farber. The little round figure looked utterly determined. "Not till you tell me what's happening."

G I L L I A N :

F R I D A Y   N I G H T ,

N E W P O R T ,

R H O D E   I S L A N D

Instead of the customary prerace restaurant dinner, *Kassandra*'s crew had gnawed on leathery pizza and toasted the voyage in acid chianti, while huddling together in the cockpit, wrapped in blankets and sleeping bags. Nico Butler, who'd sailed the yawl up from New York with old Otley and the even older Paul Marsh for crew, had arrived in Newport only that morning, to find the yacht clubs and marinas jammed with racers and all the best moorings in the big, crowded harbor taken. What was left tended to be either exposed or far from shore, and Nico had opted for protection from the gusting southwesterly rather than access to the piers and waterside eateries. As a result, *Kassandra* lay well down in Brenton Cove, half a mile from the bright lights and gay music, and surrounded by a scattering of other latecomers.

Not that Gillian missed the magical ambience of Newport on the eve of the Bermuda Race: along pretentiously named America's Cup Avenue, raucous crowds would be elbowing each other off the narrow pavement, overpriced restaurants would still have block-long lines outside their doors, and sodden, peanut-brained foredeck hands would already be throwing up in the men's rooms.

There'd been a time—it seemed like a century ago—when she'd reveled in being a part of that crowd, a part of the roistering fleet that was facing one of civilized life's few remaining physical adventures. Looking back, it all seemed so innocent, so childish; but then she hadn't had Patrick's life eating at her spirit. And Barr's, for that matter. And Sarah's.

She could handle responsibility and even fear, she knew, but helplessness was what drove you crazy: not knowing and not being able to find out. She'd managed to place one phone call to *Glory's* number from Mystic, late in the afternoon, when she and Win had pulled off I-95 for coffee; and another two hours later, from a booth at the Newport rent-a-car, while Win was turning in their feeble little econobox. The first time the line had been busy, the second time no one answered. Did that—could that—mean Barr might have located Patrick and gone after him? She stole a look at her watch: 11:00 P.M. This was maddening, having to chomp away in silence with a radiotelephone five feet from where she sat. Might have been five miles, for all the good it did.

Get off it, she told herself sternly. Don't let hope drive you up the wall. Think of something else.

He almost kissed me, last night. Twice: A girl can tell. Was it just the sympathy vote? And what held him back?

Control yourself, woman. The man you need to win over is sitting right across from you. Win Win: That still looked like the only way she could crack open whatever was going on. *Roger's scam* she'd nicknamed it, just to have a mental handle, though she reminded herself that K.C. was certainly involved, and Win himself had to know something.

While they ate, *Kassandra* began sidling around the mooring buoy, jerking at the pickup line, as the afternoon sou'wester, instead of dying with the sun, edged into the north and began to push sharp-edged little swells down to their corner of the harbor. Unlike *Glory*, *Kassandra* had no fabric dodger to shield the forward end of the cockpit, and the top of the deckhouse was too low to offer any practical shelter from the wind's bite. Conversation had never gotten off the ground, and now it withered completely. Gillian was almost too exhausted to eat but far too wired to be sleepy; shrouded in her sleeping bag she fiddled with a single slice of pizza and covertly weighed the four men with whom she would spend the next six hundred and fifty sea miles.

She knew she lacked Patrick's natural empathy for other people and their moods, but she'd spent six months tuning her perceptions to the group dynamics of charter parties; she could sense when people were ill at ease, and these men certainly were. Win was the most visibly nervous—talking too much, in quick, unrelated bursts of enthusiasm—but that was only right in a man making his first ocean passage as skipper. What struck her as odd was the way he treated the New Zealander, Nico Butler: not the deference of amateur for professional, which she would have expected, but a sort of wary defiance, as if the two men had papered over some deep disagreement between them.

Nico's behavior toward her was even odder. During her years with a sailmaking firm Gillian had encountered a great many Aussies and Kiwis, the spear-carrying mercenaries of the yacht-racing fleet, and she had learned to deal firmly with their roostering maleness. Prepared to answer a sexist putdown in kind, she found herself virtually ignored. Direct questions to Nico pried loose direct—and abbreviated—answers. Something was clearly occupying his mind, and racing to Bermuda wasn't it.

She couldn't really tell if the other two members of the crew, Otley and Paul Marsh, were more affected by the human or the atmospheric chill. They sat side by side, like a pair of ancient, wrinkled tortoises, silently mumbling their food and slugging down incredible quantities of bad wine. Otley, at least, made some effort to be convivial, but his idea of dinner conversation, a monologue on the side effects of seasickness (to which he was immune), had just trailed off with a couple of anecdotes that clearly unsettled Win.

In the uncomfortable silence that followed, Nico spoke up unexpectedly: "What about the watch bill, skipper?"

"And the berth assignments," old Otley added. "We've got four sea berths and five bodies."

"Oh, right," said Win. "I've got it all on a chart, in my briefcase."

"Why don't we move down below," Gillian put in. "I'll do the washing up while you talk, Win. Anyway, I'm freezing my tail off up here."

In the warm glow of a single low-wattage bulb, Kassandra's accommodation looked cozy and inviting—varnished bulkheads of some light-colored wood (Ash? Barr would've known) and a white-painted overhead made the cramped quarters seem more spacious than they were. The layout was basic, designed to serve equally for racing or cruising. Up forward, the V-shaped fo'c'sle was much like the one on *Glory*, with a pair of berths and lockers beneath them. For tonight, Otley and Paul would share that cabin, but once *Kassandra* was under way most of the space would be occupied by bagged sails, now heaped on the foredeck. Aft of the fo'c'sle was a narrow passage, with the unpleasantly claustrophobic toilet compartment to port and lockers for the crew's personal gear to starboard. The main cabin was about ten feet square, with six-foot headroom beneath the skylight (traces of old leaks around the frame, her trained eye saw), and contained folding upper and permanent lower berths on each side, with a rickety dining table blocking most of the narrow passageway between them. Win was seated on the starboard lower, his open attaché case next to him, while on the facing berth Nico, Otley, and Paul sat in a fidgeting row.

Gillian found herself obscurely unwilling either to join the class or sit next to the teacher, and positioned herself at the galley, which ran the width of the cabin's aft end. It was divided by the companionway ladder, so that the top-loading icebox and the too-small sink were to port and the grimy two-burner stove was to starboard. As in most galleys Gillian had seen, counter space for preparing food was minimal—apparently boat designers operated under the illusion that meals emerged fully formed from icebox or frying pan—and when Gillian had rinsed the five mugs there was scarcely room to set them out to dry. The lockers had seemed plentiful, until she discovered that two of the most convenient had been given over to a brand-new loran set and a VHF-FM transmitter, and the next she'd opened contained all six volumes of the familiar maroon-bound Sight Reduction Tables. The cooking utensils, when she finally tracked them down, had clearly been discarded from an apartment kitchen some years before, and the cups and dishes looked like the residue from a garage sale.

As Win, muttering under his breath, spread colored diagrams out on the dining table, she found herself wondering what Patrick would have said to a galley like this one, and without warning her memory produced an unexpected picture of him standing at *Glory*'s big four-burner stove, wreathed in garlic and radiating competence. If he was alive, she assured herself, Barr would get to him.

If he was alive . . .

"All right," said Win. "I think everything's here." He beamed uncertainly at the three men across from him. "Oh, would anyone like
a drink? Gillian, perhaps you'd do the honors."

"I'll take a greenie," said Otley.

"Me, too," Paul put in.

"Make it three, love," Nico added. "And Win, if you could scurry
along, I've got an errand to run ashore yet."

She handed the Heinekens across, watched the three sailors raise
their stubby green bottles in near-unison. Nico's swallow was the
longest, and he chased it with a slug from a pint he'd had in his
foul-weather jacket. An acrid trace of cheap brandy wafted across
the cabin, and the two old men eyed their colleague with silent,
doglike expectation, but he capped the bottle and stowed it back
in his jacket.

Win, pointedly not looking at his starboard watch captain, had
reshuffled his papers twice, and now at last he seemed ready to
begin. "I've decided to put Otley with Gillian, since they've sailed
together. That's port watch. And Paul and Nico will be starboard
watch, of course." He looked up from his list, as if ready for disagreement, but none came. "I'll be out of watches, since I'm navi-
gating as well as being skipper, but of course I'll be ready to take a
hand whenever necessary. The actual watch schedule, hour by hour,
is on these pages. Maybe I ought to explain—"

He proceeded to, at length, and followed his discussion with
another on the yacht's provisioning. Gillian would have thought it
impossible, but as Win's even, good-natured voice droned on, she
began to feel sleepy. Otley, she saw, actually *was* asleep, with his
mouth slightly open; Nico, sitting beside him, was twitching with
impatience. Following Gillian's eye, Win colored and brought his
speech to an awkward conclusion: "And that takes care of my part
of things, I think. Nico was at the navigators' meeting this afternoon,
but—"

"Why don't I do my number in the morning," Nico interrupted,
with a meaningful glare at the clock mounted on the forward
bulkhead.

"That's just what I was going to propose," Win agreed, sounding
just faintly huffy. "You had an errand you wanted to run ashore? I
hope it's not too late."

"So do I," Nico replied. "I'll take the dinghy and row in."

Gillian was a second slow on the uptake but recovered as Nico brushed by her on his way up the companion ladder. "If you want company, I'll spell you on the oars."

"What?" He looked not so much surprised as appalled. "No thanks, love," he added, with an unconvincing smile. Before she could press her offer, he was gone.

"I'm not a very good skipper, am I?" Win asked cheerfully. "A rhetorical question, by the way—I know the answer perfectly well."

"Briefing the crew isn't the whole of being a skipper," she said, choosing her words with care. They were sitting side by side at the forward end of the cockpit, wrapped in a single sleeping bag. Down below, Otley and Paul had grumbled their way to sleep, and the cabin lights were out. Gillian was aching with fatigue, but something told her that Win's invitation to share a glass of wine was important.

"Diplomatic as always." He passed the bottle (an elegant St. Emilion, light years beyond what they'd drunk at dinner) and she poured a little into the plastic cup she was holding. "I've had rather a lot on my plate in the past few months, beginning with Roger."

She had the feeling he needed encouragement, but in what form? "It must've hit you hard, his death. Hard on the magazine, too, of course."

"Of course."

Well, that didn't seem to be the right opening. She waited until he'd taken another sip of wine before trying again. "Those files of his are something else, though."

She thought he stiffened slightly, but it was hard to be sure through several layers of sleeping bag. "An unusual system, you mean?"

Here goes nothing. "Not half as unusual as TNF's funding," she said, keeping her voice casual. He was silent, waiting, and she had to go on. "The whole thing's supported by—what?—twenty-five big donors, at the most. The other income, from the pledge drives and the classifieds, is just eyewash."

"Not at all." It sounded to her like a pro forma objection. "The readers' pledges give them a sense of personal involvement in our work."

She nodded. "Saving civilization from itself."

"I said that the other night, didn't I." His familiar self-deprecating smile was almost audible. "I couldn't very well tell those men and women it's too late."

They were sliding away from the direction she wanted to go, but she had to give him a little more rein: "You don't mean the bomb, do you? Not anymore."

"The bomb's still there, just the same," he said reflectively, "but I was really thinking of a more whimpering finale to our . . . post-Roman decadence."

"Post-Roman?" This was a new theme.

"America—the West, if you prefer—has all the earmarks, surely: an aimless upper class obsessed by trivia, a hopeless lower class kept in check by bread and circuses, timid governments concerned only with staying in office. An utter failure of commitment, of vision, all along the line."

His calm certainty shook her. "You make it sound as if there's no changing things."

"There isn't. History is cyclical, and we happen to be living at the crumbling end of a particular civilization. Something's got to be preserved for those who will come, and that's *TNF*'s job. My job."

Again, she watched the phenomenon: Win had shed his diffidence like an old shirt; absolute conviction hardened his mild voice to steel. Survival, he explained, was the most important duty of those few who perceived what was going on. Survival, and providing a light of reason to guide the silent minority through what was sure to come. One couldn't, he told Gillian earnestly, tell the whole truth even to one's supporters; they weren't ready to accept it, even though in their hearts they recognized the irreversible decay. The best that could be done was unremitting attack against the worst barbarian excess, and sometimes it was necessary to make use of methods or allies one didn't like to acknowledge. . . . His voice trailed off. Gillian could just make out his defiant profile against the winking, glittering lights ashore.

This guy's here on a green card from Mars, she thought. Crazy as . . . as whatever you like.

"Megalomania or paranoia?" Win said evenly. "Maybe both? I don't blame you, Gillian. But before you close the books on me, just take a look at the front page of any metropolitan daily paper. A fresh, unprejudiced look. Ask yourself, is this the record of a civilized society? Children shot at random from passing cars, college athletic teams indicted for mass rape, two million people living on the streets of the world's richest nation—and that's just the surface. We have an immense educational system that doesn't educate, a federal Department of Housing that doesn't house. . . . I could go on indefinitely, but the most damning thing of all is that nobody cares—"

"Now, wait a minute," she interrupted, but he waved her silent.

"Quite right. I stand corrected: a few care. A few always have. Sometimes more than a few, as in the late eighteenth century, when the American Age began. It didn't last long, though—history moves a great deal faster than it once did. The positive part of our cycle really ended with the 1940s, though momentum and wealth carried us on another twenty years. But the wheel keeps turning, and the world will have to go through a long, bad stretch before the next dawn. If it ever comes."

She was just too tired to take apocalypse seriously. Even so, she wanted to keep him talking. "And in the meantime?" she asked.

"In the meantime we exercise what influence we can, but mostly we just—what's the phrase?—we hunker down and keep the faith. Like the lonely scholars during the Dark Ages. That's what *TNF* is all about, preserving the flame."

"Does Roger feel the same way as you?" she asked quickly.

She had thought to catch him off guard, but he picked her up: "*Does* Roger? You know my brother's dead, Gillian."

"Is he really?" she flung back. "You make him sound very alive, you and K.C. both." She gave him two long seconds to digest it and added, "It's none of my business, of course."

"You seem to be making it your business," he observed. "Why?"

"Because I care," she snapped. "Not about your keeper-of-the-flame stuff. About you, Win Huddleston."

"I see . . ." He sounded, she was relieved to hear, unfazed. She had the feeling he'd been told this before.

"And from what I can tell," she pressed on, "your brother and K.C. are ripping you off. There, I said it." She crossed her arms defiantly and turned her back on him. Her heart was pounding as she waited to hear his reply—not the words, but the music.

"You astonish me, Gillian."

But not a whole lot, she decided. "You must've had some idea how I felt," she said. "I thought you—"

"Oh, not that," he interrupted. "When did you decide Roger was . . . taking advantage of me?"

"Just in the last couple of days," she replied. "K.C. had me updating the business files, and I began adding things up. A lot more money comes into TNF than ever gets deposited in our account, and all of it's in those big donations."

"What exactly are you saying?" He sounded to Gillian almost supernaturally calm, but she sensed that he was weighing her every syllable.

"Well, it's not as if I was looking for trouble," she began. "God knows what an auditor would find, if someone like me stumbles over discrepancies—"

"Such as what?" he demanded quickly.

"Letters acknowledging donations of such-and-such an amount to the foundation, only when the money gets to the magazine's account it's shrunk by half. You're being skimmed blind, Win."

"It's a difficult position you put me in," he said slowly.

"Never mind me," she replied. "Think of the IRS."

"Oh, I have," he said. He sounded as exhausted as Gillian felt. "Believe me, I agonized for days, when I first found out."

Of course you knew, she thought, but the disillusion was no less sharp. "Roger?" she asked.

"Yes." He poured himself a nearly full cup and drank off half of it. "I might as well tell you the whole thing," he said, addressing the cup. "See if confession's as good for the soul as they say it is. When Roger came back from Vietnam, the magazine was dead on its feet. We'd opposed the war, naturally, and the FBI—Lyndon Johnson's private Gestapo—made things very difficult for us. Not just the phone taps and break-ins, but the insinuations to our suppliers and advertisers. . . . Anyway, donations were at a standstill, subscriptions were way down; we were still being read by absolutely everyone in Washington, but all of them were on the free list. Well, Roger pulled us out of bankruptcy. He was a certified Vietnam veteran, you see, so when he called on potential donors, they'd listen. Somehow, he talked enough of them around so we could go on." Win's voice, tense when he began, eased with the recollection of that hard-fought victory. Now, as he continued, the bitterness crept back.

"When the war ended, I thought our troubles had ended with it—and for a while they had. Every allegation we'd made was proved out; surely we'd be listened to in Washington, especially by a Democratic administration." He paused for so long she thought he'd forgotten her.

"But you weren't," she said quietly.

"In Washington everybody knows everything, and they hate nobody more than someone who's right when all of them are wrong." Gillian had the feeling he'd said it before, but never with more feeling. "And after Carter, the country went completely into what one of my colleagues calls the Me Mode. Oh, we have young, devoted readers—more of them than ever—but they're not the ones with money. The ones with money don't read. Or if they do, it's some one-syllable magazine about the peccadillos of television actors." He managed a twisted smile, but she could feel him shaking with anger. "*TNF* wouldn't have been the first worthy enterprise to be sunk by demographics. God, how I hate that word, and the meretricious thinking behind it."

She could see him struggling for control, and then he began again: "We needed donations more than ever. And the more we had to have, the more Roger produced. He'd really found himself, I thought. I didn't know how much he was getting for us, I was just grateful. But last year, just before the race to Bermuda, I found out he'd been . . . what was the word you used? Skimming. He'd been skimming, and so had K.C. But it was Roger who broke my heart."

Win's voice checked, and Gillian thought for one awful moment he was going to cry. "You see, he'd been such a mess when he came back from Vietnam. Oh, not physically. Spiritually: he was eaten by cynicism, didn't care about anything except getting . . . except women," he corrected himself primly. "Alcohol, drugs—I didn't know what to do. And then he came to work for *TNF* and just . . . turned around. Or so I thought."

"What was he doing with the money?" Gillian asked.

"Most of it went to the donors themselves," Win said. Sensing her question, he explained: "Kickbacks, I suppose you'd call it. Mr. X, the grantsman—what a wonderful term—the grantsman for the

Y Foundation, authorizes a contribution of, say, ten thousand dollars to *TNF*. Except that Mr. X has a private understanding with Roger that he gets anywhere up to half of it back, under the table."

So *that* was why they donated. Something for everybody: it answered everything. And a pretty shifty little scam, too. "What did you do?" she asked.

"I confronted him, of course, before my righteousness burned off. Told him I was going to break his scheme wide open." Win shook his head sadly. "I probably wouldn't have done it. But apparently he thought I would. He went on the race three days later, and when he disappeared, I thought he'd drowned. Thought he'd killed himself, to tell you the truth."

"Weren't there other people on Roger's boat?" Gillian asked. "His girlfriend, for one?"

"That dreary child, yes. And two others. They staged the whole thing. Sank the *Sea Horse*, with another boat standing by. Then it was off to South America for the lot of them."

"Roger told you that," she said.

"When he got in touch with me," Win agreed.

"So he's still running his racket, through K.C.?"

He nodded wearily. "I've known for two months. Roger wants to come home, you see. He can't be extradited from where he's been hiding, but he's afraid to reappear in the States. I've promised not to prosecute if he returns the money he took with him—*TNF*'s money. There's quite a lot of it left, he says."

I'll bet there is, she thought. "What happens to him then? And his accomplices?"

"I don't know, I just don't know. Of course I ought to go to the police—but will I? As for Roger . . . do you have any sisters or brothers?"

"No." The only child of a loveless marriage, she could barely remember her mother: the German girl who'd married a young American officer in the army of occupation and left him, and their infant daughter, the same day she'd received her final citizenship papers. Until her father's death, in a car accident three years before, Gillian had given that sweet-natured, impractical man a fierce devotion that never wavered. Maybe Win loved Roger the way she'd loved Pop; certainly she would've lied or cheated or stolen for him. Anyway, it wasn't her job to judge.

"Roger's why I'm sailing to Bermuda." The words went right past her before she realized what he'd said.

"*Roger?*" she gasped.

"He'll be there, with that stupid little paramour of his. He'll get in touch with me, and we'll settle things once and for all."

She was stunned. Win had to be told about Patrick. Maybe he could help—

Her tumbling thoughts were broken by the cushioned thump of *Kassandra's* dinghy against the side. Nico Butler scrambled awkwardly over the gunwale. Seeing Win, he snarled, "Dunno what's adrift, skip. I can't get through to the office. Bloody phone's out of order. I tried K.C., but the silly cow's not at home. We're really—" He pulled up short. "*Hel*-lo, love: Didn't see you there at first."

"The office?" Gillian said. "At this hour?"

Nico seemed to hesitate, then explained, "Night watchman. He's supposed to be on duty. Keep the niggers from stealing me blind."

"Nico, I've *asked* you not to—"

"That's what they bloody well are." He was drunker than when he'd left, Gillian realized, and he sounded ready for a fight. Win silently held his ground, though, and after a vibrating few seconds Nico mumbled, "Sorry, skip. Just a little pissed. Go below and sleep it off. G'night, love." He took a wide lurch toward the companionway, missed the first step, and only caught himself by a miracle of automatic coordination. As he disappeared down the hatch, Win turned to Gillian.

"The prototype rough diamond. He's really a good man, though. He owns a boat salvage yard in a really awful part of the Bronx, so he has some grounds for being prejudiced. Most of his crew are Hispanic, and they're far more bigoted than he is."

A salvage yard in the Bronx. She felt her stomach knot at the words. What had Patrick said the name of that place was? It didn't matter—there couldn't be two. "Has Nico sailed with you for long, Win?"

"Just this season, actually. But he knows the family, you might say. He was Roger's watch captain on the race last year."

• • •

Later, alone in the cockpit, she lay wrapped in the sleeping bag, her brain spinning in helpless circles. Above her, low clouds raced across the sky. She caught a momentary glimpse of the Big Dipper, and below its handle a single bright star that appeared and disappeared behind the wrack—Arcturus, she thought. Or is it Spica? What was the little jingle Barr had taught her? *Follow the arc to Arcturus and speed on to Spica.* Star light, star bright, first star I see tonight: I wish I may, I wish I might . . . oh, God, I wish you were here with me. She felt her throat close, pulled herself out of the sleeping bag and into a sitting position, her back against the cockpit coaming. You got yourself into this mess, she told herself angrily.

From just over her shoulder a voice whispered, "Are you Gillian?"

She whirled around, tangling herself in the bag and nearly rolling off the seat. "What?" she gasped. "Where are you?"

"Not so loud. I'm right here alongside." Now she saw him, the shadowy outline of a shaggy head above *Kassandra*'s gunwale. He must be standing in a small boat, she realized. "If you're Gillian, I've got a message for you."

"A message from who?" But the spurt of hope couldn't be suppressed. "It's Barr, isn't it?"

"He says your friend is home safe. If you want to run for it, I'll take you ashore now."

He's worked a miracle, she thought. No, two—first Patrick, and now a way out of this for me. I can get clear and it's okay. Except for Sarah.

"I don't want to hurry you . . ." he whispered.

"Sorry. Give me a second to think." But she didn't need even that; she knew the answer. "I have to stay. Tell Barr that. Tell him Sarah's going to be in Bermuda with Roger, and Win's supposed to meet—"

"Hey, hold on, sweetheart. I'm no answering machine."

"Sorry." She thought desperately, trying to boil it down. "Can you remember *Sarah's in Bermuda with Roger?*"

"I guess so. Sure."

That would give him the essence of it. "Tell Barr I'll look for him in Hamilton."

"Got it."

"And can you remember one more thing?"

"*Christ*, lady."

"It isn't complicated. I love him."

A ghostly chuckle. "Forgot to tell you: he said the same thing."

BARR:

SATURDAY MORNING,

EAST NORWALK

He replaced the microphone in its bracket and clicked off the VHF, conscious of nothing but relief flooding through his body. "She's all right so far," he said aloud, just to hear the words. He wanted to tell someone, but he could hear Farber snoring gently in the guest cabin just behind him, and Patrick was presumably still out cold up forward.

Turning off the light over *Glory's* chart table, Barr tiptoed into the main cabin. On the settee Patrick lay sprawled on his back, in exactly the same position Barr and Farber had left him six hours earlier. A navy blue blanket was pulled up to his chin, but his bare feet, caked with dried mud, protruded from the other end. He was unpleasantly gray under his tan, and Barr could see, as he bent over the sleeping figure, the purple stain of a bruise over his right ear.

The mark brought back to him the horror of the night before, the dreadful crawling figure coming out of the flames toward him. Right now it all seemed like something that had happened to another person, even though the strained muscles in his back and arms reminded him of the unsuspected strength pure fear could give a man. He had slept the mercifully numb sleep of total exhaustion, but he knew the fiery apparition of K. C. Carew would be waiting for him the next time he closed his eyes.

And Patrick: he'd gone through a hell of a lot more, had suffered physical damage—maybe mental, too—that Barr couldn't begin to assess. What was he going to be like when he woke up? Plenty of time to learn that later, he decided. Let the man rest; he's earned it. He stepped into the galley, careful to close the door quietly behind him, and made himself a cup of instant coffee, adding a shot of Gosling's to kill the awful taste. He wanted a cigarette, too, but Gillian and Patrick had long ago decreed that smoking was forbidden in the galley, and Barr, despite occasional public grumbling, had come to the private conclusion they were right. Going into the fo'c'sle, he pushed open the hatch above the V berths and balanced the steaming cup on its sill, then hauled himself up and out onto the foredeck.

Without conscious thought his eye panned across the anchorage; *Glory* lay exactly as he had intended her to, with L-shaped Copps Island about a hundred yards off the port side and, to starboard, the considerably larger bulk of Chimon, over which he could see the tall, red-and-white-striped stack of the Norwalk power plant, a mile away on the mainland. A sandspit connecting the two islands made a tidy cul-de-sac, sheltered as long as the wind blew from anywhere but the east, and in it *Glory* was quite invisible to anyone on the Connecticut shore who didn't know exactly where to look for her spars.

Barr lit his cigarette, tossed the match over the side, and scanned the sky. A little haze still lingered, but the southwesterly was already picking up; it would come in hard by noon. Up in Newport, they would be starting the first Bermuda-bound class about then. He had a vivid memory of wheeling, charging clusters of boats maneuvering for position near the high-legged Texas tower that marked the start; the final, breathless seconds as you squared off for the line; the curiously anticlimactic feeling after the gun, when you realized there were still six hundred and some miles of ocean ahead.

Gillian would be in the middle of all that confusion, all that blurred action—the perfect place for a staged accident. . . . No, you've already gone over that, he told himself. Whatever the others aboard Huddleston's boat are up to, they first have to get to Bermuda, and they don't want a lot of attention. Losing a crewmember would bring the Race Committee and reporters down on them like a flock of cormorants.

All of which was perfectly true, but it didn't fully convince him. He drained off the chilled coffee and flicked the stub of his Camel to leeward. His gaze was focused on the circular ripple where *Glory's* anchor rode entered the water, but the picture behind his eyes was of Ann, his dead wife, till now the only woman who'd been able to make him feel this unsettled, this off balance. It was odd she should come to mind, he reflected—he hadn't really thought about her in weeks, not since *Glory* had come north from the islands. He struck a match to light another cigarette, and part of him noticed as he cupped his hands around the flame that the breeze was making up even faster than he'd thought. Below the level of instinctive observation his mind was still preoccupied.

She'd been slender, like Gillian, with something of the same intense approach to life—but there the resemblances stopped, and even they were misleading. Every morning of Ann's life, she spent a solid hour (Barr had timed it) on her appearance, where Gillian might allow ten or fifteen minutes. To be fair, Ann's huge eyes, angled nose, and quirky mouth required careful highlighting, while Gillian was her same gamine self no matter what she did.

And where Gillian was driven by a need to excel everyone at everything, Ann had had a narrower focus: the pursuit of pleasure in all its forms. That was how she'd got Barr, by reawakening a sensuality he had suppressed for so long he'd forgotten it was there. In boarding school he had smoldered through a lonely puberty— smoldered without result, since he wasn't athletic or handsome or articulate (especially with girls)—until he mastered the passions that shamed him, turning his fiercely private love toward inanimate objects, particularly ones that floated.

Ann, who had perfect pitch for men, perceived that Barr's charter yacht was a substitute for something else, and when she guessed what that something was, her curiosity drove her to see if there was still a live coal under his cool surface. She'd found it, all right; nursed it back into flame; fanned it to incandescence, until Barr found himself living his own adolescent daydreams. He was the one who'd insisted on marriage, over her laughing protests, so he blamed no one but himself when her attention wandered to other men and newer sensations.

He remained obsessed by her, right until the very end, and he remembered perfectly the feeling of sick loss every time he saw her eyes light up for someone else, the bleak depressions that wrung him dry, the hopeless hope when she came back from another bed. He discovered that rum could dull his misery, though it didn't blunt his perception; as her search for yet-untasted thrills became more feverish, his need became more frequent, so that he'd spent the last three months of their life together in an alcoholic semihaze that he cringed at recalling.

And was he about to do it all over again? What was Gillian like, really? He'd spent most of the past year within a few feet of her but, as he now realized, he'd been carefully looking past her the whole time. Patrick knew her, and had responded. So why hadn't she fallen for him? Every other woman seemed to. Or for Win Huddleston? Clearly, she was attracted by him. Instead, she'd elected Jeremy Barr. He shook his head, apprehensive and at the same time strangely elated.

The sun was well up, he saw, and Mrs. Mulvey would be in Carey & Willard's office by now. She kept the VHF radio on her desk going all day, scanning automatically across the frequencies in her insatiable hunger for everybody else's secrets. It might be worth giving her a call on Channel 9 to see if any strangers had been poking about, asking questions. Anyway, he was too restless to sit on deck doing nothing.

He started back along the side deck and saw it lying there, just inside the gunwale—a big, fat, brightly colored envelope addressed to *J. Barr, c/o Carey & Willard*, in a galloping parody of Gillian's printing. He bent down and picked it up—through the padding it felt like a book, but heavier—saw the note taped to the label: *Recd. 4:45 P.M. Fri. H. Mulvey*. It must've been there when he and Sol Farber dragged Patrick aboard. No real wonder they hadn't noticed it in the dark; the only surprise was that neither of them had stepped on it in the process of getting *Glory* out to the anchorage.

Dispatched from midtown Manhattan early yesterday afternoon, according to the label. She must have managed to sneak away from the office, just before leaving for Newport, so whatever was in here had to be important. He bore his prize below and slit the packet open, spilling a mass of peanut-shaped bits of foamed plastic across the chart table and onto the deck below. Cursing under his breath, he scooped them into a heap to one side and pulled from the envelope a rectangular plastic box, about nine inches by twelve and two inches thick, with a typewriter keyboard occupying most of its face and a narrow screen the rest. Something electronic, he thought, turning the case over in his hands. Battery-powered. But what's it supposed to do? His bone-deep contempt for miraculous gadgets that whirred and flashed was based partly on experience, partly on innate conservatism, and mostly (as he freely admitted) on ignorance. He was pushed by a need to turn the damned thing on, held back by the fear of damaging it somehow.

"Hey! Anybody there?" It was Patrick's voice, weak but coherent. Relief flooded Barr as he entered the main cabin and saw that *Glory's* mate had pulled himself into a sitting position on the settee. The blanket, fallen into his lap, bared the washboard muscles of his belly, streaked with ugly purple bruises. His face—anxious, slightly dazed—broke into a broad grin as he saw Barr, then twisted in pain. "God *damn*, that hurts," he said, touching his fingertips to his temple.

Realizing he still held the plastic box, Barr set it down on the cabin table and bent forward over Patrick. The biting smells of sweat and fire clung to his skin, and a three-day blond beard fuzzed his jaw. Beneath his close-cropped hair his right temple was ugly and swollen. His eyes were streaked with red, but his pupils looked normal. "About time you woke up," Barr said. "What hurts besides your head?"

"Everything," Patrick replied. He shifted slightly, winced. His right hand went to his groin, and his eyes met Barr's. "It'll be okay," he said quickly.

"Sure. How about something to eat?"

"That'd be great. I'll—" He made as if to rise, fell back with a groan. "I guess I won't."

"Don't be a bigger fool than you can help," Barr said. "What can I get you?"

He watched silently as Patrick wiped up the last of his egg with a piece of bread. "Everything okay?" he asked.

"I never had an egg like that before," Patrick replied, chewing. "How'd you manage to burn the white and leave the yolk raw? And

I hope you remembered to put the lid on when you fried the bacon—
I'm sure not going to clean bacon grease off the goddamn overhead . . ."

"Glad you're feeling better," said Barr. "More coffee?"

"I haven't had any yet, unless you count that black syrup." And
then: "Is she all right?"

"As of midnight. I had a friend go by Huddleston's boat," he
explained. "She sent you her best."

"Did she? That was nice." Patrick shifted again. When he spoke
again, his tone was remote, detached, as if he were talking about
strangers in some far-off time: "There was a Frenchman served with
me in Chad, in old General Hals's private army. He'd been in Algeria,
during their civil war . . ." Barr watched him narrowly, wondering
what was coming; aboard *Glory*, Patrick's year and a half as a mer-
cenary soldier was a topic with off-limits signs all over it.

"And?" Barr prompted, when the silence had stretched out for
several minutes.

"Nothing." But the muscles along the line of Patrick's jaw were
set like cable. When he burst out he spoke loud and fast, staring
fixedly at the tabletop: "The French used to do that to the rebels
they captured. Like what they did to me, with wires. Afterwards,
sometimes, the Algerians weren't able to—you know—do it anymore." The sweat was running down Patrick's face, and his whole
torso was gleaming with it.

"Oh." Barr wanted desperately to say something supportive, something even remotely intelligent, but the expression on the big young
man's face stopped him cold.

Patrick looked up at him and forced a painful imitation of a smile.
"There's a lot of women would say it serves me right, I guess."

Barr waited, sensing that overt sympathy was the only totally
wrong reaction. After a few seconds, Patrick continued, sounding
faintly surprised. "Don't know why I laid that on you. I just had to
tell somebody."

"Better you did," Barr replied. He could feel the tension inside
the mate beginning to slacken.

"Say, what's that thing on the table?" said Patrick, as if the conversation had never happened. "Looks like a laptop computer."

That was its name, of course. She'd used that very term. "I guess it is. Gillian had it sent here by messenger, just before she went up to Newport."

"Well, hell, man—what're we waiting for?" Patrick demanded. "Let's crank it up and see what's inside."

Relief lifted Barr's heart, but he took care not to let it show. "I'll leave that for you," he said. "But not till we get you cleaned up. You smell like a goat."

PATRICK:
SATURDAY NOON,
EAST NORWALK

"Maybe we could call the manufacturer," Barr offered. "Get an owner's manual for this thing."

Patrick, who had been examining the keyboard, looked up in surprise. "What for? It's pretty simple—I bet we can figure it out."

"That's what you say now," put in Farber, who had emerged, blurry-eyed and bedraggled, from the guest cabin. "All I know from these things is you press one wrong button and everything inside goes to the twilight zone. Forever."

"Watch," said Patrick, with more confidence than he felt. He switched the little computer into life. To his relief, the menu came up on the eight-line screen immediately. It contained seven items, but one, labeled BARR, caught his eye immediately.

"Look," Farber whispered. "It knows you already."

Ignoring him, Patrick moved the cursor to highlight the name and tapped *Enter*.

THIS IN HASTE, the screen read. THREE OTHER FILES IN HERE ARE FROM THE TAPE I FOUND. SOME KIND OF CODE WHICH YOU WILL HAVE TO BREAK. HINT: EASTER EGG ONE OF THE $$ MEN AT UTOPIA PKWAY PARTY. ORIG TAPE TO YOU C/O GEN DEL AT BELDEN AVE P.O. NORWALK. STASH IT SAFE. I LOVE YOU.

"Well," said Barr, in a strained voice Patrick hadn't heard him use before. "That's something."

"Sure it is, but what?" asked Farber.

"Maybe we better look at those files," Patrick said, sounding to himself hostile and cold. *So she loves him—I already knew it. Why does seeing it written, even on a computer screen, make a difference? And what's it to me, after last night?* Barr was watching him with an anxious look in his eyes, and Patrick decided he really didn't need that, on top of the rest. After two impatient false starts, he got himself out of the file named BARR and back to the menu. Moving the cursor over LAST, he keyed *Enter* again.

"Open sesame," Barr said quietly.

They started with the coded names, listing them in a column on a piece of scratch paper torn from *Glory's* deck log. *Easter Egg* was Gillian's gift to them, and now that Patrick was reminded of it, he recalled the smooth-talking, oval-shaped man who didn't want the prisoner marked up too soon.

"What name did they call him by?" Barr insisted.

"They didn't say his name. Just *sir* once," Patrick answered shortly, unwilling to force his memory further back into that swirling pit. "I had other things on my mind."

"But if you ever saw him again—" Farber began.

"Face or voice, I won't forget," Patrick assured him. "Anyhow, we can track him down: like Gillian said, he's with some foundation or corporation that gives money to *The New Federalist*."

Barr made a note of it, and they turned to the next name, *Lamprey*. "That's some kind of eel, right?" said Patrick. "Maybe it means the guy looks like an eel." But no eel-shaped or -faced man came to mind, so they moved on.

Horn was even less suggestive, until Farber said, "Look, what are these names for? Why did this Roger make them up?"

"To hide the real people's identities," Barr answered, forced patience clear in his tone.

"And what else?" Farber asked.

"I don't see—"

Patrick did: "To help him and K.C. remember who they were."

"By—what's the word? Association," Farber agreed, nodding vigorously. "So it could be anything that would connect this person in their minds, not just how they look."

"Sure. But how does that help us with Lamprey? or Horn?" Barr asked.

In the silence, Patrick could hear the gulls on Chimon Island tuning up for their morning concert. Suddenly, Farber's face lit up. "Beep," he said.

It took Patrick a moment to get the connection. "Horn equals Beep, okay," he said. "But what does Beep mean?" His question ended up in a half-gasp of pain, as he shifted his body to face Farber.

"If you read New York newspapers you'd know," the old man said. "*Beep* you see a lot in the headlines, like 'Beep Nixes Cop Raise.' It means *borough president*."

"Broadway Rose Sadowa," Patrick whispered. She had stood above him, the frog-faced old bitch, looking him over like dead meat in a butcher shop. But as he remembered, an idea came to him: "We're going at this backward. Let's write down the names of the people we know are in this, and match them to the code." In a matter of minutes, Patrick himself had worked from *Missouri* to *Kansas City* to *K.C.*; Farber capped it with *Queens–Utopia Parkway–Frannie X*. And there they stalled.

"We just don't know enough of the real names," Barr said, sitting back with a sigh.

"I bet if we had the guest list of that fund-raiser we could work out half a dozen more," Patrick replied. "Anyhow, it doesn't matter: we've got an idea of the kind of people on this list. Now we need to know what these numbers mean."

"I think I can tell you," Barr said slowly. "Can you go back to the beginning of that Lamprey file?"

Obediently, Patrick punched up the first screen:

Lamprey
2 @ 150

7/15	rec 1st 150.	
7/24	.100	1.9
8/5	.050	1.85
8/15	.050	1.8
8/30	.075	1.725

"Mr. Farber, you're a businessman," Barr said. "What does that look like to you?"

"Accounts, sure," Farber nodded. He bent forward quickly and considered the numbers. "So maybe I see," he murmured. "Can I look at the next part, please?" And after a moment's inspection, "More." At last he straightened up. "Okay," he said. "Here's how I think it goes: This Mr. Lamprey, whoever he is, starts in July with two of something."

"Which he paid one-fifty apiece for," Barr agreed.

"No," Farber corrected him. "One-fifty apiece was the *price*. He only *paid* half down, on July fifteenth. Not till December he pays the second hundred and fifty."

Suddenly it made sense to Patrick, and he jumped in: "We're looking at it backward again. This is Roger's record, or K.C.'s— right? Now, like Mr. Farber said, this Lamprey bought two whatevers, for one-fifty each, and paid half down. But he didn't collect what he bought. He . . ."

While he was still groping for the word, Farber supplied it: "Banked it. With Roger Huddleston, or the woman K.C. maybe."

"Right!" Patrick exclaimed, his pain momentarily forgotten. "They hold it, and Lamprey draws against it. Look at how the numbers go: Starting with two, he withdraws .10 on July twenty-fourth, which leaves 1.9; then he takes .05 on August fifth, and sure enough his account's down to 1.85; and so on right to zero. Hell, to less than zero: he finishes with a whatd'youcallit—"

"Deficit—"

"—a deficit of .08, just a little short of a year after his account begins." Patrick looked from one of them to the other for agreement.

"That explains it, no question," said Farber. "Only it leaves a little gap."

"I know," Patrick admitted. "Why all this trouble for a lousy three hundred dollars?"

"Try three hundred thousand," Barr offered quietly. "And that's just one account. There are—what?—"

"Twenty, twenty-five more," Patrick put in. "Some smaller, but mostly bigger."

"Which means, of course, that the *what* we're talking about is drugs," Barr said. "I'm a little out of touch, but a hundred and fifty thousand dollars sounds to me like a pretty reasonable cost for a kilo of cocaine."

Patrick had never been able to figure *Glory*'s skipper completely, but dope smuggling? It didn't fit what he knew of Barr at all. To judge by the look on Farber's face, he was just as surprised: "What exactly do you mean by *out of touch*, please?" the old man asked, eyes narrowed.

One corner of the skipper's wide, thin-lipped mouth curled up. "Not what you're thinking, Mr. Farber. But if you were in the boat business in South Florida in the last ten years, you got to know something about the drug business, whether you wanted to or not."

That was it, sure, Patrick thought: Barr had run a repair yard in Lauderdale, before he'd gone to the islands with his own charter boat. But there was more to it—Barr was maybe the world's worst liar, and when he wouldn't meet your eye while he was talking, it always meant he wasn't telling the truth, or at least was leaving something out.

"To tell you the truth," Barr continued, still addressing the framed painting of *Glory* on the bulkhead, "I figured last night it was probably coke, and what's on the computer just confirms it. The whole thing fits, you see: a big, obviously illegal operation that doesn't stop at violence, but involves a lot of respectable people—men and women who don't think of themselves as criminals." His quick half-smile came and went again. "I'm not saying respectable people are especially honest, but the things they do—stock fraud, tax cheating, that kind of stuff—don't involve putting some guy in a barrel and dropping him in Long Island Sound."

Some guy, hell, Patrick thought: that was supposed to be me. "These people are buying drugs," he said, working it out as he spoke. "And doing it with somebody else's money, right?"

"Tax-free contributions that are supposed to be supporting *The New Federalist*," Barr agreed. "The contributors pay in advance, and the coke is held for them. Dispensed on demand, it looks like, a few grams at a time. Some of the cash does go to the magazine, but a lot of it probably goes for overhead and to buy the cocaine."

"So if we're talking about money, what does it come to in dollars?" Farber asked. "Read me off those figures, Patrick." Five minutes later he looked up from the sheet on which he'd been scribbling. "Twenty-seven names, and if you're right about these other numbers, Captain Barr, it adds up to eighty-two kilograms of cocaine. Times a hundred and fifty thousand, is twelve million dollars." He pursed his lips respectfully. "I guess maybe those new federals are better business-men than I thought."

"It doesn't sound real big time," said Patrick, feeling disappointed and not knowing why. "I mean, you read in the papers about these busts where the cops pick off drugs worth two, three times as much."

"What they put in the paper are street prices," Barr explained. "Makes a better story. I don't know what the prices are now, but a couple of years back a Florida wholesaler could buy his cocaine from South America at forty thousand a kilo, delivered. By the time it was cut and recut and sold in downtown Miami, the same kilo was going for ten times as much."

"So Roger Huddleston's ripping these people off," Patrick said. "Making a two-hundred-percent profit on them."

"Depends on how you look at it," Barr replied. "They're getting their highs for less than half what they'd have to pay elsewhere, and they can score without cash anytime they need to. Plus they don't have to take a chance by hiding large amounts themselves."

"I guess the stuff must be stored at that Hutchinson River Boat-works," Patrick mused. "Christ, you don't think we burned up a few kilos last night, do you?"

"If these numbers are right," Barr said, "there wasn't anything left to burn—the cupboard's just about bare."

"You think they're going out of business?" Farber asked. "Because this Roger isn't around anymore?"

"Druggies don't go out of business," Barr replied firmly. "Not ever. That list we've been looking at is called LAST—from the dates, it covers last year till now. Wasn't there another entry named THIS, Patrick?"

"You got it." He pulled the computer back to him and summoned up the document. As the screen filled, Barr and Farber crowded in on either side. "Lamprey's still a player," Patrick remarked after a moment's inspection. "Half a kilo more than last year."

"And the price goes up a little, too," Farber agreed. "What's this last line? He has to make a fifty-percent deposit?"

"To finance Roger's wholesale buy," said Barr. "In this business it's strictly C.O.D. No cash, no coke."

"But look at the next one, my buddy Easter Egg," Patrick pointed out. "He gets the same price as last year, and he doesn't have to put anything down."

"Probably because he's on the steering committee, or whatever they call it," Barr said. "Special insider rate."

"It's all orders and no deliveries," Farber said, looking puzzled.

"If I'm right, that's because their ship hasn't come in yet," Barr replied, and seeing Farber's puzzled frown added, "Delivery's not been made. Let's see the last file."

Patrick slid the cursor over SFGB and tapped *Enter*. Another list, he thought, but what the hell does it mean?

> Possibles:
> Bounty
> Challenger
> Invicta
> Robb 35
> Lion
> Reliant
> Offshore 40

From the corner of his eye he could see that Farber was as mystified as he. Barr's lean, angular face was a study in concentration and then, as Patrick watched, a smile began to reshape it.

"What is it?" Farber demanded, but Barr shook him off, addressing Patrick.

"Is there more?" The next screen appeared, even more cryptic than the first:

> Vanguard
> Triton
> A 35
> A 37
> Tartan
> Seafarer 30

Patrick looked up from the keyboard into Barr's pale blue eyes. "You see how it works?" said *Glory's* skipper triumphantly. "All old fiberglass production boats, and every one of them was available as a sloop *or* a yawl."

One mast or two, and the small one, the mizzen, behind the rudder post: so what? Patrick thought. Roger Huddleston's *Sea Horse* had been like that, he now recalled; when she'd sunk she'd been a sloop, but she sailed the race with a mizzen. He felt as if his brain were running in circles, with the answer just beyond his reach. Barr was still looking at him expectantly, like a teacher waiting for his pupil to come up with the answer. "Sorry," Patrick said at last, shaking his head. "I just don't get it."

"Well, maybe you haven't had my . . . advantages," Barr said. "I'll start at the beginning."

"Wait for a minute and I'll get us all some coffee, if you show me which way is the kitchen," Farber said.

Patrick could put up with Barr rooting about in the galley, but the idea of a stranger loose in his private preserve was too much. "I'll take care of it," he said, and slid out from behind the table. He managed to get to his feet, but as he straightened he felt as if daggers were being thrust into his groin. Barr caught him just in time and eased him back to the seat.

"What's the matter?" Farber asked Barr anxiously, over Patrick's head. "You never told me what they did to him in that place."

"Torn muscles," Barr replied, in a tone that cut off further questions. "You two sit here, and I'll take care of coffee—there's a chart I have to get anyway."

It was, in fact, a chart catalogue that Barr returned with, with a page that showed an outline of the Western Hemisphere in silhouette. "South America," Barr began, putting his palm on it. "Where the drugs come from. In the last couple of years, the favored route's been overland, up through Mexico and into Southern California, but a lot still arrives by water. It's shipped mostly from here, Venezuela and Colombia, in small freighters or trawlers or even sailing vessels. Bigger ships come straight north; smaller ones follow the line of the Antilles right up through the Bahamas and across the Gulf Stream. Land the stuff in the Everglades or West Palm Beach—

or sail right up the Miami River. Trouble is, the Coast Guard patrols the Florida coast, and they've plugged a lot of the gaps—the main passages between the islands, like Mona and the Windward . . ."

"And Anegada," Patrick put in.

"Anegada, too," Barr agreed. "If the Coasties don't pick off the drug boats down here in the Virgins, they have another swing at 'em in the nearer Bahamas or crossing the Stream. They get a lot of the marijuana shippers, because pot moves by the ton, mostly in slow freighters; but cocaine travels by the kilo, and most of the coke smugglers still make it through. Even so, there's a good deal of risk, which is why so much of the traffic's shifted to the land route, where you can buy the local cops at wholesale rates, right up to the Rio Grande. The Mexican route is fine if your customers are in Los Angeles, but what if they're in the Northeast?"

"Why not drive the boat to New York, straight from Venezuela?" asked Farber. "I don't see anything in the way."

"There isn't," Barr replied. "But that's not necessarily good news. A boat carries a big load, but it moves very, very slowly. The Coast Guard's got a lot of time to spot it from the air between, say, Venezuela and Bermuda. Then, when it approaches the American coast, they can board it with no trouble."

Bermuda. The name cut through Patrick's residue of pain. He looked up from the chart, where Barr's fingertip rested on the island. "Stop at Bermuda and change the cargo to a different boat," he offered.

"Almost but not quite," Barr replied. "Landing drugs in Bermuda itself is out. The place is too small, too compact. Word's bound to get around, and the Bermuda police get very tense about drugs." His wry smile flashed and vanished. "As witness what happened to me."

"Then what—" Farber began, sounding annoyed, but Patrick rode it down.

"Change the boat," he said. "Make it look different." And, triumphantly, "Add a mast and make it a yawl."

"Bingo," said Barr. "Even better than that, unless I miss my guess."

"So tell it straight already," Farber protested. "For a guy like me that doesn't know a yawl from a shawl."

Barr's eyes were sparkling, and he seemed to be holding himself in check with an effort. "Start by buying two secondhand sailboats," he said. "Two production—" he caught himself, grinned, and went on, tapping the table to accent the syllables: "Two stock fiberglass boats: S-F-G-B, get it? They're the same model, they look like twins. Hell, for all intents and purposes, they *are* twins, except that one's a yawl and one's a sloop. Let's say you ship the sloop by freighter down to Maracaibo or La Guaira. A fiberglass shop down there takes the deck off, pulls out the interior molding, if there is one. . . ."

"You lost me," Farber said. "Explain to me about this interior mold."

"Fiberglass boats are basically very simple," Barr said. "Two connected parts, really—the hull and the topsides, just like a big Tootsietoy. Most boats have another molding, a complicated plastic shape that forms most of the interior. You drop it in the hull, put the deck on, and there you are. But between this interior molding and the hull is a lot of waste space, most of it in little chunks—odd shapes that aren't worth bothering with, so they stay empty forever."

"Unless you fill them with bags of coke," Patrick put in.

"Right. And because cocaine is powder, the bags can be formed to fit almost any little nook or cranny. Then you drop the interior back in, seal the deck down over it, and you're all set. The boat weighs a couple hundred pounds more than it did originally, but an older fiberglass hull can absorb that much weight in seawater over a few years."

"And nobody can tell what you did?" Farber asked. "Aren't there marks to show what happened?"

"If there are, you spray-paint the interior," Barr replied. "Use a coating like Awlgrip, it'll look as good as new. Maybe better. Anyway, we've got our drug-filled sloop down there in Colombia, and she sails north by herself, toward Bermuda. Maybe she's spotted, maybe not, but the Coast Guard just doesn't have a big enough fleet to divert a cutter three or four hundred miles from her normal beat to check out one sailboat in midocean. What they'd do is mark down her description, course, and speed; set her aside to pick off later, when she closes the coast, where the Coasties have a tight cordon.

"About the same time," he continued, "the drug boat's sister ship, the yawl, sails down to Bermuda. The first couple of times Roger may have gone alone, but then he hit on using a racing fleet as cover. It's a great idea: you're talking about a hundred or a hundred and fifty racers, and they arrive in bunches. Bermuda Customs has to turn themselves inside out to process all the incoming boats. The radar station that guards the Bermuda approaches must be seeing blips all over the screen—no way they can pick out one particular boat sailing along in the fleet."

"Where's the drug boat, when all this is happening?" asked Patrick.

"Still a couple of hundred miles out, I expect. They've timed their arrival off Bermuda for when the racers begin to head back to New England, a few days after the finish. The drug boat and the sister ship make a rendezvous—set it up by radio, probably. If I were doing it, I'd meet at night just beyond the range of Bermuda Harbour radar. Off comes the yawl's mizzen, and onto the sloop it goes."

Patrick could visualize the boats, lashed together, rolling in the darkness as the crews worked feverishly. "You could rig a mast under conditions like that?" he asked. "What if it was stormy?"

"If you know what you're doing, it shouldn't be hard. It's only a mizzen, after all. Singlehanders who've lost a mainmast manage to set up jury rigs out at sea. No reason a trained crew couldn't do this kind of job in an hour or so, and tune the rig later." Barr shook his head in what seemed like admiration. "What else? Swap crews and registration papers. Switch nameboards and sails—they've got the racing yacht's numbers on them. Racers carry those same numbers on weather cloths lashed to the lifelines, so you'd change those, too. . . ."

"But it's the masts that really make the difference," Patrick broke in. "The Coast Guard might be watching for a single-masted thirty-five-footer, and the same boat with two masts would sail right past them, or just get a quick once-over. Nobody expects a sailboat to sprout another mast all of a sudden."

"It's even better than that—from the smugglers' point of view," Barr said. "The boat that isn't carrying drugs now becomes a decoy. The Coasties pounce on her, and what do they find? Nothing."

"So that's what happened to *Sea Horse*'s mizzenmast," said Patrick slowly. "They pulled it off her and put it on the other boat."

"Right," Barr agreed. "And the mainsail and boom that were shoved down *Sea Horse*'s companionway: they came from the drug boat— different sail numbers, probably, and the boom'd be too long, now she was going to be a yawl."

"But why'd they sink the real *Sea Horse*?" Patrick wondered aloud. "Didn't you say she was supposed to be their decoy?"

"I don't know for sure," Barr replied. "But I'd guess it had something to do with Roger being sick. Or maybe—"

"Never mind the boat that sunk," Farber interrupted. "Tell me about the boat with the cocaine inside. What happens next to it?"

"Next? The drug boat sails up to the Hutchinson River Boat Works. They haul her—"

"And out come the chain saws," Patrick interrupted excitedly. "In a couple of hours she's sliced open like a Christmas turkey. They take out the coke, chop the boat up fine, and toss the pieces of fiberglass onto that big heap out front. For landfill."

"You mean they destroy this . . . this whole yacht?" Farber sounded dazed. "Just chop it up?"

"For these guys it's not a yacht," Patrick explained. "It's a no-deposit no-return container." He turned to Barr, who was looking pained. "What's it cost, fifty thousand to scrap the boat?"

"More or less," Barr said. "But you're right: down in Florida the drug runners buy brand-new Cigarette boats and Magnums and sink 'em after one run. Cost of doing business."

Farber was watching Barr narrowly. "You never, yourself . . ." He shook his head. "Forget I asked. It's not my business."

"No, it's not," Barr said, with a tight, humorless smile. "If it makes any difference, I've never smuggled anything more valuable than a case of rum."

Patrick felt drained, but the prospect of action kept him upright on the settee. "So who do we call—the cops or the Coast Guard?"

Barr glanced at Farber before replying. "Neither."

"What?" Patrick was stunned. "We've got all this evidence . . ."

"Evidence to us, guesswork to anyone else," Barr said. "Even if they listen to us, what are we going to tell them?"

Patrick knew Barr was boxing him in, but he couldn't see how. "Track *Kassandra*," he offered cautiously. "Follow her when she leaves Bermuda. Look for a single-masted twin coming up from the south. Hell, she fits that profile you dreamed up: she's a yawl, isn't she?"

"A yawl, true," Barr agreed. "But she's not fiberglass." He paused, watching Patrick to see if he got it.

Not fiberglass: no inner shell, no blind compartments . . . "Then maybe the coke's in her tanks," Patrick said quickly. "Water and fuel,

must come to a hundred gallons all told." He could see from Barr's
face that he had an answer to that one.

"It's been done, over and over," Barr said. "First place the boarding
team looks is the tanks."

"Then where's he got it stashed?"

"Maybe he doesn't," Barr said. "That's my point: Win Huddleston
might not be in on his brother's racket, but Gillian's sure he can
lead us to Roger. And she just found out that Roger's with Sarah."

"And what about Gillian?" Patrick demanded, pointedly not adding
"the woman who loves you."

Barr might have heard the thought, because he turned two shades
redder under his mahogany tan. It was Farber who spoke up: "Patrick,
you should remember who's on the other side of this. Like I told
Captain Barr last night, if anybody gets arrested it's going to be him,
for killing that woman. And maybe you're an accessory."

"*Accessory?*" Patrick exploded. "I was fucking kidnapped!"

"That's what you say," Farber observed calmly. "The police listen
to the person who pays their salary."

Broadway Rose Sadowa. And those other, shadowy guys—Easter
Egg, Lamprey, and the rest—with all that money behind them.
Patrick's head was spinning. "But not the Coast Guard? Or Customs.
They're always bagging druggies on the TV."

"You ever been boarded by Customs?" Barr snapped. "I have:
goddamn storm troopers in cowboy boots, not a brain in a boatload.
If you want to see Gillian and Sarah hurt—maybe killed—calling
in those suckers is a great way to do it." He drew in an unsteady
breath, seemingly abashed by his own anger. "As for the Coasties—"

"Captain Barr, pardon me," Farber interrupted. "I'm not paying
you to break up drug rings, I'm paying to get my Sarah back. Alive
and free. I'd make a deal with a dozen Rogers, to keep Sarah from
spending the rest of her life in jail."

"But why should she go to jail at all?" Patrick asked.

Farber shrugged. "She's with that Huddleston, what can I tell you?
Look, you're a young man, I'm an old one, you take my word for
it. You get Sarah out of this mess first, then you play cops and
robbers all you want."

"I don't understand you guys," Patrick snapped. "This isn't like busting up the neighborhood crap game: these people are major criminals. They worked me over for two days, tried to kill me—you, too, Barr—and you don't seem to care."

"What I'm saying," Barr began patiently, "*all* I'm saying is there isn't anybody we can go to. Not anybody we can really trust."

"I still say the Coasties—" Patrick interrupted, but Barr was shaking his head.

"We don't dare. Look, I know your buddy Evans is okay, and we owe a lot to Susan Grover, but what about the people who boss them?"

"Christ, you don't think the U.S. Coast Guard . . ."

"I don't know," Barr said. "And neither do you."

"One wrong word," Farber put in from Patrick's other side. "Just one, that's all it takes."

He was disgusted with them both, but just too tired to fight anymore. "All right. So what *do* we do?" he demanded.

"There'll be something," Barr replied. "There's got to be."

Dawn found *Kassandra* punching through ugly little seas, rank after rank of whitecapped iron-gray sawteeth that marched up from the south. For most of the night, heavy rain had hammered on the cabin top and drummed hollowly on the bottom of the upturned dinghy over the skylight; as the rain slackened the wind rose, until it was whipping dollops of spray off the wavetops. Pretty soon, Gillian was thinking, they'd have to reduce sail again.

She was half crouched at the forward end of the cockpit, on the lee side where she could watch the jib while trimming its sheet. Otley, oilskinned to the eyes, was at the long tiller, his heels braced on the edge of the leeward cockpit seat. Though Gillian's attention was fixed on the curve of the jib, she was somehow aware of Otley's constant, delicate alterations of course that worked the yawl through the seas; she knew he was watching the mainsail's curve, reading the wave patterns, sensing the hull's movement—and at the same time attuned to the driving force from the number two genoa under Gillian's control. Over the past four hours the two of them had arrived at a nearly perfect coordination of effort, all the more satisfying for being unspoken.

When Win's face appeared in the narrow rectangle of the companion hatchway it was a jarring intrusion, and she felt Otley's concentration snap. Win looked drawn and tired, his smile forced. "You two doing all right?" he asked.

A silly question—couldn't he see? "Fine," she said. "What's it like down below?"

"Pretty damp, I'm afraid. A lot of water seems to be getting under the dinghy, leaking through the skylight."

That was just spray; if the wind kept building *Kassandra* would soon be taking regular seas over her low bow—seas that would sluice over the deckhouse and really soak down the interior. But there was no point in saying so. "You want to try for a sight? The sun comes and goes, but you can see it through the cloud cover."

Win's gaze went past her to the cresting waves. "I don't think so," he replied dubiously. "Besides, the loran's working fine."

She didn't have to be able to see Otley to sense his disapproval. And she agreed. Barr would've been on deck well before dawn, sextant in hand, on the merest chance of picking off Venus or a late star—and he would've done it, too. But that wasn't fair to Win, who spent eleven months of the year behind a desk. "What kind of speed've we been making?"

"Speed?" He looked surprised at her question. "I thought I'd plot a position after breakfast."

This time she heard a distinct growl from Otley, but before he could say anything another voice spoke from inside the cabin: "New watch coming up."

Win withdrew, and the hatch slid open. Nico Butler was first out. His quick comprehensive survey—sails, sky, horizon—reminded her of Barr, but his gleaming white foul-weather gear made him look even chunkier than he normally did. He slid past Otley and sat next to him, wedging his legs under the tiller and resting one hand lightly on the gently curving piece of laminated wood. Paul Marsh emerged more slowly, moving carefully, feeling for handholds. He lowered himself into the cockpit well at Gillian's feet, eyeing the white water that foamed past the lee gunwale, a foot or two from his nose. After a long moment he glanced up at Win, who had reappeared in the hatchway. "Too much sail," he said.

Win looked the question to Nico, who had imperceptibly edged Otley forward and was now steering the boat. The New Zealander, lips pursed, considered and shook his head. "No weather helm," he said. "None at all."

"Heeling too much," Marsh objected, and Otley chimed in, "I was just thinking something like that."

"How do you feel, Gillian?" Win asked.

What is this, a vote? she was thinking, when *Kassandra* put her spoon bow into the shoulder of a wave, shoveling half of it along the lee side deck and over the cabin top. Win emitted a startled avian squawk as a quart of North Atlantic sluiced down the back of his neck. She felt the boat shake free and rise, remembered how Barr always seemed to be able to pull an extra half-knot out of *Glory* just by getting the lee rail up out of the water. "The wind's still making," she offered diplomatically.

"Oh, all right," Nico said. "Somebody want to get the mizzen off her?"

"Working jib," Marsh snapped.

"We're still on watch," Otley objected. "You haven't relieved us."

He was talking at Marsh, but Gillian knew he was speaking to her, and heard the subtext of his warning. If she didn't stand up for herself now, Nico would fill the vacuum. Besides, she knew Nico's suggestion was wrong, and suspected Marsh's was, too. "Skipper, I think we should take a tuck in the main," she said.

Down below, the noise level had risen sharply: solid thump of seas against the bow; measured creaking of the mainmast in its step; quick, irregular whack of a slack halyard; muffled rattle as something hard rolled back and forth in a locker, with a clunk at each end of the roll; and behind it all the continual susurrus of rushing water, the note rising and falling as *Kassandra* breasted the waves. Standing braced in the narrow passage just forward of the mast, Gillian pulled off jacket and boots, wriggled out of her chest-high foul-weather trousers and hung them in the head compartment to drip. The smell of wet wool from her sweater clashed with a porridgelike odor wafting forward from the galley. "I do not get seasick, however," she said under her breath.

She worked her way back along the lee side of the galley table. Otley, wearing bright-red long johns, was sitting on the high side, spooning something from a deep bowl and grimacing with every mouthful. "Nico made this," he said. "It's from New Zealand."

She looked into the gummy pot sitting on one burner of the gimballed stove. The sticky white remains of whatever Nico had cooked were studded with what she hoped were raisins. She touched the pot. At least it was warm. She helped herself to a moderate bowlful and drenched it with maple syrup. "I do not get seasick, however," she muttered again, lifting a spoonful.

"What?" said Win, from right behind her.

"Nothing." The porridge was slippery, with flexible lumps (presumably the raisins), but all she could taste was the syrup. After the third spoonful, surprisingly, she found herself wolfing it down. She helped herself to a second bowl, saw that Win was watching her with something like horror on his face. "It really isn't bad," she said. "You have some?"

"Not just now," he replied, averting his eyes. She recognized that look; knew she ought to feel sympathy, not superior amusement. "Just out of curiosity, Gillian," he said, "why did you want to reef the mainsail?"

Otley burst out triumphantly, "Because it was the right thing to do, dammit! I told you this girl was a sailor."

She didn't want Win probing in that direction. "I don't know," she said, shrugging. "It just felt right."

Win's mouth was open, another question quivering on his lips, when a rasping voice suddenly came from the locker over the sink: "*Kassandra, Kassandra, Kassandra.* Bermuda Race Net. Over." The three of them gaped, unmoving, and just as Gillian remembered the new VHF radio Win had installed inside the cabinet, the voice spoke again: "Class E yacht *Kassandra*, this is Bermuda Race Net. We have an urgent message for your crewmember Nico Butler. Over."

Gillian knew Bermuda Race Net as a sort of radio umbrella for safety traffic, but an urgent personal message? Win seemed to be taking forever to open the locker, pick up the microphone and key it to transmit. "This is the yacht *Kassandra*. Please stand by."

He flung on a jacket and scrambled up the companion ladder. Moments later, Nico was standing by the galley counter, his foul-weather gear streaming and his ruddy face hard. "Bermuda Race Net? Butler here."

"Mr. Butler? We have a message for you, relayed from Newport." The Net operator, so crisply efficient at first, had suddenly gone reticent.

"Righto," Butler said impatiently. "Send your traffic."

"Uh, all right. It's a telegram: 'Small shed at boatworks burned to ground Friday night. Two bodies found but not identified. Cause of fire not known. What should I do.' It's signed E. Rodriguez." The blood had drained from Nico's face, leaving a sun- and windburned mask. "Shall I repeat the message, *Kassandra*?"

Nico was clearly stunned; his lips moved but no sounds emerged. Gillian's own brain was in turmoil: it had to be Patrick, but Patrick was safe—Barr had said so.

Only Otley seemed to retain self-control. Struggling to his feet he took the microphone from Nico's unresisting hand. "We'll get back to you, Race Net. Please stand by on this channel. *Kassandra* out." And taking two steps up the companion ladder he called into the cockpit, "I think you'd better get down here, skipper."

Half an hour's discussion only confirmed what all of them already knew: *Kassandra* was a day and a half from Newport and three days from Bermuda. If a helicopter could pluck Nico from the pitching deck he might be back in New York in three hours. "But it's your boatyard, Nico," Win insisted. "You have to decide."

Most of the color had returned to Nico's face and with it his composure. Even so, it seemed to Gillian that he was watching Win as if trying to find an extra meaning beneath his words. Or was she imagining it? "Well, what's the odds?" Nico said at last. "If any of my lads were missing, Rodriguez would've said so."

"I'm sure he would," Win agreed.

"That small shed was chock-a-block with inflammables," Nico continued, as if thinking aloud. "Resin, solvents, all that sort of thing. Wonder it hasn't gone up long since."

"Perhaps it was thieves," Win suggested. "Or the homeless . . ."

Nico's quick, angry glance cut Win off in midspeculation. "Could be," he said. And then, "Wouldn't prove anything, me going back."

It sounded, Gillian thought, almost like a question. "Perhaps not," Win replied slowly. "Probably not. You've got insurance, of course?"

"Too true," said Nico. "Rodriguez'll roust them out quick enough."

"I don't think I've met Rodriguez," Win said slowly. "He knows the right people to call? That sort of thing?"

"Sure he does; we've had claims before," Nico replied absently, then looked hard at Win: "No fear. He'll handle it."

"Shall I call the Race Net back, then?" Win asked. "Tell them we're staying in the race?"

Now she was steering and Otley was handling the jib sheet—the working jib sheet: they had taken the small genoa down just before lunch, and left the reef in the main. The mizzen would have to go next. Already she could feel the tiller fighting her in the puffs, and during a couple of gusts its pull had been strong enough to lift her rear right off the seat. *Kassandra* was bashing frantically through the seas, hurling sheets of spray clear over the dinghy's bottom and into the drum-taut mizzen. Just before coming on deck Gillian had made a pot of soup for both watches and put the extra in a Thermos jug for later—if the weather continued to worsen, cooking would simply be out of the question. Already, thanks to Win's notions of stowage, the cabin was a leaping, thumping, sodden shambles.

But she couldn't concentrate on the boat, at least not for more than a few minutes at a time. Two unidentified bodies. Her imagination had produced a dozen scenarios to account for them, with a berserk Patrick the star of nearly every one. And who'd been killed? Certainly not Broadway Rose or the slimy Frannie X—that kind lived forever. K.C.? Equally ridiculous. The first and most important thing was that Barr and Patrick were alive and safe; the second, that when *Kassandra* got to Bermuda she wouldn't be alone.

A solid lump of sea caught her full in the face, icy trickles running down inside her hood, soaking the neck of her sweater. She spat salt water, tried to concentrate on the helm. Otley was watching her anxiously from his post down in the cockpit well. His fingertips were blue with cold, but he'd made such a production out of scorning gloves that he could scarcely reverse himself. *Kassandra* came down off a wave with a thump that stopped her in her tracks. Time to reef, Gillian realized. Past time. She leaned forward. "Better get the mizzen off her, don't you think?"

"Better get *something* off her," Otley called back. "She's pretty good under jib and jigger."

It was the classic prescription for heavy weather, but as Otley offered it, Gillian knew he was wrong. "We'd have to fall off another point," she said. "Drop below the course. We're supposed to be racing."

Otley's grimace bared his teeth. "All right. I'll get the watch below."

She shook her head. Paul Marsh was already showing serious signs of wear. "One's all we need. And tell Nico he doesn't come on deck without a harness."

This time Otley's grin was unmistakably genuine. Cleating the jib sheet, he scrambled to the hatch and shoved his dripping head inside. No more than a minute later Nico crawled through the opening without sliding the hatch open. Ostentatiously ignoring Gillian, he snapped the carbine hook of his safety harness to a bronze padeye on the deck and worked his way past her. From the corner of her eye she was aware of him uncleating the mizzen halyard. "Ease the sheet?" she asked.

She thought he wasn't going to answer; then—"Yes. Now."

He was very good, she thought, as he fisted the smooth, hard fabric down and fought it into submission. The instant the wind was out of the sail *Kassandra* leveled by five degrees. More important, Gillian could feel the strain on the tiller fade dramatically. Without being asked she horsed the mizzen sheet in with her free hand and cleated it, so that Nico, straining out beyond the yawl's transom to furl the clew of the sail, had something firm to lean against. "Well done," she said, as he inched back past her.

"Right," he said. He slid back through the hatch belly down and feet first, avoiding her eye until the last moment.

His look of cold hatred was as palpable as a blow.

The wind was no stronger that night, according to the anemometer; less, if anything, than in the afternoon. But the blackness all around—no light anywhere, except for the red glow from the compass—gave the wind a mysterious ferocity it lacked when you could match its force to visible seas. Gillian crouched at the tiller, steering by the compass alone, her senses pulled in to a tightly personal circumference. She was acutely aware of the leak in her left boot, of the now painful rasp of wet wool against her throat, of the constriction of the safety harness across her breasts. Most of all, she concentrated on the vibration of *Kassandra's* tiller in her cold hand. She was trying to guide the yawl among the waves, sensing the invisible moving shapes around her from the way the boat sidled among them or, when she lost concentration, slammed into or off one. Barr should see me now, she told herself. God, I wish he could.

Otley was a shapeless bundle huddled against the cabin, taking what shelter the deckhouse offered. He was nearly exhausted but refused to go below, and she would not send him—as Nico, in the previous watch, had contemptuously dismissed Paul Marsh. Win had been seasick for several hours, ever since his second gulp of Gillian's soup had collided with the first one coming back up. But he was still in control of himself, and well he might be, Gillian could not help thinking: he'd barely been on deck since he'd relinquished the tiller immediately after the start. And a damn poor start, too—wrong end of the line and thirty seconds after the gun.

Forty minutes ago, as the yawl topped a wave, Gillian had spotted a green running light to windward, startlingly bright. She looked quickly up at *Kassandra's* masthead, was relieved that she could still see the green and white sectors of the combination light glowing strongly. The other boat, whatever it was, carried its running lights down on the hull, so she could only see them when the yachts were simultaneously on wavecrests. It was five long minutes before she saw the light again, noting with suddenly sharpened attention that the one light had become two—a green and a red—and seemed even closer.

She dropped the tiller long enough to push the hatch open. Below her, in the dimly lit cabin, Win and Nico were standing braced against the galley counter. Nico was holding Win's bicep and speaking in his ear, and when he looked up and saw Gillian his face seemed contorted by rage. Or maybe just by bad light, she told herself.

By the time Nico had stuck his head out the hatch, the other boat's aspect had changed. Now she was showing only a white light, definitely farther off than the others had been. "Probably lost his steering," Nico suggested. "Blundering about like a bloody cow." She tried to imagine what it would be like in these seas with the rudder gone, decided she didn't want to think about it. Instead, she stole a look at her watch. Thirty-five more minutes to relief. The lower half of her sleeping bag was soaked by a leak running down the chainplates. Cold, soggy sleeping bag. Ugh. On the other hand, the upper half was still dry. It all depended how you looked at it.

• • •

Gillian lay wedged against the canvas lee cloth of her upper berth on the windward side, trying to ignore the thin, watery light coming through the porthole over her head. Finally she levered herself up on one elbow and looked out. No horizon at all, just long, white streaks down a moving surface as gray and ugly as elephant hide. Then *Kassandra's* bow burst through the wave crest in an explosion of spray, and for a few seconds she could see the marching crests and the scurrying wrack that seemed to cling to their tops. She reached over and grabbed the handrail bolted to the inside of the cabin roof, swung herself over the lee cloth, over the unconscious Paul Marsh in the lower berth, and landed barefoot on the cold, wet floorboards.

Across the cabin Otley had got to a sitting position, but he was slumped back against the upper bunkboard, eyes closed and mouth open. When he felt Gillian sit down next to him, his eyes opened. "No point in both of us getting soaked at once," she said, forcing cheer into her tone. "I'll take the first half of the watch and you can relieve me."

The old man nodded, too numbly exhausted to show emotion. In the berth above and outboard of him, Win lay on his side, his back to the cabin. Gillian strongly suspected he was awake but found she really didn't care. She got cautiously to her feet—*Kassandra's* motion had become almost completely unpredictable, and every few seconds she would stagger from the impact of a wave, then lurch ahead. Thinking unhappily of coffee, she drank off two small cans of V8 juice and stuffed a couple of chocolate bars in the pocket of her jacket. The high-seas chart for their passage was folded and taped down on top of the icebox, with a streak down one side that might have been blood but was probably ketchup from Nico's sandwich of the night before. *Kassandra's* last noted position, presumably a loran reading, was six hours old.

"Asshole," she muttered under her breath, not caring if Win heard her or not. She retrieved the logbook from the deck at her feet, saw the most recent entry was the one she had made nearly four hours earlier, coming off watch. Shaking her head in disgust, she stepped up the companion ladder and pulled the hatch open. The air outside had a raw bite to it that emphasized the stale, wet warmth below decks.

Nico had run the jib sheet up to the windward winch, where he could reach it without leaving the tiller. His red-rimmed eyes were narrowed against the spray, but he seemed alert enough as he eyed her coolly. "Coming up, then?" he asked.

"That was the idea," she replied. "No one's plotted a position since midnight—you want to do it on your way to the sack?"

He rewarded her diplomatic *no one* with a thin smile. "Tell you what," he said, "why don't you do it? And switch the batteries while you're down there. I want to run the engine to charge them."

She'd quite forgotten about that, she realized, as she ducked back into the cabin. She flicked the main battery switch to the backup, and opened the locker that held the loran. Someone had shut off the radio transmitter, and she turned it back on, tuned to the Race Net's frequency.

What you really needed for plotting fixes in a bouncing boat, she decided, was a sloth's ability to swing from the overhead, and a couple of extra hands. Twice she had her pencil poised to mark *Kassandra's* position, only to have the deck swoop from under her each time. Finally she achieved a ragged mark that would have to do. (Even in gales Barr's charted fixes were supernaturally neat—tiny, meticulous printing completely unlike his everyday scrawl.)

As she was zipping and snapping her foul-weather gear closed, sealing the sweat and old seawater inside, the VHF came alive. One by one the boats in *Kassandra's* class checked in with the Race Net, disembodied voices slurred with fatigue. Gillian picked up the mike and chimed in, but instead of the customary acknowledgment, the voice of the controller snapped back angrily: "Where've you been, *Kassandra?* We've been trying to raise you all night."

More news about Nico's fire, she thought, as she stammered an excuse.

"Relayed from New York via Newport," said the unmollified voice out there someplace. "Received yesterday evening at eighteen-thirty. The message is for your skipper. Over."

Win had rolled over, his startled eyes wide above the top of the lee cloth. "We're ready," Gillian said quickly. "Send it, please."

"Message as follows. 'K.C.'—that's how it's spelled, Kilo Quebec—

'K.C. didn't show for work today. Called her home number without result. Will keep you advised.' It's signed 'Ringgold'; do you want me to spell that?"

Win's expression was faultless: initial surprise fading through responsible concern and ending in baffled annoyance. His eyes never left hers, as he started to pull himself out of the bunk.

"*Kassandra*, Race Net control. Are you there?"

What's he seeing on my face? That I know? But what *do* I know?

"I can't imagine what's come over Ringgold," Win said, taking the microphone from Gillian's unresisting hand. "I thought we were above internecine talebearing. But then he's always been jealous of K.C." Keying the mike he continued, in quite a different voice: "Race Net control? That won't be necessary, thanks. *Kassandra* out."

"... And continued gale-force southerly winds over the area through Thurs—" He snapped the high-seas weather forecaster off in mid-word and turned back to *Glory*'s chart table, on which he had been tracking the huge weather system that now seemed stalled over the Gulf Stream. They'd had three days of fresh gales aboard *Kassandra*, he reflected. And in the Stream, too: the little yawl's interior must be like earthquake day in the Turkish bath by now. At least the wind wasn't blowing across the set of the current. . . . Resting his elbows on the chart, he reviewed his estimate of *Kassandra*'s progress. Wind and current combined would be setting them well to the north of the rhumb line; would Huddleston have anticipated that, or was *Kassandra* clawing to windward, trying to make up her leeway?

"Where are they now?" Patrick was standing in the main cabin doorway. He'd insisted on getting dressed that morning, and in freshly laundered khakis looked like a slightly ascetic version of his usual self. But Barr had quickly observed the slow-motion care with which the mate moved around the cabin, the way he seemed to place himself within grabbing range of vertical supports. Once, in an oil lamp's highly polished brass smoke shield, Barr had caught an unguarded reflection of pure agony when Patrick had incautiously shifted position on the settee.

"Come take a look," Barr invited, and Patrick stepped down the passageway, avoiding Barr's eye. The constraint between them had grown since Saturday until it was a sour miasma that seemed to fill the boat. At first Barr put it down to Patrick's exasperation at being physically helpless; after a while he began to sense in the younger man an angry disapproval that perplexed and then annoyed him. A couple of oblique remarks suggested that Patrick still angrily disagreed with Barr's and Sol's decision to steer clear of the authorities, that he resented the way he felt they had pressured him into agreement. But surely a difference of opinion about tactics couldn't account for his attitude. No, it went deeper than that, and Barr was damned in four colors if he was going to spend any more time trying to tease the answer up to the surface.

Patrick was staring over Barr's shoulder at the sailing chart. From Nova Scotia to Florida, the East Coast made a ragged yellow diagonal down the left-hand side, and all the rest was open water except, in the chart's lower right corner, one lonely clump of islands. A line of tiny scarlet crosses, marking Barr's presumptions of *Kassandra's* progress, struggled southeastward toward them.

Barr stepped aside to give Patrick a better view. The plot was largely guesswork, of course—begun to pass the time while *Glory* lay hidden at anchor off Copps Island and continued when they had moved the ketch back to her marina berth. Yesterday's New York papers, brought by Sol Farber, had carried a sizable story on the fire at the salvage yard and the discovery among the ashes of two unidentified bodies. What had happened in the burnt building was still a mystery, according to a police spokesman, and Barr wondered how long it would be. He knew from experience that a fire feeding on resin and acetone could melt a lead keel like butter, so the bullets from K.C.'s automatic might be gone for good, but the empty gun was presumably still recognizable, and the ejected brass cartridge cases.

"You figure *Kassandra's* here?" Patrick asked, indicating the final cross on the chart.

"No, that was noon. Another fifty miles now," Barr replied.

Without comment Patrick picked up the brass dividers and walked the distance off, adding his own X to mark the position. "More than two thirds of the way," he murmured. "Looks like about two hundred miles to go."

It was more than Patrick had said at one time all day, and seemed to call for a pacific response. "If we're right," Barr offered, "and if they keep that pace up, they should finish Thursday afternoon."

"Don't worry," he snapped. "I'll be ready."

"I'm sure you will." And screw you, too.

"At least I can get into Bermuda. Nobody's waiting to nab me at the airport."

"Not at the Bermuda airport, no," Barr replied coldly. "You might find the cops waiting for you at JFK or La Guardia, though."

"Cops." Patrick bit the word off. "You hate the police, don't you? Always calling them cops—"

"So do you."

"That's different. My uncle was a—was on the force. And it's true: you do hate them. You hate everybody who's, you know . . ."

"In authority?" So that was it, Barr thought. What a strange thing to fight about.

"Authority, that's right. What's with you, anyway? You think all these people—police, Customs, Coast Guard—they're all crooks?"

"Don't be stupid: of course not. But they make a living doing what they're told, and sometimes that's worse." Now that the storm had burst, Barr found himself eager to slash back, even as he recognized how foolish it was.

"I suppose you think druggies are better," Patrick said. "Like they're free spirits? Nobody tells them what to do, right?"

"I never said that."

"Your wife was one, wasn't she?" Patrick continued relentlessly. "You never did anything about her, and she put your boat on the rocks and damn near killed everybody aboard." In the sudden silence, Barr felt as if his face had turned to stone. Patrick was visibly taken aback by the effect of his words. "Everybody at English Harbour knew about it," he protested. "I must've heard the story six times."

Truth rang in the mate's voice, and Barr's anger vanished as he realized, in a single numb moment, that he had been kidding himself for nearly three years. At the inquiry into *Windhover's* stranding, the physical state of her charterers and crew had never even come up. Now, with crystal-clear hindsight, he saw how nimbly the lawyers had dodged around the question. The whole of Antigua—the whole charter fleet—must have been in on it, and they'd been smiling behind their hands ever since.

"My wife's not part of this discussion," he said, aiming at icy dignity (and, he knew, missing it). "As for drugs generally, I don't tell the whole world what to put up its nose."

"You still don't get it, do you," Patrick said. "The whole world is somebody's wife or husband. Or kid. I'm no kind of father, I know that, but my little girl's eight years old now, and I read in the paper where eight-year-olds are selling dope in school."

"Well, that may be, but if people who think like you had their way—"

"Is this a private fight, or can I join in?" Sol Farber's cheerful voice echoed down the companion ladder, and his round head was silhouetted in the hatchway. "I could hear you two from the shore." Barr and Patrick watched silently as he backed down, feeling for each step. He achieved the bottom successfully and turned to face them. "So what's the problem? I think maybe I know." Farber's moonlike face was only partly illuminated by the light from the chart table, and Barr found his expression impossible to read.

"I know what you said, Mr. Farber," Patrick began. "Just the same, I still think we ought to tell *somebody*." But you're a lot less certain about it than you were with me, Barr thought sourly.

The old man hushed Patrick with a raised hand. "We will," he crooned. "Like I promised you. Just get my Sarah—and your Gillian—back first."

Patrick said nothing, stood waiting for the old man to continue. What's Farber got that I don't? Barr asked himself. Is it respect for age? Or because he's our client? Well, what's the difference as long as it works.

"You'll be glad to hear I agreed to go along with what Mr. Farber wants," Patrick said, as Barr came back into the main cabin with the old enameled coffee pot and three white mugs lettered with the yacht's name. The mate sounded resigned, if a little sullen, but Barr had more than a suspicion that his submission was only temporary.

"Is that so?" He slid a mug across the table to Patrick, set another in front of Farber.

"Yes, we have a plan," Farber said. His avuncular smile lit the cabin but not his eyes. "No coffee, thank you. At my age it makes me go twice, maybe three times in the night."

Barr half-filled his personal cup—the Antiguan potter had dropped the *L* from GLORY—and topped it with a shot from the unlabeled pint bottle he kept in the locker over the settee.

Farber and Patrick had watched silently, one with cheerful interest, the other with revived disapproval. Barr took a deliberate sip and set the mug down. "Tell me about this plan," he said.

Stripped of Farber's mannerisms, what remained was simple enough: Barr and Patrick were to fly to Bermuda Thursday morning, arriving well before *Kassandra* was due. They would go to race head-quarters, at the Royal Bermuda Yacht Club, where Barr's connections would enable him to learn of *Kassandra*'s arrival the minute she crossed the finish line off St. David's Head, and at least two hours before she actually turned up in Hamilton Harbour, fifteen miles away. Mixing in with the mob at the pier, they would spot Gillian and, at a suitable moment, let her see them. From that point they would play matters by ear until, as Farber put it, "my Sarah pops up." Then they were to swoop down and grab both young women, after which Patrick was free to call the Bermuda police, the American Coast Guard, or anyone else who occurred to him.

"So what do you think?" Farber asked anxiously. "Maybe needs some details pressed out, but have we got basically the right idea?" Patrick was leaning over the big mahogany table, his eyes daring Barr to object.

"Well, there's one problem I can see right off," Barr said. "You remember I had to leave Bermuda in a hurry. By now, they've prob-ably noticed that the visiting Mr. Barr has vanished without officially leaving the colony."

Patrick had thought of that one: "Easy: you just use a different name going back in. Bermuda doesn't ask for much ID. A voter registration card'll do—and the Connecticut card doesn't even have a photo on it."

Not bad, Barr thought. "You know somebody who's willing to part with one?"

"Give me a couple of bills and fifteen minutes in a South Norwalk bar, I'll buy you a handful of 'em."

That was probably true enough, but there was another half to the same problem. "And when we get to Bermuda—"

Patrick hadn't overlooked it: "I'll change your face so your own mother wouldn't know you, never mind a bunch of hick cops." A second too late, he saw Barr's eyebrow shoot up. "Never mind, you know what I mean."

Farber looked from one of them to the other. "It's okeydokey, then? It'll work?" he asked Barr.

"Okeydokey is one word for it, Mr. Farber." Except that if Barr was right Sarah Farber was never going to set foot in Bermuda at all.

GILLIAN:
WEDNESDAY MORNING,
33° 50' N, 65° 54' W

Just before dawn the southerly wind dropped away to nothing and left *Kassandra* rolling wildly among the steep seas. In her bunk, Gillian sprawled facedown on the sodden mattress, arms and legs spread to keep from being tossed like popcorn. From below her came a heavy crash followed by the sounds of rending wood, and she risked a quick look over the lee cloth. Win was half-lying on the deck amid the final ruin of the rickety cabin table. Seeing the upper half of her face, he gave a weak grin. "This is almost more fun than I bargained for," he said, barely audible over the cacophony of creaking rigging and slatting sails.

"Shut up, for Chrissake," snarled Otley from the bunk below.

A quarter hour later Gillian felt the first hint of the new wind coming in—a moment's respite from the dreadful corkscrew roll, as the sails filled and the boat gathered way. The breeze faded, and *Kassandra* stuck her bow into a wave tall enough to send a sheet of water clean over the deckhouse. Gouts of it spurted down around the edges of the skylight, rewetting everything in the cabin. But the next puff lasted longer, and the next, and then Gillian heard the squeal of blocks as Marsh and Nico eased the sheets. She pulled herself up to look out the port over her berth, just as *Kassandra* seemed to leap forward in response, white water surging past the lee gunwale, little more than a foot from Gillian's nose. A westerly at last, she thought, and fell back into a dreamless sleep.

Dreamless, and so more terrifyingly shattered when Nico ripped the washboards from the main hatch and bellowed, "Win! On deck, quick!"

Gillian beat the skipper up the companionway by three steps. Astern of them the wall of stormclouds towered harmlessly; above, the low scud was breaking up, a streak of pale blue showing off to port. As she scrambled out the hatch she scanned quickly about her, nerves on a hair trigger for snapped rigging, a torn sail. But *Kassandra*, with a bone in her teeth, was in perfect trim. Off the lee quarter, cutting easily through the seas, a gleaming white vessel was keeping pace with the yawl, close enough for Gillian to make out the Coast Guard seal, blue and white, on the wide red slash across her bow.

Shaking visibly, Nico stared wide-eyed at the white ship, while Paul Marsh, clutching the tiller with fleshless old man's claws, gaped up at him. "What is it?" Gillian cried. "What's wrong?"

For a moment Nico seemed not to hear. Then his head turned slowly. "You!" he snarled, and crouched as if to leap at her throat.

She flinched away from the rage in his reddened eyes, and Win leaped past and over her, cannoning into Nico's chest. The husky young New Zealander, taken off balance, fell backward. His bare head struck the heavy oak tiller with a solid thump, and he sagged to the bottom of the cockpit.

"My God!" Win gasped, drawing back in horror. "Is he all right?"

For answer, Nico groaned and struggled to sit up. He was clearly dazed, and his lips moved soundlessly. "Better stretch him out on the bridge deck," Gillian said.

As Win, with Gillian's help, was arranging the semiconscious Nico on the narrow strip of raised decking at the forward end of the cockpit, the voice of God boomed out: "Aboard *Kassandra*! Do you require assistance?" Gillian looked up and saw the Coast Guard cutter ranging alongside, yellow-slickered figures on her flying bridge. One of them raised the loud-hailer and spoke again. "Is everything all right?"

"Fine! Great!" they cried, their voices sounding tiny and shrill. Even Nico managed to sit partway up and give a feeble wave. The cutter fell back to her previous position.

Paul Marsh, Gillian noticed for the first time, had removed his teeth. Without them he looked more like a belligerent tortoise than ever. "Oo phtand watph w'me?" he demanded.

"What was that?" Win replied absently. Nico's eyes were half open, but he seemed content to lie where they had put him.

"Will you take Nico's watch?" Gillian translated. Her body was aching for the smelly, soggy berth, but she sensed Win's answer even before he gave it.

"I'd love to, Paul, but with this wind change . . . new course . . . better work up a position . . ." Still mumbling, the skipper slid back down the companionway and vanished.

"Here, I'll trim the jib," Gillian said, uncleating the sheet. Old Marsh was staring avidly at her, his fallen-in mouth stretched in a demented leer. Glancing down, she saw her flannel shirt had fallen open, and in the chill morning air her bare nipples were rose-colored bullets on her white, goosepimpled breasts. She allowed Marsh another three seconds, while she cranked in six inches of jib sheet, then deliberately buttoned the shirt. "Back to work, Paul—you're supposed to be driving this bus," she said.

His awful, gummy smile stretched until she thought it might engulf his ears. Without taking his hands from the tiller, he nodded to the Coast Guard cutter down to leeward. Its entire foredeck was black with small figures; Gillian wondered how many pairs of binoculars a ship that size carried. As she watched, gray smoke puffed from the ship's exhaust tubes, and she spun on her heel, presenting her squared-off stern. The name lettered on it—WHIDBEY—was quite close enough to read.

At ten of eight, when Otley appeared in the companionway for the next watch, Nico abruptly sat up. Gillian, on the helm, was concentrating so tightly on the jib luff that she'd forgotten the New Zealander, who had lain motionless along the narrow bridge deck for more than an hour. As the powerful young man stretched and surveyed the horizon, where nine sails were now visible, Gillian and Paul eyed him nervously. "Okay," he said after a minute. "I'll take it now."

His attitude was so matter-of-fact, and Gillian so exhausted, that she had given him the tiller before she realized what she'd done. Without a word, Otley took the jib sheet from an unresisting Paul Marsh. "You'd better get some rest," he told Gillian. "Looks as if we'll cross the finish line in the dark."

After the clean wind and gleaming daylight on deck, *Kassandra's* cabin seemed even more fetid and destroyed than Gillian remembered. Someone had removed the splintered wreckage of the dining table, and the waterstained sole that was now revealed presented a grim relief map of food scraps, sodden bits of paper, and wadded-up clothing. Holding her breath, Gillian staggered forward to the toilet compartment. From the too-small mirror over the tiny sink, a scraggy young termagant with frizzy hair glared wildly back at her. She stuck out her tongue at the image, removed her washcloth from its hook, and began methodically to reduce the damage.

Win was waiting for her when she emerged. "I've got to speak to you," he whispered, with a nervous twist of the head toward the open companionway. "About . . ."

"Has Nico gone batty again?" But she could see him, holding the tiller and looking as normal as any red-eyed, bristly-faced derelict from the New York streets.

"It's not a matter of *again*, I'm afraid. Come back where he can't see us." Win moved aft toward the galley, out of the sightline from the cockpit; drawn by curiosity, Gillian followed. When they were standing braced against the galley counter, with their faces six inches apart, Win said, "I didn't tell you earlier—perhaps I should've—but Nico seems to think you're somehow connected with that fire at his salvage yard."

"That's plain crazy!" Gillian exclaimed, guilt lending vehemence to her denial. "Didn't it happen Saturday night? I was right here the whole time."

"Of course you were," he said soothingly. "He doesn't mean you actually set the fire, I'm sure."

"Then what *does* he mean?" she demanded. And where, she nearly added, do you fit into all this?

"I just don't know," Win admitted. "I'm quite out of my depth." His boyishly helpless half-smile, so charming ashore, was beginning to get on her nerves.

"And Nico's only got one oar in the water," she snapped. "Good thing this race is almost over." Do I sound as angry as I ought to?

"It certainly is," Win agreed. "Because then our real job begins."

"Ours?"

"I need you, Gillian." His faded eyes bored into hers. "I've realized

I can't deal with Roger alone. He could always talk his way around me. Say you'll help me through."

It was exactly what she'd hoped for. More. He'd give her a free hand, she was sure of it. How stupid she'd been to suspect him. "Of course I will," she said.

Dusk brought a strong, steady wind lying just a little north of west. *Kassandra* was surging ahead, with every stitch of canvas filled to bursting. For the last two hours she'd been running alongside a fifty-foot sloop, and the visible competition—the first for six hundred miles—had brought all hands on deck, regardless of near-exhaustion. Nico was at the tiller, as he'd been since morning, trimming the mizzen and mizzen staysail with his free hand. Down on the lee side of the cockpit Otley was crouched like an ape over the genoa winch, while braced above him Paul Marsh handled the main. Gillian had led the twanging-taut sheet of *Kassandra*'s brand-new spinnaker between Otley's legs, across the cockpit and past Paul's narrow chest, up to her vantage point on the weather rail.

"Now, *this* is the way it's supposed to be!" she cried to Win, who was standing in the companionway, sextant in hand and a bemused look on his face.

"Is it really?" Win observed dryly. "I was just thinking, if the spinnaker sheet lets go it'll geld Otley, behead Paul, and knock you overboard—all at once."

He was right, and all of them knew it, but in that larger-than-life moment his remark drew the first wholehearted laugh of the voyage. Even Nico's grim face yielded a reluctant smile. "How're we doing?" he demanded. "When do we see Gibbs Hill Light?"

On a night as clear as this was going to be, she thought, they'd see the beam itself—a single stab of white every ten seconds—at its full twenty-six-mile range. And the loom of it against the sky from even farther out. "I'm not sure," Win was saying. (Incomprehensibly: Barr would've known to within ten minutes.) "The loran says we're doing awfully well, but I'm almost afraid to believe it."

"Then check it, man," Nico replied, impatience hard in his tone. "Forget the bloody Dial-a-Prayer box and use that thing in your hand. You've got Venus on the quarter, and bloody Polaris right behind my head."

"Of course," said Win, looking at the sextant, a battered U.S. Navy model, as if seeing it for the first time. "I'm not terribly good at star sights, though." An idea seemed to strike him. "How about you, Gillian? I don't suppose . . ."

Before caution could stop her she heard herself say, "Give it here." She cleated the spinnaker sheet, accepted the sextant from Win's outstretched hand. Should I blow it? Screw up the sights? Damned if I will.

She zeroed the instrument on the fast-fading horizon to check it: about five minutes' error on the arc, less than it might've been. Above them the Big Dipper sailed in the cloudless sky. She followed the pointers to the just-visible gleam of the North Star, called out: "Stand by." With one foot against the gunwale and the other hooked under the edge of the seat, she brought the star down fast. "Steady, please," she said, but Nico had Kassandra perfectly in the groove, swooping easily over the seas that marched down on the quarter. "Ready? Mark," she called. "Thirty-three nineteen point three. And mark. The same. And one more for luck . . . mark. Nineteen point four." She looked up, to see four astonished faces. "What's wrong?"

"Wrong?" said Win, staring down at the stopwatch and notepad in his hands. "Three sights in fifty-five seconds. It's amazing."

Well, that's blown it, she thought, seeing Nico's black, appraising stare. "The man who taught me would've done it in forty-five," she said defiantly. "Stand by for Venus."

Standing at the galley counter, she worked the result through twice, averaging each set of sights to be on the safe side. Though she was not about to admit it to the crew waiting on deck, it was reassuring to see that her results and the loran's reading agreed to within half a mile. "If we can hold this speed," she told the four expectant faces, "we'll cross the line in seven and a half hours."

"Four in the morning," said Win, five seconds later.

"An hour before dawn," added Nico, sounding thoughtful.

She climbed out of the berth at three, unable to sleep any more, pulled on jeans and her jacket with the built-in safety harness and went on deck. It was nearly as damp and warm outside as below, and after a minute sweat began to prickle her body. Ignoring Win's ironclad rule, everyone on deck was without harnesses, and she tugged the jacket off and tossed it down the companionway, telling herself as she did so that Barr never wore a harness in anything less than a full gale. The wind seemed to be stronger than in the previous watch, though that was probably imagination, and it was certainly gusting—short, hard puffs that laid *Kassandra*'s lee rail right down to the water and dipped the genoa's foot, lit red by the port running light. Every couple of minutes the boat staggered under a sudden, jarring *whump!* as the spinnaker, inexpertly trimmed by Win, lost air and then refilled.

The cabin had been inky, its only light the glow of the loran screen and the VHF radio, but the cockpit was darker still. Clouds had erased the bright stars and the new moon, and the red glow from the binnacle was barely strong enough to light the compass card. "Take the spinnaker sheet, would you?" said Nico, sounding as if the words were coming from between clenched teeth. As she scrambled cautiously up to the weather rail Win lost the trim again; *Kassandra* yawed uncontrollably for a moment, then straightened out as the chute filled with a sullen, explosive thump.

"Bloody *hell!*" Nico muttered from his position below her.

As she took the sheet from Win he gave her hand a quick, invisible caress, and she returned an equally invisible smile. Creeping back to the companionway, he stepped on Otley, tripped over the spinnaker sheet, and kicked the compass. Win Huddleston might be the man to preserve the light of Western culture, she thought, but he certainly didn't belong in a boat.

She had been trimming the sheet for fully ten minutes when she realized, with a stab of dismay, that the night ahead was as black as death, except for a single flashing white light off the starboard bow. Even at this hour the whole southwestern horizon should have been aglow by now, a warm welcome punctuated by the high red aero lights of Kindley Field and the white beams from Gibbs Hill and St. David's. Could she have been that wrong, she and the loran both? No, the crew, and Nico especially, would have been foaming at the mouth. "Rain squalls up ahead?" she asked.

"Lots of 'em," Nico grunted. "They move across the bow, but this one's a big old bugger." He raised his voice to Win, down below:

"We'll have North East Light abeam in two minutes. I want courses from there to the finish."

"Four-seventeen!" Win exulted, looking at his watch. "I still don't know how we did it."

In the galley, where she was wrestling the cork from the obligatory bottle of champagne, Gillian heard him. She had been considering the same thing, and had come to the conclusion that *Kassandra* must have been picked up by one of the Gulf Stream's immense south-bound eddies and carried along in it for a hundred miles or more. That, and the consistently strong, steady winds, would account for their rapid passage—not a record by any means, but as good as a serious racer's. If only it had been *Glory*, she was thinking, as the cork exploded from the bottle, narrowly missing Paul Marsh's head.

"Better get some of this shit off her!" Nico bellowed, above the babble in the cockpit. "Bloody great squall coming right our way—"

The next fifteen minutes were chaos—order and shrieked counterorder lost in the thunder of canvas and the stinging rain. Sails were fought down, inch by clawing inch, only to surge back up stay or track as the wind refilled them; at one point *Kassandra* was nearly flat over, with water pouring over the lee coaming. It ended as quickly as it had come, with *Kassandra* shying desperately away from the reefs that fringe the west end of St. George Island, her crew soaked, manic, and exhausted.

Gillian took a long, long swig of warm, diluted champagne and passed the bottle to Otley. "Aren't we heading in?" she asked, indicating the mouth of Town Cut Channel dimly visible between its steep headlands.

Win's mouth was open to answer, but Nico cut in: "Why bother? It's only an hour to dawn—we might as well start around for Hamilton."

"In the dark?" Win sounded surprised. "The Race Instructions say to wait till daylight."

"That's suggested, not required," Nico retorted. He wasn't waiting for the skipper's agreement, Gillian saw: *Kassandra* was already running before the southwesterly, headed for the entrance to the channel that traversed the north side of the islands, inside the barrier reef.

"Well, I don't know," said Win. "What do the rest of you think?"

"I don't give a damn," said Otley, hit hard by champagne on his empty stomach. "Sink her if you want. I'm hitting the sack."

A snort was Paul Marsh's only response, from the corner of the cockpit where he had collapsed. "And you, love?" Nico said. His tone was a challenge, and she had never yet refused a challenge.

"I think," said Nico thickly, "what I think is . . ." he seemed to lose track of the thought. "Fuck it anyway."

He obviously had no head for booze, Gillian decided. Or maybe it was the beers on top of the champagne. Anyway, he was stinking. It seemed to make no difference to his steering, though—they had rounded St. Catherine's Head, the northern extremity of St. George Island, and squared up with precision on a fine, fast reach about two miles off the scattered lights of the north shore.

Gillian herself was more than a little sleepy, though she'd only had three swallows of the champagne. Maybe four. Of course, she *had* been sailing hard for twenty hours in the last twenty-four, and the previous three days hadn't been exactly restful. . . .

"Smaller jib," Nico announced. "That's what I was thinking, love: ought to set a smaller jib."

"Why?" she objected. "She's handling the genoa just fine."

"Is now," he replied. "Once we swing round Spanish Point, though, she'll be on her ear. C'mon, sweetheart, it'll just take you a wink. You can do it easy—you're twice the sailor ol' Win is."

So he's one of those that gets friendly with a skinful. Maybe I'd be better off on the foredeck. "Oh, all right," she said.

"That's my girl. I'll put her before the wind, give you a lee to drop the jenny in."

She got to her knees, feeling stiff and old, and began groping about the unlit cockpit for her harness. No—it was down below, she remembered now. "Just a sec," she said.

"Come *on*, then," he snapped. "It's a bloody millpond."

Screw it. She started forward along the side deck as Nico brought *Kassandra* around in a long, easy turn, the main boom swinging wide over the far side as he let out the sheet. The full genoa collapsed in the wind shadow of the main, fluttering impotently. Not too far,

Nico, she was thinking—just as the yawl steadied on course, headed away from the shore with her stern into the wind. A strong wind still, in spite of being dead aft.

"Look there! Off to port!"

She whirled, nearly losing her balance. "What?" she called out, seeing nothing but the velvet horizon and the diamondlike stars above.

She never heard the boom come across as *Kassandra* jibed, but below the blurred level of consciousness her sailor's instinct was still sharp. She turned quickly, saw the gray-white of the sail rushing at her, and flung up her hands—there was no room or time to duck. The sweeping boom hit her palms with an echoing smack, plucked her off her feet, and tumbled her backward over the low lifelines.

She hit the water hard, almost knocking the wind from her lungs, but over the sound of her own splash she heard the boom strike the lee-side rigging. Then she was under the surface, surprisingly warm water flooding up beneath her shirt and into her nose and open mouth. She came up choking and gasping, saw *Kassandra*'s narrow stern already fifty yards away. "Overboard!" came a cracked bellow she recognized as Paul Marsh. "Man overboard!" Nico echoed.

Her first reaction was amused annoyance: Careless bastard, she thought, as she trod water, spitting and coughing, waiting for *Kassandra* to jibe again and head back. No, *two* careless bastards. And it's woman overboard, you sexist Kiwi twerp.

Cries and shouts, beginning to fade a little with the increasing distance. Use the strobe light, she was thinking. Damn, it's on my jacket. Now the yawl was turning—she saw the stern light kick around. But turning in the wrong direction. Nico, you really must be fried. Or—oh, no: He couldn't be. . . .

Kassandra, having jibed away, tacked and headed back. She could hear a furious argument raging in the cockpit. Stop yelling and start looking, she thought. "Over here!" she called, amazed at how small her voice sounded. "I'm here!"

"I hear her!" It was Win's voice, strained and anxious. "Gillian!" he cried. "We're coming!" She splashed furiously, renewed her shouts. Another Gillian, floating slightly apart from the woman in the water, was aware that her strength was ebbing at alarming speed. But the yawl was nearly on top of her now. Heading right at her, in fact. That son of a bitch Nico—she thrashed desperately to windward, heard Otley yelling, "Head off! Head off!"

Kassandra rounded up some twenty feet away, glowing white in the faint predawn light. "What're you doing?" Win shouted.

"She won't be able to climb aboard," Nico cried back. "I'll help her." She saw him balancing on the cockpit coaming, looming above her. He'd stripped off his jacket and shirt, and his head swung back and forth as he searched the water.

Gillian was certain now. And there was nothing she could do but wait for him. No, she corrected herself: there was one thing. She might have forgotten her harness and her strobe light, but there was one sailor's tool she never left behind. As Nico spotted her and sprang out from the side, she was groping in her jeans pocket for her knife.

The hired limousine slowed and the chauffeur half turned to address Patrick. "Which airline?" he asked.

The mate consulted the piece of paper in his hand before replying, and Barr, in the quavering old man's voice he'd been practicing all the previous evening, quickly said, "American, please."

"Yessir. American."

Patrick, whose mouth was already forming the P of Pan Am, glanced sharply at his companion. Before he could speak, Barr's left hand, below the chauffeur's angle of vision, clamped like a vise on the mate's knee. "American Airlines," Barr repeated.

"Yes, *sir*," the chauffeur said, louder this time. "American Airlines it is."

"Always fly American," Barr creaked, to forestall the objection he saw on Patrick's bewildered face. "Make the reservations m'self." He felt the tension in Patrick's leg relax just slightly, and released it.

"Is that so?" said the chauffeur.

"First Class. Only way to fly, especially at my age."

"Better food, I guess. And roomier seats," the chauffeur agreed. Barr tilted his head to catch a glimpse of his own face in the rearview mirror, but his thick-lensed glasses unfocused the world almost completely. It was still hard for him to believe the results of Patrick's three-hour makeup session. The white hair alone added three decades to his age; artful lines and grayed skin boosted the total by twenty more years, and the puffed cheeks, crusted lips, and artificially bloodshot eyes gave a convincing aura of ill health. For final touches Patrick had come up with paired hearing aids, now gouging Barr's ears, and white cotton gloves, to hide his scarred and powerful hands. He'd even rented an aluminum-framed walker, but decided against it at the last moment: "If you look any worse, they might not let you on the plane."

The chauffeur braked the limo smoothly as they approached the unloading area along the curb. "Well, here we are, sir. Let me help you out."

As he circled the car to open the passenger door on Barr's side, Patrick whispered, "What the fuck's going on?" from the corner of his mouth.

"Play along," Barr whispered back. "Tell you in a minute." And, in his querulous stage voice, "Where's my wheelchair? I told them I'd need a wheelchair."

"Well, that was some goddamn performance," murmured Patrick, once the plane was in the air. Exasperation was clear in his voice. "I didn't know whether to shit or go blind back there."

"You did perfectly," Barr whispered. And he had, picking up Barr's every lead, no matter how unexpected.

"But what was it all *for*? I mean, I already got us a pair of ID cards, and old man Farber went to the trouble of making reservations for us on Pan Am, and then all of a sudden—" Patrick stopped short, as the possibilities finally sank through. "You've got to be kidding. He's paying for this. Why would he set us up? And for who?"

Barr emptied his champagne—a disappointing taste, as it always was—and the attentive steward appeared at his elbow like a djinn. "More, sir?"

"Why not?" He watched the glass fill for the third time, before turning back to Patrick, fuming in the seat beside him. "I don't say Farber's up to something. Chances are he was just being helpful. It's just . . ." He couldn't explain to himself, let alone to Patrick, but when Farber had offered, then virtually insisted on making the plane reservations and calling the limousine service, Barr suddenly found himself wondering. "The thing is, it'd be so easy for the cops to pick us off at the ticket counter, if somebody gave them the names we're going under, and the airline."

"So it's cops again," said Patrick heavily. "And our client, too. You want to know what I think?"

"Paranoia," said Barr. "But it makes me feel more secure." Or it did before I started analyzing, he thought. Now I feel like an idiot.

"Well, it made me feel like an idiot," Patrick grumbled. "I went to a lot of trouble to get those two cards."

"Did you?" Barr asked. "Took me fifteen minutes, just the way you said it would. Fifteen minutes and fifty dollars. What's the matter?"

"Really fifty?"

"Sure: twenty for Woodrow Wilson White and thirty for Blasco Esquivel. Why?"

"I paid eighty for the two I bought." He paused in thought. "I guess you got the tickets then, too."

"Travel agent downtown," Barr confirmed. He'd walked in and paid cash: no fuss, no muss, and best of all no trace.

"You know, you're pretty good at this kind of thing," Patrick offered. "Tell you the truth, I'm surprised."

Not sarcasm, Barr decided; and worth answering, in the interest of repairing their bruised relationship. "I used to do some of that kind of hocus-pocus, for people in Washington," he explained. "Down in the Windwards and Leewards, when I owned *Windhover*."

"Washington? You mean, like the CIA?" said Patrick, clearly torn between interest and disbelief.

"I don't know," he replied. And he didn't, even after all this time. "Could be," he continued aloud. "They kept trying to convince me they were British, but it didn't go with what they were asking me to do."

"Like what?"

"All kinds of things." He still wondered, sometimes, what they'd really been up to. "Put half a dozen men ashore someplace, in the middle of the night. Survey a roadstead without the harbormaster noticing." He smiled reminiscently. "A lot of it involved moving stuff from island to island—big items, sometimes: I remember once we made a thirty-five-foot Chris-Craft just appear in Antigua. Duty-free." The local authorities had had difficulty ignoring that one, he recalled. But they'd managed, with some financial encouragement.

"Sounds like you might've been working for the Mafia," Patrick said. "Or the—what's their names?—Medellin Cartel."

"No, it was too stupid and pointless to be anything but a government operation," Barr said. "I guess it made me kind of cynical, after a while—but it was cynicism based on observation."

"Yeah. I saw some things in Salvador, when I was an adviser . . ." He let it trail off, his face twisted in perplexity. "But we were doing our best, you know? Trying to help those people. That's what I meant about cops."

"I know," Barr said, and for the instant he did. "I'm sure your uncle's an honest man—"

"My uncle the cop?" Patrick colored, laughed aloud. "Actually, he tried to make me marry Joanie, my kid's mother. Swore he'd cut my balls off if I didn't do the right thing by her. His words. But he's honest, all right." He picked up his still-full glass of champagne and took a sip. "Listen," he began, paused, pushed blindly ahead: "About your wife. I said some things I shouldn't have."

"But you were right," Barr heard himself say. "I should've kept her from putting *Windhover* on the coral. I could have, too. . . ." Three naked bodies writhing in the cockpit; would he ever be free of that memory? He looked down, startled, at the broken plastic champagne glass in his hand; continued without raising his eyes to meet Patrick's. "What I still don't know is how to deal with someone you love who's out of control. Turn them in? Would you?"

Before Patrick could construct an answer, the cabin steward materialized again, clucking his concern. "Let me get you another glass, sir."

"What?" He caught himself, added the quaver required by his new appearance. "Oh, thanks. And some more of those nuts, please."

"No," said Patrick firmly. "No more." He leaned over, addressing Barr's powerless hearing aid. "We have to watch our cholesterol, Mr. Esquivel. And our fats." He looked up at the hovering steward, his face a perfect mask of attentive concern. "Have you got any veggies? Carrot sticks, maybe, or celery?"

"Of course, Mr. White," the attendant burbled. He bent too close to Barr's head. "How about some nice celery sticks, Mr. Esquivel?"

Through the thick-lensed glasses the steward's face was a custard blob. "Sonny," said Barr, "you can take your celery sticks and shove them up your ass."

"What's that you're writing?" Patrick asked, a few silent minutes later.

"Just some numbers," Barr snapped, distracted in the midst of calculation. He stared down at the result scribbled on the cocktail napkin. Was that really possible? He began to redo the figures, then turned the napkin over and started from the beginning. When he had compared the two totals—nearly identical—he turned back to Patrick, who was ostentatiously looking out the port at a very ordinary carpet of cumulus below them. "Sorry if I bit your head off. I suddenly had an idea about how you could do it with a Concordia, and I wanted to see if it'd really work."

"Do what with a Concordia?" Patrick said to the windowpane. But curiosity overcame resentment, and he looked around. "And what's a Concordia, anyway? The name's familiar, but I can't place it."

"It's the class of sailboat *Kassandra's* one of." He had Patrick's full attention, moved the napkin where the other man could see it. "It dawned on me where you could put the cocaine. Look, this is a cross-section of a wood boat's hull: the planking's maybe seven-eighths mahogany, and these frames are inch-and-a-half oak, spaced eight or nine inches apart."

"Like *Glory*, only smaller scale," Patrick agreed. "Where's the interior—the berths, that stuff?"

"I didn't put it in. What's important is the air space between the frames," said Barr. He saw Patrick's bemused concentration and snatched the paper napkin back from him. As he talked, he sketched with broad, rapid strokes. "Here's a different view, from above. Look, between each frame is a cross-sectional space nine inches wide by an inch and a half deep. Thirteen and a half square inches—not a hell of a lot. But if you think of it as three-dimensional, running from the deck clamp down to the keel, you get a long, narrow slot—" His audience was becoming restless, and he summed up quickly: "Anyway, if you filled up those frame spaces in just the cockpit and the forward cabin, it'd come to something like nine cubic feet—or about three hundred and fifty kilos of any fine, white powder you care to name."

"I guess so," Patrick said slowly. "Sure. But what's the point? You lift the hatch, look down in the cockpit locker, and you can see the boat's side—planking, frames, the whole thing."

"Right. But what if you took really thin plywood planks—quarter-inch, say—and laid them over the existing frames, and then screwed down false frames on the inboard side of that false planking? You'd reduce the inside beam of the boat by three inches, total. Make her hobbyhorse a good deal, with all that extra weight in the ends, but I'll bet there's not a boarding officer in the Coast Guard who'd spot it. Remember, we're talking about some twenty-two-year-old bosun second, not a naval architect."

Patrick examined Barr's freehand drawings for a couple of long minutes, then went back over the calculations, his lips moving silently. "How come only the cockpit and the forward cabin?" he asked at last.

"Because they're the easiest to work with," Barr said. "In the fo'c'sle you'd just have to pull out a couple of berths and the lockers under them. Floorboards, too. They're only screwed down, so the wood could be saved and replaced. Under the cockpit would be harder for your carpenter to get at, but if you had a guy my size, reasonably wiry, you probably wouldn't even have to yank the engine. And so what if you did? It'd be a tedious piece of work, but nothing really tricky."

"So Win Huddleston's in on this thing after all?" Patrick demanded. "Is that what you're saying?"

"No. I'm only saying you could hide a lot of cocaine in a boat like his. We won't know about him unless we can find *Kassandra*'s twin and get aboard her."

"Oh, is that all?" said Patrick. "I thought it might be something hard."

From the airport they took a cab to the Bermudiana, a vast, rambling hotel overlooking the harbor. In the main-floor men's room, Barr tossed his glasses and hearing aids into the trash, and began hurriedly changing into the khaki trousers and short-sleeved shirt that Patrick produced from their joint carry-on bag. "What's the rush?" the mate said, as he unbuttoned the high-collared white tunic he'd worn on the plane.

"Too many boats in the harbor," Barr said. "Small boats. Must've been a very fast passage."

"You think *Kassandra's* here already?" Patrick demanded.

"That's what I'm afraid of," Barr replied. He balled up the old gray suit and jammed it into the cloth valise. "They'll know at the yacht club. Come on."

"At least stick your head under the faucet," Patrick said. "Wash off as much of that gunk as you can. If we see anybody who knows you, he'll think you died last week."

With Patrick laboring to keep up, Barr raced through the big, high-ceilinged lobby, and his heart sank farther. Troops of boisterous, lobster-faced young deckhands in their boatcrew polo shirts were surging in and out of the restaurant, while older sailors, weatherbeaten and gray-headed, their hairless, pipestem legs exposed by brand-new Bermuda shorts, stood about telling solemn lies. Too many of them, he thought. Too many by far.

"Wait!" The anguish in Patrick's voice turned heads all around them. Barr followed the mate's stare to a stack of fresh newspapers a hotel employee had just set down. The heavy black letters ran the width of the page, the ink still gleaming wet:

RACE SAILOR DEAD AFTER FINISH

And beneath it, in letters large enough to read from ten yards away:

Kassandra Watch Captain's Body Is Recovered
"A Heroic Self-Sacrifice"—Race Committee

A buzzing crowd was already homing on the papers, but Patrick smashed through them with Barr, head swimming, at his heels. A tall man with a vaguely familiar face was just straightening up, paper in hand, and Patrick snatched it from him. "Hey, what the hell . . ." He saw the mate's face and the words died on his lips.

"I can't read it," said Patrick wonderingly. "Here." He handed the paper to Barr, who saw his eyes were brimming.

I killed her. I let it happen. Just like Ann. In a minute, he knew, the pain would start. He forced himself to concentrate on the typeface, as if its shapes could cushion the meaning of the words. It worked so well that he was into the second paragraph before any of it penetrated. Then he exclaimed: "It's all right! Here, see for yourself."

Patrick was goggling at him. "But she's dead. It says so."

"Not Gillian." At that moment, the two most beautiful words in the language. He was dimly aware of the astonished faces, but he didn't care. "It's right here: Nico Butler. He's the one who died."

"That son of a bitch!" Patrick exploded. "Great!" The faces turned toward them were suddenly shocked and hostile, but the mate was oblivious. "She's okay, then?"

"Doesn't say." Barr scanned quickly down the page. "Happened this morning, just as they were coming in from the finish. According to this, Gillian fell overboard when the boat jibed accidentally—"

"I'll bet it did—"

"And Butler jumped in after her. It was still dark." As he read on, the scene came alive—dazed, still-exhausted men in the cockpit, staring with desperate concentration out into the blackness; sounds of splashing and voices close alongside. The boat was dead in the water by then, but they'd heard her calling for a line. . . .

"What is it?" Patrick was tugging urgently at his sleeve. "Where you going?"

Barr was already moving toward the lobby entrance. "She collapsed after they got her on board," he said over his shoulder. "They didn't find Butler for a couple of hours."

"Wait for me!" Patrick cried. "Dammit, I'm coming."

The compact, pink headquarters of the Royal Bermuda Yacht Club was virtually surrounded by an exuberant, sunburnt throng, three quarters of it male and fully half of it already glassy-eyed. On a balcony above them hung big white notice boards, one for each class, on which the finishers were listed in order, but by now everyone who cared knew the results by heart, and only when a new boat's name was posted did anyone even glance up. Beneath their feet the lawn had been trampled to rum-smelling mud, and the anecdotes were becoming more disjointed and less likely by the minute. Barr worked his way through the crowd, ignoring the few old friends who recognized him—"Christ, Barr, what happened to you?"—as he threaded his way toward the long pier, where the racing yachts lay anchored stern-to in a long, bobbing row.

Kassandra seemed deserted at first, though her companionway was open. Like many of the boats, she was hung with still-damp sleeping bags, sheets, and clothing, pinned to the lower rigging and flapping noisily in the brisk wind off the harbor. On a cockpit seat, spread neatly in the sun, was an orange jacket Barr recognized as Gillian's. "Aboard *Kassandra*," he called. "Anybody home?"

A hard finger tapped his arm, and he turned to find himself face to face with what looked, for a mad instant, like an elderly ape in gray flannel trousers and a white shirt. He refocused, and the ape became a short-haired, bowlegged old man with an amazingly broad upper lip and no chin to speak of. "You a reporter?" he demanded. "We've had enough reporters today."

Patrick, his forehead beaded with sweat, gasped up. "Where is she?"

"We're looking for Gillian Verdean," Barr said. "We're friends of hers."

"That's what the others said." The old man took a step backward, perhaps in response to the glowing impatience on Patrick's face.

Barr stepped between them. "Gillian sails with us," he said. "On Long Island Sound, back home."

The old man peered at him from reddened eyes. "You're a sailor?"

"Believe it or not," said Barr, acutely conscious of Patrick's heavy breathing at his back. "I gave her that jacket," he added. "The one on the seat, with the harness built in."

"Which she should've been wearing when she went overboard," said the old man. His simian face suddenly wrinkled in a broad smile, and he thrust out a leathery hand. "My name's Otley."

". . . So that was about it," he concluded, ten minutes later. "It was Win who saved her life—he was looking on the right side of the boat, jumped in when he saw her splashing in the water. We didn't find Nico, though—Bermuda search and rescue did. He must've hit his head on *Kassandra*'s hull." They were seated in *Kassandra*'s devastated cabin, which smelled to Barr like a very ancient swamp. Otley seemed less than grief-stricken, Barr thought, but maybe he was just too tired to show emotion.

"What about Gillian? The paper said she was suffering from exposure."

The old man apparently heard the doubt in Barr's tone. "Well, she was just about done when we hauled her aboard, even though she was only in the water five, ten minutes. I wasn't really surprised when she passed out."

"Passed out?" Patrick asked. He was poised uncomfortably on the edge of a lower berth, one of the cabin's few dry spots.

"That was what Win said," Otley replied. "Win's doctor friend was the one who talked about exposure. He said she needed bed rest, so he carted her off to his place."

Patrick's jaw dropped, and Barr quickly spoke up: "His hospital, you mean? He's a local physician?"

"Oh, this man's not local," Otley corrected him. "He's from New York, but he has a vacation place down here. Kind of a flashy-looking type, if you ask me."

On a sudden inspiration, Barr said, "I think I've met him—tall, a little heavy, straight hair combed back. Got a tan that looks as if it came out of a jar. Name's Martello, I think."

"Out of a jar, that's good," said Otley chuckling. "I didn't catch the name, but that's him, all right."

Patrick, who had been glancing about the cabin, remarked, "Looks like you've been packing up. I guess you're ready for a night in a hotel room, after this."

To Barr's surprise, Otley's face clouded with irritation. "Flying home this afternoon," he said. "Paul Marsh and I. Win asked us to —said he's sailing back tomorrow."

"And you're not crewing for him?" Barr asked. "Won't he be awfully shorthanded?"

"He didn't say," Otley growled. "And I didn't ask. But he's got some silly electrical autopilot." A thought seemed to occur to him. "That Gillian's a good girl."

"Yes," said Barr and Patrick together.

"A pretty little thing," Otley went on. "Hard as nails, despite her looks. Still, I can't say I like the idea of her and Win sailing old *Kassandra* back alone."

"Oh?" said Barr, with a quick warning glance at Patrick. "The boat looks all right, under the, ah . . ."

"She's a shithouse," Otley snapped. He looked surprised at himself, but continued doggedly: "That's the only word, I'm afraid. You might say it underlines what I'm getting at."

Patrick was visibly puzzled, but Barr felt himself comfortably within the old man's wavelength. "This the first high-seas passage you've made with Win?"

Otley nodded. "You understand. Thought you might. I've sailed with Win—oh, for twenty years. But always coastwise; never more than two nights." He looked infinitely sad. "The ocean can really search a man, you know?"

"I know," said Barr quietly, though he knew the old man's words were really for his own ears.

"I was very disappointed," Otley added. For a moment Barr was afraid he might cry, but he shook his head as if to clear it, looked up at his two visitors. "I want you to talk her out of sailing back with Win," he said firmly. "Don't know how you'll do it—she's a stubborn child—but I'm relying on you."

Patrick was on his feet. "Yes, *sir*," he said.

GILLIAN:
FRIDAY NOON,
DEVONSHIRE PARISH,
BERMUDA

She couldn't see under the water, but she knew that Nico was up above the surface, balanced on *Kassandra*'s rail, ready to jump down on her. She had to get at her knife, but something was holding her hands. And her feet, too. She thrashed desperately, dragged an agonizingly deep breath into her lungs . . .

A deep breath? Not underwater, Gillian. She stopped trying to swim, forced her muscles to relax. For some reason it was terribly hard to concentrate—her brain refused to fix on anything, and unwanted images seemed to rush into her head from all directions: Nico poised, Nico jumping. Nico thrashing in the water, grabbing at her with a terrible strength, pushing her head under the surface. Then it wasn't Nico but Win, with his arm around her chest, holding her up and calling for a rope. In spite of everything, she'd noticed it was rope he called for and not line; you may have saved my life, Win Huddleston, but you'll never be a sailor.

Without warning the images flipped back. Again she was struggling in Nico's grip, but she had the knife open at last, stabbing wildly at him. She must have got him, because he gave a choked yell and flung himself away from her. When his head hit *Kassandra*'s side, she felt the solid thump of it transmitted through the water.

Relief had undone her. She'd heard of that happening: drowning people who felt the grasp of rescuers, relaxed their struggle, slipped away. She was sliding under just as Win landed in the water beside her. He'd saved her life. Now the rest came back to her—Win dragging her below, and the agonizing pain as her shins cracked against the companionway steps; the squelching embrace of the mattress as he stretched her out on it. She was just thinking, I'm alive, thanks to Win, when she'd felt the sharp stab in her upper arm. What fool had broken a glass in the berth?

But I'm not in a berth now. And I can't see, and something's still holding my arms and legs.

Panic cut through the cobwebs wrapping her brain, an adrenaline rush like fire through her veins. Calm down, Gillian. Think. Make a list: what do I feel?

Eyes: they open and close all right, but I can't see. Eyelashes brushing against something. Pressure on forehead and cheeks; funny texture, like stiffly starched fabric.

Mouth: wedged open by something round and flexible between my teeth. A rubber ball? Can't spit it out—seems to be taped in place.

Fear began to rise in her throat, but she fought it back down, continued her ritual.

Nose: seems to be working. Land smells—plants, distant burning, used bedclothes. Strong overlay of stale perfume. Correction: men's cologne or after-shave or whatever they call it—heavy, creepy stuff.

Hands: immobilized behind my back. Prickle of cut-off circulation, but my fingers seem able to wriggle. Wrists could be lashed with sail ties.

Feet: the same, at the ankles.

Body: some pulled muscles, sharp pain from my poor shins, otherwise seemingly okay. Dressed in what feels like a sweatsuit, much too large.

Conclusion: I'm ashore, but where? And tied up—hell, packaged would be closer to it. Why?

I don't know. And I'm scared.

Wait a minute—what's that? Her body had begun to tremble uncontrollably, but she was able to ignore it as she strained to hear. A slamming door, some distance away, and rapid voices, one voice in particular. She tried to scream, but the only sound that got past her gag was a sort of muffled mewing.

It was Win's voice, and getting nearer. She still couldn't make out the words; he sounded angry and frightened. Maybe the same people who'd grabbed her had captured him, too. Another door, very near, opened and immediately slammed shut. She heard the squeak of rubber-soled shoes on waxed wood, and suddenly she could see.

The room was dim and gray, only a little sunlight finding its way between the shutter slats of a tall window. Win was leaning over her, his expression solicitous. He was wearing a terribly rumpled old seersucker suit, and he hadn't shaved. "How are you feeling?" he asked.

She wanted to snap *How do you think, dummy?* but it was hard to snap with her mouth full. He smiled pleasantly at her. *Doesn't he see this goddamn thing in my mouth?* She thrashed into a new position, in case her face was in shadow, but he only shook his head gently. "Please don't do that, Gillian. You'll just hurt yourself."

She sank back onto the bed—a big double, with rumpled sheets— as a new and far deeper sense of fear began to chill her heart. Win seemed to read her eyes. He nodded, the smile still glowing on his careworn face. "Yes," he said. "I'm afraid so."

But he'd saved her life. Even with her brain still reeling she was certain of that much. If only she could speak, she'd be able to get to him. She bit furiously down on the yielding gag, trying to tear it apart, but the rubber only gave a little and sprang back. "You're wondering why I saved your life, I expect." He laughed—the same modest laugh that so endeared him to his employees. "The fact is, we need you, my dear. Poor Nico forgot that. Quite blew a fuse, in fact. He saw you as the source of all our problems, when of course you're going to be part of the solution."

He sat on the edge of the bed, and Gillian twisted around to keep him in view. Behind her back she levered one hand against the other, trying to force a little slack in the hard, slippery ties around her wrists. She twisted and turned until she could feel the fabric bite into her skin, but it was no use.

"Actually, we need you twice over." He seemed to be musing aloud, but Gillian had the feeling his words were aimed—and not at her. "Since you're so valuable, it's only fair you should know why."

Now she was sure of it: he kept glancing quickly at the door, which was open a crack. "First, of course, you're bait," he was saying. "By now, your friends should be on the way here, unless both of them are insufferably thick, and I can't see you having *two* stupid friends."

Friends. Both. Two: just enough weight on each word so she knew he meant to make her writhe. She wouldn't give him that satisfaction, but even so she couldn't drag her eyes from his.

"Of course, we wondered about you from the moment you strolled in *TNF*'s door—a very nervy performance, by the way." The condescension in his voice had corroded her fear to rage, which made her feel somehow better, though she knew one emotion was as dangerous as the other. "You had K.C. fooled right to the end, if you care," he went on, reminiscently. "Or, rather, you had her guessing. She was like you: an efficient, straightforward mind, without perception. Or should it be vision? Both, I expect. But she was damned useful—a pity she had to die, just as it was a pity to lose Nico. Really, my dear," he laughed gently, "you and your friends have been a dreadful trial to us. You might have derailed our entire enterprise—Roger was quite worried."

He glanced down at his watch. "I hope I haven't overrated Captain Barr's intelligence. We certainly went out of our way to leave a trail for him." He must have seen the dawning horror in her eyes: "How do I know his name? Well, there's no harm telling you now, especially—"

A knock on the door at his back cut him off. "They're here? Good." Quickly he stepped to the tall window and opened the louvers of one shutter just enough to stripe the bed and Gillian with sunlight. "There," he said, stepping back and surveying his work. "That should do it nicely."

PATRICK:
EARLY AFTERNOON

He was crouched awkwardly in the bushes, trying to ignore the pain—diminished, but still very much there—and concentrate on the big, shuttered house. With bright sun glinting off the pair of freshly waxed sedans parked in the crushed stone drive, and the tall, manicured foliage all around, the place looked like a magazine car ad. At Patrick's back loomed the wall he and Barr had scaled, rough coral blocks covered with thin moss, and from behind it the muted noise of traffic on the North Road. In front, through the thick shrubbery beyond the house, he could see bright blue glimpses of the north shore shallows, and hear the splashing of wavelets on the beach. At a tap on his shoulder he looked quickly around. Barr, kneeling at his side, was pointing to the second window from the end, whose shutter was open about six inches. Patrick had already noticed it: perfect, which made it too much like a trap, especially when every other ground-floor window seemed to be sealed tight.

Maybe on the other side. He eased to his feet, motioned Barr to stay where he was. The skipper ashore couldn't move three feet without bumping into something; trying to creep silently through brush he sounded like an elephant having a fit. As Patrick drifted soundless as smoke among the chest-high bushes along the wall, his eyes darted from the branches to his feet and back again, alert for tripwires. Ordinary watchfulness wouldn't have spotted their approach: they'd paid off the taxi a hundred yards beyond the house, around a sharp bend, then come back on foot, using the wall itself for cover. The spot where they'd climbed over was shielded from the house by a whole clump of low tree.

These days, of course, there were so many ways of guarding a place like this, and most of the electronic ones were invisible. For all Patrick knew, he and Barr had been closed-circuit TV stars for the last half hour.

He pulled up short at a suggestion of movement in one of the open upstairs windows, then saw it was only an edge of faded curtain, fluttering in the small breeze. Below it, though . . . He considered the ground between him and the house: five steps to that bush with the thick, yellowish leaves, then three more to the blind corner. A big risk, but the louvers on the ground-floor window next to the corner seemed to be just slightly open. He drew into himself, counted down: three, two, one, *go*; and sprinted for the bush.

He was ready for slashing pain up the inside of his thigh, and in fact it wasn't as bad as he'd expected. Second dash and he was against the wall, feeling naked as a jaybird in the afternoon sun. But the shutter's wooden louvers were open, all right. He floated along the wall, moving extra slow, until the side of his face overlapped the frame and he could put one eye to the shutter.

At first glance he missed her entirely. The room was in shadow, and Gillian was lying motionless in the middle of the big, rumpled bed. She rolled over, and he saw her face, distorted by the gag. As his eye slowly adjusted to the twilight inside, he saw the odd position of her arms and legs and realized she was bound. She was staring wide-eyed at him; she must see the silhouetted curve of his face. At God knew what cost, she struggled up on her elbows. Muffled sounds came through the gag, and he saw she was shaking her head violently, back and forth.

So it *is* a trap, he said to himself, and took a cautious step back. From immediately overhead came a high, familiar voice: "Hold right there, cocksucker."

"So you're Barr," said Win Huddleston, standing over the three heavy armchairs to which they'd been lashed. "The gallant captain of this ruined band, to coin a phrase."

Barr's head was cocked back and to one side, and he watched Huddleston with no change in his expression. He should have looked silly—a short, skinny guy with matted hair and smears of makeup still showing around his eyes and ears—but he had a private kind of dignity that Patrick found himself envying. Not that it would do them any good. Strong-arming Patrick into the house, Golem had managed to whisper, "You're gonna get it, all three of you, but you I'm saving for myself."

"You can take that thing out of Gillian's mouth," Barr suggested calmly. "She's not going to do anything embarrassing, like beg for mercy."

Huddleston colored, but he nodded to Golem. "You think I'm a monster, don't you."

"Not in the usual sense, no," said Barr.

Golem bent over Gillian, hiding her from Patrick's view. There was a harsh ripping noise, and a muted cry. The big man stepped back, holding a broad strip of silver tape with a red rubber ball stuck to it. Gillian was glaring up at him, her eyes wet and blazing.

Huddleston winced at the angry path the tape had ripped across her face; he turned quickly back to Barr. "As opposed to Golem, you mean. Now, he's right out of the New York Post."

"That's right," Golem put in. "I was on Page Six once."

Huddleston's eyebrows shot upward in surprise, but he caught himself quickly. "Yes, well, it's certainly where you belong," he said. "But as for me, Captain Barr, what kind of monster am I?"

"Maybe you'd better tell me," Barr replied.

"Perhaps I shall, since we've got plenty of time."

"Before your brother's boat arrives—from where? Colombia? Venezuela?" Barr asked.

Huddleston smiled refusal. "That would be telling."

Barr shrugged. "But you did get into Bermuda a little ahead of schedule. And a lot more publicly than you'd planned."

"What a contretemps!" Huddleston agreed. "We came within a hair of winning our class, too—that would've been the final touch." Annoyance crept across his face. "As it was, I had to waste most of the morning eating crow in front of the Race Committee. Dour, self-righteous blockheads. But I suppose you'd disagree."

Barr seemed uninterested. "Don't know that I ever thought twice about them," he said. "Of course, I've never been part of that crowd."

"Penrod at the dance?" said Huddleston. Barr seemed to catch his meaning. A ghost of a smile came and went. "That's always been my own inclination," Huddleston continued, with a sigh. "It's never been possible."

"I guess not," Barr replied. He looked amazingly relaxed to Patrick, especially considering the way Golem and Frannie X had lashed him and the chair into one big snarl. On Patrick's other side, Gillian, who had been smoldering visibly, opened her mouth to speak, but Barr was first. "D'you know the expression *to get athwart someone's hawse?*"

"I think so," Huddleston said, looking puzzled. "Drift down onto another person's anchor line, isn't that it?"

"With the implication of its being accidental," Barr agreed. "By extension, to get in someone else's way generally. That's what we've done with you, really. We were hired to find your brother's girlfriend, Sarah Farmer—"

"Farber," Huddleston corrected automatically. "I know that."

From his vantage point at Barr's side, Patrick saw the skipper's clenched fists go white across the knuckles, but he continued in the same hesitant tone: "That's still the only thing we're interested in. I'm sorry it all got so bloody, but it was your associates who stirred up Sarah's father, and your associates who panicked afterwards."

"You're too generous, Captain Barr," Huddleston said. "I was the one who turned Mr. Farber away so ineptly, so I suppose I started it."

"Well, it hardly matters now," said Barr, and Patrick wondered at the offhand way he could talk about two—no, three—violent deaths. "My point is—"

The door burst open without warning. Golem spun around to face it, dragging at the pistol jammed in his belt, but the intruder was only Frannie X, who had vanished after helping tie down Barr. "I heard him!" Frannie gasped.

Huddleston looked down his nose at his panting assistant. "You're sure?"

"Sure I'm sure. He came up on the four-meter band, just the two words 'first call,' like we planned." He waited, chest still heaving, for Huddleston's approval.

"And you said?"

"*Nothing.* Of course not." Frannie was hurt. "I just scratched the mike twice, with my fingernail."

"Good," Huddleston said absently. And then, seeing that Frannie expected congratulations, "Very good. You've done well." For a second, Patrick expected him to pull out a dog biscuit, but he had a better reward for his helper: "You can have one snort, Frannie. From the contingency bag. But only one, mind."

"All *right*," Frannie beamed.

Huddleston watched the door shut behind him, murmured, "One works with what one has, I suppose," to the ceiling. Glancing at his watch, he turned his attention back to Barr. "You were starting to say?"

"All Sol Farber wants is to be reassured his daughter's safe. If you can produce her, I'll fly Farber down here. They meet, and that's that."

It sounded so natural, the way Barr said it, that Patrick was hardly surprised when Huddleston replied: "You're not insisting on Sarah's return? Her deprogramming, as it were?"

Patrick found himself holding his breath, but Barr sounded almost bored: "She's over twenty-one. I assume she went with Roger because she wanted to. . . ."

"God *damn* it, Barr," Gillian breathed, but he ignored her completely.

"Besides," he went on, with a twisted grin that reminded Patrick of Huddleston himself, "we're not really in a position to insist."

"A hit, Captain Barr. A palpable hit."

"Seems an acceptable compromise," said Barr, as if commenting on somebody else's suggestion. "Farber gets as much reassurance as a parent ever sees, and you get him out of your hair." He paused. "What do you say?"

A broad smile spread across Huddleston's worn face, and he broke into applause. "Wonderful! Superb!"

"You agree, then?"

"I agree you're the most plausible man I've met outside the State Department," said Huddleston cheerfully. "But you know as well as I do that I've got to kill you and your friends."

Barr seemed unsurprised: "Well, it was worth a—"

Again the door slammed open, and the short, round form of Sol Farber appeared, struggling to tear himself from Frannie X's grasp. "You can't!" he cried. "You promised!" He took in Gillian's bruised face, apparently for the first time. "This is awful! You promised she'd be safe and sound."

Patrick heard Gillian whisper, "Uncle Sol, you *didn't!*" and saw Barr's face knot up in pain. Only then did that *you promised* sink in, and he felt as if someone had just put the boots to him.

"On the contrary, Mr. Farber," Huddleston was saying, "I told you *Sarah* would be unharmed. And so she will." Shaking his head in mock dismay, he turned to Barr: "I'm afraid he betrayed you."

"So it seems," Barr said, and Patrick realized from his tone that he'd already known.

"It wasn't like that!" Farber shouted, wrenching away from Frannie X. "As God should strike me down! I didn't want anybody to get hurt. If you and Patrick went to the right plane, you'd be safe now."

"Safe in jail," Patrick heard himself growl.

"I was afraid for Sarah," Farber pleaded. "You kept talking—police this, Coast Guard that. I couldn't bear to think of my little girl in jail. . . ."

"And what about Gillian, you little prick?" Patrick snarled.

"He promised me," Farber insisted. "He did. Everything would be all right: you and Captain Barr out of the way—just for a few days. Gillian could go home, once she saw Sarah. It would have worked. . . ." His voice failed under Patrick's steady glare, and he turned to Gillian, his hands extended, but she only shook her head and closed her eyes.

Barr had turned to Huddleston. "Farber called you when? Yesterday." How could he be so calm? "But not for the first time." The old man, staring wide-eyed at Barr, recoiled as if he'd been struck and collapsed in a chair, his face in his hands.

"Mr. Farber and I did have one rather oblique discussion just before I sailed," Huddleston admitted. "He's been in touch with Mr. Martello all week, though. Mr. Farber was afraid you were going to bring the authorities down on his daughter."

So that was what triggered it: I scared him into the arms of this bastard. Red rage blinding him, Patrick hurled himself vainly against the torn strips of sheet that held him down. He saw Golem's fist poised, but Huddleston shouted, "Stop it!"

Patrick sagged back, helpless, heard Barr say, "Well, I guess maybe we should have. Sorry, Patrick."

"You're not safe yet," said Gillian suddenly. "Remember the Coast Guard cutter we saw, the one that scared Nico so much? How do you know they're not down here looking for Roger?"

"They're looking in every direction at once, these days," Huddleston said. "That's our best protection." To Barr: "I really regret having to . . . do this, but you see the necessity."

"No, to tell you the truth, I don't."

"Stalling for time, Captain Barr?" asked Huddleston, smiling. Patrick could feel Golem, just behind him, move a hair closer.

"Why not? But I really am surprised that someone like you's involved in the actual dirty work."

"Why not, indeed?" said Huddleston. "We've got a few hours— that call told me Roger's boat is sixty miles out; we won't be able to rendezvous until late tonight . . . which reminds me: Frannie, call up Bermuda Customs. Tell them *Kassandra* will be clearing from Hamilton this afternoon, to sail this evening."

"You got it." Frannie X took a step toward the door.

"And then stay by the radio, please." Huddleston smiled apologetically at Barr. "Roger will call again when he's thirty miles away. We have till then."

"Another two-word message," Barr suggested.

"And on a different frequency," Huddleston agreed, nodding. "It's really quite clever, don't you think?"

"Simple and effective. And that's when you kill us, right?"

Farber, who was slumped in the armchair, staring glassily at nothing, gave a reflexive whimper; Huddleston's face wrinkled with distaste. "There's no point rubbing it in. You won't change my thinking."

"Your *thinking*?" Barr's tone was detached, but one eyebrow was raised in the manner that had always bugged Patrick. Apparently it annoyed Huddleston, too.

"This isn't some criminal panic, it's sheer necessity." Huddleston bit his words off cleanly, but he didn't seem to like the taste. "I've already told Gillian why it's so important *The New Federalist* survive. I even thought—foolishly, I see now—that she understood."

Gillian still seemed to be groggy from whatever Huddleston had jabbed her with, but at the sound of her name she sat up. Barr threw her a warning look, which she missed, and addressed their captor. "Maybe you'd like to tell me."

"I doubt that someone like you would appreciate it . . ." Huddleston began, and Patrick heard what sounded like wistfulness in his voice.

"Why not try me?" Barr asked.

Huddleston eyed his shabby captive thoughtfully. "What do you think of the state of the nation?" he rapped out suddenly.

Barr blinked. "Don't think about it much," he said. "Out of control, for the most part. The government's in business for itself, and everybody else just wants first place at the trough."

Huddleston was eyeing Barr suspiciously. "Almost too pat, Captain. What's your answer?"

"I haven't got one, except to mind my own business." He seemed to consider his words, gave Huddleston a sour smile: "Not exactly noble, is it? Sounded better in *Candide*, somehow."

"Well, not everyone's Voltaire," Huddleston said. "But basically you're right. Of course, I tend to have a global view of things, being situated as I am . . ."

"Of course," Barr murmured.

". . . And from that perspective, our government's no worse than most—it just has more opportunities to make the worst of." He paused, as if to make sure Barr had taken it in, and allowed himself a dry chuckle. "Make the worst of. And they certainly do. It's the same with the American people: they look greedier because they've got more to be greedy with. The condition—the Gadarene stampede, if you will—is worldwide. But"—his posture, his raised hand, reminded Patrick of Father Fahey, years ago—"but it won't last forever, any more than the Dark Ages did. That's where *TNF* comes in: to preserve something from the impending wreckage, to provide an example for the future."

"Then you don't see yourself as a . . . savior," said Barr, deadpan.

"Savior? Goodness, no." He sure liked the word, though, Patrick thought. "Of course, one wouldn't mind recognition eventually, but one doesn't expect to see it. No, not a savior—the word's got an unfortunate connotation—nor a prophet, which sounds even worse. A *preserver*, of the best things our civilization has created."

"So they don't have to be reinvented, you mean," said Barr. How the hell was he following this nuttiness?

"Exactly." Huddleston beamed his approval, but then his face clouded. "And that's what you and your friends are threatening:

Without a channel, without the very specific channel of *The New Federalist*, our message won't be heard. And today, with Gresham's Law running amok, a publication like ours can't hope to achieve commercial success."

"I guess it's not easy to find the money," Barr offered.

"Only the meretricious gets fully funded," Huddleston answered. "That's why we've been reduced to this."

"*This* being dope smuggling," said Barr.

"You're needling me, I see. Yes, our mission is supported by illegal drugs. By *trafficking*: there's the pejorative you're groping for." He laughed harshly, maybe to show what he thought of pejoratives. "We pander to depravity—just look at my associates. But ask yourself this: Does cocaine do a tenth the physical damage legalized alcohol does? Is it a fraction as morally corrupting as commercial television? Does it kill anywhere near as many people as Detroit's automobiles?" As he went on, Huddleston's voice rose and strained, and the veins at his temples stood out, blue and pulsing. "No, Captain Barr, cocaine is just a part of the culture, a symptom of accelerating collapse. You could say it's a paradigm of our age—instant gratification and gradual self-destruction, with overtones of megalomania."

He was breathing hard, his mouth wet at the corners. Gillian, Patrick saw, was watching him as if he'd turned into a tarantula before her eyes. "Use it yourself, do you?" Barr asked innocently.

"Of course not," Huddleston snapped. "And I regret that Roger couldn't find a more elevated way to support us. But I've simply had to rise above it. And I have the endorsement, as you might say, of our nation's most eminent Founding Father."

"Tell me," said Barr.

"*Exitus acta probat*. You're obviously an educated man, Captain Barr. Does it ring a bell?"

"No Latin and less Greek, I'm afraid."

"George Washington's motto. And its inescapable translation? *The end justifies the means*." With that, he flung out of the room, leaving Golem to keep an eye on his three prisoners and on the distraught, collapsed Sol Farber.

Patrick watched the light coming through the louvers dim slowly, until it was a pearly gray. "What time is it?" he asked Golem, who had been sitting without speech or movement for two hours.

"Shut up, asshole," the wrestler grunted. But he looked at his watch. "Six-thirty. Not much longer."

Gillian broke half an hour of silence: "If I don't have the chance to say it later, I'm sorry I got you guys into this."

"I'm sorry I didn't listen to Patrick," Barr said thoughtfully.

And I'm sorry I can't get my hands on that Sol Farber, Patrick thought. Golem, too. From outside, Frannie X's angry voice drifted clearly through the shuttered window: "I said you're not sticking me with that, and I mean it."

The door opened and Frannie appeared, looking tired and anxious. Sweat stains made splotches on his rose-colored shirt, and his white pants had stains like tar on both knees. "Where you been?" Golem asked. "Where's Mr. Huddleston?"

"He's outside," Frannie growled. "We had to bring the boat around from Hamilton. First the goddamn spade Customs man kept us waiting half an hour, and then it took Win half an hour more to convince him that sweetcakes here was too sick to get on board at the yacht club. Did Roger call in?"

Golem's broad face registered first surprise and then dismay. "Shit, I don't know, Frannie. I was in here the whole time."

"Fucking *hell!* This whole operation's nothing but the goddamn amateur hour," Frannie snarled. "Wasn't like this with—"

"With my brother running it?" Win Huddleston suggested, stepping through the door. He was dressed for the sea, Patrick observed, from his new-looking Top-Siders to the navy blue watch cap that balanced on top of his thinning hair. In his hand was what looked like a portable transmitter. "Just remember," he continued, his voice acid, "Roger's self-indulgence caused the mess we're in now. If he hadn't sniffed himself into collapse last year, he wouldn't have taken two strangers aboard. Two *witnesses,* Frannie. And Escobar—"

"Trigger-happy spic," Frannie interrupted.

"What else could he have done with them?" Win demanded. "Though sinking the decoy boat to cover it . . . *that* was clumsy. But," he shrugged, "what's past is past. We have today's problem to solve now."

Patrick knew his time had come, knew he was even more helpless than he'd been back on Nico Butler's hateful table. The knowledge had somehow drained him dry. He hardly felt scared anymore, just bone-tired. He turned his head for a last look at his friends, just as two voices shouted "No!" together. Frannie and Sol Farber were both on their feet, both red in the face.

"You can't!" Farber cried, throwing himself at Win.

"Not in my goddamn house!" said Frannie, grabbing the old man by the collar and hurling him, breathless, back into his chair.

Huddleston looked quickly to Golem, who had dropped into a half-crouch, his head swinging expectantly from side to side, and said to Frannie, "What's this, a mutiny?"

"The whole way around from Hamilton you haven't been listening," said the nightclub owner furiously. "I've been telling you this is a tiny goddamn island. You can't hide four fucking bodies here, they'll stick out like . . . like I don't know what. And even if you could, I'm sure as hell not going to do it alone." He stopped, out of breath, and waited for Huddleston's answer. Getting none, he continued in an angry rumble, "Anyhow, there's six hundred miles of ocean out there, plus a lot of hungry sharks."

"You've got a point," Huddleston replied. "But what do you mean, *four* bodies?" He smiled on Farber, whose sagging jowls were a mask of horror. "Sol here is our ally. He's going to live and prosper. And he's going to see his tiresome daughter—back in New York."

"Three's still too many," muttered Frannie. "One'd be too many. I told you, this place—"

"All *right*," Huddleston snapped. "We'll do it your way. I certainly don't want Gillian's body turning up here when she and I are supposed to be clearing Customs in New York." He looked into Gillian's stunned face, and dropped into phony regretfulness: "I'm sorry, my dear, but Sol's daughter will be using your passport, which makes you rather *de trop*."

"So that was why you pulled me out of the water?" she said slowly.

"You had to arrive in Bermuda so you could be on *Kassandra*'s crew list going back north." He smiled happily at his own cleverness. "Of course, Sarah will be taking your place—amazing how much you two look alike, at least in a passport photo."

Farber gave a choked cry of despair that drew all eyes. They were still staring at him when the small radio in Huddleston's hand crackled: "Second call," said a man's voice, speaking slow and clear.

BARR:

FRIDAY NIGHT,

OFF NORTH ROCK

Kassandra dug her bow into a swell and momentarily lost way. The sudden lurch threw Patrick off balance, and he slid six inches aft along the berth, bumping into Barr, who braced to stop him. The previous time it had happened, all three prisoners had wound up in a heap on the cabin sole, affording Golem the amusement of man-handling each of them back onto the starboard lower berth. That was at least two hours ago, Barr figured; since then, the wind had risen, pushing the seas into intransigent heaps and making the yawl's abrupt movements less predictable. Barr could feel Huddleston, at the tiller, repeatedly edging *Kassandra* too far into the wind, until she went into spasms of pitching that killed her speed almost completely.

The companionway hatch was nearly closed, to keep the light from belowdecks out of Huddleston's eyes, and the resulting shortage of fresh air was having its effect on Golem, sitting across from his bound and muffled victims. Barr had watched the big man progress from vague uneasiness through the whole range of classic symptoms; he was sweating visibly now, wetting his lips every few seconds and swallowing hard. Under the single, dim bulb his skin seemed an almost luminous green.

Not that Barr—or Patrick or Gillian—would be able to do any-thing about it, even if Golem became violently ill. Before they'd been brought aboard *Kassandra*, the three of them had been trussed into near immobility, their ankles taped together, hands tied behind their backs, silver tape gags covering their mouths. If by some miracle he got out of this, Barr knew he would never forget the bitter taste of tape.

Patrick had given up; considering his condition it was surprising he'd kept his spirit as long as he had, but it cut Barr to the heart to see his friend slumped hopelessly against the berth's backrest, eyes dull and unseeing. Gillian, by contrast, was still struggling against the line around her wrists. Whatever Huddleston had given her had completely worn off now, and Golem's pawing, as he dragged her off the cabin sole, had brought her to a pitch of outrage. If her wrists were as securely tied as Barr's, she was burning energy uselessly, but anything was better than despair. There might—just might—come a chance to strike out; if it came, Barr intended to be ready. Since he couldn't keep himself on a hair trigger hour after hour, he explored in his mind the ways Huddleston, Golem, or *Kassandra* herself might be damaged, but all the possibilities depended on having at least one hand free for a few seconds, and that seemed less and less likely.

He knew how they were to die—Huddleston had briefed Golem twice, yelling instructions down the hatchway as they motored along Bermuda's north shore. Nothing fancy; they'd simply be wrapped in lengths of *Kassandra*'s anchor chain and heaved overboard. The chain itself lay on the floorboards before them in three innocent-looking piles, chinking gently as the boat pitched. Barr recognized it as standard five-sixteenths-proof coil, about a pound per foot of length; plenty to drag a bound and writhing man down into the black depths, struggling helplessly until his lungs couldn't—

Stop that.

He forced himself to concentrate on the yawl's movements, on the sounds of the water against the hull, the wind in the rigging. *Kassandra* was working harder now, no question. They must be nearing the stationary squall line he and Patrick had seen from the plane this morning. Only this morning—it was hard to believe that twelve hours ago they'd been making fun of the cabin steward, and now they were on the edge of death.

The storm was a gift to Huddleston—not that he needed any more help. Once beneath those towering thunderheads, engulfed in torrents of rain, *Kassandra* and her single-masted sibling would be practically invisible to chance passersby, and to radar as well. All the two skippers had to do was find each other.

But what if they couldn't? A new line of possibility opened up to Barr's fevered thoughts, and he flogged his exhausted brain down its track.

Kassandra headed up into the wind, sails volleying wildly, and then fell back on the old tack. As the sails filled she lay over steeply, spilling the prisoners to the deck once more and toppling the miserably sick Golem over backward. The hatch slid open, and Huddleston's face, streaming water, appeared in the black square. "It's Roger!" he yelled, raw nerves edging his voice. "Get up on deck, quick!"

Golem clawed his way up the ladder, treading heavily on Patrick. *Glory*'s mate doubled over in pain, grunting through the layers of tape that sealed his mouth. Gillian was lying jammed against the ladder, her back to Barr. With the strength of desperation he squirmed over a spilled pile of chain, rolling so his back was to hers, his numbed fingers groping for her wrists. He could feel her arms twisting under his grasp, realized she was trying to free him. For a moment he fought her. His hands were much more powerful; he could get the knots loose quicker. But once freed he would be the more dangerous attacker. He relaxed, willing his own skill into her small, hard fingers.

Rain or spray or both spattered down the companionway. Barr could hear confused shouting from the cockpit. *Kassandra*'s motion abruptly eased—she was hove-to, he could tell—but from the occasional shuddering heave that dragged her backward, he guessed Roger must have secured his boat's bow to the yawl's stern.

The knots Golem had made around Barr's wrists were as tight as sadism could pull them. He felt one of Gillian's fingernails snap off short, but she was still probing, tugging when Barr sensed a figure looming above him and looked up.

The man framed in the hatchway was gaunt, even under his streaming foul-weather gear. His sharp nose stuck out above what might have been a handlebar mustache when it wasn't plastered to his face; his chin was overgrown with straggling beard. Unlikely tufts of thin hair spotted his scalp, but his brows were thick, drooping down over tired, deepset eyes. He swung himself easily through the hatch and dropped down the ladder; without a word, his bare foot kicked Gillian's hands free of Barr's wrists. His eyes met Barr's without blinking. "What a mess," he said.

Stepping carefully over Patrick, who had rolled onto his back, the newcomer dropped on one of the berths and surveyed the cabin. "What happened to the table?" he asked, directing his words up the companionway.

Win Huddleston had replaced his brother in the hatch, but he showed no desire to come below. "It got smashed during the storm. Does it matter?"

"Hell, no. It was a piece of junk anyway. Just remember to pull the table out of my boat, soon as you have a minute." Roger leaned back, clearly pleased. "Aside from that, looks like a perfect match."

"Hadn't we better get to work, Roger?" his brother asked. "What if somebody stumbles on the two boats tied together?"

"In this weather? Not likely. Besides, I'm beat. I've been sailing that bastard eighteen hours a day for two weeks—without a mizzen she's got a lee helm that drives the autopilot nuts, and I don't dare trust Sarah at the tiller." He looked pointedly at his brother. "Which is something you want to bear in mind."

"Not trust her? Why not?"

"The fast track was a little too fast for her, I guess," Roger replied wearily. "Christ, I don't know." He considered the three mute, staring figures on the cockpit sole and shook his head. "Looks like you really fucked this one up, brother dear. Tell me about it."

Win Huddleston's report, delivered with reluctance, veered from self-serving to abject and back again. Things might have been different ashore, but at sea there was no question which Huddleston was dominant. Roger briskly channeled his brother's meanderings, cutting off the excuses, pinning the evasions. At the end, he shook his head. "So I've got old Golem for my sailing buddy, instead of Nico. Could be worse, I suppose. Well, we'd better get to work."

They left the damp, partly recovered Golem on watch below and went on deck to deal with the rigging. Barr, tossed back on the bunk like a bag of laundry, followed Roger's shouted orders with a sinking heart. It was all too clear that this was a man who knew boats, and who had perfected the routine for unstepping and restepping a spar in midocean. The whole operation took no more than an hour, and then a half hour more to switch the two yachts' personal gear, from pots to books to clothing. Roger even extracted the VHF transmitter and the loran and passed them up the hatch to his brother. Turning, he saw Barr's eyes on him. "That's why I got plug-in units," he explained. "Nothing snows the government mind like numbers, and now they all match—serials on these gizmos, documentation carved into the main beam."

Sound of light steps in the cockpit, and Roger's face darkened. "What're you doing here?" he demanded. "I told you to stay back on the other boat."

The young woman feeling her way carefully down the ladder ignored him, as she ignored the three bound figures on the bunk. "You forgot this," she said, holding out a clumsy, cloth-wrapped bundle. She looked taller than Gillian by a couple of inches and older by a decade, but the resemblance was still striking. Remembering the bleary photo in Gillian's passport, Barr knew no one would notice the difference. With the documents Huddleston had taken, Sarah Farber could be Gillian Verdean for as long as she wanted.

"I didn't forget," Roger snapped. "That's just an excuse. You won't learn, will you?" His right hand went up quickly and she flinched. As the cabin light flooded her face, Barr saw the bruise over her cheekbone; Roger clearly saw it, too: "Oh, Christ. I'm sorry," he said, his voice gentler. "That's no way to say good-bye." He took the parcel and cut the twine binding it. "Document board," he murmured, "name boards, ship's papers, ship radio license. All present and accounted for." He looked up at Sarah, who was standing silently waiting.

"Please," she said, her eyes filling with tears—brown eyes, like Gillian's, but bloodshot and circled with fatigue.

"It's not a good idea, kid." She didn't move, and he shrugged. "Okay: They're your nightmares."

Quickly Sarah turned to Gillian, whose eyes, wide and despairing now, were locked on her friend. Sarah leaned forward, lost her balance and caught herself, and embraced the smaller woman. "Good-bye, dear," she whispered, kissed her quickly on the cheek, and stood. Gillian had fallen back on the bunk, her eyes tightly closed. Tears seeped from beneath the lids. "Good luck," said Sarah, and fled up the companionway.

"What good did that do?" Roger asked sadly.

His brother's head and shoulders appeared in the hatch. He was haggard and wild-eyed, and Barr, whose nerves felt as if they had been sanded raw, sensed that the reality of what he'd embarked on was just now sinking in. "We're ready to sail, Roger," he said.

"Good," Roger answered. And as his brother's head began to pull back, continued quickly: "Wait a minute." He stood by the companion ladder, swaying gently with the motion of the hove-to boat, pulling his thoughts together. "Now listen up, Win. One," extending his forefinger, "I told Sarah about her father, so she knows: any trouble from her, and he gets it. But she's not in the best shape lately, so make allowances. Two, don't forget to tighten up the mizzen rigging once the wind dies—and pin those goddamn turnbuckles, or you'll lose the whole mast." He paused, thinking hard. "What am I forgetting? You called Rodriguez at the yard, and he'll be waiting for you, so that's okay. Oh, yes: one other thing. Did you see anything that looked like patrol activity, coming down here? Choppers or Falcons—the little Coast Guard jets—buzzing you? Any Coast Guard cutters at all?"

"I don't . . ." Win Huddleston began slowly. His eyes suddenly sharpened. "As a matter of fact, there was a cutter, a little more than a day before the finish. But it's all right: I saw her again, tied up in Hamilton Harbour, just this afternoon. Why do you ask?"

Roger's matted beard hid his expression, but his voice was calm, even soothing. "Nothing, probably. The competition down south is getting a little ugly, that's all. The big Panchos want to squeeze us little guys out, and the easiest way is to tip off the American DEA. I heard a rumor, just before I left . . ." His brother seemed to be slipping from concern to fright, and Roger caught himself. "Forget it. Just remember, if you see a Coastie, sail right at him. Call him on the radio and ask for your position. If you're boarded, give him your Court of the Hapsburgs shtick. Remember: if they're looking for anything, it'll be a sloop, not a yawl—and you've never been south of Bermuda."

The other managed a weak smile. "I'll deal with it. But you . . . I hope you won't waste any time. . . ." His eyes drifted uncontrollably to Gillian, darted away.

"As soon as you're out of sight," Roger assured him. "Now, head for the barn. And the bank."

Golem rolled up the sleeves of his shirt with elaborate care, tucking the cuffs under and then tugging at one sleeve until it was exactly the length of the other. He got up, balancing awkwardly against *Kassandra's* smooth, loping motion. Patrick had come out of his lethargy and was glaring at the huge wrestler, but Golem had put a sail tie around his neck and lashed it to the bunk rail, so that *Glory's* mate could barely twitch without throttling himself. "You watch," said Golem happily. "You get to see it twice."

So now it really was over, Barr thought.

He craned his neck to look past Golem, standing over him and flexing his huge paws. Gillian, seemingly unconscious, lay on her back, her eyes still closed. He would have given nearly anything to look into those familiar brown eyes one more time, but he knew it was infinitely better that she not see what was coming. Her face was curiously peaceful, and Barr filled his heart with the sight of her, until Golem moved between them. "You killed K.C.," he said, his voice thick with emotion. "You think about her." He put his hands around Barr's throat and began to squeeze.

PATRICK :

0 2 0 0   S A T U R D A Y ,

33° 01′ N, 64° 45′ W

Beyond thought, beyond hope, beyond anything but blind rage, Patrick threw himself forward again and again, brought up short each time by the choking jolt of the Dacron strip around his throat. He could see nothing but Barr's face, nearly purple, eyes bulging, as Golem carefully brought him to the edge of strangulation, then allowed him a few wheezing breaths before beginning again. Patrick's own focus was narrowing, his own field of view darkening from lack of air, when from the corner of his eye he saw Gillian sit up, her hands miraculously free, and slash at the tape around her ankles with something that flashed brightly.

Golem, his back to her, was dividing his pleasure between the thrashing, choking man between his knees and the helpless Patrick on the bunk before him. But he must have seen something in the mate's face—in the half of it visible above the broad strip of silver tape—because he dropped Barr with a thump and half-straightened, turning as he rose.

He was an instant too slow. Gillian, tape still clinging to her freed legs, had clambered to her feet on the bunk and flung herself onto the broad back just in front of her. Patrick, transfixed, saw her right hand come down hard, stabbing again and then again with a stubby knife, while her left arm locked around Golem's throat. The wrestler heaved himself fully upright, squealing like a pig as he tore at the thin, wiry forearm across his windpipe.

Then his training took over. Reaching back over his own shoulders with both hands, he grabbed Gillian's wrist and bent quickly forward, pitchpoling her into the bulkhead. She landed on her back, feet in the air, winded and helpless. But she was still holding the little knife, and her hand was red to the wrist and dripping. Golem crouched, staring at his own blood; in that second Patrick drew back his feet and lashed out in a kick powered by despair and fury.

His heels—hard-edged city-shoe heels—took Golem just above the left cheekbone, hurled him across *Kassandra*'s cabin to crash into and through the inch-thick oak rail of the upper berth. He hung limp for a moment, his head awkwardly wedged in the splintered wood, and then sagged.

But Gillian was already struggling to her feet, eyes blazing, knife poised. Patrick bellowed at her—more like a bleat, filtered through the gag—and she caught herself, turned to him. He nodded furiously toward the companionway. Come *on*, Gillian! Roger's got a gun, the only one in the boat.

It seemed forever before she got Patrick's meaning, and started hacking the tape from his ankles. He had flipped over onto his stomach, felt her sawing at his wrists, when the companion hatch slid forward with a crash. "What in hell was that—" Half-blinded by the light, Roger stared open-mouthed at the shambles below him. It took him a full two seconds to sort out the tangle of bodies; eyes widening, he staggered back out of sight, his hands groping at the zipper of his foul-weather jacket.

Patrick forced himself to kneel motionless, straining against the strips of fabric that dug into his wrists. He felt something give, jerked hard, and his hands were free. No time to worry about pain, about circulation, about the blood running down his fingers. He was across the cabin in one leap, swarming up the ladder. He hit the hatch's washboards with his shoulder, smashing them out of their channels, and exploded into the cockpit—just as *Kassandra* jibed all standing. The mainsheet squealed and the boom whizzed across, slammed into the lee rigging with a twanging jolt that laid the yawl over on her side. Roger, struggling to extract his pistol from beneath jacket and chest-high trousers, was tossed against a cockpit seat. His yell of pain rang out, with the ugly *snap* that Patrick recognized as a bone breaking clean.

First things first. Ignoring *Kassandra*'s sickening lurches, the crash of spars against rigging, Patrick tore open Roger's foul-weather jacket and pulled out the gun—a beautiful, long-barreled .38. The semi-conscious man moaned and thrashed feebly, but Patrick found it easy to harden his heart. Checking the safety, Patrick shoved the revolver in his hip pocket.

Kassandra was still on her ear, struggling to right herself as wave-tops whipped into the half-filled cockpit. Patrick braced himself against the lee-side coaming, craned his neck till he could see down the companionway. Golem was still lying in a crumpled heap, across the lower berth to starboard. No sign of consciousness, but that wasn't a surprise—he'd felt the man's skull give under the force of his kick. Gillian, kneeling over Barr, glanced up at Patrick. Her eyes were alight, and he needed no more assurance than that. Patrick gave her a thumbs-up sign and pulled the hatch closed.

So much for the easy part. Now he had to make *Kassandra* heave to before she slatted the rig right out of her hull. Over the previous winter, Barr had demonstrated the operation over and over again; made it seem as simple as breathing. But there was—Patrick discovered in the next ten minutes—all the difference in the world between the perfectly balanced *Glory* and poor *Kassandra* freshly shorn of her mizzen. At last, torn by impatience, Patrick hauled down both jib and main and let the boat lie nearly broadside to the seas, rolling uneasily.

Only then, returning to the cockpit, did he begin slowly, delicately picking at the silver tape that was driving him crazy. After a few seconds he knew that half-measures weren't going to work: the gag was pasted too firmly to his skin. He grasped the corner he'd managed to pry free and, pursing his mouth to protect his lips, tore the tape off. The pain was blinding, and the drops of rain and spray burned like dry ice on his lacerated skin. At last he wiped the tears from his eyes and looked down at Roger Huddleston.

He lay quietly on the cockpit floorboards, wincing every time *Kassandra* rolled; his loose foul-weather trousers hid the break, but the way he braced himself to ease his right leg told Patrick where the damage was. To make sure, he knelt at Roger's side. The other man stiffened in apprehension. "What're you doing?" he gasped.

Without answering, Patrick ran his fingertips upward from the right knee. At midthigh he felt it, through two thick layers of cloth. *I should tear this guy's leg off the rest of the way, and laugh at him,* he thought. What's wrong that I don't want to? Roger was holding his breath, every muscle taut, watching Patrick's face for a sign. "If I was Golem," Patrick said hoarsely, "I'd drag you down the companionway, just for the fun of it."

"But you're not," Roger replied, between clenched teeth.

Patrick grimaced experimentally, feeling the raw skin around his mouth tingle. He leaned through the companionway hatch, keeping a wary eye on Roger. Barr was sitting on the cabin sole, his head rolled back on the lower berth, eyes closed, his throat striped with the purple marks of Golem's fingers. Gillian, on her knees beside him, sensed Patrick's presence and looked up. Her lower face was cruelly raw, but her eyes gleamed triumph. "He can't talk," she said, "but he's okay."

Barr's head lifted, and his eyes opened. As he saw Patrick his thin lips formed words—formed them with such exaggeration that he had to do it twice before Patrick deciphered *where's Roger.*

"He's up here. Seems to've broken his leg."

Barr's laugh escaped him before he could stop himself, and his eyes reflected the pain of it. Turning to Gillian, he made quick writing motions in the air. She brought him *Kassandra's* logbook and, as he scribbled, called his words up to Patrick: "We've got to make sail. Get on Win's trail before he's too far ahead to catch."

"Why bother?" Patrick said. "We can radio that Coast Guard cutter back in Hamilton. Let them do it."

Barr shook his head impatiently, began writing again, but Gillian laid her hand over his. "We can't risk a shootout," she explained. "Sarah might get killed from either side."

"*Sarah?*" Patrick couldn't believe his ears. "Fuck Sarah. I saw that Judas kiss she gave you."

"You didn't see all of it, then," Gillian replied calmly. "That was when she slipped me the knife."

All Patrick really wanted was eight hours in a real bed, though he would willingly have settled for half that in one of *Kassandra's* damp, rancid berths. Instead, he found himself heaving Golem up into one of the upper berths and strapping him in, then helping Roger down the companion ladder and into the matching bunk on the opposite side. (He was a hard man, Patrick had to admit: barely a moan out of him.) Gillian, meanwhile, was clearing away the loose trash on the cabin floor, so they could move without tripping, and up on deck Barr was running a quick check on the standing rigging.

It seemed like days before they were done, and *Kassandra* ready to sail again. Patrick, who'd drawn the first off-watch, slumped onto one of the lower bunks; his feet, still in now-soaked city shoes, were beginning to ache, but he knew he couldn't possibly stay awake long enough to untie the laces.

He was just lifting his feet up and over the guard rail when he heard an urgent thumping on the closed hatch. If I look around, he thought, I'll be sorry I did. The thumping came again, louder. With a sigh, he rolled over and propped himself on one elbow. Barr's wet face appeared in the hatchway, and Barr's even wetter arm motioned him up on deck.

Patrick crouched at the helm under Golem's foul-weather jacket while Barr—wearing, Patrick reminded himself, no jacket at all— crept about the pitching, slippery decks, tweaking the forestay, twanging the shrouds, and tightening or slacking their turnbuckles according to some mysterious schedule of his own.

Whatever he was doing seemed to work: Gradually the knot-meter's needle crept up the scale, from five to five and a half to six. At the same time the tiller slowly came alive under Patrick's hand, until he had the sense of controlling *Kassandra's* progress rather than just aiming her. Barr finally came aft and took the tiller, allowing Patrick to spread the tentlike jacket over him. *Glory's* skipper held the curved wooden bar with his fingertips, shook his head in dis-satisfaction. "It's good enough for now," Patrick insisted, but Barr had him trim and then retrim the sheets before waving him below. "You sure?" Patrick asked doubtfully. "You okay alone?"

The look on the other man's face was all the answer Patrick needed. As he started down the companion ladder he suddenly became aware of an incredible, delicious, unbelievable smell coming from a pot clamped into place on the gimballed stove. When had he eaten last? Patrick asked himself. Twelve hours ago, he decided, though it seemed far longer. Gillian was grinning up at him. "Grab a seat. It's almost ready."

He collapsed on the nearest bunk, watched her ladle thick soup into oversize plastic bowls. "It's only from a can," she said, passing him a bowl.

The first spoonful burnt his tongue, and he set the bowl down beside him to cool. Chicken base, his seared tastebuds told him; clam chowder in it, too. Not enough pepper, though, and some chives would've helped—he slipped away with the thought unfinished.

He woke up slowly, his fogged brain sorting the medley of creaks, thumps, and splashes that came from all sides. Behind them he was conscious of a quick, hoarse, chugging sound, like a leaky pump, from right above his head. *Kassandra* must be going to windward, he thought; a little bitch of a sea, too. But what was that other noise? Then he became aware of a slender, bluejeaned knee braced on the mattress beside his head. He rolled partway over, looking upward. Gillian was leaning over him, staring intently into the upper bunk. In the gray light she looked worried as well as exhausted. "What's up?" he asked.

"Golem," she said. "Can you hear that breathing? He won't wake up."

Patrick pulled himself up, swung his legs over the side of the bunk without thinking. Only when he was sitting upright did he realize that the pain from his groin was nearly gone. His wrists, his hands, all the muscles in his body were throbbing in unison.

The pumping sound was coming from Golem; quick and shallow breaths, almost as if he were panting. Patrick reached past Gillian and touched the big man's forehead. It was burning.

"What's wrong with him?" she asked.

He knew well enough but was reluctant to name it. "Well . . ."

"Skull fracture," grunted a voice from across the cabin. It was Roger. "He's dying—" *Kassandra* mounted one sea, was slapped by another. "Oh, Jesus!—and so am I."

Golem's breathing paused for a second; then picked up, louder and hoarser than ever. "What can we do?" Gillian asked. "I can't take that noise much longer."

You won't have to, Patrick thought, looking quickly away to keep her from seeing it in his eyes. "Not much we can do," he said. "Not if we're going to keep chasing after Sarah."

"That's it, then," she replied, straightening up. "Patrick, can you relieve Barr? He's been on for five hours now. He's got to get some sleep."

Five hours—and after what he'd been through. Patrick pulled on Roger's foul-weather jacket, straining tight across his shoulders, but dry. He remembered the bowl of soup, looked around for it.

"Sorry," Gillian said, reading his face. "It kind of evaporated. How about a couple of chocolate bars?"

He started up the ladder. "What about you?" he asked her.

"Don't worry about me," she said. "Barr's the only one who can find Sarah. We've got to keep him going."

He pulled the hatch back and stuck his face out into the wet. A miserable dawn was turning the eastern horizon the color of lead, and the wind, coming over the starboard bow at about twenty knots, was hurling rain across the deck in sheets. Looking toward the uncertain light, Patrick decided he could see about a hundred yards. "Go below and get some sleep," he said to Barr, who looked like a child inside Golem's jacket. Patrick half expected an argument, but Barr nodded, indicated the course on the binnacle compass, and hoisted himself stiffly through the hatch. Patrick settled uncomfortably on the weather side of the cockpit and unwrapped a candy bar, reflecting that at least the wild goose chase wouldn't last long. There wasn't a hope in hell of their finding the other *Kassandra* in such next-to-zero visibility. Barr might be good, but there were times—and this was one of them—when modern technology had cards and spades over intuition or second sight or whatever went on inside Barr's head.

"I'm not sure," Patrick was saying. "I only saw her for a second, but it was a yawl, on the same course as our boat."

"How close was she?" Gillian asked. "D'you suppose he saw us?" She was standing on the windward side of *Kassandra*'s cockpit, balancing against the boat's quick, corkscrewing plunges while she searched the shifting gray curtains of rain ahead. Barr, still rubbing the sleep from his eyes, had no doubts at all—no intellectual doubts, anyway; the knot in his stomach was pure irrationality, and Patrick's answer untied it: "A mile ahead, maybe. The rain just opened up for a minute, and there she was."

A mile ahead and on the same course. Barr, who was standing on the companion ladder with his head and shoulders protruding from the hatch, pulled from his pocket the pencil and wad of paper that were substituting for his voice. *Ease mainsheet*, he scrawled, then stopped to reconsider: Win had set exactly the course Barr thought he would—close-hauled to the northwest, on a direct line to Montauk Point, six hundred miles ahead. He'd been under way for a good hour and a half before *Kassandra* set out in pursuit, so they'd made up five miles on him in the last eight hours. And that in turn meant that *Kassandra*, even without her mizzen, was moving through the water a half-knot faster than the other boat.

Barr scratched out the words he'd written, printed *Reef main*, and passed the paper to Patrick, standing at the tiller.

"Reef the main?" Patrick said, his eyebrows rising in surprise. "What for? We've almost got him."

God damn this throat. Barr shook his head, jabbed his forefinger at the paper.

"You don't want to catch him?" Gillian asked, from over his shoulder. "Oh: You don't want to catch him in daylight?"

Good girl. He grinned approval and watched her face light up in response. Patrick was still looking puzzled; Barr formed a pistol with thumb and forefinger, mimicked shooting Gillian, then pointed beyond *Kassandra*'s bow.

Patrick's face cleared: "You think he might shoot Sarah. Does he have a gun?"

Barr shrugged ignorance, but Gillian said, "There was one on Roger's boat. I heard him tell Win."

"Then there's no problem—I've got it," Patrick replied. He pulled up the front of his jacket to show the pistol butt sticking out of his waistband. "Stainless steel .38. Perfect for a boat."

"Is it what they call a Mac 10?" Gillian asked. "Because that was the name Roger used."

Patrick's dismayed expression supplied her answer, but he amplified: "Folks, if Win Huddleston's got one of those, we are in deep shit. A Mac 10's a submachine gun, very compact, very simple. Sprays bullets like a hose sprays water." He stared thoughtfully at the horizon. "I don't really want to go up against something like that. Not with just a handgun."

No more do I, Barr reflected. Roger might be a cold-blooded killer, but his brother was even more dangerous. To a loony like Win, playing Samson in the temple might seem very attractive, especially if he was cornered.

"But Sarah saved our *lives*," Gillian began, her jaw set obstinately.

"There's the boat again!" Patrick exclaimed. "On the starboard bow."

And a good deal less than a mile away, Barr was thinking, as he scrambled forward. Close-hauled, all right; something odd-looking about the mizzen. And another goddamn shower was about to march between them. . . . He felt Gillian at his side; she was holding out a pair of binoculars. He snatched them from her, blew her a kiss. "I'll collect on that later, Barr," she said, as he clapped them to his eyes.

He had only a glimpse before the rain blotted her out, but it was long enough to show him that the mizzen was luffing, the spar itself slightly out of line with the main: Huddleston either hadn't got around to tuning the mast, or else he'd botched it. Only one person on deck—presumably Win, but impossible to be sure—standing up by the windward shrouds. The yawl's cockpit was empty, so she must be sailing on the autopilot. It figured, shorthanded as he was and with a crew he couldn't trust.

Barr hung the binocular strap over his shoulder and swung his way aft, calculations tumbling over themselves in his mind. The first thing to do was reef, no question—otherwise they'd overrun their quarry in another couple of hours. How far back to lie? If Huddleston stood on his own boat's cabin top, his head would be about ten feet above water level, which meant his visual horizon would be some three and a half miles away. Add another two and a half miles' distance to shield *Kassandra*'s hull and cabin, and that made a total of six. And her sails? He looked up at the gleaming Dacron triangles; a random sunbeam would light them up like spotlights. Nothing to be done—as long as *Kassandra* lay close-hauled in Win's wake, her rig would be as unobtrusive as it could get.

For the rest, Barr had the strongest intuition that Huddleston would hold his course, make no correction for the northerly flow of the Gulf Stream until he was well into it. Unless the wind veered to the north and headed him, in which case he would surely tack westward, to lee-bow the current. It'd be a mistake to underrate the man just because he happened to be crazy, Barr reminded himself. He was a bright guy out of his element, and that meant he might be capable of something really unpredictable.

Gillian was still up at the spreaders, clinging to the mast with one hand while she surveyed the horizon ahead of them. The false *Kassandra* had been hull-down beyond the earth's curve since noon, her course unchanging, and Barr, standing at the tiller, was beginning to feel reasonably confident about the coming night. The weather was changing, but *Kassandra* should still be able to make her final approach behind a rain squall, come booming down out of it at the last moment. Barr thought he had a fair chance of laying his boat

alongside before Huddleston could react; and if fortune really favored the good guys, their enemy would be sound asleep in his
cockpit.

He sensed a lift and steered *Kassandra* up to meet it. Even with
her mast raked aft, she was still unhappy without her mizzen, and
it was hard to give her the delicate steering she deserved. Win, up
ahead, was clearly getting nothing at all out of his mizzen—and
wouldn't, unless the wind backed around to a reach.

Dusk was coming on fast, and as Barr was beginning to think of
waving Gillian down from her observation post, she untied the spare
halyard that held the bosun's chair and began lowering herself to
the deck, guiding the chair's downward progress with her feet. She
had bounced back amazingly since yesterday, but Barr knew she
might easily drive herself to collapse.

She slid out of the chair and tied it and the halyard off to the
mast. As she worked her way aft along the side deck, he saw she
was moving stiffly, and trying to hide it. "Other boat's still there,"
she reported. "He's turned on her masthead light, so we should be
able to find her later."

He smiled acknowledgment and, opening his mouth, pointed his
forefinger first into it and then at her.

"Eat?" she replied. "I'll make something for both of us."

Her reappearance, some thirty minutes later, was preceded by a
tantalizing smell of stew and another, even more welcome odor that
drifted out the nearly closed companionway. The steaming mug,
passed up by a seemingly disembodied hand, confirmed Barr's hopes:
rum and hot chocolate in equal parts, with a trace of cinnamon. Any
thought of sipping vanished with the first taste, but before he'd had
time to set the empty mug down, the hand appeared again, this time
holding a large bowl with a spoon sticking out of it. "Grab that,"
came Gillian's voice, and he did. A moment later she hoisted herself
up through the hatch; in the dim light from below he could see that
she'd done something to her hair and, he thought, to her face. "I'd've
changed my shirt, too, only that bastard took all my clothes to use
on Sarah," she announced, swinging her legs into the cockpit. "You
eat; I'll drive."

The smell rising from the bowl destroyed any reluctance he might have had about turning over the helm. He tasted, then began shoveling the stew into his mouth, and only after the first few spoonfuls remembered to sit down. When he did, he found that his calf muscles were achingly tight, and realized he'd been standing in much the same position for over five hours. Barr set the empty bowl down on the bridge deck with an audible sigh and an inaudible longing for a cigarette. At his side Gillian, intent on the mainsail luff, seemed oblivious to his presence. Her profile was red-lit by the binnacle light, and he noticed with amazement that she had somehow become beautiful.

Without looking at him she asked, "When did you plan to go after Win?" Her tone made it sound as if a night assault on an armed lunatic in the middle of the ocean was something they did every day.

Barr felt in his shirt pocket for his pad and wrote $+/-$ 0130, holding the page where it could catch the light from the compass.

She glanced down at the number and lifted her eyes back up to the sail. "One-thirty in the morning, more or less?" He nodded, pointed up at the sky. "During a rain squall: of course. That's what Patrick said you'd do—we talked about it while we were eating." She fell silent, but he could tell she was groping for a way to go on. "I feel bad about Patrick," she said at last. "I kind of bullied him into agreeing to . . . you know, go after Win."

Go after: what she meant was *kill*, and she knew it. Of the three of them only Patrick was trained for this kind of thing, and she was hating herself for reminding him of the fact. Barr wanted desperately to comfort her but knew there was nothing he could say, even if he'd been able to speak. He put his left arm around her shoulders; she surprised him by leaning against him almost eagerly, and he surprised himself by taking her small chin between his fingertips and tilting her head back.

Her lips were cool and salty from the spray coming back over the decks, but her mouth, when it opened under his, was warm and welcoming. He was holding himself in check, and he could feel her doing the same, but their brief union was nonetheless complete. When they pulled apart, both of them were trembling. "I don't want it to be because you feel sorry for me," she said.

"It's not," he croaked.

"You talked!" she exclaimed. "Well, more or less."

And it hurt, too, but he was too euphoric to admit it. "New therapy," he said, grinning.

"One more, then you go hit it for a couple of hours." This time she pulled his head down to her. The sound of the luffing jib finally broke them apart. "Go," she ordered, yanking *Kassandra* back on course.

Patrick was pulling Roger's foul-weather gear trousers over his boots as Barr came down the companionway. Golem, still panting unevenly, was a massive lump in the starboard upper, and across from him Roger lay quietly on his back, apparently asleep.

Patrick saw Barr's surprised look. "Passed out. I gave him a slug of rum," he said.

Barr raised an eyebrow, and *Glory's* mate reluctantly continued: "When I was splinting his leg. It's just I don't like people moaning while I eat."

Turning away to hide a smile, Barr shed his jacket, his sodden shirt, and was unbuckling his belt when he saw Patrick looking at him oddly. "What is it?" he rasped.

The big man wriggled his way into Roger's pullover jacket; his face emerged wearing a twisted grin. "A lighter shade of lipstick would suit you better, Skip."

The line squall hit about eleven, dumping Barr out of a rhapsodic dream and onto *Kassandra's* damp, cold cabin sole. The boat was laid over nearly on her beam ends, so that when Barr got up he was standing on the face of the starboard lower berth, while Roger, groaning through clenched teeth, was held in the port upper only by the tightly stretched lee cloth. As the first shrieking gusts subsided, Barr could hear rain drumming violently on the decks and roof, and *Kassandra* began to stagger back upright. He climbed the ladder and pulled back the hatch just enough to put his head through. The boat was on a screaming reach, rain coming across the deck almost horizontally, with stinging force on his bare skin. The chill wind out of the west was already beginning to puff itself out, though there might be a few dangerous gusts still left in it. Patrick had the tiller in both hands, one foot braced against the leeward seat, and Gillian was crouched down by the sheet winch, retrimming the jib.

"We're okay," Patrick yelled, barely audible over the wind. "Under control."

Barr nodded, pulled his head back down, and slid the hatch closed. He climbed into the lee-side lower, knowing that sleep was done. In two hours they might all be dead.

"Any questions?" he whispered. To spare his voice, he'd written the instructions out, and Patrick and Gillian had just finished reading them—Patrick twice. Though occasional handfuls of spray were still whipping aft, the mate had taken off the constricting foul-weather gear and replaced the borrowed boots with sneakers. With a watch cap pulled down over his forehead and the dully gleaming pistol in his waistband, he looked ready for anything.

"I've got one question," Gillian said. "What's happened to the rain?" Clouds were still thick above them and to the east, but a scattered handful of stars were already visible up to windward.

"Sailed through it," Barr replied. "Sorry."

Patrick looked quickly upward, and even more quickly brought his gaze back into the boat, as if staring at the clouds might dissolve them further. "One thing," he said. "I'm going to tape Roger's mouth, just in case he decides to try something clever."

Gillian's face twitched with distaste, but she said, "Do it," and Barr nodded his agreement. As Patrick slipped below, Gillian picked up three red phosphorus flares and stuck them in the pocket of her jeans. "Let's make sure I have this right, before I go up the mast," she said. "When we come alongside, I light these and toss them down into Win's cockpit." She waited for his nod, and continued: "You sure I won't set his boat on fire?"

"Probably," he said. "But we can put it out." The first goal, however, was to distract the man, and Barr could think of no better distraction than fizzing, spitting, blinding flares rolling around at one's feet. Besides, if Huddleston did manage to get at his machine gun, Gillian would be a lot safer up at the main spreaders than down at deck level. It was a point that Patrick clearly appreciated, too, though he was far too sensible to say so. His head and shoulders reappeared in the hatch, and Barr said, "Lights out below?"

"Right. Want me to hoist her up now?"

"Please." And to Gillian, "Soon as you're settled, give me a bearing

on his lights." His larynx was on fire again from talking; he wished
he had another mug of hot chocolate, but it'd have to wait. The
pain in his throat made him think of Golem. The big man was
certainly getting weaker, and twice he'd broken into meaningless
babble. If they didn't get him to a doctor soon he'd die.

And if I was a Christian, I might care.

Gillian's clear voice cut through the breeze: "Nothing. No lights
at all."

Damn. He waved acknowledgment, but his brain was already
racing through the possibilities: Win had changed course, sometime
during the five hours since sundown; or his masthead light had failed;
or he'd just turned it off. . . .

Patrick hurried back along the side deck and dropped into the
cockpit. "She'll keep looking."

"Good." Maybe he'd made a mistake on the chart; he had to
double-check. "Here, keep her on this heading."

He'd run through the figures three times, starting from the loran
fix at sundown, and come up with the same answer each time:
Kassandra should be right on top of Huddleston's yawl. He stuck his
head up through the hatch, noting that the patches of starlight had
multiplied amazingly and the wind had slackened, backed almost
into the west. Gillian had somehow pulled herself to the very masthead. "Still nothing," she called down. "And there's good visibility
everywhere but southeast."

Barr slid back down into the swampy dampness of the cabin, switch-
ing on the overhead light; no point in keeping the boat dark now.
Roger's pain-filled eyes glittered as they followed Barr's movements.

Would Win have headed back? Or changed course at all? He
might have seen *Kassandra*'s sails at dusk, though the chances were
strongly against it—but what if he'd seen them earlier, and waited
till night to turn off his lights and change course? Barr was already
moving the parallel rules across the chart when common sense fought
its way through: This guy isn't Horatio Nelson, for God's sake; he's
a weekend sailor. If his boat isn't where it's supposed to be, it's more
likely accident than cleverness.

What kind of accident could you have out here, though? We're
well outside the shipping lanes, and the nearest reefs are six miles

below the keel. Fire was a possibility—*Kassandra* was powered by an elderly gasoline engine, so Win's boat must have the same. Or a flareup from the alcohol stove. If there'd been an accident, whatever it was, maybe he'd called—was calling for help. Barr opened the radio locker and snapped on the VHF. The model was unfamiliar, but after a few minutes' experimentation he had figured out how to make it scan all the channels across its band. Silence.

Wedged between the VHF and the loran was a black crackle-finish casing that looked familiar. He pulled it out: a hand-held transmitter, he saw, battery powered. He was on the point of replacing it when he remembered—this was the radio on which Win Huddleston had received Roger's two-word message back in Bermuda. Yes. And it didn't operate on the marine frequencies at all. He switched it on.

Someone was talking, very faintly, in a flat, hopeless tone. Barr turned the volume all the way up, but the signal was still weak, immersed in static. And then, for no reason at all, he heard Win Huddleston's strained voice, loud and clear: ". . . went right over. Not my fault, Roger. Not my fault."

Frantically Barr pressed the mike button, but Huddleston would have to stop transmitting before the hand-held could break in, and Win was clearly in a mood to talk. His voice came and went, rose and fell, but Barr could make practically nothing of what he said. Part of it even seemed to be in a foreign language, or maybe two. In all the sometimes tearful, sometimes angry meandering, one fragment emerged: During the night something or someone had gone over, presumably over the side.

Sooner or later Win had to run out of breath; perhaps his thumb would slip off the push-to-talk button. When that happened, there was only one person who could certainly get his attention. Barr looked up from the radio, became aware that Patrick and Gillian must have been watching him for some time. "Tiller's lashed," Gillian said quickly. "I headed us back south."

Damn the woman, but she was right. "Get that tape off Roger's face," he croaked to Patrick. "He's going to help us."

It was easier than Barr had thought it would be. Roger still seemed a little high as Patrick helped him out of the upper berth and into an awkward sitting position on the lower, grasping the portable transmitter. "Poor old Win's gone fuzzily wacko," he observed. "Better get to him before he hurts himself—or damages my ex-sweetie, the little cunt."

About half an hour after Barr had first picked up Huddleston's voice it suddenly stopped. Roger keyed the hand-held quickly: "Win, you out there? Come back to me, old buddy."

"I'm sorry," Win cried. "I didn't mean it, Roger." His voice was definitely fainter, Barr noticed, and so apparently did Roger.

"Of course you didn't," he answered. "I won't blame you, Win. Just tell me what happened." He looked up at Barr. "Juice is running out of this thing. We'd better use the VHF, if I can get him to switch over."

"Are you sure, Roger?" Win was saying. "Tell me you promise."

"I promise, Win. But look, I want you to turn on the other radio. The VHF. The battery on this one's almost gone."

Barr propped Roger against the galley counter, while Patrick held the microphone—"Just in case," he said. In moments Win's voice came through, much louder. VHF transmissions were line-of-sight, Barr reminded himself. With two fifty-foot antennas, it meant that the false *Kassandra* was no more than about twenty miles from her namesake.

". . . I was going to put pins in them," Win was saying. "I just didn't get around to it, and then that black squall came down on us out of nowhere. . . ."

Pins? That must be it—Win had forgotten to follow Roger's orders and put cotter pins in the mizzen turnbuckles. Without them the screw ends of the turnbuckles would just back off under repeated loads from wind and sea, until the mast toppled over the side. Unnerving, for sure; maybe even frightening, but it was only the goddamn mizzen.

"I didn't make her do it, Roger. I just asked her to hold on to the boom." His words were spaced by gulping sobs, but he never stopped transmitting so Roger could break in. There was nothing to do but listen. ". . . tried to heave to, but the boat kept heading off and jibing and I was afraid the main would go next, and when I looked over the side again the mizzen was gone, and Sarah was, too . . ."

From the companionway Gillian gave a choked cry, and Patrick stood stunned—but Roger grabbed up the dead hand-held set like a hammer and with one sweep of his arm smashed in the front of the VHF. "Up yours, Sarah!" he exclaimed. "And up yours, too, motherfuckers. You'll never find either of them now."

GILLIAN:

SUNDAY,

0600

"Here," Barr croaked. "Begin here."

Gillian looked about her at the waste of water on every side, last night's swells from the north crosshatched now by new seas from the west. If by any chance Sarah was still alive she was out here someplace. The empty gray wilderness chilled Gillian's hopes, but she ignored her growing despair. "I'll take the first lookout," she said. "Patrick, would you help hoist the bosun's chair?"

"Sure," he replied. She hated the compassion in his eyes; he didn't think they had a chance of finding Sarah, either. Barr was different. He hadn't tried to minimize the odds, but the intensity of his concentration, as he'd pored over the plotting sheet, lifted her heart more than any words could've done. She had stood beside him as he set up the search plan, watching intently as the big, battered hands—God, how she adored those hands—moved over the paper. Even torn by her anguished concern she was consumed by her feelings for him, constantly amazed when she recalled the watered emotions she'd previously thought were love.

And yet he certainly was a funny-looking Romeo, especially now: hollow-eyed, bristly, the raw spots on his thin face an angry red. He sensed her gaze boring into him and looked down at her; how could she ever have thought his pale blue eyes were cold? "You want to see?" he whispered.

She was willing to take his word for it, but happy just to stand next to him for a couple more minutes. He smelled of sweat and saltwater and, thanks to Patrick, tobacco: a stale tin of Win's Prince Albert, discovered by chance and converted into homemade smokes. Who but Barr would've moistened the dried-out flakes with rum and rolled them up in strips cut from the *Coast Pilot?* They burned with a smell that would knock you over, but Barr had consumed five already, and his raspy whisper no longer seemed to pain him at all.

"Here's our position at eleven last night, when the squall hit," he said. "And here's where Win was, six miles ahead and to leeward. Storm probably reached him about fifteen minutes after it hit us. I'm betting his boat was laid over the way we were, lost the mizzen right away. He said on the radio that he tried to heave to"—Barr's forefinger described a quick series of swoops on the plotting sheet—"but the bow kept falling away. Anyhow, I figure he'd come up and head off again, make a few hundred yards to leeward. And somewhere in there's when Sarah went overboard. So we start at this point and search outward, nice and slow, taking plenty of time."

"What are the chances, Barr?" she asked, holding his eyes with hers. "How long could . . . can she stay alive in the water?"

"It depends. The water's warm, and that's the biggest factor. After that . . . Is she hurt? does she have anything to hold on to, or does she have to swim to stay afloat? And then there's . . . other things." He dropped his eyes; the word *sharks* hung unspoken between them.

She wanted Patrick to raise the bosun's chair all the way to the masthead, but Barr demurred. "He says you're better there at the spreaders," Patrick called up to her. "Remember, you're looking for something's only as big as a coconut. Don't range too far from the boat."

Three times in the first hour she saw an unnatural break of the water's surface and cried out. With meticulous seamanship Barr laid *Kassandra* alongside a glass fishnet float covered with weed and barnacles, a watermelon with a big chunk out of it, a dead gull. She'd almost given up after the third false alarm, but he must have known it because he had Patrick shout up to her, "Keep hailing, Gillian. For anything at all, he says. Remember: She's depending on us."

Ditzy Sarah, depending on us. Gillian pulled herself upright in the bosun's chair and took a fresh focus on the sea below.

• • •

Patrick relieved her at nine, and Barr ordered her below. "What d'you mean, *below*. I'm doing fine," she snapped.

"Sure you are," he said. "But rest your eyes for two hours, and then make us something to eat."

"Since when am I the cook?" she demanded, half joking.

"Since the real cook went up the mast," he replied. "And roll me a few more of these, would you?"

"Are you serious? They'll tear your throat out." Though in point of fact his voice was stronger than before. She turned to go below, was startled to feel his hand pat her behind. She whipped around, saw blank amazement on his face.

"I never did that before in my life," he said.

"Just don't do it to anyone else." As she went below, she could still feel her grin stretching the lacerated skin of her cheeks; before she lay down, she took a tube of first-aid cream and smeared the greasy stuff on her face.

They completed Barr's search pattern at three in the afternoon— and began again. At six, when they were changing watches, Patrick asked Barr, "We going to keep this up all night?"

"If we have to, yes."

"The search, sure—I'm with you there," Patrick said quickly. "I meant, do we want somebody at the masthead?"

Gillian had begun to think of Barr as being immune from fatigue, but when he took an extra beat to reply she realized his reserves weren't unlimited. "What? Oh, no. Two people up at the bow and one steering, once the sun goes down. At night you need ears, not eyes."

"What about Win's boat?" Gillian asked.

"What about it?" he retorted. "It's out here someplace."

Useless new moon, and even that was veiled in a haze just thick enough to blank out the stars. Gillian was on her knees at the rail, staring blindly to port, as *Kassandra* slid through a shapeless, hypnotic nothingness, with only a seabird's cry to break the rustle from beneath the forefoot.

A seabird's cry? But was it? The sound came again, and she was calling at the top of her lungs: "Port bow! Port bow! I heard something!"

Kassandra glided up into the eye of the wind, under the mainsail alone. "There!" said Patrick, from her side. "See the splashing?"

"I got it," Barr rasped. "Easy does it—this is when you can lose them."

As no one knows better than me. Before Patrick could move, Gillian had one foot on the lifeline. She hit the water in a racing dive, with Barr's anguished "No!" ringing in her ears. The floating mizzenmast was closer than she'd realized, and she had to fight her way to the surface through a tangle of wire and rope that caught at her clothing and tried to drag her down. Sarah was draped across the spar with her head on the junction of the spreaders. Two feet away down the mast, a large feathered shape looked Gillian in the eye and emitted a weirdly human squawk. My God, she thought, it *was* a bird.

Watching from the water alongside, she decided that Barr must have thought it all out in advance: The floodlights mounted on the spreaders suddenly glared, turning *Kassandra*'s decks to high noon. Her mainsail came down at the run, and Patrick leaped on it, furling desperately, even as Barr unshackled the mainsheet from the car running across the bridge deck. He and Patrick swung the boom out over Gillian's head, with the lower sheet block dragging through the water. "Pass a line under her arms," Barr called. "Good and tight."

Sarah raised her head and tried to say something. Her face was horribly burnt and swollen, her cracked lips bloody. "For God's sake, get her a drink!" Gillian cried.

"Lift her up here first," Patrick called back. The mainsheet blocks squealed, and Sarah rose dripping from the sea. Patrick swung the boom inboard, and Barr eased her limp, dangling body over the lifelines. Then Gillian grasped Patrick's powerful hands and felt herself raised straight up, dragged over the gunwale and through the lifelines. Barr was kneeling on the cockpit sole, supporting Sarah's head while he held a cup to her lips—the water he'd remembered to bring up on deck, just in case.

"She'll be all right," Patrick said to Gillian, holding up the lifelines so she could crawl beneath them, over the coaming. The water seemed to be running from the corners of Sarah's mouth, and Gillian felt a sharp pang of fear beneath her breastbone. Could they have been too late? Had she died as they were pulling her aboard? Sarah spluttered and choked; tears of relief started in Gillian's eyes—and Patrick's hand slammed her across the shoulders, knocking her flat.

Wood ground against wood with a squealing, rending crash, and *Kassandra* heeled, shuddering, to leeward. Gillian, who had landed facedown across Sarah's thighs, saw Patrick, on his side next to her, pull out Roger's shiny pistol. "Stay down!" he roared in her ear, as a second crash shook the boat, followed almost immediately by an explosive, ripping noise. Patrick was sighting along the gun barrel, trying to take aim at something behind Gillian's back, but the second impact knocked him down. She struggled partway up and saw, piercing the almost tangible curtain thrown by the spreader lights, a boat's white bow riding up over *Kassandra's* windward rail. As she stared, open-mouthed, it slid back and down, gouging itself and *Kassandra* impartially.

A bony shoulder spun her around, and she caught a glimpse of Barr, sliding like an eel over the companionway sill; a moment later the spreader lights winked out. She heard again the strangely percussive ripping sound, this time accompanied by a drumroll of tiny shocks felt through the cockpit sole. Out the companionway echoed Barr's strained yell: "Engine!"

Gillian's comprehension came an instant before Patrick's, maybe because the instrument panel, recessed into the aft side of the bridge deck, was only inches from her nose. She wrenched the ignition key over, and Patrick's forefinger stabbed the starter button. The engine caught with a scream—someone must have fallen against the throttle—followed by a dreadful *thunk!* as Patrick slammed the shift lever forward. But then *Kassandra* was moving, picking up speed.

"Hard over starboard!" cried Barr, from the hatchway. The other boat's bow, scarred and torn, thrust out of the darkness. Gillian grabbed *Kassandra's* long tiller and, scrabbling for purchase with feet and knees, pushed it all the way over. Slowly, slowly *Kassandra* began to turn, pulling her stern away from the attacker. As she swung, the other boat struck her starboard quarter, thrusting her so that for a few nightmare seconds the two boats' sides were only feet apart, as they headed in opposite directions.

Kassandra's spreader lights flicked on again, and there was Win,

on his feet in the other boat's cockpit, with a strange-looking gun
in his hands. His eyes were wild and unseeing, and he was shrieking
something that sounded like verse, but his voice was nearly gone
and the words stumbled over each other. He was pointing the gun
directly into *Kassandra's* cockpit—Gillian, feeling nothing, looked
right down the short muzzle—but the blinding light from above
seemed to take him by surprise, and he hesitated. She heard the
sharp *crash* from just behind her, saw Win picked up and hurled
backward out of sight. *Kassandra* forged ahead, still gaining speed,
and Patrick scrambled to his feet, holding the pistol in both hands,
and fired five more times.

PATRICK:

MIDNIGHT

Not till he hung up the microphone did he realize why the cabin
felt so familiar and at the same time so unreal. The low, varnished-
wood compartment was exactly like the one in *Kassandra*—but exactly, right down to waterstains around the leaky skylight. Just the
way *Kassandra*'s had been, that is, before Win Huddleston's Mac 10
had stitched the hull with bullets, five of which had gone through
the unconscious Golem as he lay dying in his berth. Now *Kassandra*'s
interior was shredded, berth cushions soaked with blood, bulkheads
splintered and torn by ricochets. The real marvel was that Golem
was the boat's only casualty, unless you counted a flesh wound in
Roger's arm. Win himself lay where he had fallen in the cockpit of
Kassandra's twin, under a spare jib to keep the gulls off.

Patrick had his foot on the ladder when the thought struck him.
He stopped where he was and pulled open the drawer that, in
Kassandra, would have held the engine tools and spare parts. They
were there, all right, and looked to be perfect duplicates, right down
to the extra carburetor for the old Atomic 4. And rebuilt, not new,
he saw—just as in the original boat: Roger might be a little short
in the humanity department, but he sure had an eye for detail.

The carburetor wasn't what he wanted, though. He stirred the
collection with his finger until he spotted a big screwdriver and took
it out. Where had Barr said the stuff would be? Under the cockpit
and all the way forward; the fo'c'sle was a lot easier to get at.

Exactly as in *Kassandra*'s, this boat's fo'c'sle planking was covered by battens of light-colored wood, screwed to the frames and spaced a half-inch or so apart for air circulation. When Patrick saw this inner sheathing his heart sank: it looked as if it'd been there for years. He chipped at a screw head and dislodged a layered flake composed of three slightly different colors of paint. Then he reminded himself of that rebuilt carburetor, and began to back the screw off. It came out easily enough, and it was only three-quarters of an inch long—exactly the length it should have been to secure the thin protective batten to the frame beneath.

So was the next one, turning Patrick's disappointment to real apprehension. The third screw, however, took far more effort to start, and even when it finally began to turn it moved reluctantly. More and more of its bronze stem appeared, until finally it fell free to lie, fully three inches long, on the bunk. A quarter inch for the sheathing, Patrick figured, plus an inch and a half for the false frame, plus another quarter inch for the false planking, and the final inch to drive into the real frame underneath. He calculated the number of screws that would have to be pulled in order to remove a single false plank. Without a power screwdriver it'd take all day.

Still, he had to know: If there wasn't a load of cocaine under these planks, he—and Barr and Gillian—wouldn't have a prayer of talking themselves out of this. He ripped out a couple of the light battens, relishing the way they cracked as he levered them free with the screwdriver. Between two of the planks thus exposed he rammed the screwdriver's blade and, putting all his weight behind the tool, worked it back and forth, feeling it bite through the wood. When the whole blade was buried he paused, thinking, I'm going to look like the fool of the world when saltwater squirts out this hole. Fuck it. He grasped the screwdriver in both hands, braced his foot on the edge of the berth, and pulled.

It came free more easily than he'd expected, and he staggered back a step. For a moment nothing happened, and then a thin trickle of white powder sifted down onto the faded blue canvas of the mattress. Patrick extended a finger to touch it. Looks just like flour, he thought, feeling strangely let down.

The two boats bobbed about ten feet apart, tied bow to stern. *Kassandra*'s spreader lights shone brightly down on her cockpit where

Barr sat with a beer in one hand and his arm around Gillian. *Glory's* skipper looked up as Patrick made his way forward along the other boat's side deck. "You took long enough," he said, when Patrick had got to the stemhead and began taking in the connecting line. "Did you get hold of them all right?"

"Coast Guard cutter *Whidbey*," Patrick replied. "At the pier in Hamilton. They'll be on their way as soon as they call the Bermuda cops to pick up Frannie X and Farber." His eye went to Sarah, lying across the aft end of *Kassandra's* cockpit. Her expression, under layers of zinc oxide, was unreadable. Patrick fended *Kassandra's* transom off with his foot, then stepped aboard. "They should be alongside in a couple of hours. I told them we had the spreader lights on, but they asked me to hang a strobe in the rigging, if we had one."

"There's a strobe light on Gillian's jacket," said Sarah, her words blurred by lip salve. "In the hanging locker forward. I can show you where."

"In a few minutes, thanks," Patrick said, lowering himself to the seat beside her. "Are there any more of those beers?"

"Whole icebox full," said Barr. "I could handle another myself."

"I'll get them," Gillian offered, starting to her feet. She put her head into the companionway and recoiled. "Oh, God—I forgot about Golem."

Patrick pulled himself up again. "Stay where you are," he said to her, thinking that he should've remembered: *Kassandra's* main cabin was no place for a woman just now.

Gillian sank back down beside Barr. "Sorry, Patrick." She grinned at Barr and he smiled back, his head cocked to one side. Patrick had never seen him look like that before—his thin face lit up with what had to be love; it was almost as if he'd been wearing a mask all these months, and now he'd taken it off.

When Patrick came back up the ladder, carrying the dripping six-pack, Gillian was the first to see his expression. "What's funny?" she demanded.

"I just got offered a million dollars," Patrick said, shaking his head in bemusement. "First time in my life, and probably the last."

"What'd you have to do for it—let Roger go?" Barr asked, reaching for a beer.

"You got it," he agreed. "After we killed the three of you, of course." He opened a can for himself, then remembered the woman at his side and offered it to her. She shook her head, but her eyes— much darker than Gillian's—seemed to be weighing him. "He said the Coast Guard and the DEA and all of them would never believe what happened," Patrick added, trying to keep his voice light. "Said they'd hang all of us." He'd laughed in Roger's face, but he couldn't help wondering just the same.

"This whole thing's going to take a little explaining," Barr said, flashing Patrick his quick, sardonic grin. "But now we've got the most important pieces—the tape recording, the two boats, Roger. If the Bermuda police are on the ball, they'll have Frannie X, too." He popped the beer can and took a long swallow, pursed his lips thoughtfully. "I have the feeling Frannie's the kind of guy who'll make the best deal he can, as soon as he sees the odds against him. Roger, too, now that Win's dead."

"And I'll bet the *TNF* files will have a lot more evidence in them," Gillian put in. "All the customers' names."

"I suppose it'll work out," Patrick allowed reluctantly. "I still wish we could just sail away from all this. But I guess . . ." he waited, hoping Barr would contradict him, "I guess it'd be too much of a risk, sneaking back into the States with either of these boats."

"This from you?" said Barr. "These are the good guys we're waiting for, remember? Think of your uncle the . . . the police officer."

He had been. That was what was worrying him. "So you think it was the right thing to do, calling the Coasties?" he persisted.

"Hell, it was the only thing we could do," Barr said, firmly. "*Kassandra's* a sieve and her cabin's an abattoir, and our consort back there's got a cockpit full of blood and enough coke down below to pop every skull in a small city." He paused. "At least, I hope the coke's down below."

"Oh, it's there, all right," Patrick replied. He intercepted Barr's unspoken question. "I couldn't stand it, not knowing. I checked the fo'c'sle—it's just where you predicted it'd be."

"Three hundred and twenty kilos," Sarah agreed brightly. "And three hundred and eighty under the cockpit. Roger hired the nicest little man to do the work—it took him two whole months, and we had to hang around every day, watching him. A new chapter in the

annals of boring, let me tell you." As Patrick stared at her, unbelieving, she undid the top two buttons of her shirt, its fabric taut
across her breasts. "He gave me this when he was done," she went
on, pulling out a carved mahogany crucifix on a silver chain. "I
bought a little something for him, in return, but he just vanished—
poof!—and I never had the chance to give it to him."

Nobody seemed able to think of anything to say until Gillian,
with a shaky laugh, said: "Sarah, if I were you I wouldn't wave that
trophy around when the Coasties get here. I think you want to aim
at outraged innocence, even if it's a little late."

"Of course I'm innocent," Sarah said. She seemed to have moved
a good deal closer to Patrick. "After all, I was Roger's hostage, almost,
for a whole year." Gillian's eyebrows shot up, but she remained
silent. "Well, I *was*. And I can tell them how the whole thing worked.
That should count for something."

"Oh, I expect it will," Gillian answered. "I wouldn't worry if I were
you. Skirts are back up again, and no judge in the history of the
world has ever sent a pair of knees like yours to the slammer."

"That's unfair," Sarah objected. And three seconds later: "They
are? Skirts, I mean. You wouldn't believe how *isolated* I've been
in the last year. If I never see another embroidered cotton shirt
again . . ."

"What d'you think's going to happen to them?" Patrick asked,
cutting right across her. "Broadway Rose, all those backers of
Roger's?"

Barr's thin smile didn't seem to have a lot of humor behind it. "If
you want my candid opinion, not a whole lot. Roger and Frannie X
will take most of the heat, but they'll get off in exchange for giving
evidence. Their customers? Unfortunate, misguided victims."

"I can hear the judge now," Gillian put in. "Two hundred hours
of community service apiece."

It was the answer Patrick had half expected, but it angered him
anyway. Before he could object, though, Sarah said: "I almost forgot:
Daddy. What about him?"

"Uncle Sol?" Gillian sounded surprised. "What can they prosecute
him for?"

"Oh, not *that*," Sarah answered impatiently. "I just meant, I hope
you guys aren't mad at him or anything."

She really is fantastic, Patrick thought. From the look on Barr's face, he thought so, too. Gillian took a deep breath before she spoke: "He was worried about you, ducky. Too worried to trust us—and now I kind of understand why."

Barr made a choking noise and quickly sluiced the rest of his beer down his throat. He got stiffly to his feet. "Maybe I'll hoist that strobe light. You feel like a walk, Gillian?"

"Absolutely." She bounced up.

Sarah was silent until Barr and Gillian had disappeared down the other boat's forward hatch. "I love her dearly," she said to Patrick. "I really do, but she's so *judgmental*. Like your mother, you know?"

Patrick thought of his mother, back in Bay Shore. "Not like mine," he replied.

She was appraising him with unconcealed interest. And open calculation. "You're about the most gorgeous man I've seen in thirteen months," she remarked. The shadow of a thought wrinkled her forehead. "Say, you and the two of them aren't . . . I mean, the three of you don't—"

"No," he said firmly.

"Just thought I'd ask." She eyed the can of beer in his hand. "You know, if I tilted my head way back, could you pour some of that in my mouth, without touching my lips?" She positioned herself, waiting.

Patrick thought for a second about Susan Grover; he owed her a lot of things, but he couldn't see that celibacy was one of them. Besides, she was six hundred miles away and Sarah was right in front of his nose. "Let's give it a try," he said.

ABOUT THE AUTHOR

TONY GIBBS, whose home is in Santa Barbara, California, was born and brought up in New York City, and lived in western Connecticut for many years. He has always spent as much time afloat as possible, in places as widely separated as Long Island Sound, Nova Scotia, Bermuda, Florida, and California. Having worked first in book publishing, he turned to marine magazines as a form of gainful sublimation; he became executive editor of *Motor Boating & Sailing* and then editor of *Yachting*, while at the same time writing a number of nonfiction books, all but one about boating. Until moving to the West Coast a couple of years ago, he was for some time executive editor of *The New Yorker*, to which he is still a frequent contributor; his many nonfiction pieces for the magazine include an extended examination of the U.S. Coast Guard and coverage of the three most recent America's Cup regattas.

Mr. Gibbs is now a full-time writer. His first Random House book, *Dead Run*, was published in 1988; *Running Fix* is his second adventure story with a nautical setting, and he is hard at work on a third.